Pleasing Arie

Bad Boys Book Six

Christine Young

Published by Rogue Phoenix Press, LLP

ISBN: 978-1-62420-599-6

Credits
Cover Artist: Designs by Ms G
Editor: Sherry Derr-Wille

Published in the United States of America

Chapter One

June 1824
Glasgow Scotland

Victor, Arie's best friend and confidant, sat back in the plush chair with a glass of brandy in his hand, grinning, feeling like a besotted fool. "I took care of the little matter at hand. I believe you will be somewhat pleased. She is rare. A fine gem."

"So, the lady is ready to see me?"

Arie Demir had been too long without a woman. The little redhead he saw in the restaurant caught his attention. Victor always made sure he got what he wanted. The moment he saw this woman all thoughts of Chelsea vanished from his head.

"I wouldn't go that far," Victor laughed, his mirth rolling off his tongue, his gaze and smirk focused on him. "Unless you want a battle on your hands. Alison Donovan is a spitfire. Her personality seems to fit the color of her hair. You'll have a devil of a time taming that one. In the end you may not want to. She will talk to you but anything else..." Victor shrugged his broad shoulders, a wide smirk still on his face appearing to enjoy his friend's discomfort. "My advice, proceed with caution. Perhaps at this point, bribery should be contemplated. Possibly you can win her over with the promise of jewels."

"Jewels? By all that's holy, I own the woman."

"She is Scottish to the core. Doubt if she has the same belief."

"My ladies are not able to teach her what will be expected of her? What you will expect when you go to see Alison. Still... there is potential. Hers is a beautiful woman's body, ripe to give pleasure a man will remember and come back for more." Arie rose, striding around the room, his gaze traveling upward to the rooms above. "They are not doing their job?"

"As I said, she is a redhead Scotswoman, born and bred, stubborn to her very core. Thinks she is free." Victor followed the direction of Arie's gaze. "This will take time and untold patience. I'm confident in the end she will see you as you wish her to see you."

"I should talk to her." Arie headed toward the staircase. A loud thud reverberated throughout, rocking the walls of the house then a scream that rent his pore eardrums. "What the bloody hell was that?" He started forward, held back by Victor.

"Hold it right where you are. I'll see what just happened. I'm assuming, nothing good." Victor didn't wait to see if he followed his directions but raced to the top floor.

All Arie saw was Victor's back as he sped upstairs. With a huge breath of air, Arie sat down, sipping his drink while he waited for news. He didn't have the patience for this. What did he expect? She was nothing like the women he was used to dealing with. In her home men might have dominated her, but she probably was able to come and go as she pleased. She'd been his prisoner now for days, held captive in the rooms on his third floor.

He'd already endured a lecture from Chelsea MacEwen, his friend, about buying women. Old habits were hard to break. Just because he was a foreigner in Scotland, didn't mean he could change his true colors with a snap of his fingers or a lecture from his favorite lady. He would have wed Chelsea if she'd been willing to become his fourth wife. She was not. Arie didn't think she was even willing to be his first wife if that had been possible. The lady was deeply in love with Cam MacEwen, her husband.

Restless, Arie didn't want to remain inside the stuffy confines of the house. He stepped outside, leaning against the porch railings, staring at the stars and the moon. Chelsea told him about the stars along with the facts her husband Cam taught her. He'd been impressed. Cam had more facets about him than Arie realized at first. He wasn't even a sailor. He knew more about the stars than most sea captains. Arie had been surprised to discover Lord MacEwen was an expert in his field, astronomy, giving many guest lectures at the university. As well as possessing a title, he was recognized for his intelligence.

A few minutes later Victor stood beside him, leaning on the railing, gazing at the brilliant night sky. Silence echoed around him for several minutes, dark brooding silence even drowning out the animal sounds. When he turned, Victor had a broad grin on his face, which belied the mood he found himself in.

"I take it everyone upstairs is still alive." Arie heard his deep breaths as well as the beat of his heart.

"Perhaps you should talk to Alison now. You've more patience than I have," Victor said laughing as if he knew something about the lady's present mood. "You should hear her words for yourself. A second-hand rendition is never good. No, it's just never a good thing to hear about something from another man's point of view."

"Not sure I've the courage to confront the Scotswoman. She's a delicate wisp of a thing. I'm down here cowering in my boots wondering about her mood." Arie let out a long breath of air before finishing his drink. "I want her too much. Doubt if I can be objective where she is concerned."

"She doesn't like the lock on the door or the clothing you've granted her. Doesn't seem to realize she has it a hell of a lot better here than in the whorehouse you rescued her from. Don't know how you're going to go about enlightening her though. She doesn't see things the same way you do."

"Doesn't appreciate the finer points of slavery." Arie's laugh didn't reach to his soul.

He'd promised Chelsea he'd treat this lady right. She was human. Well, it had been several days since he bought Ali. At this point in time, she was still far from compliant. He gave her more than any other women he owned. He thought she would understand that fact but she didn't.

"She has no idea what waits for her and even if she does, what she doesn't understand is the difference between you and serving several different men every night. To her it's the same. Both scenarios are repellent to her. She thinks she should have some say in her future."

"Perhaps I should leave her alone for a few more nights." Arie turned his attention to the light shining out the third-floor window. He put her on the third floor because he knew if Chelsea was in that room, she would find a way to escape. He prayed Ali wasn't like that, reckless to a dangerous point, willing to risk anything as well as her life to flee from him.

"Not all women are the same as the MacTavish girls," Victor reminded him pointedly, following Arie's gaze. "She might be feisty, but I doubt if she'll try to shimmy down that wall to the ground. It's a sheer drop and few would survive unscathed."

"She'd most likely kill herself if she tried. I don't think Chelsea would have tried this one either."

"No, there aren't enough sheets in Alison's room for her to tie them together so they would reach to the ground. I made sure of that," Victor grinned wickedly. Arie was sure he was thinking of something amusing about this situation. "Well, if you want to talk with her, you should probably go now. If I were you, I wouldn't wait."

"Why? What difference would an hour make, or another few days?" Arie watched her, unsure of himself for the first time in his adult life. She was standing in front of the window, staring outside. Candlelight from her room caressed her hair, displaying the multitude of brilliant colors. He had an urgent need to run his fingers through the wild vivid strands, wanting her more now than the first time he saw her. Chelsea's beauty dimmed when he looked at Alison.

Victor lifted his shoulders nonchalantly, his smile broad. "She might be angrier in another hour. Who knows what she could be like in the morning, a redheaded Scotswoman? A tigress? Right now, she is somewhat biddable. I believe she's had several glasses of wine although she didn't touch her food. Might work in your favor, might not."

Arie ran his hands through his hair, frustrated by the situation, understanding all the rules he lived by for twenty-five years would not be applicable now. Ali lived by a different set. "Don't know what I'd say to her. Just want her in my bed, willing to give herself to me."

"Tell her why you bought her. Make her position in your life clear so there will be no second-guessing. In time, she will come around to your way of thinking. She needs to comprehend how much better her life will be with you than in a whorehouse or on the streets. After all, you have her best interest at heart." Victor strode into the house, pouring another glass of whiskey, chuckling softly, still clearly amused.

"Doubt if she'd like my reasons any more than she enjoys being locked in that room, even though I've given her the entire floor. More than any other concubine I've owned." Arie figured he'd never be able to get close enough to the girl to seduce her to his way of thinking. "Maybe you have a point, but I expect you to be outside the door to rescue me if anything turns violent."

"You could bring her a gift," Victor repeated his earlier suggestion, holding up his hands to make his point. "Don't ask me what. No, wait a minute. You could bring her real clothing. Something you can't see through. I believe she would appreciate the gesture."

"Doubt if baubles or clothing would ease her temper. She doesn't seem to be a lady who wants monetary things." Arie was stroking his chin, wondering what he could bring that might soothe her displeasure with him, completely ignoring the suggestion of clothing.

"She might like some clothes." Victor nearly laughed, repeating himself again.

His suggestion didn't go unnoticed by Arie.

"Then she might be more inclined to find a way down the side of the house. I don't intend to offer her the chance to kill herself."

Arie was wondering about a dress for her. She might not be appreciating the harem clothes he'd given her. They were, after all, meant for a man to appreciate, not the woman. As for appreciating her, he hadn't even seen her wearing the soft lavender harem pants and bolero top.

"You don't want to chance her escape. She'd die on the streets," Victor said, all amusement vanishing. "We both understand that fact. If you point the fact out to her, I'm sure she'll comprehend what you are trying to tell her, perhaps even come around to your way of thinking. You are a true savior to that girl. She has no one else."

"How will I know? I can't just give her a dress and unlock the door." He was thinking of the MacTavish girls. They would bolt the second they got the opportunity, see through clothing or none at all.

Allison would die on the streets, either that or find herself abused by men. He meant to treat her special.

"You have to go to her and explain why she is here as well as her options," Victor said.

"She has none," Arie said, glancing upward once more.

"Exactly."

"I rescued her." Blood pounded in his head, the ache growing which each thud.

"That you did," Victor said agreeably.

"She should appreciate me."

"All true."

The silence between the two men was long and drawn out. Arie reconciled to meeting with Alison. She would come to recognize and accept her fate then he would treat her with the care and respect she would deserve. He thought on everything Chelsea told him days ago. It was nothing he wanted to hear, but he did listen and her words changed the way he meant to deal with Ali. Giving her the freedom Chelsea suggested was never an option in his mind.

He gave her time and space to adjust to her new circumstances. Shouldn't she be adjusted by now?

He was a coward, he surmised thoughtfully, afraid of a tiny redheaded girl who stole his breath the first time he saw her. Victor had done well by him. He followed her and procured her for him before she was forced to entertain her first client in the whorehouse. Ali's circumstance decreed she would fall into his arms. From his vast experiences when given the chance, all women fell into his arms. But...

She fought Victor and railed against him, holding herself aloof as if she was royalty. Still he stood at the bottom of the staircase, sweat dripping from his brow to slither down his cheek. He'd never felt this way before. If he could, he'd give Ali everything she asked for.

Except her freedom.

He could never do that.

Victor stood beside him, one hand on his shoulder. "Perhaps you should give Ali her autonomy then she'll fall into your arms. That's what you want, isn't it? Let her know she can come and go as she pleases."

"She would run. She has nowhere to flee; no money, no clothes, no nothing. She'd die on the streets or be violated," Arie said, wiping his brow with his sleeve, his hands shaking.

"Alison is not stupid. She has figured out that someone, most likely her stepfather, sold her to the whorehouse. She knows you bought her. She will also understand she cannot make it in the outside world without help, most likely from a man. Perhaps you will have some bargaining chips with her if you present these facts to her."

"You think so?"

"No, but it's worth a try. Right now, Alison is not thinking clearly. She does want to run from you and from all the bad things that have happened to her this last week. She might not have led a sheltered life, but I do believe she is an innocent in many ways. If you want her, you need to treat her as a virgin as well as give her your respect. She deserves nothing less."

"A virgin?" Arie didn't understand the words coming from his friend. This was a surprise to him, and he wasn't sure he wanted to deal with another innocent. "No wonder she is protesting so vehemently. Still I cannot believe she has never known a man intimately."

"I think so. However, I've been wrong about other things. When you first saw her, I was sure she would be quite willing."

"So, where did we go wrong?"

"We didn't know the circumstances of the sale. I do now. It seems Fletcher Donovan and his nephew sold her. Apparently, the mother was in agreement. However those two men turned on Alison's mother. Sold her home and left her penniless. As we speak, she is destitute and on the streets."

"She probably got what she deserved. They all need to be punished. It was Donovan and Leod who captured Chelsea and sold her to the same whorehouse. We should find the mother so we can see how she is faring. On second thought, I'm sure the Madam can find a suitable position for her at the brothel."

"The Madam too?" Victor asked a brow arched in obvious disbelief. "Not sure she had any idea what was happening."

"She was greedy and wanted the money. Was contrite when I

confronted her. This information about Ali is new to me."

"All the more reason to make sure Leod and Fletcher disappear forever. Leod apparently did not learn the first lesson I gave him."

"All will be taken care of," Victor said flashing a huge grin. "Just give the order."

"I want them taken and sold to a man who prefers men," Arie said, a smirk on his face. "I do believe that to be a fitting punishment for the two of them who are willing to abuse women for their own gain." He nearly stopped himself on those words because he understood that unknowingly he abused his women. He had three wives. All but one barely tolerated him. The third wife said she loved him nevertheless...

Maybe that was a lie too.

"I will take care of it in the morning. I'm going upstairs with Tessa for a few hours. I do think you should at least introduce yourself to your new concubine and decide for yourself on the next course of action."

Arie inhaled a long deep breath of air, downing his drink in a gulp before heading up the stairs. By the time he reached the top, he was breathing hard and sweating more profusely than at the bottom of the steps. The climb wasn't the cause. The fear of the confrontation was. He had a lot to prove to himself. He didn't know if he could change that much.

He nodded to the man stationed in front of the door, "Don't come in no matter what you think you hear. Not unless I tell you."

"Are you sure?"

"Positive."

Arie stared at the doorknob for a few seconds before he slowly opened the door. Alison was still standing at the window, dressed in the see-through lavender harem pants and bolero jacket he gave her a few days past. Without a second thought, he grinned, appreciating the view, the finely sculpted curves. From the back she was just as beautiful as he imagined, her vibrant red hair spilling to below her waist, curling around her, tested all his senses.

"Alison?"

"Go away."

"Afraid I can't do that." He stepped inside the room, closing the door behind him. The outside lock turned as he walked toward her. "We need to speak, to understand each other. I need you to comprehend why you are here rather than the brothel."

"Who are you?" Her voice quivered when she spoke.

Her shoulders were stiff. Still she didn't turn around. He didn't need to see her face. Her visage was etched in his memory.

Arie understood this would not be easy between them. Now, he wasn't sure if she was terrified or angry, perhaps both. He hoped it was anger causing her body to shake. Anger he could deal with much easier than fear. He prayed she didn't cry. There would be no tears. Despite the lecture from Chelsea, Alison wasn't going anywhere. She was his for as long as he wanted her.

In any case, Ali had nowhere to go. Donovan sold her house after selling her to the whorehouse. She had nothing save what he would give her.

"My name is Arie."

He stood beside her, looking out the window, his body barely touching her shoulder. A crescent moon stood out in a cloudless sky while brilliant stars emerged as the city lights dimmed even more with the hour.

"Then, Arie, what am I doing here?" she asked, her voice tense. "You have no right to keep me prisoner."

"Do you want me to be brutally frank?"

He smiled, wondering exactly how she would react when he gave her the truth of her existence now.

"Brutal?" she queried, her eyes wide as she turned to look at him, her hands fisted at her sides. "Everything that has happened to me in the last couple of days has been brutal. I'm a free woman. You've no right to hold me in this house."

"You didn't answer my question. I find I cannot continue on without an honest answer from you." He smiled, realizing this woman was not afraid of him; defiant yes, angry yes, but not afraid.

She turned away from him, her hands on the windowsill seeming to support all her slight weight. He was afraid when she learned the truth she would no longer be able to stand on her own.

"Why would you be anything less than honest?" Her voice

quivered while her shoulders trembled.

"Perhaps you should sit down first." He turned to the pillows and bedding gracing the floor behind them. "Have something to eat, a sip or two of the fine wine I've procured for us. You should relax."

"I'm not hungry or thirsty. I don't want to relax." She moved to look at the pillows then him. "I'll stand, thank you."

He shrugged wishing she would at least eat something even while he was enjoying the beautiful play of emotions on her face, "Suit yourself." Striding to the pillows set out for them, he held his cup out and a servant poured wine.

Relaxing and making himself comfortable, he sipped the liquid, watched her as she swayed slightly. She must be exhausted. He wanted nothing more than to make her life more comfortable, yet she was refusing at every turn.

"You really should sit down before you fall down," he said, patting the place beside him.

Slowly she walked toward him. For a few seconds she stood. Finally, she sat down as far away from him as possible. "I need to know the truth. What is it you want from me?"

"Ah, finally." He poured her wine and motioned for the servants to leave to an adjoining room. "You should sip it slowly."

She held the wine in shaking hands, her green eyes huge. She coughed slightly with the first sip. "I've never had wine or any spirits."

"A delicacy you might learn to enjoy. I can give you anything you want." He held his breath waiting for a response. "Your life with me will not be a bad one."

She seemed to bristle, her chin rising. "What I want is to leave this place and you behind me."

For a moment his heart sank. He slowly smiled. She would come to his viewpoint when he explained the facts to her. "Where would you go? How would you eat? You have no clothing."

Her body seemed to wilt at his words before she stiffened with seeming determination. "I'll find a job."

"At the whorehouse?" he asked smoothly, hoping to make his point.

"No, I'm not a whore." She drank the entire glass of wine. He filled it again, hoping she would begin to relax.

"Do you have any skills?" He wished she would understand she had few alternatives except whoring. "If you go out on the streets, you will only end up in a whorehouse or worse. I suppose if you were lucky you could find employment as a nanny or a wet nurse if you gave birth to a child of your own. Do you have an education?"

"There are worse things than a brothel?" She inhaled a long shaky breath appearing to think over what he said. She asked again. "What do you want from me?"

He no longer knew what to tell her. If she thought this was worse than a brothel, she was sadly mistaken. It would be hard to convince her she was wrong. "You could be out on the streets with no roof over your head, no food and no clothing." Frustration filled his soul. He needed to shake some sense into her. "I offer comforts I'm sure you never received at home. Inevitably, I would like you to warm my bed. I do not give things without expecting something in return."

It seemed she did not listen to him. "I'm your prisoner though. What is it you want in return? All men do." Her fists were clenched at her sides and if there had ever been a threat of tears, it vanished.

"If we please each other you could become my wife." There it was an offer he had not meant to introduce to her at least not now. He didn't understand why he blurted that out to her. The suggestion wasn't tenable.

"Is that what you want me for? Another wife?" Frown lines creased her brow. "I won't be a fourth wife."

"How did you know?"

Gossip had never been something he could abide. It seemed his servants were doing just that. Gossiping. There was no other explanation for her knowledge.

"There was talk, silly chatter from the women who were trying to teach me things you would want me to know. There was nothing intentional or malicious about the facts they talked about. It was just women talking about men."

It seemed to Arie she sensed his anger. "So you say." They were all women. Of course she would defend them. "Well," he paused, thinking it was time for a change of subject, "do you care to show me what these fine women taught you?"

She blushed sweetly before turning her face away. He almost laughed. Dancing in the way of his people was not easy.

"I've two left feet. My hips don't move the same way theirs do. For that matter they don't move at all." Her voice was lighter. It appeared she was laughing at herself.

For a second it seemed to him she forgot her anger as well as her desire to escape him.

His chuckle was soft, not meant to laugh at her. This was the first break in their serious conversation. "You should show me what you learned." He poured them both more wine, hoping she would loosen up some more, at least enough to show off her fledgling skills.

"I don't think so."

She sipped the wine, leaning back and pulling a pillow across her front, hiding the delightful swell of her breasts below the tiny jacket meant to reveal more than conceal. "You would only laugh or be appalled."

"Soon then," he prompted, disappointed she would not perform for him but encouraged that soon she would be more at ease.

Perhaps this talk with her was a good thing. Victor had been right.

"What will you do for me if I dance? Not really sure one can call what I do dancing but..." She was smiling, her laughter soft.

"What do you want?" He picked up a strand of her hair and held it in his hands. "So soft, silken, fire in my hands. Is every part of you this soft?" he murmured, staring at her lips, wanting desperately to kiss her, feel the moistness of her mouth.

"Soft...?" She swallowed hard. "I don't know what you mean."

"Your hair is like fire and it burns my soul."

She pulled back, "What will you give me if I dance for you?"

"I repeat, what do you want?"

"To go for a ride on my mare."

"Your mare." Arie rubbed his chin, thinking. "Your entire household was purchased. Everything. Doubt if the mare is still there."

"You have the means. I'm sure you could offer whoever bought her enough money to buy back my mare. Please find the dear girl and buy her back."

"Dance for me and I'll do it first thing tomorrow."

~ * ~

Alison had not expected the swift compliance to her wishes. Strangely, she wasn't terrified of Arie. One could say she was more fascinated by him than she could have ever imagined. She'd never met anyone like him. One could say he was unique.

Frustration and confusion had filled her since she first woke up in the brothel where she found herself dressed in a flimsy see through gown. It seemed to her she jumped from one fire into another when Arie bought her at the auction. She ended up in this third story room several days ago. Now she had some hard decisions to make.

Ali didn't want to be attracted to him. No, she wanted to despise the man who sought to make her a prisoner, a concubine. His personal whore. How was that so different from being confined in a whorehouse? Ah, his smile though sent a jolt straight through to her heart seeming to melt it.

Now that she'd seen him, talked to him, she could never hate him. His deep brown eyes shimmered with humor, some knowledge she wanted him to tell her. She just didn't know what it was he hid behind those dark brown eyes of his. They seemed to draw her to him. She'd never met anyone comparable. His muscled chest was also something she'd never seen before. The sight left her with a nearly uncontrollable urge to touch him, to run her hands along the smooth, hard muscles.

Mesmerized by him, she had an uncanny need to please this man, wanted to reach out and touch him.

Dancing for him would not please him. "If you promise not to laugh at me." The thought of failing as miserably as she knew she would left her shaking not with fear but with feelings of humiliation even while she wanted to laugh at herself.

"I would never laugh at you." Arie was grinning though.

He had no idea. She knew he would laugh. It would not be possible for him to keep the amusement behind his teeth. "Then you are a saint." She rose then and inhaled a sharp breath, flashing him a smile. "Do I get music?"

Arie clapped his hands and two of his servants appeared. "Music for Ali."

With that said the music played. Alison began to move her hips as she believed she'd been taught. She was awkward. In no time she was winded from the ungainly attempt at belly dancing. The tempo picked up speed. She knew a shimmy was next, but not one part of her body seemed to work. Humor seemed to fill her then as she saw the look of utter shock on Arie's face. No, he wasn't laughing at her, he was horrified by what he witnessed.

"You're not pleased." She stopped, dragging in deep long breaths of well needed air.

The look on Arie's face was nothing she'd seen before. All her fears about the man vanished, at least for the moment. She fell on the pillows next to him, unable to stop the laughter bubbling up from deep inside.

"I want you to know I'm not laughing, but under the circumstances I'm having a devilishly hard time fulfilling my promise." He choked on the sip of wine, the liquid sputtering across his chest as a deep humorous rumble shook him.

She wanted to touch him, clean the liquid, reaching out she almost stroked him before she drew back her hand. His grin now was broad. His even white teeth glistened in the candlelight.

He nodded for the other women to leave and filled her glass again. "You know what you just did?"

"Earn my mare?" She accepted the glass but set it on a nearby table, feeling as if she shouldn't drink anymore, her mind a bit hazy.

"More than that. I will also bring you something else to wear when we go riding. I enjoy your smile as well as your laughter. I want to spend more time with you. I also want you in my bed." With the back of his hand, he tenderly touched her cheek.

"Thank you." She looked down, hiding her surprised expression from him, unwilling to show him her gratitude. What he didn't know wouldn't hurt her. "I don't know what to say."

"Thank you is quite enough," he told her, rising from the pillows. "You look tired. You should sleep. I've the feeling you've managed very little sleep since you arrived here."

She sat up, staring at him, at the broad expanse of his chest, wondering what he would look like without clothes. "What if I don't want you to leave yet? I've been lonely."

"You want me to stay?" He sounded astonished.

Ali moistened her lips. "If you don't mind. You could tell me something about yourself."

"We do need to speak about why you are here and your options. It seems you might be settling in now. That is good, very good. I'm pleased. I would like you to be happy and if not happy at least content."

"I still want my freedom," she bristled. "You will never own me."

"So much for progress," he mumbled.

"I didn't mean to give you the impression I wanted your attention."

She suddenly didn't feel the least bit magnanimous. Her earlier anger simmering deep inside she realized the emotion would never be assuaged by a gift from a man who could afford anything.

"I understand. You only want me to buy your mare for you, but you don't need or want anything else to wear." He stroked his chin, his grin disappearing.

It seemed to Ali she had lost what little ground she made by dancing for him. He would not come around to her way of thinking. She stood then, accepting another glass of wine despite the fact she didn't want to drink it. At the window she gazed at the moon. It appeared the same as when she looked at it from her window at home, no longer her home.

From behind her he spoke. "You've gone through a great deal of trauma in the last few days but Ali," he paused seeming thoughtful, "you are mine and the sooner you accept that fact the happier you'll be."

She whirled on him. "Never!" With a great deal of purpose, she strode to him, tossing the liquid onto him and dousing his shirt. Her breath caught in the back of her throat as she realized what she'd just done to the man who held her life in his hands.

For a few seconds he appeared shocked then a slow smooth grin spread across his too handsome face. A moment later his shirt was on the floor and he was bare chested, standing his hands on the fasteners of his soaked britches. Ali gasped at the pure male beauty she saw. Then her eyes widened as he was suddenly very nearly naked, his britches on the floor beside his shirt.

He clapped his hands and a woman appeared from a side room. "Would you please bring another pair of pants?"

"A shirt too?" she queried.

"Don't believe I want one. I find it's incredibly warm in this room tonight, perhaps getting hotter."

It seemed to Ali he searched her face for some sign of contrition. She didn't feel anything but awe as she stared at him unable to remove her gaze.

She pulled her lips together, retreating to the window and the incredible manly view. The long breath she inhaled was shaky, her knees trembling as she felt his presence so very close to her. Although he didn't touch her, she felt the heat emanate from his large, muscular body.

"What do you want?" she asked, her voice shaking, afraid of retaliation. If she'd done something like that to her so-called father, Fletcher Donovan, she would have been thrashed. He would have enjoyed taking a whip to her back.

"Only your sweet compliance, but I'm resigned to the fact I will have to work harder to achieve that which I seek."

Still he didn't touch her, just stood beside her. "It was an impulse. I know I shouldn't have tossed the wine."

"Of course," he left her side. When she turned around, he was sitting on a freshly made pallet with new coverings and pillows. "We talked about brutal honesty. Come sit." He was patting a spot beside him. "You should know what I need from you, yet I'm afraid you're not ready to hear the words or accept your destiny."

She was shaking her head no, even while she strode toward him, sweat sliding between her breasts. Ali didn't want to sit. Standing was preferable when he held her future in his hands. Standing was preferable when she wanted to reach out and touch his chest, find out if it was as hard and unyielding as it appeared.

Then she did sit down, scooting as far from his as the pillows would allow. “Why am I your prisoner? Why did you say I was yours?”

He settled back, his arms spread wide on top of the pillows, his legs stretching out in front of him. “Because I bought you.”

“It’s not as simple as you try to make it. People cannot buy people.” She didn’t understand any of this even while she’d heard that Fletcher sold her to the brothel.

“People with power and money can do anything they please. It pleases me to own you and eventually reap the benefits of other purely sexual things. Whether you agree or not, you are mine. Now, no more discussion of this sort. Tell me more about yourself.”

She needed to figure out what all he said meant to her. “If I say no, what then?”

“It doesn’t matter what you say. I do care what you want but not where it concerns my ownership.” His words were calm yet measured. “You will always be mine. Unless of course, I grow tired of you of this silliness and sell you to someone else.”

“You can’t do that!”

His smile told her otherwise. A shiver of fear slipped down her spine. At least here she was safe. It didn’t seem he meant to abuse her.

For a few seconds, she looked away from him, remembering her life from a few days’ past. It had been fraught with hard work and sometimes not knowing if there would be a next meal. Looking around the room, she was amazed at the opulence, the food and everything else that adorned the space she lived in and wondered what his quarters looked like.

“It is better than the whorehouse, I assume. I would have been able to walk out those doors though. As you say, as your possession I’ve no choices.” She thought that might be true but wasn’t sure.

“Not until you worked for the Madam long enough for her to make a profit. She would also keep your door locked. You would be forced to service several men each night.”

“Do you have an answer for everything?”

She found she was bitter, not at Arie for taking what he wanted but for her circumstances, for Fletcher who set all this in motion. He spoke the truth. She didn't want to admit it. "So, I would have been kept behind a locked door."

"Yes." He sipped his wine and ate. "You should try the food. It's really quite good, much better than at the brothel. My cook is excellent. The spices he adds enhance the flavors."

"How would you know?" she shot back, angry once again at his arrogance and all-knowing grin.

His chuckle sent her nerves on edge. "I've partaken of the food at said brothel several times. Now, if you don't mind, I'd like to learn something about you besides your love for your mare."

"She probably won't be there if you still plan on buying her for me. She is very old and can't be ridden." She was plucking at the sheer pants she wore. "I'll miss her even though she is a worthless nag. Obviously, I could not have ridden with you anyway."

He leaned forward then, his hand on top of hers, stilling her restless motion. His fingers wrapped around hers and she was startled by the gentleness. "I will do everything in my power to find her for you. I'm not an ogre. She will be kept in my stable and whenever I've the time, I'll ride with you. Not on your nag though. You must have a mare worthy of you. I'll see to that too."

"Promise?"

Her optimisms lightened. Perhaps he spoke true. She could only hope even though she understood there would be a price to pay for his generosity. In time he would collect. He wanted more than an awkward dance.

"Yes, what would you like to know about me?"

"Anything you would want to share. What makes you so confidant you can buy a woman and no one cares?" She didn't want to sound belligerent but she couldn't help herself.

"Ah, people do care if it's the right woman. You have no man in your life. So, no one cares about your fate except me."

"I've no one to care about me," she repeated.

She found her heart was breaking. Once not so long ago she

thought her mother cared about her.

"I'm confidant because I've always done what I pleased. I've lived my life in luxury with any woman who caught my fancy. You, my dear, catch my fancy." He placed his finger beneath her chin, "Don't ever believe that I don't care about you. I do more than you will ever know. I want only the best for you. If you are pleased then I'm a man well pleased."

"I caught your fancy?" Once again, she repeated his words, not really wanting to hear him agree yet beginning to realize she was better off than if she had not been a woman he wanted.

"The Madam told me you are not a virgin. Is that true?"

"Do you care?"

She bristled again, remembering a time when she had been forced to kiss a man but she had not been violated. Fletcher had watched, grinning like a besotted fool. He did nothing to stop the man who would not accept her no. Yet, he finally did step in and pull the man from her.

"No, but the truth will dictate how I proceed with you."

Ali inhaled a shaky breath, watching Arie intently. "A man who lived nearby."

She stopped then, turning to the window to stare outside at the stars. The moon was no longer visible from her position.

"Go on," he urged.

"Fletcher thought I should wed this man so he brought him to me. I didn't even know his name. He kissed me and I shoved him away. I don't know if I'm a virgin or not."

Once more she was plucking on her pants, pulling at the fabric. She tried to stop her trembling fingers.

"Just a kiss," Arie's voice was gentle and soothing.

"No, he didn't like the fact that I pushed him away. He hit me, punched me in the stomach. I never knew anything could hurt that bad."

His hand tightened around hers. "What did Fletcher do?"

"He ushered him from the house. I was surprised by that. He always hit mother when she did something he didn't like."

Arie's fists tightened, his eyes growing so dark they seemed to turn to ebony. "I have guesses about that but none of them are important.

I'm sure you are still a virgin, Ali. Think hard and see if you can remember the man's name. I would like to speak with him. Is that the only kiss you've experienced?"

"Yes."

He brought her hand to his lips and placed a kiss on the back then he looked at her. "Was it that horrible?"

She blinked a few times before facing him. "I liked your kiss."

"That was hardly a kiss," he laughed.

She looked away, unable to meet his gaze tugging at her hand, which he kept prisoner in his. "Still I liked the way your lips felt on my hand."

"Perhaps before I leave tonight you would let me kiss you." He moved from the pillow to stride around the room.

His back was broad and his flesh well-tanned such a contrast from her paleness. He was strong and proud. "I might like that."

She was beginning to understand that her options were limited. Getting along with this man might serve her better than fighting and denying him the things he wanted. Perhaps she wanted them too.

"Good."

She was sure he was waiting for her to come to him. Her feet wouldn't move. "If I kiss you, can I have something else to wear, that dress you spoke of maybe?"

"I promised you your mare tomorrow because you danced for me as well as clothing if we are to ride."

He laughed then and she wondered what he was thinking.

"What I did was hardly a dance."

She smiled at him, felt the mood suddenly lighten again. She was heartily pleased with that.

"Perhaps I'll give you two dresses then. Come here, one more if you kiss me." He motioned for her, beckoning to her.

Her body seemed to have a mind of its own and refused to move. Catching her bottom lip between her teeth, she inhaled a long deep steadying breath of air. She knew she would like that kiss, understood once she gave into a kiss, she would never be herself again. The only way to have control over this totally confidant man was to deny him.

"I believe I changed my mind," her words squeaked from her tight throat. "I don't think a kiss would work. I'm sure two dresses is too extravagant. One will suffice for now."

For a fleeting second his grin vanished. Suddenly, it was there on his face broader than ever before. "If that's what you wish."

He leaned on the windowsill, his back to her. She needed to know what he decided, how he was feeling about what she told him.

Ali stood beside him now, close to him, too close she decided when he turned suddenly his hands around her waist pulling her close. She knew she could break away if that was what she wanted. Instead, Ali closed her eyes for a moment before she let her lashes flutter open and gazed into his dark brown eyes, eyes that seemed to shimmer with raw passion.

His desire was evident.

Her heart raced so hard, she could not look away, could not refuse him as he slowly lowered his face so they were mere inches apart. "Do you want to kiss me? I would allow it if that is what you want?"

"Me kiss you?" she squeaked, her words barely audible.

"I would bring you some delicacy you might crave."

Her hands settled on his chest, moving, exploring, prowling as if she did this every day. Beneath her fingers his muscles flexed. She was acting like a ninny. Something needed to be done here before she lost herself to this man who demanded things of her she wasn't yet willing to give or even understand.

I can control him.

Controlling Arie would only happen when she kept her fascination with this man in check. Arie was everything in a man Ali ever imagined and knew was beyond her reach.

Beyond until now...

What would she have to do to gain his trust and respect? She would have to meet him part way and tempt him the other half.

Ali had no knowledge in the art of tempting a man. She didn't even know the rudiments of flirting. Perhaps others in his employ would be willing to give her some hints, teach her. If they understood her motives though, they might relay the information to him and that would defeat her purpose. They seemed to tell him everything.

She inhaled a long-ragged breath, gazing into his eyes. "I can't do that. Kiss you. I don't know how."

The moment the last words were said she regretted them. He would find some way to turn them around to his advantage. She smushed her lips together, thinking, wondering just what would happen next.

The only thing she craved was discovering what his kiss felt like, if his lips were as soft and warm as they appeared. She wasn't about to let him know her thoughts and she had no reason to show him how inept at kissing she was, just as inept as dancing. He would be repulsed with her awkward kisses, send her away, give her to another man. She knew she didn't want that.

Thinking she was way in over her head she pushed away from him, turning and walking toward the door.

"I'm tired now. It's been a long day." What a blatant lie. "Don't you think it's about time you left?"

She stood beside it, hands clasped in front of her, watching his grin widen and she wondered just how that was possible but it was a fact.

"Not until I get my kiss."

He sat down on the pallet where she would sleep, relaxed, watching her intently. Still watching her, he lazily stretched out, his long legs taking up the length of the bed.

She pushed hair from her face, exasperated by this arrogant and very stubborn streak. "You should learn to take no for an answer."

She remained by the door, wishing she dared walk the distance and give him what he wanted.

"If I recall you didn't say no, just that you didn't know how."

"You should leave when asked."

"Why, when I don't have to? Perhaps I'll stay the night." He leaned back closing his eyes, his large hands behind his head. "This is comfortable. I made sure of it because one night, I hope in the not too far distant future, I'll spend the evening here with you."

"More distant than I'm sure you want to believe." She nodded her head toward the door. "I'm also sure you would like me to act more docile, but it's not in my nature."

"Neither docile or subservient would satisfy me. Now, I'll do what you ask as soon as I get that kiss."

Her eyes narrowed while she stared at him, "I suppose you'll have to stay the night." At the same time, she was speaking the words she was looking around the room for a place where she could sleep.

"As you wish."

He rose. For a moment she thought he meant to leave. He unfastened his pants.

"You can't do that." Her voice strained with emotions. She wondered what devil got inside her to challenge him this way. He didn't care if he slept with her. It was after all what he wanted all along.

Now he wore only his small clothes. Her throat tightened when she thought... "No, I'll kiss you then you can leave."

"Ah, but I think it might be too late for that. I find this bed quite comfortable."

"No, it's not." She rushed toward him, stumbled on the rug in her haste. Together they fell on the bed, his arms wrapped tightly around her. The skimpy bolero jacket she wore rose. She felt the naked flesh of his chest against her breasts. Her nipples tightened with the contact. A tiny sound erupted from the back of her throat.

"I like this position. You on top of me. I didn't even have to ask." He smoothed hair away from her face. "Are you going to kiss me?"

Her mouth touched his. Quickly she withdrew. "There."

"That was not a kiss."

He laughed, his throaty chuckle sending shivers down her spine as she squirmed against him. His hands roamed the length of her back, up then down again, to finally stop on her bottom, pressing her against him.

"I told you I didn't know how to kiss."

"Try again. Make it last a wee bit longer. Perhaps you can give me a taste of your tongue. That's right. I'd like to taste you. You would taste of the sweet wine you just drank."

"My tongue?"

Her body pressed against his trembled with raw passion. How the devil was she supposed to control him when she couldn't control herself?

"If you like."

"If I like?" she parroted.

I'm smarter than he is, stronger, too, at least my will is stronger. I'm faster, my mind can be if I work at it.

"Press your lips against my mouth. I'll show you how it's done."

Ali pushed away from him, the tiny bit of distance making it easier for her to breathe. "Now you'll show me."

He grinned. "Any time."

"Alright then."

She lowered herself so close to him she felt the whisper of his breath across her cheek. She touched her lips to his, closing her eyes and wondering how much a bit more time was. Gasping, her lashes flew open. His hand was behind her head, holding her close. His tongue swept across her lips. She was tempted to touch his with hers but held back, wishing she understood more. A tiny sound mewed in the back of her throat as her hips moved against his belly. His other hand swept up her back, touching, exploring naked flesh. When she gasped again, his tongue met hers then withdrew.

Alison found herself sitting next to him, her clothing askew. Quickly, she righted her pants and jacket Everything happened so quickly. Now it was like nothing happened except she was hot, so very hot. Her body ached in places she never thought about before.

"Thank you," he told her before slipping on his pants and walking through the door shutting it behind him. "You can sleep alone tonight."

Breathing hard she raced to the door, tried to open it then collapsed onto the floor. Of course he locked it.

~ * ~

Victor relaxed in his room, Tessa, his favorite lady, handed him a drink before sitting down next to him. Wrapping an arm around her, he pulled her close. He figured he had about an hour before Arie gave up on his third-floor quest and knocked on his door.

Arie's mood would be questionable. So unlike himself in his dealings with this new lady, Victor found it difficult to read his friend. He didn't understand how this one redheaded woman had Arie twisting within himself, tying himself into knots. She was beautiful, yes. But...

He needed to bed the woman, show her he would treat her with the respect she deserved. After that he could get on with his life. Instead, he let his good friend Chelsea MacEwen tell him how to relate to this new woman, a new concubine. He was so off kilter it would be amusing if his temper wasn't frayed. A man could lose control in sensual matters. What he saw led him to believe Arie handed the control over to the redhead.

"You seem preoccupied. Have I done something wrong?" Tessa asked, stroking Victor's chest and placing tiny kisses where her fingers had been.

She raked her nails across his belly. His body hardened again with the need she generated so easily.

"Just worried."

He picked up her hand, kissing the palm, running his tongue there before nibbling kisses the length of her arm.

"About Arie?" she queried. "I know it's none of my business but..."

"Hush." He placed a finger on her lips before tracing them. "What you think or what I think will not change the way he goes forward with this new acquisition of his. She is different somehow. He is not his usual self."

"I'm sorry." She was immediately contrite. "I'll go."

He reached out to her, "No, we've time yet."

"I don't know what you want."

"Kiss me and I'll show you."

She was more than eager to satisfy him. She trailed her tongue across his lower lip, prowling inside his mouth along his teeth and deeper. Thrusting her tongue inside, he toyed with her, the sensual play delighting him.

More than an hour passed before the knock on his door woke him. Tessa left, quickly wrapping a robe around her and walking by Arie with a nod.

"I see you've had a better night tonight than I have." Arie chuckled which surprised Victor.

"You're in a good mood?" Victor pushed the covers back, rising and slipping on his pants. "Do you want to tell me anything?"

Arie was shaking his head while he poured them both a drink. "Would have liked to have stayed the night with her but..." He held his hand up, "Never expected that to happen in the first place. All in all, the visit went surprisingly well."

"Maybe tomorrow?" Victor laughed, watching the man he'd called friend since they were just lads playing in Arie's father's harem.

"Not tomorrow. I'm going to make her wait for me. I'm going to take control away from her, take charge of the direction this is going between the two of us. Right now, she believes she has the upper hand. Is dictating to me. Not any longer."

Arie tossed his head back and laughed, leaving Victor bemused and wondering what happened in the third-floor room tonight.

"What have you promised her?" Victor said, searching through the tray of food that was left over from earlier in the evening for something to eat. "Hopefully not the stars and moon."

"Her mare. Told her if she danced for me, I'd see if I could purchase it for her."

"Her mare? That's all?"

"Yes, the horse is old so I'm afraid the people who bought her home might have done away with it even though it's only been a few days since the property was sold."

"What do you want me to do?" Victor asked, knowing that Alison most likely won the first round between them.

"First thing in the morning you should go to the farm and talk to the owner. Pay him anything he wants. Then see if there is anywhere you can purchase another horse for her. One she will be able to ride. I'd like to take her outside the room, give her a small measure of independence. She needs to feel sunlight on her face and fresh air to scent."

"A taste of freedom?"

He arched a dark eyebrow in speculation. Arie was smitten.

"Just enough to let her appreciate what she has with me."

"You plan on buying her suitable clothing?" Victor asked laughing.

"I promised her a dress for a kiss."

Chapter Two

Arie strode outside the house watching the two mares as they were led into the stable. It did not take Victor long to purchase the horses as well as the other necessary item, a dress. Ali had earned the mare and the gown several nights ago. He decided he wasn't going to see her that day or the next. He meant to let her wait and wonder, also needing the time away from her to regain some semblance of control over his unruly man parts.

Thoughts of Ali in the harem pants and now the new dress gave him reason to smile. Then, heaving a huge sigh of resignation knowing the day would not be easy for either of them, he looked upward to the window, something he'd done every day since his last encounter with the beautiful red-headed siren. Today he would give her the first taste of freedom, find out how she dealt with it. He'd taken every precaution understanding she might bolt.

Alison had no one except him to rely on.

She would come back if she did leave, but he wasn't going to take a chance on his hunch.

"What are you waiting for?" Victor laughed, seeming to follow his gaze to the upstairs window. "The day is beautiful. I assume everything is set for you and your new concubine."

"She's going to be angry when she sees me. I shouldn't have stayed away so long."

His heart raced in anticipation of the passion that might follow if he induced the right emotions. Anger could swiftly change to passion.

"Wouldn't you be furious?" Victor countered with the obvious question and a lifted eyebrow. "Locked in a room and subservient to a man's whims. Just when she believes she will receive a breath of fresh air the man decides to stay away."

Arie chose to ignore Victor's question, the answer obvious. "I've taken every possible scenario to task. I've a plan for each one."

Really, he didn't, figured he would have to take each second and analyze his reactions and what should be done in order to serve Ali in the best way possible.

"I'd like to watch this but don't want to be responsible for your life. Make sure you don't leave anything sharp within her reach."

Once again Victor chuckled, his gaze riveted on Arie as if he thought to read his mind. "What exactly do you have planned for the afternoon? I assume you intend to see her."

"An outing, a picnic of sort at a secluded place on the river. We need to be alone together so we can see what transpires."

Arie's thoughts traveled to the way her body felt against his the other night, the way she tasted during that brief kiss.

"Are you going to allow her to ride the horse you purchased? Take the chance she'll try to leave you?"

"She can try and I'll let her."

He'd thought about this situation so many times his head ached from all the possibilities. Perhaps he was the biggest fool ever, a besotted fool.

"You sound confident," Victor said, "You want some help keeping track of her when she takes off, and you know she will."

"I've men stationed in strategic spots to keep an eye on her. I plan on giving her as much distance and time she wants or needs in order to come to the logical conclusion."

Arie was staring into the distance, contemplating her reactions and how she would feel when she gave up on the idea of freedom in a world ruled by men.

"Her place is with you."

"Of course it is. Was there ever any question?"

Arie felt suddenly lighthearted, ready to get on with this day and discover the truth of her feelings as well as just how long it would take for her to return to him when she left.

She would leave.

"You're making light of this." Victor sounded surprised even while there was also a note of approval in his voice. "I'm glad you've come to your senses."

"No, I'm very serious." Since he first brought Alison to the house, Victor did nothing but disapprove. "I want her to understand she can leave me at any time and that staying with me is her choice."

"Think she can leave you," Victor corrected. "You're not really going to tolerate the fact if she chooses autonomy."

"What I can say is that I will keep her protected and safe no matter what her decision. Best you get your rest while you can." With that said, Arie started for the house, his package for Ali in hand. He wanted to give his gift to her and watch the expression on her face, his heart leaping to his throat in anticipation.

"Good luck," Victor called out. "I'll make sure Tessa is close by just in case you need us."

She could be angry it took him so long to fulfill his promise or she might feel appreciative and ready to grant him favors. He grinned ready for whatever would transpire. He would treasure favors of any sort. He would even hold a smile close to his heart. Victor was wrong about him as well as his intentions. He watched Cam try to woo Chelsea in just this sort of way and where Chelsea's heart was concerned the unconventional process had been quite productive. After a few weeks, Chelsea was begging Cam to make love to her.

Perhaps he should ask if he could take her to Cam's beach house so they could stargaze.

He could wait a few weeks for the same outcome. Hell, he could wait a month if that's what it took. After all, if he didn't mess up, they had the rest of their lives ahead of them. She was innocent and untried in the ways of men. She would fall at his feet, beg for his touch and tender concern. All he needed to do would be to show her his gentle side.

Once again, his heart raced as he stood at the door, hesitant at first to knock or to just walk inside. He chose the latter.

"Alison?" He stepped into the room, thinking he would find her in the main salon. His breath caught in the back of his throat when he realized the room was empty. She wasn't there. Quickly he strode to the window, peering downward. What he saw was a straight drop to the ground.

"Arie."

He turned, his body tense yet when he saw her, he relaxed momentarily. His body hardened at the sight of her, her breasts full, the pink tipped nipples bursting on the fabric of her jacket. The red hair of her woman's mound was quite obvious through the thin fabric. He cleared his throat, his voice rough before he blurted, "Would you like to go for a ride this afternoon? With me?"

She smoothed her sheer pants before looking at him, "Not in this. You wouldn't make me, would you? I know you can see every part of me. I understand that's what you wanted. Do you truly want everyone else to see me like this, totally revealed?"

"No, of course not." He cleared his throat again then, thinking he would like to stay right here and make love to her.

"Then," it seemed she prompted.

"I brought you the dress you earned for the tender first kiss you gave me." For some reason he didn't like the way that sounded. Too briskly he was sure he finished by saying, "Anyway, here it is. I'll be downstairs when you're ready." He didn't wait for an answer or even a thank you, which he wasn't at all sure would be forthcoming. He set the package down before he turned and left the room with the door open.

He was halfway down the first set of steps when he heard her footsteps behind him then her hand on his shoulder. Her breast brushed against his arm. Good God but he was acting like an untried youth.

"Thank you. I'll hurry."

The slight flush on her face pleased him as well as the fact she ran after him with the sole purpose of thanking him. She would be absolutely beautiful in the lavender day dress, embellished with darker lavender Belgian lace. He enjoyed picking out the dress and a few other things a few days past at the dressmakers. He held them all in lieu of possible favors she might bestow on him. Truth of the matter was he enjoyed buying things for her.

"You're welcome, don't be too long."

His gaze followed her back to her quarters before he turned and strode to the drawing room. Once inside the room he poured himself a whiskey, fortitude for the long day ahead of them.

Too many minutes ticked by. He was suddenly afraid she had changed her mind about the outing. He stepped into the hall, focusing his gaze upward.

One of her serving ladies rushed down the stairs. Breathless, she spoke. “So sorry, she is almost ready. We had to make her beautiful for you. There were too many things to do and her hair...” The lady sighed, “It is unruly at best.”

“She is already beautiful. She needs nothing, no enhancements.”

He wasn’t sure he liked the thought she was donning makeup to augment features that needed nothing. Her hair needed no adornments either.

“Well, we had to, well you will see when you make love to her.” With that she curtsied and rushed up the steps. Reaching the second floor she turned, “Wait there and I promise you won’t be disappointed.”

When he made love to her, probably not today but he had a guess as to what the lady spoke of. He wasn’t at all sure how he felt about that. He was trying to customize himself to the ways of the Europeans. In any case, he changed his mind liking the idea of Ali doing things to please him.

He heard her before he saw her. Her footsteps from the third floor were slow and measured, perhaps a bit hesitant. Holding his breath, he watched her dissent. When she stepped in front of him, she lowered her lashes for a moment before meeting his gaze.

With a smile, he held out his arm for her, “Shall we go to the stables first?” he asked pleased that she accepted him. Placing his hand on top of hers he waited for an answer.

“You bought my mare?” she queried softly. “I was sure...”

“Sure?”

“I didn’t think you would be able to purchase her. She’s really quite useless, but she was my friend in a time when I needed one. I used to sit in the stables, confiding in her. Told her all my secrets.” Her green eyes shimmered with moisture, tears threatening to slip from her eyes.

He was taken aback by her words, touched by the depth of

emotions she showed him. "I promised."

"They might have sold her..."

"Don't think about her demise. She will now live a very docile and well-fed life in my stable. All you need do is ask. If I'm able you can see her. You said you don't ride her?" They reached the stables. He opened the door for her.

When she saw the horse, she raced to her, stroking her and hugging her. Tears did fall, turning into silent sobs of despair. He wondered if the tears weren't more for the situation she now found herself in rather than seeing her horse alive.

Arie watched for some moments from a distance, realizing she thought the mare was one more thing that was dear to her that she thought she had lost. He did well. His reasons to give her the mare reaffirmed.

Pleased with himself he stepped forward. "Come, I want to show you something else I bought you. I'm hoping you will like this gift as much as the first two."

Placing her hand in his he strode with her to another stall. She stopped midstride with a small gasp. "What is this?" She turned, her hand on her chest. "Arie?"

"A horse you can ride. How can you go riding if you don't have a horse?" He smiled at her, wishing she would wrap her arms around him and stroke him. "Tulip the second?"

Perhaps today she would take the chance he meant to offer. He would discover just how long it would take her to return to him when she fled.

She would flee. He knew it as surely as he knew the sun would set in the west.

"Thank you again. Do I have to ride her right now? I'm not sure... it's been so long."

She was threading her fingers through the fabric of her gown, her eyes narrowed in concentration.

"No," he paused wondering at the strained tone of her voice. "You don't want to ride her?"

"It's just," she swallowed then lifting her delicate shoulders upward, "It's just that I'm a bit rusty. Tulip hasn't been able to carry someone in quite some time and this horse... Oh, my heart is beating so fast it feels as if it might just jump out of my chest."

"I'm sure you'll remember how as soon as you sit her. I'll tie the new horse and my stallion to the back of the curricle and we can ride later this afternoon. If you like you can go out by yourself."

He wondered if she understood what he offered. How much it would cost him if she disappeared or was hurt in any way. He reminded himself his men would be there, would follow her, would help her find her way back to him.

"You don't have to do that," she insisted, laying her head against the little mare, stroking her with her small white hands.

He wanted to feel her stroking him. When he closed his eyes, his imagination took over. "Of course I do. It will make you happy, and that in turn will make me happy."

To make sure his plans were fulfilled today, he needed to give her the opportunity to leave him. This was his strategy, her freedom to come and go as she pleased as soon as she realized she was better off with him than without him.

She nodded a few times wiping the tears from her eyes, smudging some of the makeup the ladies had painted on her face, "Thank you," she said again, seeming unable to think of anything else to say this afternoon.

"Here, let me help you," he said taking a handkerchief from his pocket and dabbing at her eyes until the blackness disappeared. "Don't want you to look as if you have two black eyes." He grinned shamelessly, very pleased with himself as well as his idea to grant her some freedom.

After helping her into the buggy, he handed her a parasol. "You're so fair. Don't want you to burn your skin."

"Thank you," she said again as his frustration began to escalate even though the responses were appropriate.

The longer he was with her the more he wanted to forget all the pleasantries he planned. He needed her, burned for her.

He yearned to hear words other than thank you. They rode in silence for quite some time. Uncomfortable with this situation he put in motion, Arie wasn't sure what he should say or not say. Sometimes nothing was better. He could always leave it up to Alison to begin the conversation, yet for the longest time she seemed content to remain mute. The silence didn't last much longer.

"Where are we going?" she asked then, tugging on her skirts she began to ramble. "I didn't tell you how much I like the dress. I've never had anything like this. It must have cost a small fortune. The horses, well, they are so perfect. I don't understand why. All I did was kiss you once. One would think I should have done something more to have earned so much from you."

He enjoyed hearing her voice and learning little things about her even if he'd guessed them before. Oh, but she would do more than kiss him, much, much more. What he suddenly didn't enjoy hearing was that she thought she should have done more to have earned the second horse. He supposed though her first impression had been almost correct. He had been bargaining sex for gifts. Eventually, she would give him everything he craved.

"So," he began when she finished rambling. His thoughts were changing. "We are going to a nice spot on the river, a picnic of sorts. Do you like picnics? There are no obligations whatsoever from you. I just want you to have a good time, enjoy the beautiful sunshine. The weather could change you know."

Ali looked down again, her dark lashes fluttering softly against her face. "Don't think I've ever been on a picnic. What's expected of me?"

"Nothing is expected of you. Well, perhaps one is expected to eat and drink what my cook packed."

"You mean that?" she sounded astonished and in a bit of disbelief.

"This will be your first lunch outing among other things I'm going to enjoy with you for the first time. By the way, I'm glad you like the dress. I thought the color would be perfect to go with your red hair."

She stared at him, her bottom lip caught between her teeth, "but," she hesitated, "I don't mean to be disrespectful. I don't understand why. It was just a dress."

"Just a dress," he repeated then, shrugging his shoulders, "a dress was what I promised for the kiss, a horse for the dance." He knew what she was asking but needed to hear her say the words.

"I know. The other ladies told me I shouldn't sound ungrateful but..." Her fingers wove in and out of the fabric of the dress.

"But..."

He truly didn't want to hear what exactly the other ladies told her. He would have to have Victor make sure there would be no more gossip about him or the things he might expect from Alison. The ladies meant well. He was sure of that. However, he would decide what and when she would know things.

She waved her hand in the air, clearly frustrated. "Never mind. Forget I said anything. In any case it doesn't matter. The dress is nice and I'm grateful. Did you know I've been wearing no clothing at night when I sleep so the harem pants and bolero can be washed?"

His grin widened at the image of her sleeping naked and created new thoughts of their bodies intertwined together. He placed a hand on her thigh, wishing he was touching tender flesh. "No, why would I know something like that?"

She lifted her slim delicate shoulders a wary expression on her small face, "I can't say, just thought you might have dictated something like that."

"I would gladly answer any of your questions if you would ask."

Gazing at her, he tried to encourage more queries. He realized she was shy. Spending time with a man was something new to her. The slight rise of color painting her ivory skin made him smile. It must have cost her to ask the question then tell him she slept naked. She would have no idea what exactly that image would do to his already strained emotions.

"I don't think I know how to say it," she told him. "It's really quite embarrassing, a lot embarrassing."

"Well, if you change your mind you can ask me anything. You could just blurt out your question."

"I could but I won't."

She smiled at him then, her dark lashes lowered for a moment against her flawless skin, nearly flawless there were a few freckles sprinkled across her nose and cheeks.

He pulled the curricle to a stop. "We are here. What do you think?" He gestured toward the structures he'd ordered as well as the river meandering in front of them.

She looked over the scene he'd set. If all went well, he meant to spend the night here, perhaps more than one. He was sure he'd figured in every contingency; the awning for this afternoon, the tent for this evening. Both contained all the comforts of home. Later, Victor would arrive with a feast for them.

"Is this the way of all picnics? It seems you've gone to a great deal of work; an awning and a tent, all the pillows." She waited for him to walk around the carriage and help her down.

"Your comfort as well as my own are important to me."

His hands around her waist he thought to pull her close, feel her breasts, the soft rounded globes that were fully covered as they pushed against his chest. Low in the back of his throat he groaned as raw mouthwatering sensations filled him, coursed through his body. He knew he shouldn't push this sensual side of their relationship, needed to let her feelings for him come to its gradual and logical conclusion, at Ali's pace not his.

She would come around in time. He just had to invoke the patience he was not known for. In time she would beg for his attentions just as he dreamed.

For a moment too long he held her, reveled in the closeness before he let her go, content in the fact she didn't push away from him. If he was not mistaken, she leaned into his chest, her fingers clenching his shoulders for a second.

"The awning is for you so you won't burn your fair skin just as the parasol was necessary for the ride here. The rest, well, I like to be elaborate when people I care about are involved."

Lightly he touched her cheek with the back of his hand, wanting so much more yet determined to allow her to set the pace in this relationship.

"You care about me?" she queried, sounding surprised then indignant. "You haven't even come to see me in so many days. You've a strange way of showing how you care."

"Maybe not in the way you expect. What I feel is far from platonic. I want you, Ali, and sometimes seeing you tests my control beyond my powers. I'm not going to take what you're not ready to give. Hence the distance of the last few days. Trust me, I stayed away because I wanted you too much."

"I'm not too sure I understand what you are trying to tell me." She walked toward the awning then standing beneath it, slowly twirled in a small tight circle. "Are we just going to sit here all afternoon and eat? A person could get fat doing that."

"I hope not," he grinned feeling as if she was perfect, perfect for him. He did appreciate everything about her. "Don't want either of us to get fat." He stifled the grin that was forming.

"It's hot today." She sat down on the pillows his servants laid out for them, running her fingers along the tops, seeming to absorb the ambiance.

"There is a breeze off the river."

He wasn't feeling particularly hot but appreciated the fact she was heating up and they had barely touched. This could be good, very, very good.

She played with the buttons on her dress, plucking at them until a few came undone. "I don't know why I feel so hot." She waved a hand in front of her face, creating a tiny breeze.

He sat down next to her wondering if she understood what she was doing. Surely where she grew up, unbuttoning one's bodice in front of the opposite sex was frowned upon.

Yet he couldn't resist the subtle if unknowing invitation. "Let me help. This does have a high collar. I suppose I should have picked out something with a lower corsage but I thought, well I thought you'd be more comfortable in something that covered more of you."

Quickly he undid several buttons, pushing the fabric aside then, unable to help himself, he ran his finger across her collarbone, enjoyed the swift inhalation of her breath. Again, she didn't move away or tell him no.

He was a man well pleased.

Just how far would she allow his advances to go without refusing him or moving away?

"I'm not sure that helped very much," she sighed, waving her hand in front of her face. “Perhaps the fan will help,” she told him picking it up and waving it in front of her.

“It’s cooler by the river,” he told her then stood holding his hand out to her. “Want to see?”

“You think so?”

Her eyes were wide green pools, questioning and curious too.

She pleased him.

Pushing his shoulders upward in silent speculation. “We could test the theory.”

He headed down a path toward the river hoping she would follow him. She could turn to the horse and leave. There was no one here except for the two of them. In some ways, he hoped she would take the opportunity. He needed to have her wholly committed to him and ready to get on with their lives together.

To his brief disappointment she trailed behind him.

“Wait. Wait for me.” Now she was running after him.

He turned. She stumbled into his arms. He righted her. “I didn’t know I was walking too fast, didn’t know if you would follow me.”

He was trying not to apologize for his rudeness. After all he should have waited for her, helped her down the path. Chivalry was not something that was a normal part of his everyday life.

She smoothed the fabric of her dress in a very feminine action, lowering her lashes at the same time. “I didn’t want to be left alone here.”

“I never thought...” After a short pause he circled an arm around her, drawing her close, “Come then, we’ll walk together. See what’s down that path and if it is cooler close to the water.”

“I’d like that. I don’t mean to be so clingy.”

Ali pressed against him surprising him further as she wrapped her arm around his waist. Good Lord but he needed to know what was in her mind right now.

They walked then. If it were someone else beside him, he would have stopped and kissed her. He wasn’t sure what to do. He thought how difficult it was to behave and not seduce. At the moment Ali was completely seducible. He needed for her to kiss him as she did before. He would follow her lead, try not to encourage a more sensual contact.

He stopped, his hands behind his back, rocking on his heels while she stood beside him. Unable to stop himself, he stared at her lips as they parted slightly. They appeared warm and soft, moist as her tiny pink tongue danced across them, enticingly.

"I don't understand what you want. The ladies told me you would kiss me and make love to me today. Am I being impatient? Too nervous? Have you planned something for tonight?"

He grit his teeth together. "Is that what you want?"

"I don't know."

He heard the thin wail of her voice, cringed at the sound. Then, "No, I want my freedom. Need to know I can come and go as I please before I commit to anything from you. I don't want to live behind locked doors. You've made it clear that's what you want from me."

He turned toward the awning and the pillows that implied seduction but to Arie meant so much more. "Then why didn't you mount your new horse and ride from here when I gave you the chance?" His voice was rough, shaky as the implications of what she told him became clear.

~ * ~

She was taken aback not just by the words but the harsh tone that followed. "You want me to leave you?" Her voice was shaking as moisture pooled in her eyes. She breathed in deeply hoping it would settle her nerves. He had convinced her. She couldn't leave him. She had nowhere to go. What was he up to?

"I want you to kiss me."

He smiled at her, gently running his finger down her arm and back up, his eyes darkening to ebony. Clearly, she saw the desire, which confused her even more.

"Let's not think about any of this now. We started our walk so let's finish it. Perhaps if there is shallow water we can wade and cool our feet, hmm..."

"My feet aren't hot," she shot back, wondering what his plans were now.

Confused to the tips of her toes, she didn't understand anything. One minute he implied something then the next second, he acted as if nothing the exact opposite had been said. She'd been yanked from a home, an unloving one. In any case it was her home. If that wasn't enough, placed in the situation she knew nothing about. The women told her one thing while he acted in a completely different manner.

Men, they were contrary people.

"Then I'll wade. I find all of me is hot. Perhaps we should swim instead of dabble our feet in the water. I could get totally comfortable," Arie said, his grin wicked.

"I dinna ken how to swim."

Once again, she was in a position where she had no idea how to proceed. She felt inadequate, terrified as well.

"Something else I can teach you if you will allow me. I believe the list is growing."

He stopped suddenly, turning her, pressing her against him, his hands enfolding her buttocks. Slowly he lowered his head toward her.

She watched, fascinated by the play of his features, the hardening of his jaw then his lips brushed across hers, so softly at first, she wasn't sure it wasn't the wind. She felt his breath, the scent of mint fresh in the air around him. The moisture as well as his touch fascinated her as did the softening of her lips as he caressed her. His touch was gentle and sweet, coaxing her to give something she felt unsure about, something she yearned to give him, something she wasn't quite understanding. In all her life she'd never been treated gently.

His tongue swept across her lips. Her body trembled with a deep raw passion, the sensation enchanting and magical. Shyly she touched his mouth with her tongue, tentatively at first, growing bolder as the seconds passed. Then he reciprocated the gesture again, sweeping across her teeth then deeper inside. With no hesitation, she pulled him closer, her fingers winding into the fabric of his shirt then beneath the expensive fabric to touch flesh. Having no idea what possessed her, she slipped her tongue between his lips, dancing with his until tiny sounds rippled from her.

He pulled away, pushing strands of hair from her face, watching her intently. His smile showed a wealth of straight white teeth. Puzzled again, she wanted to ask him why he stopped. She didn't dare.

He touched the tip of her nose. "Come, let's walk some more before I ravish you right here on this spot."

"Ravish?" She swallowed the lump in her throat, leaning against him. "What does that mean?"

Never before had she felt so incompetent and lacking. Surely, she should understand what he was saying as well as what he was asking of her. She tried to remember what the women told her about him, what he wanted, what he would do with her when they were alone. Her head was filled with dust. She couldn't remember anything.

"It's getting later. The sun will go down in a few hours. A breeze will cool us."

He was still gazing at her. She had the distinct feeling he was staring at her lips then lower to her bosom. Heat inside her grew to an inferno.

She ran her tongue across her mouth. "I don't know why I'm so hot. Don't ken why you stopped the kiss? Don't you like the way I do it?"

"Too much, way too much. Your innocence excites me to no end. Let's wait a few hours before we try this again." He paused seeming to think then, "Ravish, it means to overwhelm or enchant, even to bewitch. Which meaning do you like?"

She nodded a few times not really understanding what he was saying. Liked it too much. What the devil does that mean? "A few hours? Then you will bewitch me?"

"Perhaps enchant." He grinned, his smile broad, seeming to know everything.

"Enchant," she mused thoughtfully, liking the sound of the word.

"Maybe after dinner you can bewitch me." He grinned pointing ahead. "A shallow spot. I dare you to go wading with me. Take a chance. You can learn to swim tomorrow or the next day."

She held back unsure of herself and him. Pleasing Arie was the first thing on her mind. It seemed she either failed at every turn or didn't understand what he was saying or asking. The women told her that her happiness would revolve around how much she pleased him, if he accepted her into his life. She didn't know what that meant for her. She always tried to please. It seemed to her she'd never succeeded.

Perhaps it would be best if she left him. He was giving her the opportunity with the horse, even implied she could have left him earlier. He wouldn't stop her. No, he changed his mind about her. Instead of claiming her as his, he was giving her the opportunity to leave him. At that thought her heart sank.

What to do now?

So, he didn't really care for her, didn't like her kissing. She was inept, inexperienced. Perhaps she should do as he thought she would. Just another case of a man not wanting her, stiffening her spine and inhaling a long drugging breath of air, she decided it didn't matter what he wanted. What was important here was what she wanted.

"I used to wade when I was a child," she murmured, looking over her shoulder. "There was a tiny creek near the farm. I would go there with a neighbor." With some fondness she remembered those idyllic summer days.

"How old are you now? Has it been so long?"

He laughed and the sound uplifted her spirits a bit. "Can't say I've done anything like that in years."

"I'll be nineteen in December."

"That old?" he asked as he slipped his boots off before rolling up his pants. Slowly he walked into the water. A swift gasp then looking over his shoulder, "I think my toes are freezing. Whose idea was this?"

She couldn't help herself, she giggled, slipping off her shoes and skipping into the water to join him. "You're right." She kicked up water splashing him, forgetting he held her life in his hands, forgetting she didn't know what would please him and what would not. For the first time in too many years she felt carefree.

"Ah, you dare too much now." He bent low and with his hands sprinkled her with water then more when she retaliated. He let out a low belly laugh, seeming to enjoy the play, his grin wide and infectious.

"No, you don't." She ran from him, trying to lift her feet from the water, slipping on the rocks littering the river. She waved her hands in the air, trying for balance.

"Ali." His voice resounded behind her, his arms lifting her and steadying her before she could fall into the river. "What were you thinking?" He brushed hair from her face, his hands gentle, concern in the dark depths of his eyes.

"That I didn't want to get drenched."

She touched his mouth with a finger then quickly withdrew her hands, afraid of her boldness, what he might think. When he grinned at her the trepidation, she felt lifted from her heart.

She was giggling as he turned her and with a harsh voice. "You need to learn to be more careful. You could have been hurt."

Again, the subtle slap in the face with his words took her by surprise, yet it was just like him to confuse her further. "What? I didn't mean to..." She pushed away from him, struggling in the confines of his arms, furious now that she felt his wrath for no reason.

Slipping on her shoes, she stomped back to the awning he set up for her to keep from burning he told her. She was angry now, more furious than she ever could remember. Her new mare, Tulip the second, was tethered by a tree, munching grass. She wasn't too sure how she was going to mount her, but she would figure it out. Staying with a man who thought so little of her, confused her at every turn was not something she could do, a man who didn't like the way she kissed him. Well, she didn't have any practice.

What did he expect?

Alison reached the mare, stroked her sides then whispered to her, telling her she was going to ride her. They would leave this place and this man behind them forever. She understood Arie would follow her. His ego would allow nothing less. He would probably catch her and bring her back.

Why he would do that, she couldn't comprehend.

It was what she wanted. Her feelings puzzled her even more.

With the help of a nearby rock, she was mounted and riding. All she knew was that she headed toward the road she remembered arriving on. When she looked over her shoulder, he was standing in front of the awning, feet braced apart his hands on his slim hips, an odd look on his face.

She would remember the way he looked at that moment forever.

Tears slipped from her eyes as she raced away intent on putting distance between them. A few minutes later she slowed Miss Tulip. Thinking of a new name was beyond her capabilities right now. Miss Tulip would just have to do.

The sun was still high on the horizon. She had time to get back to Glasgow, but she didn't know what direction that was. She could be heading away. She'd not thought to pay attention to the direction they traveled when they left his house. She had not expected to be returning by herself. Nothing was happening as she supposed it would.

Every second she thought she heard pounding of hooves behind her, wished he would come for her. Well, she made her choice. It didn't appear he cared that she left him.

So much for his claim on her.

So much for everything he told her.

She wasn't his, never was. Ravish, enchant, bewitch, what was he thinking? He'd made her feel wanted for the first time in her life. Now he was just like the other men she knew. He found out she couldn't kiss very well so now he didn't want her. Not for one second did she believe him when he implied, he liked her kiss too much.

He didn't like it at all.

Seconds turned into minutes, turned into hours, Ali couldn't be sure. Fear clenched her gut. She didn't recognize anything.

Tears clouded her eyes as she rode not knowing, and in any case, not caring where she was going. Insecurities swamped her. She turned down another road then another. Shadows danced on the lane. Shivers of fear swept up and down her spine. Normally she would have enjoyed the play of light and the dancing leaves on the trees and the path below. The small animal noises surrounding her would have caused her to laugh. A soft wind tugged at the pins in her hair.

She was beginning to think she had turned the wrong direction. Getting to the city should not have taken this long, yet she truly didn't know how long she'd been riding. Her fingers gripped the reins tighter even as they shook so hard she thought she might not be able to hold them any longer.

For a moment the sound of hooves pounding the ground behind

her startled her. "He came for me." Her heart lightened then air caught in her lungs.

When she turned to look over her shoulder, the man on the horse was not Arie. He grinned. She didn't like the way the man looked at her.

"Why did I leave? I knew nothing good would happen," she spoke to herself trying to make sense of everything.

Her life this last week had taken way too many turns and except for Arie buying her, they had all been for the worst. Her mother and stepfather had betrayed her.

"You're a ninny and unthinking." A little voice in the back of her head spoke up.

Usually that voice was her voice of reason, but until this moment logic escaped her. Fear wove a tight curl in her belly.

"Where are you going, lass? I could be of assistance." The man pulled up beside her, a strange look on his face.

She sat up straighter deciding not to show her fear. "None of your business. Best you get on your way. My husband will join me in a few minutes. He is just a few seconds behind me. You just want to take things I don't want to give." Her mind as well as her words were rambling now. Coherent thought evaded her.

"You're lying but I'll forgive you. Come I'll take you with me, protect you from the sultan and all the bad things that might happen to you on the road." He held out his hand to her.

"No, don't believe you mean anything good for me. Arie will come for me. I know he will." But she didn't know anything. If he was interested in bringing her home, he would have caught up with her a long time ago. He allowed her to ride away with his blessing.

The man grabbed her reins from her hands, tugging on the horse. She fought back, retrieving the reins again and turning the horse away. How had she got into this trouble? A few hours ago she was laughing and enjoying the outing, the freedom Arie offered. She bargained for gifts with her kisses despite her inability in that area.

Racing in the opposite direction she tried to breathe, collect air into her lungs and absorb as much energy as possible. For some reason the man didn't pursue her. When she looked over her shoulder, she saw him slumped to the ground, his horse wandering close by.

Alison didn't know what had happened. At the moment she didn't care. She continued to gallop her horse until Miss Tulip's sides were heaving. "Sorry."

She leaned over patting her sides and slowing her to a walk. Ali knew Miss Tulip was hurting. She slipped off the horse, walking her and wishing she had food for the little mare or at least some water to give her.

They both needed rest but there was nowhere to stop, nowhere she would consider safe. She didn't know what to do or where she was.

If she knew how to get back to Arie and the romantic little picnic area he set up earlier this afternoon, she would head that way. The sun hovered on the horizon and even though the day had been warm, the breeze was cool as the sun began to dip behind the hills.

She rubbed her arms, wishing she had a jacket or a shawl. Goose bumps rose on her arms as she began to shiver uncontrollably.

"I'm so sorry, Miss Tulip. I acted foolishly. Now look at the mess I got us both into. I don't even know where I am or what direction to go. I'm lost, Miss Tulip. It's getting dark. Are you as hungry as I am?"

Miss Tulip shook her head before she went back to grazing.

"No, I suppose you're not hungry but you have to be thirsty. Should we stay here for the night or keep going? I won't ride you. We can just walk. The road has got to go somewhere." Ali felt defeated, inept. She didn't know where to turn or what to do. She would welcome help from Arie if he would just show up. Deciding then and there if he did come to find her, she would give him anything he asked for.

Miss Tulip shook her head again.

"Somewhere might not be a good place. Is that what you're trying to tell me? I should know where I'm headed before I start expending energy by walking."

Now she was talking to her horse. Who else could she talk to?

Ali rubbed her arms, shivering. She thought at least if she walked, she could stay warm. "Come along, Miss Tulip. We're going to walk until I can't put one foot in front of the other." Moisture filled her eyes. Wiping them away with the backs of her hands, she refused to let the tears fall. She got herself into this mess. She would get herself out.

One step then another, minute after minute passed. She didn't know how far or how long she walked. It seemed she made progress but to where? Finally, she sunk to the ground unable to cry. She was so exhausted and hungry her body shook with spasms of pain.

Closing her eyes, she rested then she must have slept. She woke looking into Victor's eyes, not Arie's. At least she was safe. Victor would take her back to Arie. He came for her.

Finally, someone came for her.

Or would he just walk away? Would he tell her she needed to get back on the horse and ride?

"Are you alright?" he asked, his voice gentle but he wasn't Arie.

She wanted Arie's arms around her. Needed Arie to soothe her shattered nerves and spirit. Yearned to have him tell her that he wanted to ravish her, enchant her. She wanted a golden aura of magic to surround her.

Sitting up straighter, "Just hungry and cold," she whispered, pushing hair away from her eyes. *Terrified.*

"I'm glad you aren't hurt." Victor still sounded gentle and caring.

Victor had always been that way with her. When he first brought her to the house, he spoke softly, tried to encourage her, telling her that everything would turn out fine. Told her she would be pampered and indulged.

He lied.

"Did Arie send you to find me?" she asked, hoping and praying the answer was yes. Nothing in her life was turning out fine.

"What do you want me to say? He was worried about you, the way you took off, riding wildly across the countryside. He was afraid you would get lost. But no, he didn't send me to find you and bring you back. If you wanted freedom, he wanted you to have it."

"And here I am not knowing where I am." She inhaled swiftly. "Does he want me back? Even though I don't know how to kiss. Even though he practically told me he thought I should ride away. I didn't want to, you understand."

Victor looked away for a moment. After several seconds he looked back at her, "Where do you want to be?"

She was taken aback by his words, not believing she ever had a choice. She felt weighted down by the enormity of her decisions. "I can't survive on my own. It's obvious I need help. If Arie doesn't want me, I don't know what I'll do, where I'll go."

"That doesn't answer my question little one. Where do you want to be?"

"I don't have an answer for something so preposterous."

She had only one place she could be. With Arie.

"What if I offered you safe haven?" he asked, as he wrapped his coat around her. "A place for you to live safely, away from the sultan."

Immediately suspicious, "Like the brothel?"

She would never go back to any place like that as long as she had a choice.

"No, if you choose not to go back to Arie, I'm sure he will help you find a place of your own and support you as well."

"I would earn my way."

"On your back?" Victor asked. This time his voice was harsh just as Arie's was at times. "What else can you do?"

She didn't know what to believe any longer. That was so unlike the message Arie gave her before. If she admitted anything, she would have to come to terms with the fact that Arie wanted her to be in his bed. Wasn't that the same as surviving by sleeping with a man or many men? She held her breath for a second before letting it out in a long whoosh. "I want to be with Arie if he still wants me."

Victor chuckled then, "Even if you can't kiss very well, I'm sure he wants you to come home to him. I'm also sure he will treat you gently, give you anything your heart desires."

"You think so?"

Her heart lightened for a moment then, thinking of all the skills she lacked she doubted herself again. She was a foolish ninny.

"I know so. He's been quite taken with you from the first time he saw you in that restaurant in Glasgow. He wanted you the moment he saw you. Unlike the man I've considered friend for years, he's treating you in a different manner than his other women."

"I don't remember the restaurant or seeing Arie," she said, trying though. Everything those first few days was foggy a haze in her mind.

"I'm not surprised. You were drugged and didn't know what was happening. He had pressing engagements that night. He bid me get you for him at any cost. He said he had to have you."

"The other ladies know so much. They've been telling me what to do and how to please him. I do want to please Arie," she murmured drowsily as he lifted her.

She was standing now but she wasn't at all sure she could ride the horse.

Victor seemed to have the same misgivings. He whistled. From nowhere the curricle they drove to the picnic appeared with a driver. With ease he lifted her and she sat in the buggy. She wondered where Arie was and why he didn't come for her.

He said a few words to the driver and they left. Victor following beside them with Miss T by his side. He leaned over. "We should be there in a few minutes. Try to stay awake. Don't judge Arie to harshly. He is just as confused as you are. He's a man who has never been confused in his life about a woman. He doesn't know what to do, doesn't understand his changing emotions."

She didn't think that would be easy at all. Keeping her eyes open was a struggle she was losing. "So, I wasn't that far away?"

"No, it seems you were traveling in circles. A few more hours and you might have found the camp all by yourself." Victor laughed softly.

"Traveling in circles?" she asked, wondering how he would have known that if he just came across her. "But I couldn't even walk."

"By your tracks. By his orders I did set out to follow you. He was worried, you see. When you didn't come back. He does care for you."

"Worried? Arie worried? About me?" She didn't understand why her words were slurring. "I think I like that."

What Victor told her did not have a ring of truth. To Arie, she was beginning to realize, she was merely a possession.

He would keep what he deemed was his. This afternoon was a game to him meant for her to realize she was better off with him. It was true. She would have to admit that fact and deal with him the best she could. Now she understood the game he played with her.

"You should. Arie cares about you more than I've ever seen him care about another woman."

"I suppose I should like that." She didn't know how she felt. "Don't think I can keep my eyes open a moment longer."

"Look," Victor pointed, "the light from the camp is there. If I'm not mistaken, Arie is standing beneath the awning now, waiting for you to come to him. He will have things to say to you. Don't take everything too seriously. Don't doubt yourself. You hold great power over him. Learn to use that power wisely. If you do, your life will be a pleasant one."

She did look up. Victor was right. He was striding toward her. All the light was behind him. She so wished she could see his expression read the shimmer in his eyes. Needed to gain some clue as to how he was feeling. But she could see nothing to help her decipher his emotions. He was sure to be angry with her. She grimaced as she stole a quick breath for courage.

"How is she?"

His hands were on her waist. Suddenly she found herself pulled from the buggy and cradled in his arms. His lips pressed lightly and only for a moment against her forehead.

"Cold, probably hungry, scared but otherwise fine. She will recover with a meal and a good nights' sleep." Victor's last words were pointed and somewhat harsh.

"Where did you find her?" he asked as Victor joined him.

Others appeared to take care of the horses.

"A ways down the road. In the morning we need to talk about what transpired. I understand she is your main concern at the moment."

She leaned into Arie, soaking up his warmth and strength. He would be furious. She dared to leave him. She hoped he would forgive her. She never meant to get lost, had intended to return here. Actually, she'd believed he would chase after her in order to bring her home. None of this was supposed to have happened.

Allison understood so much more now. Arie would have his way in everything. From time to time, he might even let her think she controlled a situation or two. The lesson he provided for her today was learned.

When they reached the tent, he whistled. Two women came forward. “Sir? What can we do?”

“You need to make sure Ali is dressed in something warm.”

“She has nothing except what she is wearing now and the garments she wore earlier,” one of the ladies told him.

“Then put her in one of my robes. I believe Victor would have packed at least one.”

He set her on the pallet in the tent with another brief kiss to her forehead, “I’ll be back in a few minutes. Your ladies will let me know when you are ready for me then you can tell me what happened.”

Until that moment he’d been gentle and almost loving, well she thought loving. She’d never been loved before so she could only guess at the feeling.

~ * ~

From a distance Murray Frasier watched as the man they called the sultan played with Alison in the water. He remembered that day when he had to leave her behind with her mother. She’d been a little girl then, hardly the beautiful young woman she turned out to be. She’d filled out nicely. He should have taken her with him, should have made sure Fletcher Donovan knew he wanted her.

Too bad he didn’t defy his father.

Too bad he left her to fend for herself. He would rectify that as soon as he could.

When he heard of the sultan’s purchase, rage built inside. He would never allow his daughter to be used in such a way. Alison was bred from nobility.

All he needed now was to get her away from the sultan. His daughter should have never been put in such an untenable situation. Alison would have been happy living with him.

Alison was beautiful, more beautiful than her mother. He understood the sultan’s draw to her. After all, he’d been unable to leave Alison’s mother alone.

When he watched her race away from the sultan on that little mare, he wondered what was happening between them for a few minutes. He grinned when the man foolishly did not go after her. He knew then he might be able to get her away from the man who so easily degraded her.

He promised himself he would find a way to get her safely away from Arie Demir. Quickly, he strode to his horse and set a course he figured would intercept Alison's wild ride. His heart thundered in anticipation of the meeting.

An hour later he pulled up, searching the road in both directions for any sign that Alison had passed through the area. He saw nothing. Still he figured he had a bit more time to search before the sun set.

Then he saw her. He grinned as he rode up to her, thinking in a few more minutes they could be in his home and safe.

"Where are you going, lass? I could be of assistance."

He pulled up beside her, his grin widening surprised she didn't seem to understand he could help her. She was his now. Alison would always be his daughter, his to protect.

She sat up straighter, a decidedly grim expression on her face. No, she was more beautiful than her mother, her cheekbones high, her lashes dark and full. He eyes were stunning a beautiful green, just like her mother's. No wonder the sultan wanted her but he wouldn't have her. Frasier heard he bought her from a brothel just for his own purposes. Blessed hell, how did his daughter end up in a brothel to be rescued by the likes of the sultan?

"None of your business. Best you get on your way. My husband will join me in a few minutes. He is just a few seconds behind me. You just want to take things I don't want to give." Alison waved her hand in the air gesturing for him to leave.

He wasn't going to do anything like that leave her. Bloody hell, he was going to take her home with him tonight. She would never be placed in this type of danger again.

"You're lying but I'll forgive you. Come I'll take you with me, protect you from the sultan and all the bad things that might happen to you on the road."

"No, don't believe you mean anything good for me. Arie will come for me. I know he will."

He grabbed her reins from her hands, tugging on the horse. She fought back, retrieving the reins again and turning the horse away. Valiantly she kicked at the horse urging the mare forward.

Frasier felt the bullet hit him, felt the earth meet his body hard. He closed his eyes. Next thing he knew he was bandaged and sitting with his back against a rock, his horse grazing nearby.

"What the devil happened?" he murmured, but he was pretty sure he knew.

The sultan had not let Alison ride away from him. It would be harder now to claim the girl, but he meant to try. Alison was his daughter and by God he was going to see her life set to rights. Perhaps the sultan would let her go for the right amount of coin.

Chapter Three

"What the hell happened? My men were supposed to keep her safe." Arie raked his hands through his hair pacing the distance between the tent and the awning he set up earlier in the afternoon. "Ali was not supposed to be hurt or lost."

He was angry, furiously so. Waves of ever-changing emotions swept through him until he felt the greatest urge to hit something.

"We did keep her safe. The closest man to her shot someone who approached her and stopped to make sure he didn't die on the road," Victor spoke calmly further irritating him.

Shot someone. This was supposed to teach her a well-needed lesson. No one was supposed to get hurt.

"Seems she got lost anyway. How do you explain that?" Arie looked to the tent, needing to go to Ali, wrap her in his arms and tell her he was never going to give her a chance to leave again. He would take the key to her freedom and throw it into the Firth of Clyde. He sucked in a long draught of air, hoping to gain control of his fury as well as his terror. His heart still thundered beneath his chest.

This was not well done of him.

She could have been lost to him.

"She was never lost or in any danger. I made the choice to go to her and bring her home rather than having one of your men frighten her. I was told she was terrified the first time someone she didn't know approached her." Victor was looking at him as if nothing went wrong with this ill-conceived plan of his. He was trying to placate him with sweet meaningless words.

Terrified, he'd thought if she was frightened, she would never want to leave him. He was not pleased with himself. He should never have left the horse waiting for her, never implied he would allow her to disappear from his life. In the name of Allah what the hell had he been thinking?

He'd not been honest with her and he needed to rectify that.

He vowed then she would never be terrified and alone again. She was ill equipped to survive the world by herself. That was why he saved her from the brothel. *No, I saved her because her red hair and pale skin fascinated me. I prayed, too, her desire and passion would rival mine.*

"You should go to her," Victor's voice was soft and gentle. "She might not admit it but she does need you. I think the lesson you intended came through loud and clear. Tonight, she might well shock you, pleasantly."

The sound of Victor's gentle voice surprised him. It was a side of Victor he wasn't familiar with. Now his curiosity exploded. He felt bound to know everything that went on between the two of them. "What did she tell you?"

"Know that she has doubts and is feeling insecure about your wishes for her. You have sent her different messages, confusing her. She doesn't know what to make of her feelings for you. It's best she tells you herself. A second-hand account is rarely the best source of information. Don't you agree?" Victor was smiling now, grinning from one ear to the other.

"I don't know what to say to her."

Arie felt self-doubts himself. He wanted to please her, not frighten her. He needed to introduce her slowly to sex with him, not seduce her. He yearned for her to come to him first but he had doubts of that ever happening. He smiled then, thinking of all the possibilities that would entail. If she came to him willing, holding out her slender white arms for him. He walked to the edge of the awning and back, thinking, contemplating his course of action.

His time here in Scotland was changing him.

Now that he had time to think about his actions, he'd gone about this all wrong.

Now it was time to fix the situation. He wasn't sure how. She was nothing like his other women. Never would be.

That was why he wanted her so much. The difference apparent from the set of her slim shoulders as well as the way she held her chin high, her regal bearing obvious.

Ali was different. That fact intrigued and captivated him, left him spellbound and overwhelmed. It wasn't just her red hair and sparkling green eyes. No, it was her personality when she wasn't second-guessing his intentions. At times she left him tongue-tied and weak-kneed.

What to do?

He inhaled several long deep breaths, a ploy to calm his nerves. Where Ali was concerned, he felt as if all his body was ripped apart, unknowing. Where she was concerned, he was an infatuated fool. He didn't like that feeling of helplessness she instilled in him. It would be best if he took her to his bed and let her know what was expected of her. Get the bedding over with and she would lose her hold over him.

"Just be forthright, tell her how you feel, your expectations where she is concerned. I think you'll be surprised at her response," Victor said still grinning from ear to ear as if the man understood his thoughts.

Arie didn't know if he could do that, be forthright to a woman about his feelings. He'd been taught women were put on earth to ease a man sexually and provide children. Women weren't there to confide in or have discussions with. They lived to provide comfort and whatever else a man needed. The women he met in Scotland didn't believe that antiquated notion.

"Don't know if I can do that," Arie murmured staring at the tent again. "Do you think she is ready for me?"

"Tell her how you feel," Victor insisted. "In any case if I'm done for the evening, I'd like to spend the rest of the night with Tessa. I'll wait here until she comes out."

Arie nodded walking toward the next meeting with Ali and praying it would not be a confrontation that left them both wanting.

"Tessa," Arie said passing her on the way.

He knew Victor had no misgivings about bedding Tessa or any other of the women under his protection. "Have a nice evening."

She paused tilting her head a bit sideways, grinning. "Yes, you too."

Arie thought he heard her wish him a good night but had no reply. Inside the door to the tent he stopped, searching the room for Ali. When he first noticed her, she was sitting in an overabundance of pillows, sipping wine and dressed in one of his plush robes. With one hand she clutched the opening to keep it closed. Still one alabaster shoulder was bared to his view as the fabric slipped along her arm.

He grinned, suddenly feeling more self-assured telling himself it didn't matter what she thought. "How do you feel?" He poured a drink before sitting down beside her. A need to touch her shoulder and more swept through him.

He was in control. The power was his.

"I think I'm still cold," she murmured, staring at the liquid in her glass, unwilling to meet his gaze. "I'd rather have something hot to drink."

He wasn't going to force anything, remembering Victor's advice. Perhaps the man was right. "I'm sorry."

Apologies didn't come easy for him. This might even be the first. Well, hell, it was the first. He wasn't sure if he liked the tenor of this meeting. "Hot coffee?"

That wasn't enough to say but it caught her attention and she looked at him, candlelight shimmering in her eyes.

"Sorry for what? No, I don't like coffee." Her words sounded accusatory seeming to understand he didn't mean his words. The apology was filled with air.

He bristled, feeling defensive, still needing to get inside her head. With both hands he ran his fingers through his hair, the leather thong he tied it with falling to the pallet. "I suppose everything. Just don't know where to start. Not used to telling anyone I'm sorry."

He shrugged his shoulders, staring at her, intent on taking what was his. Just how to go about it now that he'd acted so strangely eluded him.

"How about why you implied I should leave. Take the horse and leave you. Why do you want me gone?" Her voice wavered then grew stronger.

The hurt in her tone was evident. Candlelight shimmered in her hair, golden highlights threaded with the deepest reds.

"I don't." His heavy sigh caught her attention. "What I want is to have you in my bed and beneath me. That is, after all, why I purchased your beautiful body. Don't know what I was thinking or doing."

She gasped in a sharp breath, her eyes flashing emerald fire. "You have a strange way of telling that to me. One second, I'm locked in a third floor room. The next you are giving me a horse and telling me to ride away. Now you tell me you only want my body. You're my captor. What is it you want from me?"

"That's one of the reasons I'm sorry."

He did touch her shoulder then, stroked and caressed what was visible to him. He moved back watching, debating even as his smile curled into a mocking grin.

She pulled the fabric over her shoulder, her gaze returning to the drink she held. "Do you have other reasons?" Her voice was still shaky and strained. It seemed she was searching to understand to make some sense of her situation.

Momentarily his heart went out to her. Then with a swift intake of air along with an attempt to keep his grin behind his teeth, "What can I say? I'm used to getting everything I want. I wanted you. So, I took you. Then I tried, albeit unsuccessfully, to be someone I'm not."

"You didn't know what to do with me?"

"I know exactly what to do with you, however I tried to make a friend happy. In the process I lost my identity. Where you are concerned, I floundered, hoping to make this lady, who is only my friend, happy as well as you. If not happy, you will be content. I promise you that."

Finally, he felt as if he was regaining his equilibrium. With every breath inhaled relief flooded him.

"You had me then sent me away." She downed the potent glass of wine, turning away from him.

"I've never had you. It was just a kiss," he gritted out unable to remain calm despite his efforts.

She sparked emotions in him he didn't understand, couldn't control when he was around her. He was tempted to take what he yearned for and everyone else be damned. A year ago, he would have done exactly that. Thoughts of her coming to him arms open wide seeming to vanish with the evening.

She turned toward him, her eyes wide, shimmering pools of green. "What exactly does that entail? Had me? If it's not a kiss, what is it?"

A distinct edge to her voice made him smile even though he tried not to. This was why he wanted her, why he needed Alison beyond reason, beyond anything he felt for a woman before. She was special, unique and untried. She questioned. "Should I be crude or put it in more poetic, romantic terms?"

"By all means suit your fancy," she mumbled while her breasts rose and fell with the rising passion he was invoking in her by simply caressing her with his ardent gaze.

He adored her in his robe and decided she would wear it every night and nothing else since he was in control of her possessions. Strangely, he didn't feel a moment of guilt at his decision.

"If I had you, I'd have spread your legs and filled you with my rod until you cried out with the ecstasy I gave you. I would have made sure you felt something so deep and strong you'd beg me for more. Never forget you are mine, Allison. You were put on this earth for my pleasure. You will be grateful when I give you yours."

He liked it when she bristled with emotion, when her cheeks flushed with anger. She would never provide a dull moment for him. With his words he sparked an array of wild emotions.

"That was the crude version?" she queried sarcastically.

He was sure she almost smiled. Instead, she turned away.

"Perhaps I'd like to learn more about this ecstasy you believe you can give me. It most likely doesn't exist."

Allah, he wanted to know what she was truly thinking. "Am I softening your heart a wee bit, lassie, not that it matters over much. I promise you a woman's pleasure does exist."

He placed a finger on her lips, thinking he should end the torment, put his mouth there, taste her, feel her tongue against his. The heat from her would certainly set steel on fire. She needed to vent all her emotions and reservations as well.

Perhaps he deserved that and more. Chelsea MacTavish would cheer Ali on if she was here and she would light into him, explaining in vivid detail every despicable thing he said to Alison. At the moment, he was reverting back to his old ways. Well, a man doesn't change overnight, especially when a beautiful woman is waiting nearly naked for him in his boudoir.

"I think I would have preferred the poetic romantic rendition."

A quick smile did form on her lips, but it vanished in a blink. She tilted her head slightly, seeming to study him, her eyes caressing him.

"I might not understand it better, but I wouldn't be more confused."

"Then," he turned her face to look at him, "I would make love to you. I don't know any poetry. I'm not like some others who read it voraciously." He shrugged, thinking of Cam MacEwen and when he sent poetry to Chelsea changing some words so they described her, "What I told you first is more honest and direct. I promised Victor I would be telling you the truth, blatant or otherwise. Also, told him I would be gentle as well. Though why I owe him any promises is beyond me. Perhaps it is because he secured you for me."

"You'd spread my legs and come inside me?"

Her eyes were wide pools of desire and passion. He read curiosity there as well. She was questioning everything he said. That was good.

"With my manly parts." His grin grew wider as did her eyes. "My rod. I will come inside your body, delight you."

"I know I'm a farm girl but..."

"But?" he prompted waiting for an answer or a question.

"I do know you're built different from me, but..."

"But?" One eyebrow rose waiting for the 'but' to be defined.

Quickly she stood, hanging on to the oversized robe as she stepped toward the door. He wasn't sure if he should go after her or if she would stop of her own accord. What the hell did she want him to do?

She did as he hoped, turning before she left. "I never know if I should take you seriously or not. You confuse me all the time. Just like now. I don't understand why that would give me pleasure. It sounds as if it would hurt."

"Something else I suppose I should be sorry for, Ali. I want you to stay with me. I want to make love to you and give you pleasure. Will you do that tonight?"

"You don't like the way I kiss or you like it too much so you don't want me to kiss you again. What exactly does that mean?" she asked, her lips parted slightly, eyes wide.

Her arms rose then suddenly fell to her sides.

Her words were a stark reminder of the afternoon, which could have turned deadly for her.

He didn't know what to say. "Is that why you ran away? Because I told you I liked your kiss too much?"

"I left because you told me you wanted me to go," she blurted out then turned away again as if she thought she might have said too much. Her slight body trembled as she stood at the opening, looking outside then back to him.

He wondered if she was thinking about running again. "Locked in, no freedom, wanted something different for you. Needed for you to have a choice."

He could hear Chelsea's words in the back of his head telling him he couldn't treat women like chattel, couldn't buy women and expect them to obey his every command. Yet they always did. He was pretty sure he could persuade Ali to his way of thinking with little to no effort. Instead, he made a mess of things by trying to be someone he wasn't, do things he wasn't comfortable with.

"This has all become a confusing puzzle for me, one I can't solve. You don't say anything that makes sense." Her voice riddled with confusion, she wandered toward him.

"It seems as if I haven't solved it either. Perhaps we can join forces and figure out what comes next."

He still meant to take this slow. He still wanted Ali to set the pace of this relationship. That was why he backed off the kiss, but she didn't understand. Showing her the effect her kisses had on him was out of the question. Despite her upbringing he guessed she was innocent when it came to men.

"Solve this together? I need everything you've said explained. I'm not sure about anything except you don't want to kiss me and now I've a choice as to whether or not I want to leave. I don't have anywhere to go. I'm sure you're aware of the fact. You don't act like it."

He needed to show her what she said wasn't true but unless she was ready to have sex with him tonight, kissing was out of the question. Placing her hand in his, he walked with her back to the bedding.

"Come here." He sat down, pulling her into his arms. "You're probably tired and need to sleep. You should sleep," he murmured as he ran his fingers through the length of her silken hair, wishing he could wrap it around him. "Yes, I'm sure that's a fine idea. Sleep." Allah, he still sounded like a love-struck fool.

"I am tired but I'm anything but sleepy. Before Victor found me, I slept some. He woke me up and brought me back to you."

With the tip of one finger she touched his chin, explored his jawline. She ran her finger down his neck, stopping where his pulse thundered. Her eyes lit when she realized what she was doing to him.

"He did. I'm glad he brought you to me. I would have been lonely without you." Winding a strand of hair through his fingers, he held it to his cheek. "Your hair is so soft, silken to the touch. You smell like roses." He'd like to wind it around his body, bask in the silken fire.

"Victor did ask me questions. Told me he'd take me somewhere I'd be safe from you if I didn't want him to bring me back here."

"What did you tell him, hmm...?" he queried, smiling assuming the answer was what he wanted to hear since she was in his arms.

The pleasure of her small body next to him amazed and intrigued every sinew. How could one tiny woman generate such raging passion in him that he was hard pressed to control?

Turning in his arms, she continued the tentative exploration of his face. Letting her sooty lashes fall closed for a moment, "Told him I wanted to be with you. Didn't want to go anywhere else."

His breath rushed out in a long sigh, his body tightening further. The experiment worked. He'd taken a huge chance but it worked. She was his now. "Do you want to go to sleep now? I'll leave."

"No, don't go. I want to fall asleep in your arms. It seems unless you're holding me, I'm still cold, still afraid of the sounds outside."

Trusting him, she rested her head against his chest, her soft curves molding against him.

"I'm not sure that's a good idea, for me to stay here with you, in bed with you. I might not have the strength to resist." Thoughts of her naked under the robe and how easy it would be to slip it off converged in his head. Even now his fingers were finding a way beneath the fabric covering her.

"You don't want to sleep with me? Did I just misunderstand?"

She looked at him for a moment before setting her head on his chest once more, her fingers close to his heart, heating and enticing him.

"I want to sleep with you and so much more..." he murmured, stroking her collarbone where the robe slipped from her shoulder, enjoying the little shivers of desire he felt ripple along her body. He ran his hand along her shoulder then down her arm to return before doing the same again and again.

"Is that like you not wanting to kiss me? I'm willing to take the chance simply because I don't want you to leave me."

When she pushed away from him to stare into his eyes, the robe slipped farther. He was treated with a view that left him groaning.

"Yes, and I'm not willing, not yet. Not until I know you want me more than I want you." *Until she begs me to make love to her.*

"I think I do."

"You have no idea what you're asking. Perhaps we'll kiss a bit more. I will try to control myself. You have to promise not to be offended if I stop suddenly. If I pull away it doesn't mean I don't want you."

"Promise," she murmured softly, her lashes fluttering gently across her high cheekbones.

"Promise me you won't believe I don't like your kisses. They are sweet and innocent, so exciting, nothing like anyone else I've ever kissed."

He was a jaded man, having lost count of the women who had been brought to him, the women he made love to. Ali was unique. Sighing contentedly, he brushed tangled hair from her eyes, noticing the ladies had taken time to paint her face with a tiny bit of makeup. Thankfully the tiny dusting of freckles across her face were not hidden.

"Promise."

She pushed away from him, her hands on his chest. He turned her so he was above her, his hands on either side of her head. Slowly, slowly...

Tenderly his lips brushed against hers, the taste so sweet and tantalizing it stole his breath, air caught in his throat. He closed his eyes, his body tightening, hardening with just that small caress. Then her tongue swept across his lips, a groan rumbling through his chest. He fought the urge to discover the silken flesh beneath the robe. Fought his powerful desire.

"You learned," he told her, grinning as he stared down at her. "Perhaps you are learning too much too fast."

His tongue caressed and parted her lips, delving inside for a moment. He tasted the wine and the sweet essence of the woman.

She responded, slipping her hand beneath his shirt, running her fingers across his chest, rubbing her palms against his nipples.

"Teach me something else."

Her fingernails ran across his back, sending swift mercuric heat throughout his body. His groan of desire and pleasure rumbled up from deep inside his chest.

"What do you want to learn?"

He pulled away slightly but her lips were so close and they beckoned, their sirens call unable to resist. He kissed her again and again, each kiss a little deeper, more heated, excruciatingly painful, achingly delicious. Her passion bubbled up from deep inside her into him. His hunger for her was fierce and savage. He was beside himself with the knowledge he could have her now. If he wished he could take her.

She wouldn't resist.

"If I knew I wouldn't have to ask," she breathed out when he pulled away. Her words were more of a question than a statement. "You do want me?" Her eyes held a question that needed answering.

He laughed then, a deep belly laugh. "No, I suppose you wouldn't have to ask. My sweet treasure, I want you more than you could ever guess."

Gently he separated the robe, revealing more flesh, tender skin just waiting for his attention. Her breasts were perfect rounded globes, so very white, tipped with tiny rosebud nipples tightening even while he stared at them.

Bracing himself above her he slowly sketched a line across her collarbone then between her breasts. He followed the path his fingers made with his lips, teeth and tongue. Gently caressing, nipping and kissing until tiny sounds of pleasured rippled through her. The sounds were softly muted, giving every indication of her enjoyment and passion a passion he knew he could draw forth to the expected conclusion.

He would stop soon. Yet he didn't like leaving her wanting. He needed an end to this lovemaking just as much as she did. Already her hips were reaching for him, moving upward in a silent primal dance of yearning. The magic of her enchanted him, a tempest of fire and passion. Her body wanted his but her mind needed to be in synch too. She didn't understand but he did. He couldn't take her until she understood more, until she asked him, no, begged him to make love to her, to ease the burning need he so easily brought forth. Before he came inside Ali, she would be desperate in her need.

He moved back from her, pulling his shirt off. "Touch me." He placed her hands on his chest.

"Really?" she asked, her eyes wide with anticipation.

She was hesitant at first then she began to explore him, her fingers dancing. Running her hands up then down his body, she stopped each time at his waistband to look at him as if for approval. He wasn't too sure how much more of this he could endure. He nodded his encouragement. He inhaled sharply, stunned and rigid instantly tense, instantly aroused beyond anything he'd known before. With each pass of her hand, the inferno raged higher.

She was just a woman, nothing more.

He held her hands in his, kissing them each so he could contain himself. "I love what you are doing but..." He held her hands on either side of her head.

"But you love it too much?" She blinked a few times, scrunching her lips together. "Does that mean you like for me to touch your chest?" Her warm pink tongue ran across her bottom lip.

He tried to stifle the groan wishing that tongue was inside him.

"Yes, and eventually other parts."

Then with his teeth he pulled the robe open again. Still her breasts waited for his attention. He knew he was testing the limits of his control if he kissed her breasts. They were so tantalizing, hardening further even as the cool air caressed them.

"Should you see me," she swallowed seeming unsure of herself, "See my... my breasts."

"Only if you want me to see them. Do you?"

He held back then, thinking he'd taken this too far tonight.

"You're so different from me," she murmured as she stroked his chest. "Your skin is so dark, the hair crisp and curling around my fingers."

"Thank God," he said, grinning at her, watching the tantalizing expression flit across her face. Her eyes darkened with the passion she was feeling. "Do you like the difference?"

"Yes, a thousand times yes."

She closed her eyes as he lowered his head to touch the tip of one breast with his lips before nipping it with his teeth.

"Open your eyes, my sweet treasure. I want you to see me when I kiss you. I need to see your eyes when my lips close over the tip of your breast. Want to hear your sweet response. Those tiny sounds I hear coming from the back of your throat."

Arie watched her as he slowly closed the distance. His mouth found the nipple again, caressed and laved, bit gently. Mesmerized by her innocent reactions he switched to the other breast.

In the candlelight, he saw her shimmering eyes and her naked breasts as well as the gleam of moisture where his lips had taken possession. She was like a flower unfolding its petal to the sun. He gritted his teeth together, forcing himself to a calmness he didn't feel. Hoping to control himself, he swallowed quickly, felt the speed of blood as it raced and bubbled from the pulse beating at his groin and echoing throughout the length of his body.

With a huge sigh of regret, he closed his eyes and pulled the robe closed. "You stopped?"

He brought her hands to his lips, tenderly kissing each finger. "Because that's the end of the lessons for tonight."

"I don't want you to stop." She was shaking her head, her lips parted in an invitation she was yet to understand.

"You don't know what comes next. Besides, it's time to sleep. You need your rest for tomorrow."

"Why? What are we going to do?"

"It's a surprise. I assure you will like what I've planned."

"Will you sleep with me?"

"Later. I've a need to speak with Victor now."

"All right then but I want to wake up in the morning with you beside me."

"I want the same thing." He bent over kissing her quickly on the forehead before slipping his shirt on and striding outside.

Arie wanted to talk to Victor but forgot he was going to be with Tessa. He was sure Victor's night would not end chastely as his did.

He didn't know how long to stay outside mulling over the evening's transgression. For several hours he sat beneath the awning, contemplating his body's reaction to the special woman inside. He rose, stretched, stared at the tent. With a heavy sigh, he sat again. The horizon was beginning to lighten before he stepped inside the tent. At the tempting sight of her, his breath caught in his throat.

~ * ~

With eyes still closed and unwilling to escape the reverie of her dreams, Alison rose and stretched muscles that had never been used before she rode a horse in circles. She felt the coolness of the morning air caress her skin then heard the soft masculine gasp of surprise.

When she opened her eyes, Arie knelt beside her, his hand tenderly touching her cheek. She smiled at him then met his gaze, her eyes fixated on his lips as she moistened hers. His were full and damp. She remembered how they felt and tasted last night when he was convincing her he wanted her to stay with him. She understood the power he held over her. She didn't believe it was such a bad thing. Her life had been difficult, hard. Until Arie came into her life, she labored from sunrise to sunset.

It seemed she always knew she'd be given to a man. Married she'd be used by her husband. This was not much different. On one hand she needed to be loved and married. On the other she thought no man would want her. Now she was coming to realize her fate as a woman was sealed. She would be owned. This man was different from the previous men in her life. No man offered for her hand in marriage. No man wanted her until Arie.

Why shouldn't she give him anything he asked for? He would treat her well in exchange.

Perhaps...

Well, perhaps life with Arie might not be so bad, might indeed be better than what she would have known if Fletcher found a husband for her. Instead of a husband he chose to sell her to a brothel.

Quickly he slipped out of his shirt and settled in behind her, holding her close. His hand cupped one breast. His lips scattered kisses across her shoulders and neck before following a path down her spine. The sensations were unspoiled and delectable, creating feelings she didn't understand.

"Arie." His name squeaked out as she felt the same primal and so very mercuric sensation gather deep in her core that she felt last night.

Between her thighs she burned with a desperate need she sensed only he could ease.

"I know. I should stop, but..." He continued his explorations, seemingly unrepentant.

She pushed back against him, seeking his warmth and more of the relentless stroking of his lips and teeth. Trying to turn in his arms, he held her still. "I don't want you to stop. Please."

"We have to. I've a surprise for you, and the curricle will be waiting for us in a few minutes. What would the poor horse think if we kept him waiting?"

He touched the tip of her ear with his tongue then his teeth. It seemed he was having difficulty stopping.

"Then you cannot keep torturing me," she said indignantly. "I..." she swallowed wondering just how much she could share with him. She didn't dare tell him how his touch made her feel, tell him she felt swollen and wet in the most private parts of her.

"I?" he questioned as if he did want to know everything she was thinking. "What is it you want to say?"

She ran her tongue across her lips, tiny sounds rippling from her throat as he rolled the tips of her breasts between his fingers. "I... Arie, I'm so hot and wet..." she finally blurted. "I've never felt this way before except the other times you kissed me. Why is it?"

"That is good, my sweet, so very good, but we still must get up."

He pressed kisses down her neck as he continued to play with her breasts, one hand settling on her belly. Currents of need raced through her as her muscles contracted. She closed her eyes, wishing there was time to explore this further.

Suddenly the heat from his body vanished. Cold air caressed her where his big body had been only a second before. Looking more handsome than sin, he stood over her, his grin wide.

"That was not fair of you," she told him, pulling the sides of the robe together to cover her nakedness.

"Don't." He reached out to stop her, smiling. "I enjoy looking at you. Besides you need to dress yourself unless you want me to do the honors."

"As I do you, but I'm cold."

She pushed his hands away. It seemed he drew back, allowing her the need to cover herself.

"Is that the real reason?"

She paused thinking and playing with the lapels of the robe.

"Be honest."

"No, and yes. It embarrasses me to have you look at me with no clothing on. Even the harem pants covered me though I knew you pretty much saw all of me. I lied to myself and tried not to think about it."

"I'll allow it for now," he told her, walking away, whistling to himself. "I'll be outside waiting for you."

She nodded still holding the robe closed over her breast, thinking it was one thing for him to touch and fondle her but something entirely different for him to stare at her while she was naked. He teased, taunted her body with promises of pleasure then left her.

Tessa poked her head inside the tent. “Arie says you are ready for a bath.”

“I am,” she said wondering how much Tessa would guess about last night.

“Good. Your dress was washed last night. It is dry now. Was your evening good with Arie?” she asked.

Her smile was soft. Her question seemed innocent enough, but Alison wondered how much she knew. “It was fine.”

“You don’t sound so fine. I spent the night with Victor. Perhaps in time Arie will sleep with you. He is so unsure of how to deal with you, he is not himself,” Tessa rambled on, her grin wide as if she knew some secret about Arie she wanted to tell.

“Did Victor make you feel so hot you wanted to scream? Did he create an ache deep inside you in female places?” Ali asked.

Tessa paused in thought, watching her with her dark brown eyes. “I didn’t think he made love to you. At least he acted like a man who needed sexual release.”

“Is that what you call it, that ache that has no end? He leaves me wanting more and says I’m not ready. He walked out the door. Left me in the bed by myself. I wanted to run after him, bring him back to me.”

Tessa laughed softly, “Victor has told me that Arie is a driven man. He is trying to keep his friends happy. In doing so, he is making both of you miserable. I’m sure he will figure it all out shortly. You have reached something inside, Arie, some place that he doesn’t know what to do. He wants to act the gentleman yet he doesn’t know how. Arie is a man used to taking what he wants when he wants. This is as new to him as it is to you.”

“What am I not ready for?” Alison wasn’t about to let her question go unanswered. Tessa seemed more than willing to answer whatever she asked, to give information she needed.

“For sex with him,” Tessa said bluntly.

“That is when he spreads my legs and comes inside me. He told me there is a delightful sensation like nothing else imaginable. A woman’s pleasure, he called it.” Ali was shaking her head, still confused, irritated as well at the man’s audacity. “Why am I not ready?”

“Did he tell you that? I should box his ears for you. Well, I would except Victor would have words with me if I dared do such a thing.” Tessa laughed, clearly amused with something.

Ali couldn’t help but smile when she looked into Tessa’s eyes, realizing there was a lot she didn’t comprehend. “I did ask him for the crude version when he offered to explain what ravish meant. I don’t care too much for romance and poetry.” Alison slipped into the hot, rose-scented water thinking on all that Arie told her while Tessa busied herself around the room.

Tessa stepped outside for a few minutes while she finished bathing. Alison could hear voices, but she couldn’t make out what was being said. Tessa seemed a bit angry though as her voice rose and fell, any trace of amusement if it had been in her voice was gone.

She heard Arie’s laughter. He was kneeling beside her, taking the sponge and soap from her hands. Before she could voice a protest, he’d soaped the sponge, was running it along her legs then around her breasts, stroking and teasing, taunting her, cajoling her to those sensations she felt the night before. Her body heated, responding to him. She burned for him.

“I can wash myself,” she told him, her voice thin, shaky, unable to hold back the ragged emotions coursing through her.

“Lean over so I can soap your back. After that I’m going to wash your hair.” He ignored her, disregarding her words while he batted her protesting hands away. It seemed to Ali he would not respect her objections.

“It will take an hour to dry. Aren’t you in a hurry to get on with the day? At least you said as much a few minutes ago.” She felt like pouting, refrained though.

“You could sit in the sun while I comb it. I’m sure it will not take that long.”

Suddenly a bucket of water was poured over her head. She shrieked, closing her eyes, sputtering and holding her breath until the last drops slid across her face.

“You didn’t have to do that. You didn’t even give me a warning.” She pushed the excess water from her face and eyes, angry once more with the egotistical man.

He chuckled. “You would have complained.”

“Well, I can’t sit in the sun. As you said yesterday, I might burn.”

She closed her eyes again when he started massaging the soap into her hair. The feel of his fingers on his scalp sent a mercuric shiver spiraling through her. “Why are you doing this?”

“Because I want to. Now this time I do need you to close your eyes because I’m going to rinse the soap out.”

“Do you get everything you want?” she asked wishing he’d given her some say in this, in any of this.

“Not where you are concerned. I’ve held myself back. Kept myself from making love to you the first night I had you in my home. Now, I’m enjoying watching you and helping you take a bath. I do enjoy looking at you with nothing on.”

His easy grin turned to what appeared to be a smirk of satisfaction.

She held her breath as the next bucket of water was dumped over her head. It seemed he made sure all the soap was gone before he left her side.

“Now it’s time to get out.” He held out a large bath sheet, waiting for her to get up, grinning shamelessly as he watched her, his dark brown eyes fixated on her breasts then lower.

“You can leave.”

She suddenly realized she was naked in the tub. He’d been looking at her, touching all of her and the feelings that silent contact elicited left her breathless and mindless as well. She didn’t want to give him any more of an advantage over her than he already had.

“Don’t want to. If you stay in the water much longer, you’ll resemble a prune.”

His voice was smooth and compelling. She knew what he said was true. As Victor told her, Arie would get everything he wanted and more.

Once again, she closed her eyes and stood, allowing him to drape the towel around her. For a few seconds she held her breath, silently willing him to leave the room.

“Why did you close your eyes?” His words held laughter in them.

With a long sigh of relief that she was out of the water and wrapped in a towel, “If they were closed, I wasn’t going to see you looking at me."

"I don't want to embarrass you." This time he did sound sincere.

"Well, you do."

"In time I won't. You have to get used to me, that's all. Now, Tessa has laid your dress out so as soon as you let me help you into it, we will get your hair dry."

"Then you'll tell me what this surprise is that you have waiting for me."

"Not quite yet. You will have to wait until we reach town. You will know and I'm sure it will please you."

Over an hour later they were riding into Glasgow. They stopped in a place she'd never been. Of course, there were few places in the city she went let alone in what looked like an expensive district. She looked at him, wonder in her eyes.

"What is this?" she asked as he helped her down and settled her on the walkway in front of the shops.

"A dress shop," he told her, his eyes brimming with silent laughter. He looked and sounded pleased with himself "You don't have enough clothing. I'm going to purchase something of everything for you."

"Dresses?"

"Underthings, perhaps a parasol to go with each carriage dress although I think you will have more use for day dresses. If I have my way, which I will, you're not going to need anything to wear in the evenings."

He chuckled a grin on his face that she was coming to understand all too well.

Heat bubbled through her, rushing to her cheeks. She clamped her hands on her face. "Underthings?"

"Of course, you're sounding like a parrot now."

He laughed again a full belly laugh as he opened the door for her and the little bell announced them.

"Why?"

"More things to take off you. I'm finding I enjoy that part of sex almost as much as the rest. The foreplay, you understand. I enjoy the slow reveal as well as the little sounds you gift me with each time I see or touch a different part of you."

"No, I don't understand anything."

He bent, whispering close to her ear, "Soon you will."

"Good morning," a seamstress greeted them. "How can I help you?"

Alison jumped, startled by the sudden appearance of the woman.

He pointed to a chair for Ali, "Sit and I want you to tell me if there is anything you don't like. Otherwise I'm going to do most of the shopping. Will you promise to do that?"

"Alright."

She was nodding her head in silent surrender. Once more he made her feel unsure of herself and lacking. She certainly didn't have the ability to pick out clothing in a place like this, so perhaps his way was for the best.

She wanted to learn though.

She could learn.

"Monsieur, we need to get her measurements."

Arie sat down beside her, picking up her hand and holding it in his. "You will need to go into the dressing room so the seamstress can measure you. I assume you've never done anything of this sort before."

Shock coursed through her then leaning close and whispering, "Do I have to take my dress off?"

"Well, I suppose you will if the measurements are to be accurate." He was laughing again. She wanted to hit him.

Instead she swallowed, wishing she could dissolve into the walls of the shop. "I have nothing on beneath the dress. I'm naked."

"Hmm... I forgot about that." For a moment he looked chagrined, rubbing his chin as he seemed to search for an answer.

He rose then addressing the lady in charge. "We have a bit of a problem. She has no underthings and is embarrassed to be naked in front of others. Would it be alright if I took the measurements?"

The woman's face paled as she stared from one to the other. "Monsieur!"

"I can go somewhere else where they will be more conducive to my request. As you know this is a substantial order."

Her face red to the roots of her hair, the woman slowly nodded her head, narrowing her eyes at them as he brought her to the privacy she required. Clearly, she disapproved.

"I don't want you take the measurements either." Alison was pointedly blunt.

"You do have a choice," he said, his voice smooth as if he knew what her answer would be. "Perhaps..."

"Perhaps what?" She hoped he thought of something that would ease her discomfort.

Her rational thoughts cried out to her that he'd seen all of her, touched most of her. What difference would it make if she stood naked in front of him. Only an hour or so ago she'd done just that when she got out of the tub.

"Perhaps I can purchase an already made chemise you can wear. The garment won't hide anything but," he paused, grinning, clearly exacting amusement from the situation, "if you close your eyes, you won't know I'm looking at you. Won't know I'm taking your measurements."

She inhaled a long deep breath. "Please. I would like that."

He stepped from the privacy room, returning a minute later with two garments. He lifted his shoulders, a wicked glimmer in his eyes that didn't go unnoticed. "I didn't know your size." He held both up to her and decided on the smaller one. "I will even turn my back when you put it on."

He turned. She quickly slipped out of the dress and into the chemise. Dragging in air to her parched lungs, "I'm done."

With the measurements taken, she dressed and stepped from the room with Arie. On the tables an array of fabrics were strewn along with fashion plates. He held up bolts, asking for her approval. She felt thoroughly overwhelmed and unable to say yes or no.

"I'm happy if you make the choices for me." She waved her hands in the air, confused. "This is all so overwhelming."

"Thank you." He proceeded to purchase day dresses and gowns along with shoes and parasols, too many undergarments for her to count. Exhausted by the ordeal, she leaned against the wall, closing her eyes as Arie and the seamstress chatted and decided on her clothing.

What seemed hours later, he sat down beside her, picking up her hand and kissing the back. "I believe we are done here. You did quite well. I'm proud of you. Would you like to go somewhere to eat? I know just the place."

She nodded, not remembering breakfast. Now the time must be a few hours past noon. "Are we going back to the tent or to your house?"

"Visiting. The nice lady here has promised to deliver a few of the things tomorrow morning. When you wake you will have a choice of what to wear. Will you like that?"

"What if I want to wear the harem pants and bolero? I find I'm becoming accustomed to you seeing me naked." She realized the truth of her words. Still, she felt heat rise to her cheeks when she realized what she told him.

He let his head fall back while he roared with laughter. His eyes blazing when he set his gaze upon her lips. "I would love that. You can wear them anytime I'm the only one with you. If you like, I'll even let you dance for me."

"Never again." Heat rose to her face.

"With a few more lessons?"

"So, who are we visiting?" Suddenly realizing who he must be speaking of, her body shook with anger. She was shaking her head, unable to form the words her throat parched.

"Chelsea and Cam MacEwen." He studied her seeming to look for some reaction. When he saw only the embarrassment she felt to the tips of her toes, he said, "You will like her but you mustn't like Cam. No, that wouldn't do at all."

"She is the lady who has chastised you for your treatment of me. She is the one you care so deeply for."

"Yes, and I believe she will be pleased with my purchases." He cleared his throat as if he realized how his words could be construed. "The dresses, of course, even though she understands I bought you."

"Isn't she the cause of some of our problems. Not sure if I want to meet her."

No, Ali knew she didn't want to see Chelsea for any reason especially not for social reasons. She was awkward and knew she would embarrass Arie. The woman would know she was his concubine.

"No, I want to go home."

Truly she wasn't sure of anything any longer. This lady was someone Arie admired. She'd heard as much from the ladies who tried to teach her how to please Arie.

"You'll like her, I promise," Arie told her but he suddenly didn't sound quite so sure of himself. "Well, I know she'll like you. Chelsea will also tell me how I need to change my ways where you are concerned. Whatever happens we are going to need to sit down and talk about the repercussions of our visit before one of us does something foolish."

"Could we just forget about this and go home?"

Nerves seemed to stretch then and snap. She'd never met a lord or a lady before. Didn't have the slightest idea what to say to one or how to act in his presence. "I've had too much excitement for one day, and I don't want to meet anyone."

She understood she was being perverse, but she'd asked Arie for very few things. It seemed he could grant her this one favor. Problem was, she didn't want to beg him for anything. She did have her pride. Pride, which had been sorely tested the last weeks.

Arie helped her into the curricle, his hands on her waist reminded her of more intimacies. Things she'd like to discover with him sooner than later.

"We've been invited. I've accepted the invitation." His voice was gruff, more commanding than she'd heard it before.

She supposed nothing more should be said but she was trying, as Tessa told her, to let him know how she felt about things. At this point she was resigned. "Can we leave if things get tense?"

"What is tense?" He asked as the carriage began to move forward.

He kept his attention on the road ahead of him, refusing to acknowledge her question with an answer.

Perverse man. "I just don't want to be told what to do or how to feel. This Chelsea seems strong willed and opinionated. I've never had much experience with other females." As she spoke, her hands were shaking.

"You can stand up to her." He smiled at her as if he knew some secret. "I would enjoy that. Tell her no if she tells you to do something you don't like."

"I don't see how. I'm nothing but your possession. She is a lady, nobility."

She fiddled with her skirts wishing there was some way to convince Arie meeting this woman was not the best course of action.

"We're here."

Suddenly, her heart fell to her stomach.

~ * ~

Chelsea's gaze was riveted on Arie. It was perfectly obvious that he was smitten with Alison. No wonder he turned into a man she didn't recognize. If Ali understood the power she held over Arie, she could get anything she wanted, perhaps even her freedom. Chelsea almost laughed at that thought. Held the mirth behind her lips simply because she didn't want to explain anything to Arie. He would have to figure this out the hard way.

"So, what did you do today?" Chelsea asked looking at Ali, hoping she would speak up and by doing so inadvertently tell her something about herself.

They'd been sitting in the parlor for nearly fifteen minutes. So far Ali said nothing except nice to meet you. Chelsea was doing everything she could think of to change that. She wanted Alison to open up.

Cam stood, addressing Arie after clearing his throat then giving Chelsea a side-glance. "I've a new horse. Would you like to go look at the stallion?"

"Yes." Arie's gaze went to Alison.

"Suppose we should leave these two to talk. Chelsea has some things she wants to ask Alison," Cam said laughing while he stared at his wife. "I told her to leave well enough alone." He paused, hefting a great and very dramatic sigh. "Where you are concerned, it doesn't appear she can do that. She wants you to act like a well-bred Englishman even though she kens you are not."

"Is this your getting even with me?" Arie asked returning the chuckle seeming to remember something amusing. "I'm ready. Bring it on. I've found I've been trying to act as I believe Chelsea would want me to act, and it's given Ali and I nothing but difficulties. I'd much prefer to be myself with her."

"Yes, and before you know it, all your good intentioned plans will fly right out the window," Cam said. "Women we care about have a way of blind-siding a well-intentioned man."

Cam left the room with Arie following him. Chelsea wasn't sure how that would end. She would make a point later tonight to thank her husband for his thoughtfulness. It had not been that long ago when Cam had been intensely jealous of Arie. Perhaps he even hated him. He'd had to change though when she married the stubborn man.

"You say Arie took you dress shopping today?" Chelsea asked, sipping her tea, wishing she'd offered wine or brandy. She had a decided feeling by the time they were finished here she would need the fortification. She hoped, while buying dresses for his lady friend was nice, he was not intending to receive certain types of favors in return. A long slow breath of air drifted out. By this time Chelsea was sure Arie had already claimed this woman as his own.

"Some lavender cakes for the two of you?" Jana, Chelsea's lady's maid set a tray on the table in front of the couch. "They are fresh from the oven."

"They're very good," Chelsea offered them to Alison, wishing the air didn't feel stilted and heavy.

The moment the men left it seemed to her Alison withdrew into herself even more as she stared at the empty path the men made when they left the room.

"I'm fine." Alison sat stiff backed, her hands in her lap. "Never had lunch or any kind of dealings with a viscountess. Don't know what to say or do for that matter."

"Tell me something about yourself and don't worry about the title. I'm really just like you. I wasn't born with the tittle. I married it. For the longest time my brother thought I was a little hoyden."

Chelsea remembered when Arie first told her about this beautiful green-eyed woman and how her red hair enticed him like no other. She bit into one of the cakes, hoping Alison would relax, even take a moment to enjoy herself.

"I come from a small farm. Arie has treated me very carefully. He is so worried that he is going to offend you that he is not himself. I know Arie bought me. I'd be in that whorehouse if he didn't. My life would be very bad. Now I have things I never thought of before." She blushed prettily when she spoke of Arie. "And beg your pardon, we are nothing the same. I've never had nice things. There were times when I didn't know where my next meal was coming from, at least until mother met Fletcher Donovan." Ali held her hands up to stop Chelsea's reply. "Before you say anything, I know what he's done. Fletcher is not a nice man. Arie is. He will never hurt me."

"Really, I can't imagine Arie would not be himself. He seemed to encourage my relationships with Cam. He even kissed me once to make Cam jealous."

"Arie is so confusing. He was so worried about the fact that he bought me." She waved a hand in the air, her forehead creased with deep lines, "that I left. I managed to get myself lost. I could have died because I thought he wanted me to leave him. I was wrong though."

"What did he want? I'm sure it wasn't that." Now Chelsea was beyond curious. The very notion that Arie lost his confidence in himself over a lady was too intriguing and funny to ignore. Arie must be head over heels in love with Alison.

"What did he want? Do you really care? He's different, you know. Because of you he needed to make sure I didn't feel as if he owned me. I knew he owned me. I also kened I had no other options. In any case, it doesn't matter if I'm his slave. I like the man. I've nothing else, no other options."

"I see." But she really didn't understand the point Alison was trying to make. "Who would want to be owned?"

Chelsea decided she needed to speak with Arie again. When was the only question?

"I do know. Victor offered them to me, the options, but I only want Arie. I don't care that he bought me. Don't care he owns me. I don't care that he considers me as his. I don't care what you think."

Ali inhaled a long slow deep breath of air, appearing relieved that she spoke her feelings and got them out in the open even if she rambled and repeated herself. She had the feeling Chelsea would have to be told more than once that she was happy as things were between herself and Arie.

Chelsea's smile grew broad. She was thrilled with Ali's response. "Arie deserves someone who cares so much for him. I hope your feelings for him will never change. Do you care if you're his fourth wife?" Ali appeared startled by that question. "Have I said too much?"

"We," Alison suddenly turned red. "We haven't spoken of marriage just sex. I haven't considered marriage as an option. Didn't know one could have more than one wife. At least not at the same time."

"Well, I'm sure it will come up eventually. Has Arie behaved himself with you? He hasn't forced you, has he?"

"Don't know what you mean by behave himself," Ali said softly wishing the conversation would come to a sudden and abrupt end. "We kiss. He's touched me in..." She stopped then. Her eyes wide as saucers. "I don't think I should be talking about something so private with anyone except Arie. I don't know you."

Chelsea knew this woman would eventually be perfect for the man she cherished as a friend from the first moment she met him. In so little time, Alison challenged him in numerous ways. It wasn't because of what she told Arie. It was because he cared for her. Arie would never change his ways unless it was what he wanted. Not even for her would he change.

"Would you like some wine? Something stronger than this tea we've been pretending to drink? I know I want wine," Chelsea asked as she found a bottle and poured herself a glass, holding the bottle in the air as she waited for an answer.

"Yes."

"You know, all I wanted was for Cam to kiss me and make love to me, and all he wanted was to try to court me properly and protect me which didn't include kissing and making love. For a short time anyway, he would have been content to hold my hand."

Ali sipped the wine Chelsea handed her. "I wasn't used to wine until Arie. We have it every night, at least the last few. At first, he stayed away from me. I was glad then, at least until I met him, spoke with him."

"You have to make sure you tell him what you want, not what you think he wants. He has to say what he wants not what he believes I want. Perhaps that's where you went wrong. Neither of you were honest with each other."

Chelsea's sister Bliss had that same type of trouble. She wasn't honest. Neither was he, her husband.

"I made guesses, bad choices, assuming things that weren't true. We've told each other we have to be truthful with each other. We promised to talk after tonight in order to see what new expectations we both came home with."

"A good start if I do say so myself," Bliss waltzed into the room, stopping to pour herself a glass of wine. "Before you ask, Grams is babysitting the twins. She says they are little darlings, however Broc is molding them into his image. I dread their teenage years. They will be incorrigible at best."

"But you wouldn't have it any other way," Chelsea said with a giggle as she looked over the rim of her glass at the two women.

"I heard you speak of honesty. Sometimes it works, sometimes it doesn't." Bliss shrugged before taking a sip of her wine and sitting down. "In my case truthfulness proved to be a disaster."

Ali's eyes widened perceptibly. After she blinked a few times, she asked, "You want me to lie to Arie?"

"No, I didn't say that," Bliss spoke softly with a hesitant smile. "But my name was in question. If Broc knew what my last name was, he would have left me sooner rather than later. As it turned out he left me as soon as the truth came out. Fortunately for me, he thought better of his decision and married me."

"Well, I'm going to be perfectly straightforward with Donal if he ever decides he wants me. I'm going to tell him that I never plan on marrying anyone but I will have sex with him." Daryl walked into the parlor, joining the three of them.

"You won't?" Bliss said, appearing astonished. "You don't want to get married?"

"Of course she will. She always does precisely what she wants.

I'll wager her beau, if it is Donal will figure out a way around her."

"How will you support yourself?" Ali asked clearly listening and interested. "I had nothing after my home was sold. A brothel then Arie bought me. I would have starved on the streets since I've no skills or education."

"I'm going to have a bakery. Lacie will help me keep the books. At least I hope Lacie will help me."

"I paint," Bliss said. "I've enough money I could live by myself. Do you have any secret talents?"

"Of course I'll help. Help do what?" Lacie sat down smoothing her skirts. "You must be Alison. Arie hasn't been around the last few weeks. He must be spending all his time with you now."

Ali lifted her slim shoulders, a strange look in her eyes. "Only the last few days. Before that I only saw him once. I think he was afraid of me."

"That doesn't sound like Arie, afraid of a beautiful woman or anyone for that matter? The sultan who left a man naked in the town square because he didn't take the one word 'no' from me," Chelsea said with a giggle.

"You don't cross Arie," Cam said with a quick chuckle as he and Arie stepped inside the room. "Until I married Chelsea, I was afraid of him and ending up naked somewhere I didn't want to be."

"Dinner is ready," Jana said from the doorway.

Arie offered his arm to Alison, smiling at her besottedly. "Do you want to stay or go home? It's your choice."

"I suppose we can stay. I've learned some interesting things about you."

Arie slanted her a quizzical look.

"I'm sure you are going to tell me later."

Chapter Four

"Interesting you say?" Arie asked as they made their way down the road headed to the lavish tent they would call home for the rest of the summer. He planned this dinner in hopes Alison would come to enjoy the company of his friends in Glasgow. With a soft chuckle, he laughed, "I hope they haven't told too many exaggerated tales about me."

"I suppose." She lifted her shoulders as she pulled her shawl closer. "The sisters can be intimidating, and I'm not sure they liked me."

"I suppose is hardly an answer. Of course they like you." He knew bringing her to meet the sisters could be dangerous for him but he needed for her to gain more confidence in herself. "Did they tell you about all my misdeeds and in doing so explain how you should stand up to me?" He spoke with a chuckle, keeping his gaze riveted on Alison on her ever-changing expressions that told him so much about her thoughts.

Purposely he turned in the seat of the carriage, brushing his lips across hers then caressing her mouth with his tongue until she opened for him, knowing the horse would find his way home. He wanted to possess her completely. Felt the time was finally right, hoping she would agree. Enough of the teasing, he burned for her.

When he drew away, she sighed softly, moistening her lips with the soft pink tongue that intrigued and excited every nerve in his body. "I was told you left a man naked in the town square. I couldn't believe it at first, however by the looks on the sister's faces, it was true wasn't it? You bought me and... I don't know if I know you at all. If I don't please you, what will you do to me? You wouldn't leave me naked somewhere would you?" As he wrapped his arm around her pulling her closer, he felt the fine trembling of her slight frame.

He held her hand in his, bringing it to his lips, unable to get enough of her. He sucked in a deep breath of air. Allah, he didn't want her to fear him. It seemed the trip home took longer than anticipated. "I would never do anything to harm you. I would never leave you naked anywhere for others to look at you. You are mine. Only I will see you in all your glory." He spoke from his heart, knowing that all of this needed to be made apparent to Ali.

"You did do it though." Her hand rested on his cheek. She was staring at his lips as if she wanted another kiss. "Was the man so horrible that there was no other way to explain how you felt than by intimidation?"

"Yes. I'll never admit to anyone that I regret my deeds. I would do the same to a person who threatened you. The man would not take a simple no from a certain lady. He made it perfectly clear to me he still had every intention of seeking her out despite her objections."

She leaned into him while he pulled her closer. She set her head on his chest. "I believe you. What are your feelings for Chelsea? She's such a beautiful and strong woman. How could you let her go? Why would you want me?"

He chuckled willing to lie to her about this. While it wasn't true before he met her, it was most vividly true now. Running his fingers beneath her shawl, up then down her arm, reveling in the way she responded, the mini tremors wracking her body as he stroked her.

"She is not you. I find you much more desirable than Chelsea. It seems just as my father has, I have developed an affinity for red hair but only yours, Alison, only yours." He thought of his half-sister Hope. He had no feelings for her despite the color of her hair. He didn't think he would ever be enamored of red hair but he was now. Before now, he'd always preferred blonds.

"I find the color of your skin fascinating and your dark brown eyes are mesmerizing. Sometimes they turn to an ebony color."

She looked down at her clasped hands. He knew despite the darkness she was blushing.

Color easily painted her cheeks whenever she said anything that might embarrass her. He felt the time was right for them, for the lovemaking he wanted to share with her. He'd held back for so long and now, now this night felt perfect for the two of them. At the thought of possessing her, his body hardened with the need he'd been feeling for weeks now.

She pushed away from him, staring at his lips. He wondered which one of the sisters told her about that ploy. Before he knew it, she'd be staring at his crotch. Once again, he kissed her, held her chin lightly as he explored the dark recesses of her mouth. He questioned if he should just stop the curricle and make love to her here. She felt so good in his arms. It almost hurt to think about the sex that would follow.

At this rate, he wasn't sure if they would make it home. He did want their first time together to be perfect, enchanting and magical. He wanted the pillows surrounding them. Needed to make her feel comfortable. He knew wine would help along with some subtle coaxing on his part.

"Chelsea asked me how I felt about becoming your fourth wife. I didn't think..." Her hand resting on his chest, she studied him, stared at him for the longest time. "They said if I stared at your lips you would want to kiss me."

He chuckled softly. "What else did they tell you?"

"If that didn't work to stare at your crotch."

He roared with laughter at her innocent words and quick change of subject. "I'm not taking another wife anytime soon. I don't want to embarrass you with that discussion. I understand Europeans believe in one wife and many mistresses. That is not the way in my culture. We take many wives, as many as we like. In any case it shouldn't concern you. I am here. My other wives reside a great distance from here. At the moment I only want you."

"I'm sorry, I shouldn't have asked." Her lashes lowered concealing her eyes.

As he pulled the curricle to a stop, he made sure she was looking at him even though the fading light would keep her from seeing his eyes. "Don't ever think you shouldn't ask me something. I need to know what you are thinking and questioning. It's important for me to know how you feel."

"I'm sorry."

"Don't apologize when there is nothing to apologize for." He jumped from his seat and striding around to the other side he lifted his hands to help her from the vehicle. "Come, we've many things to explore tonight. I want to discover more of you. All of your soft curves, need to kiss every part of you."

She didn't say anything, but he felt her melt gently into him as her body slid the length of his, her unrestrained breast pushing provocatively against his chest. For a moment nerves settled in as his hands shook, not remembering the last time making love to someone felt so important and so different.

He always gave and received pleasure. Now...

Allah, he didn't know.

His hands beneath her breasts cupping them, he kissed her again then again. Through the fabric of her gown, his thumbs slowly passed evocatively across the hardened tips of her breasts. This time deepening the kiss until he felt her tongue caress his lips in answer, prowl inside, explore. He opened for her a deep rumble of contentment sweeping through him. Drawing back, he swept her into his arms cradling her against his chest. His lips found hers as he walked.

Reluctantly, pulling away for a moment, he told her his voice soft, "There will be more as soon as I get you alone. We have all night. I mean to use every second well."

He passed Victor and Tessa who were in deep conversation beneath the awning in front of the tent.

"How did your evening go?" Victor asked, sitting up, seeming to protectively arrange the quilt around Tessa.

"Better than expected," Arie grinned. "Would the two of you mind staying here for a short time?"

"If that's what you'd like," Victor said. "Any reason?

"I don't know why, but I'm apprehensive. I don't think it's just because..." Well he didn't want to explain anything to his friend. "I just want someone close by who I trust with my life."

The uneasy feeling in Arie's gut was as unexpected as it was ridiculous. Nothing could possibly happen to her here. His guards spaced throughout would keep all possible harm at bay.

Victor chuckled softly. “Except for the lack of privacy, all your men surrounding the area, this awning with the fire so close is really quite conducive to seduction. You should try it sometime, making love beneath the stars. We don’t mind do we, Tessa?”

She hit him in the chest. He respectfully grunted as an all-knowing masculine grin spread across his face. “Speak for yourself. You are not being seen naked by other men.”

“No other men are seeing you either,” he shot back seeming to enjoy the interchange between them and her sudden and quiet endearing bout of shyness. “I would have to kill them if they did.”

“They ken what we are doing.”

“Only because when I give you your woman’s ecstasy you scream out my name.”

He laughed, bending over to kiss her mouth hard and caress her beneath the cover.

She hit him again. In a quick move, he was on top of her, her hands pinned on either side of her head. “You shouldn’t have done that. Now you will have to pay the price.” His mouth covered hers again, nipped and kissed.

“And what price is that?” she giggled as the blanket covering Victor’s back slipped to his waist.

“Your delight and enjoyment.”

“Come, we should leave them to their privacy. What there is of it then we can find our own.”

He was in a hurry to find himself in the same position as Victor only with Alison beneath him. He wanted to feel her sultry warmth, touch her womb and discover all her secrets.

“They will ken what we are doing?”

Ali buried her head in his chest, his arms encircling her while his hand found their way beneath her dress. She gasped as she felt his hand stroking her inner thigh.

“Yes, but only if you scream out my name. Will you do that? Scream my name when you climax?” He pulled the tent flap aside and stepped into the room before setting her on her feet.

His hand trembled when he touched the column of her neck,

tracing a path down her arm and back up. She ran her tongue along the outside of her mouth before sucking the bottom lip beneath her teeth.

"Your soft sighs remind me of the breezes that blow gently across the desert, leaving undulating tracks on the sand. I need to hear the incredible sounds rippling from your throat when I stroke you, generate the heat and fire within you until you cry out my name."

Then his mouth molded across hers. He found she was pulling his shirt from his pants, her fingers running along his spine. Her eagerness pleased him as did everything else about her.

"Is this really going to happen tonight?" she whispered as she stepped back, staring at his lips. "Even though it's only been a few weeks it seems I've waited a lifetime."

"Whatever you want, Alison. It's yours. Do you want to discover a woman's pleasure tonight? I'm a damn good lover. Will make sure you are well satisfied." Lightly he brushed his lips down her neck, gently trailing his fingers along her collarbone.

"I'm nervous. My hands are shaking, and I feel as if I've butterflies in my stomach. Is that normal?"

"Don't be nervous."

He swept her into his arms, striding quickly to the lavish pallet where he set her down.

He reached for a glass of wine that had been poured for them, handed it to her. "Drink, you will relax at least a little bit. I promise you will..." but he wasn't' sure what to say. He meant to tell her he wouldn't hurt her but when he broke through her maidenhead, he would do just that.

She sipped then as did he from a second glass he retrieved from the other side of the bed. "I don't know if anything will relax me," she whispered yet gulped the wine, finishing the glass. "Except maybe you. When you touch me and kiss me, I lose all rational thought. I forget everything save the wonderful mercuric things you are making me feel."

"Perhaps, well, I'll pour you one more and this one you can drink slower," he laughed and handed her a grape to eat. "Should we savor the moment? Are you hungry? We can take as much time as you would like or..." He pulled her closer, running his fingers along her arms.

"I know, well, I don't want to wait and yet I'm so unsure of what you expect from me. I want to please you Arie. I don't know how."

"As do I you." He set his glass on the table then hers. "I will make this right for you. I promise."

Then he came down with her, kneeling behind her as he quickly undid all the fasteners on her dress. Through the lightweight fabric, his hands cupped her breasts, tweaking the hardened tips, his lips trailing kisses along the column of her neck. If he didn't slow down, he would have her on her back. She would find him deep inside before she could enjoy every moment.

With the buttons undone he slipped the sleeves down her arms, trailed more kisses across her back, reveling in the tiny shivers and sounds swelling from her. The gown pooled around her knees. All she wore now was the fragile chemise they purchased just this morning.

Turning her on her stomach, he feathered kisses down her spine, nipping when he reached her buttocks. They were perfect, white and quivering from his kisses. He kissed his way back, stopping to brush her hair away from her neck. The red strands seemed like fire as he sifted his fingers through them. He pulled in a long breath of air, holding himself back.

"What are you...?" Her voice was a tiny swallow of her breath.

"Yes..." He tugged on her ear with his teeth, continued to place kisses softly along the back of her shoulders until he turned her over again. Straddling her, he bent to take her mouth in his, slipping his tongue between her parted lip, his hands cupping her breasts while his thumbs played with the hardened tips. Suddenly, desire and passion collided, exploded within the vastness of his body. His pulse burst, thundering within his ears. To catch his breath he pulled away, staring down at this woman he loved

She ran her hands along his chest then wrapping her fingers around his neck pulled him closer. Tipped her neck back as his lips swept down the long column of her throat, biting gently at the furiously beating pulse at the base as blood pounded heatedly within her.

His attention turned back to her lips, kissing and sucking again, pillaging into the warm moist recesses she offered to him. He felt her hips arch against him, felt his rod pulse to be let free. Her fingernails scorched down his back.

"You need to take off your clothes." His mouth captured her words. "I want to see all of you."

He touched her intimately, finding the small silken nub that would bring her such pleasure, massaging while her hips pushed against him. He smiled to himself. Her pleasure was his. He needed to make her wild and reckless desperate in her need, bring her the greatest ecstasy possible.

"Arie," his name was a thin barely perceptible sound. Innocent and pure it aroused him as no other. "Arie, please."

"Is this what you like?" he asked, turning her again and nipping on the back of her neck then down her spine to place intimate kisses on her small perfectly rounded derrière. Moving his fingers between her swollen petals, he delighted in the slickness and the arching of her back as her body begged, weeping for more and more of his gentle caresses. "I'll give you the greatest ecstasy you've ever known," he whispered close to her ear.

"You've got all your clothes on and I..." Her words were short and crisp while he worked his magic, the enchantment he knew so well how to generate.

"Wear only your chemise," he finished the sentence for her, turning her then and placing a knee between her legs to come down between them. She was on her back and somehow, he'd managed to loosen enough pins that her hair spread across the pillows in wild abandon. He ran his fingers through the length, reveling in the silken fire scorching his fingers.

He rose above her, slipping from his shirt, his muscles flexing when she touched him, her fingers on the waistband. He sucked air, realizing in all his life he could not remember ever feeling so aroused or so protective. This woman was his life, held the hopes of his future in her tiny hands. He burned.

They would do well together.

Was this heaven in this small part of Scotland? If so, he never wanted to leave. He could see her breasts as they rose and fell with her breathing, more rapidly erratic now than before. The sheer fabric did nothing to hide any part of her from his gaze. The few candles strategically placed highlighted her features. Still he yearned for her to be naked beneath him, needed to feel her flesh caress his.

He kissed and nibbled his way up one leg to her woman's mound. Tessa must have had the ladies remove the hair. He wasn't sure why but he was disappointed. It was too soon to touch her more intimately, so he continued his discovery up her belly then her breasts, sharing his loving between the two. Through the fabric the tips hardened even more as he sucked each one into his mouth biting and laving then turning his attention to the other.

"Arie?" she whispered. "What did you do?"

"You taste like peaches and cream," he murmured softly.

His name sounded somehow different, strained. With the next moan he was suddenly terrified. Something was terribly wrong. This was not a sound of delight. "What is it?" His heart raced as she moaned and tried to curl into a tiny ball.

"I don't feel so well."

He braced himself on his forearms, staring at her, searching for a reason. Her face was flushed bright red. She was having trouble breathing. He'd recognize that coloring anywhere.

She'd been poisoned.

"Tessa!"

He strode to the opening and found that Tessa stood in front of it, Victor behind her, a worried look on her face. He knew he'd never spoken like that to her before. "Ali's been poisoned. Get your medicines. Hurry." His body shook, his head pounding with fear.

"Let me look at her first." Tessa hovered over Alison as she shook with pain.

Then she left, racing to her tent.

Arie ran his hands through his hair striding to the bedside. He sat down beside her, holding her upright. Her body was covered in sweat, her breaths strained and sporadic as she struggled for each tiny sip of air.

Tessa knelt beside them. "She must drink all of this. What did she have to eat?"

"Nothing. Only a glass of wine." How had this happened? No one had access here except trusted servants. This was impossible. His gut clenched as he helplessly watched the reality enfold in front of him.

Arie concentrated on the task at hand. He knew the potion was bitter. Alison choked on the liquid, droplets sputtering from her lips. "Your life depends on this. Tessa says you must drink it all. Please. Don't fight. I wouldn't make you drink this if it wasn't necessary."

He stroked her damp hair, closing his eyes and praying to the only god he knew. Then he began to hum, a song he first heard from his grandmother. He knew it to be a prayer. He hoped his grandmother was with him looking over Ali and making sure she survived.

He found he was shaking as she finished the last drops of the healing potion. Setting the vial on the table, he pulled her close, trying to give his warmth to her. Still her body recoiled. She burned. Her flesh coated with moisture.

"No, no, no..." she murmured then wretched into the basin Tessa brought.

"It might take all night to empty her stomach of the poison. This will not be easy for her or you." She handed Arie a damp cloth. "Keep her cool and warm as needed." Again, she pointed out, "The poison should be out of her system by morning but she will be weak. Give her as much water as she'll tolerate. I've brought a bottle of wine. It might take away the bad taste in her mouth. She must have liquid. Whatever appeals to her."

"What did you give her? Will she need more?"

Arie soothed Alison, rubbing his hand along her back as she lost more of the contents of her stomach. Never before had he felt such gut-wrenching terror. He would give his life for hers, take away the pain if he could.

"I don't think so. It is a concoction of charcoal. It works on this type of poisoning. You need to find out who did this to her and if the poison was intended for you. I doubt if Alison has enemies, while you..."

"I understand my enemies are numerous. No one would be so bold as to come into my personal space and hurt what is mine."

His anger, now that it seemed Ali would live, grew. He was livid and worried all at the same time, desperate in his need to see her well.

When Alison fell still for a moment, he looked at Tessa, "Will you stay with her for while? I need to speak with Victor."

Tessa pointed out all the urgent reasons he needed this crisis taken care of. Had to discover the perpetrator of this crime. Had to know who he was dealing with so it wouldn't happen again.

Outside, staring at the fire, Arie took a few moments to steady his shaking emotions and his shattered nerves. Alison could have died tonight. He meant to get to the bottom of this. There wasn't one doubt in his mind the poison had been meant for him. Victor would have some accounting to do. He was in charge while he was gone.

"Who was in the tent this afternoon?"

He stood with his hands behind his back, rocking on his heels. His subtle accusation seemed to hit Victor hard, deep lines furrowing across his dark brows. The man, his friend, looked away for a moment, his eyes narrowed with concentration.

He was shaking his head clearly at a loss to answer the questions, obviously as shaken as he was. "Just the usual women. I will have to ask your other men if they saw anything worth reporting. I was away for about an hour just after you left this morning."

A heavy silence fell between them. His thoughts went to Ali. Why? "The poison was meant for me. It was in the wine on the side table where I sleep. Only someone who knew us, who knew our habits would have had the foresight to place the wine there. Otherwise they would not know who would drink the poison."

"Ali drank the poisoned wine..."

"Because I handed it to her. I want the perpetrator of this crime caught and punished."

His fury grew. He couldn't shake the ominous feelings. Would have to take more care.

"You realize none of the women would have motive. An outside force must be involved," Victor said.

"Discover this outside force." Arie paused in thought for a few seconds. "Could it be the man one of my men shot? Do we know his name? Find out who he is."

"Anything is possible," Victor said, the urgency in his voice didn't go unnoticed. "And no, I don't know his name but I'm sure if I send out a few men to inquire, we can discover the truth."

"Bring him to me when you find him."

~ * ~

As Tessa told him, the poison seemed to be out of Ali's system by midmorning the next day. Yet Ali could barely walk, needed help getting in and out of bed. Victor was making little progress in finding the man however they did discover the woman who placed the poison in the wine.

Arie watched Ali sleep. Now her breaths even and deep. He trembled at the thought he might have lost her. For the last week he felt as if that was all he was able to do, watch her and pray. Each day she grew a little stronger. Today she was sitting up in bed smiling impishly at him, her vibrant red hair in tangled disarray around her.

"You don't have to hover like an old lady," Ali said as she pushed back against the pillows, a hesitant expression on her face. "If it's not too much trouble, I'd like something to eat and perhaps a cup of tea." She paused a moment, wishing she was stronger and thinking perhaps with a few comforts she might take a step forward. "And a bath. All of me needs washing."

"I'll let Tessa know." He turned and left the room.

Ali closed her eyes relaxing into the pillows, wishing with her whole heart Arie would return to being more himself. She was straightforward with him when she told him he was acting like an old lady. Yet perhaps he wasn't. Maybe she should feel pleased that he cared enough to hover, seeing to her every need as well.

"He just wants to make sure you have everything you need to get to being yourself. You understand you gave him quite the scare. He blames himself," Tessa said as she walked into the tent, a tray of food in hand followed by some of Arie's men bringing hot water for the bath she asked for. It seemed Tessa was reading her thoughts before she had them herself.

"I'm fine now. He can get back to his normal self and stop asking me how I feel. I'm not even sure any longer what that is. What I do know is that it doesn't include his standing over me every second of the day, hovering."

She laughed thinking about his actions. The man was truly an enigma to her.

Ali was sipping the tea and eying the food put in front of her. Since that night she was poisoned almost a week ago, she'd been able to eat very little. At this moment she was ravenous, ready to eat everything she saw in front of her. She broke off a piece of bread, slathering it with sweet butter and honey. For some reason wishing Tessa brought bacon too. It was all right though. She probably didn't expect her to eat.

"The bath is ready anytime you are. Arie asked me to set out a few of the new things he bought for you so you can pick out something to wear."

Tessa was humming. The sound delighted Ali. She envied those who could sing and keep a tune. She also envied those women who could dance vowing to learn if it killed her. She wanted to please Arie, needed to learn how to dance for him. Sighing softly, what she understood was that it would not be easy for her since she obviously couldn't keep one foot out of the way of the other.

Tessa was busying herself with unwrapping the packages. One by one, the garments were laid out for her perusal. "Do you see anything that pleases you?"

"I'm almost inclined to wear my harem pants and bolero jacket. It seems I miss them as well as the freedom they give me. Also miss the way Arie looks at me when I wear them."

Inhaling quickly, she felt her face heat with the embarrassment of what she was saying. To be for all practical purposes naked in front of a man, was not something she should be used to. With Arie it seemed she was. She wanted him to see her naked.

"You must be feeling better. I take it you want to continue where the two of you left off the other night." Tessa was smiling at her before she set out the soaps and the towels. "When you're done, I'll help you dry your hair and dress. Just call out when you are ready. You will be so beautiful, he will drool."

"Thank you. I was hoping Arie might do that."

She felt the heat rise on her cheeks once more. Not wishing to apologize, she was still mortified by what she told Tessa.

"I'll tell him but I think he has a short outing planned for the two of you when you are ready. He might not want to be distracted from his purpose if he sees you with nothing on. So, you should probably pick one of the dresses instead of the sheer pants and jacket. I'll make sure the harem pants and bolero are easily accessible for you when you return if that is what you want though. I believe you are staying the night somewhere else."

Her heart pounding, Alison leaned forward, hoping for new light on sex. "What is it like? Is it as good as men seem to say it is?"

"Sex? You two were interrupted that night." Tessa sat down, a tiny frown on her face. "Before you had sex? If it's the right man sex is better than the men say it is. If not, well... In bed Arie knows what he is about. At least that is what I've been told. You will find the act quite enjoyable." She smiled again, "I will put a few things in a small satchel for you."

"Is Victor that good? You don't have to answer that." Her hands rose to her cheeks mortified that she was so intrusive. It wasn't like her to be rude.

"Victor is the right man for me. He makes sex fun and different. Sometimes the things he does makes me giggle as if I'm still a little girl. I never know what to expect, and he seems to find ways to make love that are new and unexpected even though he does love to tease and embarrass me as well." Tessa laughed softly, her hand covering her mouth. "One day we made love beneath the awning. It was everything I could do not to cry out when he, well when I found my release. Everyone would have known exactly what we were doing."

"Really?"

Alison was half shocked, half not surprised. Victor was much like Arie. She supposed he would love to tease her as well. They were just beginning to know each other. Arie had always treated her as if she was a China doll.

"Really, he had me sit on him. Now I'm sure Arie wouldn't want me giving away secrets nor would Victor. Men like to think they are in charge of everything. Where their women are concerned, they believe they should be the ones to teach them everything," Tessa told her with a wicked smile on her face. "And women have to let them believe it whether it is the truth or not."

Alison mulled Tessa's words over in her mind, not quite understanding why sitting on him would create such havoc or embarrassment. After all she'd sat on Arie's lap before and nothing untoward or embarrassing happened. Perhaps it would be something for her to ask Arie about.

"Chelsea told me if I wanted to make Arie want me, I should stare at his mouth and if that doesn't work then I should focus on his crotch. Do you think that will please him?"

Any information about sex would thrill Ali, and any help pleasing Arie she could gain from Tessa would delight her.

Tessa laughed until tears ran down her cheeks. "Yes, it will please him to no end if the two of you are alone, but if you're in the company of others you should take care. He might do something to embarrass you too. You might not like the retaliation or it might disconcert you more than you expect."

Ali tilted her head slightly thinking hard about what Tessa said. Then moistening her lips, "Why would staring at his crotch embarrass him? It's just supposed to make him want me."

"Because..." Tessa looked as if she wasn't sure about what she asked then she smiled. "You haven't seen him naked, have you? Believe me, when that happens you will understand a bit more. If you don't understand, ask him. I'm sure he will be more than willing to explain things."

"All I've seen of him is his chest. It's magnificent. He seems to know that though. I would like to see the rest of him. I'm sure the sight would steal my breath, leaving me gasping for air," Ali sighed softly. "There is so much I don't know, can't fathom. You must help me and tell me everything."

"Those things are not for me to tell you. Arie will want to be the one to explain everything. I'm sure you need to wait until he's willing to show you. All men have their reasons. Arie is no different."

"I'm always having to wait. I would have found out that night."

She wandered to the bath, slipping from the robe then into the water. “Do you think he’ll make love to me tonight?”

“I’m sure you would have discovered something about his manly parts. You didn’t and that is something Arie would want to be in charge of. Just like a man in charge of everything.” Tessa laughed again, humor lightening her voice. “What else would you like to know?”

“Are you and Victor married?” she asked and... She waved her hand in the air, realizing she should not have asked. “Never mind. I’m guessing that question isn’t appropriate.”

“We are not wed. Everyone around here knows the truth of that so there is no reason you should not. Victor has no wives so...” She lifted her shoulders as if she was going to acknowledge something then appeared to change her mind.

Silence seemed to stretch on for a few minutes. “Do you know what this outing is all about? Or where we are going to stay the night? I really don’t want to visit the sisters again.”

“All I know is the curricle was brought around and is waiting for you to finish the bath and dress along with what I mentioned to you. Arie probably told me about this evening so I would know to pack a few things for you.” Tessa looked over the array of finery. “Which dress would you like?”

“I don’t know. Why don’t you pick. I’m not really very good at things like gowns or what is appropriate for what. In my life, I never had more than three dresses at any one time.” She ran the sponge along her leg wishing Arie was bathing her.

Reveling in the heat of the water she closed her eyes, dreaming of Arie along with the way he made her feel as well as the sensation he so easily created in her. Unbidden mercuric heat surged through her, centering in her most feminine parts. Her imagination taking over, she felt the gentle glide of his fingertips along her arms then legs, moving ever higher.

She moaned deep in the back of her throat as his lips found gentle purchase on her neck then her ear. His tongue whirled delightful circles inside the shell. His hands cupped her breasts, teasing the hardened tips.

“Arie?” she questioned but was afraid to open her eyes, afraid the wonderful dream would vanish if she did so. "I hope that's you and not my imagination." Yet she truly couldn't be sure. She was half asleep.

"My sweet harem girl," he whispered.

His heated breath against her flesh surged mercuric heat through her while he played and caressed, teasing her body to respond to him with tiny sounds of encouragement. The tempest inside exploded around her.

"Are you ready for sunshine? Do you want to finish what we began the other night?"

"Is it really you? I thought it was a dream, a beautiful wonderful dream." For another moment she closed her eyes. Then, "Sunshine and you? What more could a woman ask for?"

"We are going for a ride. I thought you might like to get out of this tent. I've two destinations in mind. First, I've set up a spot about a mile from here. I've food and wine. No, hush," he placed a finger on her lips, "The bottle has not been opened. I promise you there is no one near you who would think to harm you."

"Will you pick out a dress for me?" she asked nodding toward the garments on the bed. "I don't have the any idea what to choose."

He laughed softly, "You need to learn but yes, today I will choose when we've finished here."

He continued to soap and rinse her body, playing evocatively with her nerves while creating a rising desire within her. His soft strokes became more and more intimate. She hungered for him, needed him now.

"I hope you know what you're doing here." Her words were short and breathy.

She couldn't think of anything but desiring Arie, yearning more of what he was creating within her, knowing there was something more.

He pulled back, "While I hope to find some private time with you later today, this is not well done of me. It seems I'm having trouble controlling my hands as well as my lips. Tessa told me you are well enough for any pursuits we might have planned." Once more his lips found the pulse at the base of her neck, biting gently.

She closed her eyes, her breath held inside for a moment. "I'm not sure what you're talking about. If it means you will finally make love to me, I'm pleased with what she's told you. I don't mind what you are doing. Indeed, I don't want you to stop."

"Good, I'm glad you are ready for this man's body then." He stood back holding the bath towel out for her.

She rose feeling lighthearted and strangely not embarrassed. During her recovery, he'd spent time cooling her down to keep her temperature from getting to high then alternately lying with her to warm her up.

"You've lost weight and I will have to try my best to do something about that. I should feed you some delicacy every hour."

With his words she felt suddenly self-conscious. "You don't like..."

"I didn't say that. You haven't eaten in a weak so of course you would be smaller. I want you just as much no matter your size." His smile broadened, his even white teeth gleaming with what seemed like satisfaction. "You should see how much I want you."

"I'd like that," she murmured, stepping from the water.

"Then you shall have it."

He wrapped her in a towel before motioning her to sit. "I need to dry my hair before we leave."

"I believe the sunshine in addition the breeze will do that for you." He toweled the strands so they were no longer dripping. "Now would you like me to help you dress or should I call for Tessa?"

"I'd like you, please." She smiled at his look of concern beginning to understand a bit more about him and the ways of sex. "You don't want to?"

"That could be playing with fire," he murmured, striding to the bed. "But as you wish. Let me see. This green gown with the ivory lace will bring out the color of your eyes. The scoop of the neck is such that I will be able to admire your breasts when I look at you as well as think about what is beneath and the delightful things we will do tonight. Do you like this one?"

"Then this little outing is truly platonic."

She wasn't sure what to think about that, had expected Arie to have other motives.

"We will eat and drink. Then if you are not exhausted, we will spend the evening in each other's arms. It's been far too long for me," Arie said.

Ali was thinking that it had been far too long for her as well. It seemed her entire life had passed without knowing the delights Tessa and Arie spoke of. It was what she wanted. She didn't want to wait a moment longer than necessary.

"And enjoy the sunshine. I want to see some color on your cheeks although I will make sure you do not burn." He was fiddling with the underclothes, picking up one piece then letting it fall to the bed. "Perhaps we should forego the undergarments. I think..."

"That's not well done of you," she said still wondering about his motives and at the same time needing to laugh.

"No, it's very well done. While you are sitting in the shade sipping your wine, I'll be thinking about what you are not wearing in anticipation of tonight. This evening there will be nothing to interrupt us and nothing between us including clothing. I will see all of you."

"And I will see all of you."

She shivered at the thought, had waited for Arie to make love to her. To Alison it seemed an eternity. He treated her as if she was fragile. Perhaps this last week she had been. Now she was not. Before the poisoning she'd been strong and resilient.

"Have you found the person who poisoned me?" she asked thinking she should really know.

"Yes, one. Let's wait to speak of this. I'm afraid some of what I have to tell you will bother you. In my country when a person tries to kill another, we deal with them harshly. Take matters into our hands." He lifted his broad shoulders in a masculine shrug, "In this country we must wait for the law."

A shudder swept through her at his words. "What does harshly mean?" she asked, concerned yet realizing this woman could try to kill her again.

It seemed Arie read her mind. "I believe she was trying to kill me. Unfortunately for her she didn't know how skilled Tessa is in the art of medicine. You were very lucky."

Her eyes seemed to grow wide at his comment. Fear for him

thundering beneath her chest, "She was trying to kill you? Why?"

"I suppose when we find the person who paid her to put the poison in my wine, we might discover the truth. Victor is still looking. Now let's get you dressed."

Sitting in the curricle, Ali was surprised to see him turn toward the shipyards. He'd told her he had a blanket under a tree waiting for her. "Where are we really going?"

"I actually had two thoughts in mind and decided against the blanket in the sunshine. We are going to one of my ships. We will stay there. Perhaps we might even stay the night in my cabin if you don't mind the rocking of the ocean waves. If you do, I'll think of something else because I want you all to myself tonight. Don't want to share. No, sharing you is not ideal. The shipyard is a way from the ocean, but the changing tides as well as the waves give the ship a distinct motion." He turned to look at her then, "You don't get sea sick do you?"

Finally, she did laugh at him and the words. "Arie really, I've never been on a ship. So, I wouldn't know if I get seasick or not."

"Well, that makes some sense now that I think about it. Even Chelsea had never been on a ship."

Chelsea, there was that name again. While she did believe Chelsea to be nice enough, she certainly didn't like the fact Arie doted on her. Her name seemed to follow every thought. She tried to push the vision of the beautiful blonde-haired lady from her head, "What do you trade here?"

"It seems the Scots like their silks and furs. Spices are especially lucrative. In return my ships take home to the Ottoman Empire things like woolen cloth, glassware and some medicines. Sometimes we bring gunpowder home, mostly products we cannot manufacture."

"So, your ship is about to sail or no?"

He piqued her curiosity, seeming to have an abundance of funds. As far as she had seen, he pretty much did nothing.

"This one just arrived. The girl who poisoned you is on the ship bound for home. I thought you might want to speak with her while you still have the chance. You will never see her again. If I'm not wrong, you were fond of her. Perhaps she would be more forthcoming to another woman than my interrogators. Victor puts the fear of god into people."

"Who is it? I'll try but I don't know what to say. What's going to happen to her?"

Murder or attempted murder was a serious crime in Scotland. She wondered what it would be like in Arie's homeland.

"What will happen to her? It depends I suppose on what we tell the authorities. That's why I want you to speak with her before we come to any conclusions as to her punishment."

She mulled his words over in her mind for the longest time. "It depends? Then what are the possibilities?"

"If we claim she tried to murder me, she will be put to death." He stared at her. "So, you see, it's important you get her to talk. We need to know what her intent was."

"How?" she gasped, all of her was shaking.

Arie placed his hand on her leg in an attempt to reassure but nothing was helping.

"She will either lose her head or be executed by drowning." His voice and words were too calm, too impersonal.

Her swift gasp for air surprised her. The shiver snaking down her spine did not. She was shaking her head, confused yet determined. "We cannot let that happen. What could she have possibly gained by killing you? There is no reason for anything like this."

"That is why I will leave it to you to sort everything out. I believe she was a favorite of yours. Here we are." He jumped from the curricle, quickly rounding it to help her from her seat.

"A favorite of mine?" she asked puzzled. "I didn't miss anyone today," she said as she tried to think of the women who had come in and out of the tent while she was bed ridden.

"Perhaps you didn't realize because we just sorted this out and garnered a confession yesterday. Tessa figured it out and Victor brought her to the ship this morning."

"Who is it?"

"I will let you see for yourself." He offered his arm as they walked up the gangplank to his ship.

Her heart fluttered to her throat. Searching for air to draw into her lungs, she looked to Arie. "Did you want me to see that too?" She was staring at Fletcher Donovan and Leod who were stark naked and bound to one of the masts.

"Needed you to know that the men who sold you into servitude were being punished now and in the future, just as they intended for you. They will serve other men as they expected you to do."

Her eyes widened at his words. "You bought me too." She turned on him, wondering how there could be two different rules yet understanding at the same time.

Arie gave her freedom even after he spent money to keep her. She would have never earned her freedom from the whorehouse. Would have been bound to service men the rest of her life.

"The selling of you was not their only crime. They kidnapped Chelsea, sold her to the same brothel. The two of them had to be punished. The punishment is appropriate. What I'm not sure of is that death is what your young servant deserves. I'm going to allow you to decide."

This was not something she neither wanted nor asked for. The power of life or death over a fellow human was not something she could fathom. Inhaling a long deep breath and hoping for the right words, she said thoughtfully. "I don't know how I can do that."

"You are young and innocent. You've been wronged several times in your short life. I for one hope I've made amends to you. I'm also hoping you can ferret out the perpetrator of the crime and why this lady accepted the task. Now if she was coerced, blackmailed or threatened in any way perhaps the punishment is too severe. If she won't tell you, why then..." Arie smoothed her cheek with the back of his hand leaving his sentence unfinished

"Then you think she was part of the plan and deserves the punishment."

"Yes."

~ * ~

Zara stood in front of Alison, her hands clasped together, waiting to hear her fate. She knew death was possible. She prayed many times over the last days to be spared, but the harsh look on Alison's face told her that her hopes might have been set too high. Alison must know the poison was meant for Arie not her. She was sure Alison was in love with the man. She would want the worst possible punishment to be meted out. Shivers of terror bubbled up from deep in her gut.

"You should understand I'm sorry and I didn't mean any harm to come to you," Zara said, her voice soft filled with remorse.

Perhaps she should have prayed for a swift merciful death. How did she explain to Alison she was not the intended target? Arie was. She didn't believe that knowledge would help her cause.

"No, just Arie."

"I..." she began searching for the words, the right words that would not implicate her in the crime. She was lied to, was told the potion would cause drowsiness nothing more. That it was merely a prank between two close friends.

"You do understand that you need to be candid with me." Alison spoke in a quiet voice but Zara heard the edge to it. "I was shocked when you stepped into the room. Arie didn't tell me who it was that put the poison in the wine, only she was a friend of mine."

"The potion was not meant for you. I certainly didn't mean to poison Arie or anyone for that matter." Zara was quick to point out. Then she blurted, "I didn't know it was poison. I thought..." she swallowed hard biting her lips until she drew blood.

"That is not an excuse. You realize killing the sultan would have been far worse a crime than killing a concubine."

Zara stiffened her spine, unsure whether meekness was the best approach or confidence she didn't feel. "No excuses. I deserve whatever punishment is allocated to me." Even while she spoke the words, she thought her knees would collapse. "I don't want to die."

"It is my job to discover why. Why did you do it? You were..." Ali lifted her shoulders seemingly puzzled. "You have no grudge against either of us. Do you?"

"No." Zara was shaking her head no idea how much she could say. Her life as well as her sister and mother at home were at stake. She repeated her words, hoping for the best. Sometimes ignorance could pass as an excuse. She prayed in this case it would. "I didn't know it was a poison."

"What did you think it was?"

"A prank from one dear friend to another. I was told it was to make Arie sleepy." Again, she swallowed hard wishing for the courage to keep going and to tell Alison the truth.

"Then a prank? You trusted someone. Who was it? If Arie understands your motive, he might make this easier. You don't need to be sentenced to death or a life of living in hell."

"I don't know what anyone can do for me. The die is cast. I made my decision the best I knew how. Promised something I should not have."

Zara understood all too well that Arie was a powerful man, but his money as well as his power was centered thousands of miles away from here in the Ottoman Empire. She was dealing with a foe who was Scottish. For some reason she couldn't fathom why the man wanted Arie dead.

"You must realize Arie will protect you."

"He can't." She was concise and matter of fact even while she was shaking her head. "I will take whatever punishment you decide. If it's death then so be it. Know though, I'm not a threat to you or the sultan."

"Who is intimidating you? I will tell the sultan. He will have Victor bring the man here. Even now two men are staked to masts waiting for the ship to sail. Their fate is beyond. You should not have been put in this position."

"I don't know his name but I'm sure he..."

What was she sure of? Only what the man told her.

"You're sure everything he told you is true? I doubt that. I've known men who will lie to get what they want. My supposed father sold me, sold my home, left me at the whim of men. I was lucky Arie stepped into help me."

"I was sure at the time." She could do nothing but murmur and feel as if once again she put her belief in someone she shouldn't.

"Who is it?" Ali stood beside Zara clearly frustrated that she was not telling her what she wanted to know.

"I don't know his name. What I do know is that he watched you and Arie together. He knew you, knows you somehow. He didn't tell me much only that he was also a very good friend to Arie. He also watched you try to leave, saw you ride in circles, thought to help you."

"I remember a man. I saw he was shot but didn't turn around to help."

"No, I don't know. Perhaps that was a different man, maybe not. You should also know it was one of Arie's men who shot him."

"Why?"

"Because Arie had men following you to make sure you were not hurt in any way. This man threatened you."

"So, he was shot," Alison said, appearing to try to make sense of her words.

"Yes, but he survived."

"Only to seek revenge against Arie." Ali inhaled long and deep seeming to mull over all that she said. "So how did he threaten you? This does not sound like a man playing jokes on a friend."

"With the lives of my mother and sister if I didn't do what he asked. His story did change when I refused him."

"Your family is thousands of miles away."

Zara couldn't help herself, tears slipped from her eyes and she crumpled to the ground. "It's all true but he made me believe he could still kill them. He could reach them even in the Ottoman Empire."

"Let me get this straight. The man who gave you the poison was not a friend playing a practical joke."

"He was not. He did tell me it would make him sleepy not kill him."

Chapter Five

Arie waited for Zara to be escorted from the cabin before he entered. He was eager to hear what Ali discovered as well as knowing in a short amount of time he would make love to the woman who captured his heart. He'd waited weeks to finally have her to himself and comfortable with him. Of course, he lost the chance a week ago when she was poisoned.

Now they would make up for lost time.

"What did Zara have to say?" he asked, stepping into the room.

She was sitting on a window seat overlooking the sea. At his first sight of Ali his breath caught in the back of his throat. Her face was pale, her eyes swollen from crying. Tears for the woman who tried to murder him and nearly kill Ali. Sadness for that woman was not what he expected.

"I believe we should keep her here with us. She was betrayed. Even more than I was by Fletcher Donovan. Her intentions are pure. Zara was forced, threatened with her life as well as her families."

He stopped midstride. "Intentions are pure? I can hardly believe that. I think you are too sweet to see what is really happening here."

"Zara was threatened and bullied. She didn't comprehend the potion the man gave her was poison. Thinking it was a trick, a practical joke that would do no harm, she put the potion in the wine. At first, she refused. The man intimidated her until she felt she had no choice. The fault lies with the man not Zara. You have to work on finding him."

"You believe her?" Arie asked in total disbelief as he sat down behind his desk gazing at the woman who somehow was stealing his heart.

It was something he believed would never happen. He understood

Ali wanted to see the best in people, but this was going too far. He had not expected this outcome.

"I will keep watch over her. I'm sure Tessa will help. Zara is a favorite of everyone. This is a onetime incident, I'm sure." For a moment Alison looked down, smoothing the skirt of the dress she wore, appearing to think on what she was about to say. "I wanted you to see me tonight in the harem pants and bolero jacket. I see your look of disapproval. Do you still want me?"

"Nothing has changed between us, my harem girl. Are you trying to change the subject?" Arie laughed a moment, wishing he could pull her into his arms. He didn't care about anything right now but Alison. "This is far too serious a matter to take lightly. You need to tell me more. Did she tell you who the man was?"

"She doesn't know his name." Ali spoke as she fiddled with the pendant she always wore.

Several times Arie quizzed her on the significance and Ali had always been loath to speak of it. "What's the reluctance?" Arie asked leaning forward, his gaze riveted on her fingers, his gut suddenly telling him there was more significance to that pendant than Ali even knew. She was hesitating. The look on her face didn't seem to bode well for him.

"You had me followed."

For a moment she looked out the window. Arie wished he could see into her head, read her thoughts. Of course, he had her followed. He never wanted to risk her life.

"I'm not sure I understand what you mean." He would always make sure she was safe. She would never be left alone to fend for herself. He had a guess as to what she referred to but he needed her to tell him.

"That night you invited me to leave, had the horse ready and waiting, you had me followed. You were going to bring me back no matter what I decided. You didn't have any intention of giving me my freedom." Her voice seemed to grow angrier as she spoke, her hands now shaking. "How can I ever believe you when you lie to me?"

"Right on all counts. But..." he paused for a few seconds trying to figure out the right words. This was a delicate situation. "If you'd been intent on leaving me, I would have had Victor make sure you were well taken care. I didn't want you to leave though."

Gently he touched her lips, longing for her, not this argument. As far as he was concerned quarrels were a waste of time.

"I should leave right now." She stood but immediately sat down again, looking away from him, her shoulders slumping. "My dilemma is that I don't want to leave you."

She sounded so forlorn he almost grinned but decided to go along with her perhaps help her to understand more of her feeling toward him.

"You can go. Victor will bring you your horse. He will have men follow you. Not to return you to me but to make sure nothing happens to you. Although it would not please me if you left. Now, my sweet harem girl, what does any of this have to do with that night nearly two weeks ago? Something Zara said? Or is it the ornament you're playing with?"

She gasped then dropped the pendant quickly as if it was hot. "A man watched us that day, followed me when I tried to leave. He is the one who approached Zara with the poison. He told her it was a prank. Told her it would only make you drowsy. Yes, it was intended for you but not to kill you. At least that's what Zara believed. I don't know about this." She held the medallion up. "I've always worn it."

"A prank? Zara thought he told the truth? I find that hard to believe. Zara would never—"

"The man threatened her with her sister and her mother's lives. She had to believe him. There was no other choice for her but she didn't know him, never saw him before. What she did know was that he was Scottish and he wore the Frasier plaid."

"That is more to go on than we had before." Arie stood, walking around the desk before taking Ali's hand in his and bringing her to her feet. "You have done well. I'll pass the information on to Victor. He can send men to find this man. A Frasier you say? That's very interesting. Did you know that pendant you wear bears the Frasier seal?"

Quickly she looked at it then dropped the ornament. With a deep breath, "That was what Zara thought. Now about Zara before you talk to Victor. What have you decided to do with her?"

"Nothing yet. I have until tomorrow morning to make my wishes clear to Victor as well as the captain of my ship." Wistfully, he caressed

Ali's cheek with the back of his hand. It went against all he knew to leave Zara unpunished. She needed to be held accountable for what she did. If not, what would stop her the next time someone threatened or tempted her in some way. She should have come to him.

"She must be punished in the ways of our people. I will let you decide on the action that should be taken."

The moisture in her eyes nearly undid him. She was not accustomed to matters such as this. Her life, though hard, had been somewhat sheltered. She told him she was not the child of Fletcher Donovan. So, who was her father? He would pass the task of discovering her birth father onto the Victor. Perhaps one had something to do with the other.

Ali was shaking her head. "I've no idea what that would be. I would not wish to decide someone's fate particularly when the fate is life or death."

"You must. The poison was given to you."

Arie was adamant in this decision. She would have to make the decision.

"But it was meant for you and only as a sedative."

Arie cleared his throat, watching her closely. "I can give you some choices. However, you won't like any of them. One is for her to be flogged. That is common practice for lesser crimes. Another is to have her wait on my men and give them any pleasures they might ask of her." He watched as Ali's face paled.

"Couldn't you just confine her for a week or two, take away her privileges to come and go from the house?"

"That would hardly be the same. Another would be to give her some of the poison and see if she survives. If she does then it is god's will."

"What would she prefer?" Ali asked, her bottom lip caught between her teeth. "None of them sound very appealing."

Arie wanted to laugh. "A reparation is not meant to be appealing. They are meant to teach a lesson. One never asks the recipient of a crime how they would like to be punished."

"Death could hardly be meant to teach anyone anything," Ali said, her eyes blazing with passion.

"Death is for a crime so heinous there is no reason to teach."

"I don't like what you're saying. Zara did nothing wrong. Nothing, that is except believe something she should not have."

Arie's deep sigh was for patience. "Almost killing you and trying to kill me is nothing wrong?"

"What you've planned is too severe. I think she would learn what you're trying to teach if you just confine her for a short time."

"That is not the way of punishment. She grasps that concept." Arie nearly laughed at her sweet innocence. Yet, she needed to understand the ways of his people if she was to live among them. "She would most likely prefer to give pleasure to my men. If you must know, she has already performed for them and slept with most of them. Zara is not the innocent you might think she is. She would most likely take the flogging over the poison."

"I don't want any of those punishments for her. Lock her in a room somewhere. Put her on bread and water for a week. Wouldn't that be enough?" Ali seemed determined to stay her course unwilling to listen to reason.

Arie was growing tired of this conversation and wanted to move on to more pleasing pastimes with his new concubine who so far had avoided his bed, albeit not because she wanted to do so. "No, it would not be enough. Now, if you still have an inkling to wear the harem pants and bolero jacket for me this evening, perhaps even dance, I will go speak with Victor."

Despite the fact she turned away when he tried to kiss her, Arie still had a good feeling about tonight. Ali had never held a grudge. It had been a very long time since she refused him anything. Looking at the bed in his cabin, he grinned. The accommodations pleased him.

Perhaps tonight then he strode from the room.

"Victor!" he called out, shielding his eyes from the bright light of the setting sun. "Victor."

"Sir?" Victor was beside him. "What did you discover?"

"A lot of untruths from Zara and some facts that are most likely true. I'm allowing Ali to set the punishment. I've given her several choices. She is loath to do it, but she will come around. I will let you know in the morning then you can carry the task out."

"So, Ali will set the punishment?" Victor asked appearing amused by what Arie told him.

"She will. As I said, I've given her several choices, but I don't want her to see Zara until the time is right. I could keep her in my bed for a week, but I'd have to be there with her."

Arie laughed then thinking that might be a grand idea. If only... if only he had the time for such a rare and delicious event.

"Did she tell us anything useful?"

"Only that the man who threatened her, told her this was a prank between friends is a Frasier. Did we ever discover who Alison's birth father was?"

"You think this could be her father and no, I've reached several dead ends in my inquiries." Victor said.

"This man could be her father and is exacting revenge on me for what I've done to his daughter, either that or because one of my men thought to shoot him a couple of weeks ago, leaving him for dead. From what I understand now it might have been someone else. There is the distinct possibility it was this man who was shot. We've no way of knowing. Anything is possible." Arie raked his hands through his hair, searching the door of his cabin, wishing he was spending time with his concubine instead of discussing his poisoning with Victor.

"A man who abandoned his child would seek vengeance for what you are doing?" Victor asked in disbelief. "I find it easier to believe it was the man who was shot."

"We don't know if she was abandoned," Arie said wondering at the truth of that notion after all these years.

Victor shrugged slightly saying once more, "Anything is possible. If he didn't abandon her, then why was she living with Fletcher and her mother? Why doesn't she know anything about her real father?"

"Too many unanswered questions," Arie murmured.

"We'll find the answers. Your wellbeing is at risk."

"Stranger things have happened. Perhaps he found a conscious or maybe until recently he never knew he had a child." Arie mulled that over for a while. Any man who leaves his seed inside a woman should understand the fact they could father a baby. "We should look into the reasons more thoroughly. There of course could have been extenuating circumstances. I want to know exactly what I'm up against and if the man can be reasoned with."

"So, this man, Frasier, had some fun with Alison's mother, left and never looked back until..." Victor paused. "How many years later?"

"Nineteen, I believe," Arie said, smiling at Victor's assessment of the situation. "We should look into this matter, convince her would be father that Alison is better off with me."

"If he's a Scot and her father, he might insist you wed," Victor pointed out, a look of wry amusement on his swarthy features.

"Just as he wed Alison's mother? Don't believe he has any high morals to rely on here." One dark eyebrow rose in speculation. "I rather doubt he can demand anything of the sort. In any case, Alison has the right of refusal under Scottish law."

"Would it be so bad to take a fourth wife?" Victor asked. "She is beautiful and intriguing. With her red hair and green eyes, she will have a unique place in your harem as well as captivating children. The two of you would make fine sons."

"This from a man who has no wives."

Arie slapped his friend on the back, quickly turning the conversation to make it about Victor. He would take her for a wife in an instant if she would agree. Getting around to asking her would be left to a more suitable time, "You should listen to yourself and wed Tessa. She has been loyal for many years and now... have you had another woman in all this time? Tessa would make a fine wife."

Victor turned away for a few seconds, clearly unwilling to confide in him. Then, "I'll think about it. We could have a double wedding."

The conversation had suddenly grown far too serious for his taste. "Find the man and set up a meeting. I want Zara there also and maybe someone will speak the truth."

"You give the woman too much power. If she is lying, she'll continue to spout falsehoods," Victor said. "I would never trust her. Would never allow her to go unpunished. If Alison can't decry a suitable punishment, you will have to take this into your hands."

"Maybe, maybe not. Ali will do the right thing. I'm spending the rest of the evening with her. Unless you have an emergency, I don't want to be interrupted tonight."

When he entered the captain's cabin on his ship, he closed and leaned against the door. Candles had been lit and Ali sat on the bed, her knees drawn beneath her, her glorious red hair spilling in waves around her shoulders to tumble in delightful curls down her back. He remembered their first time together and the way she felt in his arms. She responded so quickly and so sweetly, her response mercuric and passionate, her desire for him beautiful. She responded to him with raw hunger that eclipsed anything he'd felt before. He was sure tonight would be no different.

Pushing away from the door, "Are you ready for me, Ali?" he asked understanding she wouldn't really comprehend what he was asking.

Allah, but he could see all of her through the sheer fabric, the tight buds and rounded curve of her breast, slanting to a tiny waist before curving to generous hips.

He was a man well pleased.

She moistened her lips, her dark lashes fluttering across alabaster cheeks before she looked at him, her eyes sparkling with passion. "I suppose so." Her voice was tight, shivering slightly with nervous energy.

He could tell she was anxious as she pulled a pillow close to her chest, covering parts of her he'd rather see. "You must know before we begin."

He smiled at her as he stepped farther into the room. While he'd been talking with Victor, servants had brought trays of food and wine. The bottles were all unopened. Tessa must have been responsible for the setting as well as prepping Alison.

He stepped to the table, picking up a bottle before setting it down to examine another one. "A Chianti or Bordeaux?"

He smiled slightly when she lifted her shoulders revealing more of her breasts, not that there was much left unseen. The need to touch and taste overwhelmed him, yet he strove to maintain a reserve he didn't feel. Taking this slowly and savoring every moment was at the forefront of his mind despite the heady desire raging inside. Tonight, there would be no doubt that she was his.

"I don't know the difference. Anything except what we had the other night," she decided, moving over to make room for him.

"Chianti it is." He popped the cork and poured them both a generous glass. "Liquid to relax. I see you are nervous. I am too. Did Tessa help prepare you? You know you are beautiful." He was rambling, couldn't help himself. He couldn't ever remember feeling so anxious as he did now.

"You? Nervous?" she queried, the sound of her voice clearly told him she didn't believe his words. "You can't possibly be nervous. How many women have you had in your lifetime?"

"Not as many as you might think. It's been a very long time since I made love to a virgin. It seems it was my third wife. That was years ago." He did look back on that night fondly.

"In any case more than me."

"Thank my lucky stars, although I wanted you when I thought you were a whore. So, nothing between us would have changed except I would have had you that night I bought you. Something held me back. Suppose I knew even then you are special." He handed her the glass, sitting down beside her, holding his crystal high. "To you and the night to come. May we both find the greatest pleasure and satisfaction?"

"I don't know what to do," she said focused on his eyes, then his lips.

He watched as she set her glass on the table near the bed.

"Drink first."

She did long and deep.

Arie did laugh then, "You are such a delight. Click my glass then drink up. We shall proceed as we did that ill-fated night."

Adrift in the thoughts of her innocence as well as the explosive passion between the two of them, he meant to make this right for her.

"Is this some kind of tradition?" She did so and this time she seemed to sip cautiously.

"Yes, I promise you the wine is safe," he said the words even though he supposed it might not be true. He couldn't live his life wondering at everything he ate or drank. “Now, I want to kiss you.” He set both their glasses of wine on the table, “Or would you prefer to kiss me?”

She ran her tongue across her lips. “You can kiss me. I’m sure I’d fail miserably.”

He chuckled softly, running his finger across her bottom lip. “You need to have more confidence in yourself.”

Yet he placed his hands on either side of her head, lightly touched his lips to hers before pulling back to look at her. Disappointment, he guessed, was the look in her eyes. He grinned. “What would you like me to do? I want you to tell me everything you like and what you don’t like.”

Her hands on his chest, Ali smushed her lips together, seemingly unsure of what he asked. Inhaling a long deep breath, she finally spoke in such a soft whisper Arie could barely hear her. “That tongue thing you do.”

When he did figure out what she said, he was pleased, wanted to laugh out loud again. “The tongue thing,” he parroted, chuckling softly, not wanting her to think he laughed at her. “Like this?”

He still held her, his lips now covering hers, tracing the line of her mouth with his tongue. She breathed in. He took the opportunity to discover and explore the inside of her mouth. The sultry warm depths were an aphrodisiac calling to his soul. His rod pulsed and pushed against his pants.

She met his caresses with ones of her own. He encouraged more by biting her bottom lip then gently tugging on it with his teeth. He delighted in the sounds of pleasure she graced him with. She was soft and supple in his arms, her breasts pushing against his chest. Now her fingers tugged on his shirt as she seemed to remember the other night when he was shirtless.

“I want to see you and feel you,” she said, pulling a small distance away from him. “All of you.”

“As I do you, but we must take our time. It would not be well done of me to rush this now would it?”

Once more he kissed her, teeth and tongue finding purchase within her willing lips. His body roared to life, an inferno sweeping through him.

For him the enchantment was new. He'd never before felt the seething delicious hunger for a woman that he did now.

This woman was slowly becoming his heart and soul and he had yet to possess her. Her secrets outnumbered the things he knew about her, yet he didn't think she'd kept any knowledge from him. Learning more was rapidly becoming a necessity. She was an enigma to him, his puzzle.

She ran her hands on his back, her fingernails making tiny scratch marks along a trail downward. He groaned when they were no longer exploring his back but now touched his nipples, rubbing them with the soft palms of her hands.

Quickly, he held her hands in his, placing them on his back. "Not yet, my sweet harem girl. Do not rush the beauty and the pleasure of these moments together even though I understand why. This first time, you must do this my way, trust in my superior knowledge about sexual things." Inwardly, he laughed at his words. This time with her seemed like a first time to him. Before the sex was about sex nothing more. Now he wondered at his feelings the incessant desire rippling through him for an untried woman.

He kissed her again and again while she seemed to move restlessly against him, her hands running along his back with needy desperation he understood all too well. Silently she was pleading for release. She just didn't know it.

"Arie, please," she whispered as he pulled away for a moment to run his hands through the now tangled mass of her hair. "Please do something, I'm so hot. I feel as if I might explode. You must..." she groaned, stroking his thighs with her legs while she writhed beneath him.

"Hot is good. It's very, very good. Are you weeping for me too?" He grinned before trailing kisses down her neck then to her ear, his tongue swirling inside the pink shell. She shivered at the caress, her hands once again moving to find purchase on his chest. His kisses followed a trail along her collarbone to her other ear.

"Will you take your shirt off?" she said through tiny gulps of air. "I need to feel you against me. I do remember the last time, the way you felt when you were above me. I liked the weight of you."

"Good, I want you to remember the parts that pleasured you. If you want my shirt off, why, then you must take it off." He held out his arms, knowing his grin was wide and expectant. It seemed she enchanted him in ways no other woman ever had before.

For a few seconds she looked askance at him then with a determined glint in her eyes, she pulled the bottom from his pants and with a tiny bit of help from him she slipped it off his arms.

She smiled, looking down for a moment. He had the distinct impression she was staring at his crotch. She looked up though, touched the palm of her hands to his chest. Smoothing them along the line between his nipples to his waist then back up.

He grabbed her hands stopping her. "Not yet. I need to see to you first. Then you can remove my pants and look at me all you want. Now, it's my turn to remove your jacket, although there is little keeping it on you. I also want to feel the hot length of you against me."

She nodded seeming to give him her approval. He found the gesture interesting yet he was heartily glad she did. He'd never sought or even cared if he had a woman's approval before. This was something very new to him. He meant to savor all the moments and new feelings. Slowly he unfastened the one hook holding the jacket together before slipping the sheer fabric from her shoulders then down her arms. He ran his hands along the newly barred flesh. Allah, he felt as if the sun just rose over the desert basking the day in its warmth.

Ali was so very white, her skin nearly translucent. The pink aureoles surrounding the tips of her breasts were unique and intriguing. With gentle care he bent to reverently brush his lips across each one before gazing into her passion dazed eyes.

He ran his hands along her sides from her breast to her tiny waist then back to cup both rounded globes in his hands. She was ready for him, he was sure. Yet he needed to discover the truth for himself, needed to make sure she would feel only that one second of pain before the blinding all-consuming ecstasy he meant to introduce her to.

Running his hands along her legs, he stopped when he reached the fasteners on the pants. He pulled her to her knees, sending the fabric to the bed. She was unclothed and beautiful, perfect to his manly eyes. He'd never wanted anyone so much as he did Ali.

He was a man well pleased with his acquisition. He would never let her go despite the words he spoke to her about her freedom. Taking his time with her had paid off for him. He would continue to reap the harvest.

He came between her legs, kissing her slightly rounded belly, then farther while he let part of his weight come down atop her. She fell back against the bed. For a moment he closed his eyes fighting for the restraint he needed to do this right, to proceed slowly to give as little pain as possible.

Beneath him, her hips rose and fell as he continued his exploration of her, delved into her softness with a finger then two. She was tight and so very small yet so hot and moist for him. Her maidenhead was intact, which delighted him also made him so aware that for her with this joining everything she felt would not result in pleasure.

"Arie," she whispered his name as he slowly caressed her most intimate feminine folds, finding the silken knot that would help give her the gratification she so richly deserved.

Slowly he entered her, felt the moment of enchantment and needed to savor the magic. She pulsed and quivered, her sheath tightening as he held still for a moment. Then he pushed forward, claiming her even more thoroughly as his. She cried out into his mouth as she beat her fists on his back.

He held still until he knew the pain had subsided. Inside her tight core he slowly began to drive inside her then her hips moved against him inviting him farther and deeper until she cried out his name. He felt the tremors of her raw ecstasy engulf her body. Again and again she writhed against him, pleasured by him as he emptied himself inside her sweet hot core.

He was a man well pleased.

~ * ~

Arie was looking at her from above, his forearms on either side of her head, his grin broad. "You will calm soon. I promise then perhaps we will do this again. Only if you like, of course." He placed chaste kisses on her forehead then a quick kiss to her lips before pushing his hands through her hair. This was more than he expected, more sunshine, she gave him such pure delight.

"I don't think I'll ever be able to walk or move." Her voice was thin and raspy, her breaths uneven. She tried to swallow but her throat was so parched she could not. She inhaled long and deep trying to draw much needed sustenance for her lungs. The slow burn, the tempest inside her... She inhaled again, long and deep.

Rolling off her, he helped her to sit before handing her the wine sitting on the table. "Drink, it will ease your parched throat. Ah, what do you think now? Perhaps some food so we can ease another very different appetite."

He sat back, the sheet around his waist, seemingly comfortable in his nakedness. She watched him, so at ease. He'd done this so many times. She felt a tiny rise of jealousy thinking about the other women to grace his bed as well as his life.

Tucking the sheet around her breasts she sipped, closing her eyes and wondering if every time would be this wonderful. This was just too new to her. "I..." she began, running her tongue across her dry lips but wasn't sure what to say, tucking her bottom lip beneath her teeth.

"I?" he parroted laughing. The sound was infectious. "I've left you very nearly speechless. I believe I like that."

From the bed he reached for a basin of water then seemed to think better of it and returned his attention to her. "Did I hurt you too much? You do understand my coming inside you will never give you pain again."

She nodded her understanding even as she finished the wine he'd handed her. "You have left me without words as you just said. I don't know what to say or think. I feel rejuvenated. My life seems much more than it was but not as much as it will be."

"Tell me how wonderful I made you feel," he chuckled then he fell silent for what seemed the longest time. "Maybe we should speak of other things, more pressing things than my manly prowess. Tell me about this pendant again. You wear it night and day."

He held it in his hands, studying it. The back of his fingers touching her, the sensation felt as if it was the gentlest caress, heating her once more. Her tiny gasp gave him another reason to smile.

"Speaking of it only brings pain and sorrow. There is nothing pleasant about it."

"Then why do you wear it?"

She was shaking her head, lifting her shoulders in a hesitant shrug before she replied, "I don't know."

"Perhaps it would be wise to discover more facts."

"What do you want me to say that I haven't told you already?"

Truly she didn't like speaking about the necklace. Talking about it had always brought tears to her mother's eyes and a faraway look. The necklace reminded her of another time in her life, one much more pleasant. Now she hoped to make new memories, ones she could cherish.

"Just whatever comes to your mind." He spoke gently and it seemed to Ali with incredible patience. "For your sake as well as my own, I need to learn as much as possible. Is that too much to ask? Is there any minute fact you can remember? A name? A place?"

His sincere words left her feeling a bit selfish. The pendant, though she wore it, left her feeling bittersweet. She knew it had something to do with her mother as well as a lost love. Truly she didn't think it had anything to do with her.

Ali smiled then, touching his chest with the tip of her finger. He caught it, bringing it to his lips and biting then the other and the rest of them after that. "If you keep that up, I won't have a coherent thought in my head. Even if I think of something, I won't be able to speak."

"Just what I like to hear." He quit though and held her hands in his. "Now, what do you remember?"

She'd rather delay this, much rather have him wheedle more of those amazingly delicious sensations from her body again. Perhaps another time after that but she knew the tactic would only delay the inevitable. He would never give up on his quest to learn the truth. "Mother told me I should always wear it and that someday I might find good luck if I followed her wishes. Suppose I have found those good things in you, but I don't think that is what she was thinking about."

"Good luck, am I that good luck?" Arie asked grinning wickedly.

"Most assuredly so, but I doubt if mother ever envisioned this sinfully, wicked moment between us. I believe she was thinking of something else, someone else."

Ali watched the movement of the candlelight on the walls of the cabin. The ship was rocking gently now with the undulating of the water. She felt mesmerized by the delicious feelings surrounding her. Moonlight played through the window, shining on them enough so she could see his beloved features.

"Perhaps your birth father gave the jewelry to her, to remind her of him. Maybe he wanted her to always think about him. Or, perchance it was to reassure her he would come back for her," Arie said thoughtfully. "I've been thinking this man who tried to kill me might be your birth father seeking vengeance for crimes he believed I've committed against you, his daughter."

She gasped, wondering at Arie's words. Her birth father; until now she'd thought very little of him. Her mother never mentioned him. "Why would he even care? He abandoned my mother and me. Left us to fend for ourselves all those years. One winter we nearly starved. Mother would walk into Glasgow and beg for food. Most days she would only bring home a few crusts of bread. Sometimes I was so hungry..." Alison couldn't bear to think of those bitter times.

"How old were you?" He cared, his words sincere and seeming to come from the heart. He brushed a tangled mass of hair from her face.

Ali tried to smile. "Five or six, I suppose. I know she always felt guilty leaving me. Whenever she was gone, she told me not to vacate the house for any reason. I didn't. I huddled in the armoire until I heard her voice. Those were the scariest times of my life. I heard imaginary noises. I was sure someone was in the house and they would find me."

Raising her hand to his lips he kissed the knuckles, running his tongue across each one. "A child should never go through anything of that sort. What will you do if this Frasier is your father? Will you accept him into your life? Will you do what he asks? You do realize he will want you to leave me."

She paused for a single moment. In any case she didn't need to think very long about how she felt. "Nothing. He means nothing to me and you should exact your punishment on this man instead of Zara. He is the real perpetrator of the crime against me. He tried to murder you, in the process nearly killed me, his daughter, if your guesses are right. I would have him flogged then beheaded."

Arie roared with laughter. "You can be a vindictive little thing when it suits you. There is a blood lust in you I never imagined. Remind me not to get on your bad side."

She turned and punched him as hard as she could in the belly, knowing the blow would have little to no impact on him. "Don't tease me, Arie. I owe this man nothing. He caused my mother too much heartache to continue on this path. The world needs to be rid of the man."

He grabbed her hands in his, still laughing. "I'm not teasing. I meant every damn word. I would be willing to bet that if you got to know this Scotsman, you would feel the same about him as Zara and would be pleading with me to confine him without food or water for a few days and that should be sufficient to teach a lesson. I won't do that for either Zara or your long-lost father if he is your father."

"I don't want to meet him or get to know him," she said, her voice shallow.

She found she was shaking. She could barely breathe just thinking about this man as well as the repercussions he could have on her life. "Why would I?" she paused. "After all these years."

Arie lifted his broad shoulders slightly appearing to study her. "To know your roots and where you came from. To find out why he abandoned you and your mother. There are a host of reasons."

"My roots are in a tiny farmhouse outside Glasgow. That's where I come from. Whatever excuses he has, I'm not interested in any of them." She was adamant in this. "You can ferret him out if you want. Find out whatever it is that is bugging you. Keep it to yourself. I don't want to know any of it." With that said, she turned her back on him, frustrated and angry that he was pushing her. Yet in the back of her mind a memory stirred. Quickly, she tried to push it to the farthest recesses of her mind.

She could not.

"I'm sorry you feel that way. I will find out the truth, I promise you simply because I need to know and understand this situation so I can make logical decisions where you are concerned."

Now, his hands around her waist, he lifted her. Pushing at the sheets, he set her on top of him.

She was straddling him now. She could feel his rod pulsing intimately against her. "What are you doing?" Her hands rested on his chest, nails lightly scoring him as she recalled Tessa speaking about sitting on him. She suddenly realized what Tessa meant. "Arie, you can't mean to..."

"Of course I can. We've ruled out a discussion about this Frasier person, so I believe I'm about to make love to you one more time tonight. No, perhaps there will be more times. We have not finished even one bottle of wine or any of the food. I find this conversation with you to be arousing, very stimulating. I must have some relief before my hunger dies."

The sheet had fallen from her. His lips were now caressing her nipple, sucking deeply, lathing with his tongue. He watched her, studying her, his eyes ablaze with tension. Lightly he touched her breast again, keeping his gaze fixed on her. He drew his fingers low over her ribs against her abdomen, down to her thighs to stroke knowingly between them. Her lashes fluttered. Tiny sounds wavered from her lips. Sounds she could not stop as his bold intentions increased.

"No," he told her softly, and she lifted her gaze to his again as he lowered her onto his shaft invading her more intimately.

She drew her lips together as the flame touched her while her body surged against his touch of its sweet desire. He laughed with sheer pleasure and triumph as he pulled her closer and his lips seized upon hers.

"Candle light," he spoke softly. "Thank God for the light spaced around the cabin as well as from the silvery moon. Tessa must know my every thought when she decorated this chamber for us. I huger for the sight of you, and will hold this night dear in my heart forever."

He touched intimately upon her, her breasts touching his chest, the heat of the sensual caress searing her as he helped her move on him. His lips covered hers. Then in wild tempest and reckless abandon they traveled to her breasts again, sucking the tips into mouth.

His eyes gleaming in the soft light, in a swift move he turned her over and once again he was above her. Then he was moving, moving against her as her hips rose to accept him more deeply into her.

The bliss was potent and heated, magical and enthralling then the sweetness embraced her again as her body rose and met his. She had never known a hunger so great or so achingly sweet. She had never wanted so urgently to please. Her body shifted and writhed and arched on his as she lost the power of thought. She stroked his flesh with her fingernails, felt the constriction and heave of his muscle and the every-greater fury of his force.

She swirled with it, she soared, she reached for the highest pinnacle. Then it seemed as if the entire world exploded deep inside her; that nothing had ever been so wondrous and enchanting in her life. She closed her eyes, seeking once more to recover from the lovemaking Arie seemed to take for granted. She would fill her life with his love for as long as possible. Someday he might grow tired of her and cast her away. She would deal with that if and when it came.

She had not expected this, a second time tonight. Had thought... she didn't know what she thought, just not this. He shouted out as he reached his climax, emptying himself inside her. Thoughts of a lasting love filled her before she shook them from her mind. There was nothing lasting about her situation. No, there was only the moment.

For a few minutes they lay together wrapped in a tangle of their arms and legs. Her body was sweat sheened as was his. His flesh seemed to glow where the candle and moonlight caressed his bronzed skin.

He rose with a purpose and brought a basin of water and cloth to the bed with him. "I need to wash my seed and your blood from you. It will not be comfortable to sleep tonight if I don't."

Shocked, she wasn't sure what he meant. She did feel the stickiness between her legs. Slowly, he pulled the covers from her. She nearly cried out. Embarrassed now that she was completely and truly naked in front of him as his hands were moved over her body.

The sensations were not arousing yet they comforted. He was gentle as he methodically washed and dried her.

Alison lay in his arms now, feeling the beat of his heart along with the slow methodic moving of his chest as he drew each breath. Peace surrounded her, a stillness she couldn't explain. She felt content for the first time in her life.

I love him.

She didn't dare say the words. He would not expect them, might even take issue with the sentiment. What was love after all? Perhaps it was lust she felt. She wondered if she'd ever known love. Surely her mother loved her but that had to be different. Before her sale to the brothel, she'd thought she loved her mother.

No longer, not after the deception.

During the last few years, she had not loved her mother, not since Fletcher Donovan came to live with them. Her life changed. Her mother was different, rarely speaking to her, giving all her attention to Fletcher.

Exhausted by the events of the evening, she yearend for sleep yet it seemed elusive, too absorbed in her thoughts to relax. She heard Arie's, deep rumblings as he fell into a restless sleep.

When she woke the next day, light filtered through the one window in the cabin. Reaching out a hand, Arie was gone. She looked at the empty bed, wishing he was still there. From the corner of an eye she saw a bath had been drawn for her. She sat up, pushing the tangled mass of her hair from her eyes and away from her face.

"Arie?"

"He has left for the morning and told me to make sure you had all the comforts of home. A bath first then food. Do you like coffee or tea with your breakfast?" Tessa's knowing smile caught her off guard. "From the looks of things, I assume you had a good night, uninterrupted this time."

"You know about our night?"

Alison wasn't at all sure if Tessa was guessing or if she knew they had made love and she'd fallen asleep in his arms. How could she not know what happened?

"Your man left with a huge smile that could mean only one thing. Without going into details there are signs that you made love for the first time. Now enough chatter. Your bath will get cold as will your food."

Tessa busied herself in the room, picking up items, putting them away.

Signs? She wasn't at all sure what Tessa spoke of, but the waiting bath looked divine. She meant to soak until the water grew cold. She was stiff. Her muscles ones she never noticed before ached.

"Do you know where Arie went?" Ali asked but she was pretty sure he would seek out the man he thought might be her father even though she told him she didn't want to meet him.

"No, he doesn't tell me about his business, just what I should do for you." She set one of Ali's new dresses on the bed then the underthings that went with the gown. "You will look beautiful in this. The color will bring out the beautiful shade of your eyes."

"That's what Arie said when he picked the fabric. I don't know much about those things."

Alison felt awkward again. There was so much she didn't comprehend, woman things, things she should understand. But she didn't.

"Well, Arie was correct in this choice." Tessa laughed then with a sigh, "I wish Victor would pick out a gown for me. It would be nice to dress as the Scottish ladies. I could go somewhere with him if I had a dress." Her words were wistful yet also resigned to what she must understand was her fate.

"Perhaps you could ask him. The way he looks at you when he's around, I'm sure he wouldn't mind. It could be he's just never thought of doing something like that."

"I could not be so bold. I do care for Victor. I think he feels the same for me. It would be too far out of my place to ask anything of him. He does own me. Now let's get you ready for your day."

Ali wanted to argue but the look on Tessa's face along with her last words told her she already overstepped her bounds. "What do you think should happen to Zara? Tell me what you would do if the decision was left up to you." Arie would come to her and expect a judgment and she needed to have one ready.

"Zara should be sent back to her country. No one should stay here in Scotland with Arie who is not loyal and trustworthy. Just the fact Zara was willing to perpetrate a prank makes her untrustworthy and puts everything else in question." Her voice was bitter and sent shivers down Ali's spine.

She rubbed her arms in an attempt to ward of the goose bumps.

"You would have her beheaded then?" Ali gasped out, still trying to come to terms with a possible execution or even a flogging, which would leave her scarred for the rest of her life.

"Flogged. She didn't kill anyone, but who knows if she will try again. Giving her to the men would mean nothing to a woman who had already done just that," Tessa said matter of factly and with no reservations.

Who would know if she tried again? "How long ago did Arie leave?" Ali asked deciding once again a change of subject was in order.

"About two hours. He said not to wake you. He also bade me tell you he'd be back as soon as possible."

"He is after information I don't want to know. Do I have to stay here until he returns? His quest could take all afternoon." Alison was ready to leave, go back to the tent or wherever Victor would take her, the house possibly. Thoughts of leaning about her supposed father made her stomach clench.

"He left the curricle and one of the men will take you home." Tessa busied herself around the ship's cabin.

"Not the tent?"

She wanted to return there. It seemed a world all by itself. She'd grown fond of the ambiance, fond of the memories. The house was a place where he imprisoned her. Freedom there had been nonexistent.

"The weather will turn soon. The rains will be here before you know it. It's almost September after all. The tent was designed for hot weather of the dessert." Tessa opened the door and a servant brought in a tray of food. When the winds are blowing and the rains fall, it will not protect you.

She was hungry, she realized, as she tried to ignore Tessa's words. The food last night had been abundant but neither of them ate much. Alison smiled, remembering the evening and the sweet way he touched her, played her body with finesse and magic.

Well, there wasn't anything sweet about the caresses. They were hot and potent and seared her soul wrenching her from her innocence. She was his now. She didn't mind admitting to that fact.

Out of the tub, Tessa helped her with her underthings and her gown. “Are you happy living here, being a servant?” Ali asked even understanding she overstepped what would be considered proper.

Tessa stared at her as if she lost her mind. “I’m a slave just as Zara is. I’m not a servant as you Scottish people seem to think. I cannot come and go as I please. If I left, Victor would find me and punish me.”

Her hand on her chest, she wasn’t sure what to do or say. “A slave.”

“Just as you are a slave, Arie’s concubine, and will remain so for the rest of your life unless Arie decides to take you for a wife. I’ve no say in when I come or go. No say in who has sex with me. My protection lies in the fact Victor wants me. When he grows tired of me, he will pass me off to someone else. There will be no questions asked. It is just way it is.” Tessa was too frank, her words brutal.

“He gave me my freedom.” Alison would argue this point to the end. “He told me I could leave anytime. That’s not a slave. I could walk out this door right now and he has no say.”

“You cannot. There are men around the ship who would stop you. The curricle driver will make sure you don’t leave except with him,” Tessa said, her voice strained as is she tried to think of all the reasons Ali was not a free woman as she believed. “It is best if you stop deluding yourself with thoughts that Arie has made you a free woman. He has not.”

Ali could barely breathe wondering if what Tessa told her was true. It could not be. This was not well done of Arie. She choked back a sob. “He gave me my freedom,” she said weakly for a second time.

“You returned to him of your own volition telling everyone you accepted your fate. You accepted Arie giving you a home and providing for you. Do you really believe Arie would ever let you go? He keeps what he deems as his and after last night... well you are his.” Tessa turned her back seeming to be finished with the conversation.

“After last night, what do you know about last night?”

It seemed her body was shaking from head to toe. They made love yes, but it was never implied or said to her that she lost her freedom by sleeping with him, by accepting him into her body. “You know nothing,” she blurted out refusing to acknowledge what Tessa told her as her fate even though she understood Tessa knew far more about this man and his expectations than she did.

She would not be any man's slave.

"I'm sure you will comprehend what Arie believes soon enough. You will either remain a sex slave with Arie or you'll become his fourth wife. If you say no to him about becoming a wife, you still won't leave his possession. Just as everyone else he's known intimately, he will keep you close until he grows tired of you. It is just the way of this world. Perhaps in some ways it's no different than the world you came from. Men have all the power. Women must find a way to accept the fact."

"I don't want to leave him. I don't want to be a wife among other wives," Alison murmured softly, wishing Tessa had not been so blatantly frank with her. She should have never given Arie her virtue. Now, where she was concerned, she really had no viable choices.

"Then you want all of Glasgow to consider you his whore, not a mistress but his whore? By staying with him and not allowing Victor to find you somewhere safe to live, you committed to Arie and whatever he wishes."

Tessa continued packing the small valise she would take with her when she left to go home. Everything going inside that bag, Arie gave her. "Don't get me wrong. He will treat you as a princess. You will want for nothing."

It seemed to Ali Tessa meant to be incredibly candid. "No, I don't want that. Don't want to be any man's whore but..."

She moistened her lips, staring at the door as if she wanted to race from the tiny room that would forever hold memories for her yet also sealed her fate.

The lighthearted happiness she felt upon waking changed to a heavy depression. Her body and mind seemed drained beyond belief. When Arie told her she could leave and Victor gave her options, she thought... well now she didn't know what she'd thought. Tessa told her she was Arie's slave yet he didn't treat her as such. Last night he cherished her. She wondered just how long that sentiment would last.

"I'm incredibly stupid, aren't I?" she asked Tessa who sat down beside her. "I never realized any of what you told me."

"Why would you? No, you are just naïve. I'm sure if my life had not been this way since I was born, I'd be naïve too. When he asks you to marry him, you must accept the proposal. There are no other options for you. Don't put any terms on the yes. Don't ask him to annul or divorce his other wives. He can't do that. It would bring terrible shame on the women he married before you, on women who bore him children. You would put him in a horrific position."

The knock on the door surprised both women. Ali's heart jumped to her throat as she ran her sweaty hands along her gown.

"It must be your driver, here to take you home." Tessa opened the door with a bemused look on her face. "Alison hasn't eaten yet. Do be patient for a little longer. She should be ready in about fifteen minutes."

"Victor told me not to wait for any reason," the man said, his hands clasped behind his back. It seemed patience was not something he intended. "It's time to go."

"Really, unless there is some pressing matter that is more urgent than Arie's favorite woman's comfort, she must eat. The sultan would not be a man well pleased if we were to starve his lady," Tessa said without blinking, the words flowing effortlessly. "Alison will be out when she is finished with her breakfast." With that said Tessa closed the door on the man.

"Are you sure that was wise?" Ali asked, looking to the door then Tessa. "He didn't seem too pleased."

"He is a servant and Victor would have never said that to him. It was not well done. He just doesn't want to wait for you," Tessa said, her smile changing to a frown as she seemed to think of repercussions to her actions. "Although an impatient man can be a dangerous man."

"Do you think it wise to get him angry?"

"Probably not," Tessa said letting out a long slow breath of air. "It's too late now. We'll just have to make the best of the situation. Now, sit down and eat your breakfast. Who knows when your next meal will come?"

"I don't want to ride back with that man by myself in the curricle. Do you think Arie would be too upset if I stayed here?"

Alison held tight to the pendant then quickly let it go as if it burned her hand. If she had the courage, she would take it off, but it seemed to her the necklace brought her luck. If she had the courage, she would walk out that door and take her chances in Glasgow. Somehow, she knew she would not get very far.

Arie would find her. He would not be pleased.

"I'm sure he would be very displeased if you stayed. The ship sails with the evening tide. You would find yourself in his homeland if you remained on board. Something you do not want to do unless Arie is with you." Tessa set Ali's small valise by the door in the cabin.

"Guess I don't have a choice in this. Will you go with me?" she asked even though she knew there was no room in the tiny vehicle.

"I will be close by. No worries," Tessa said.

"Too many worries. What if that man...?"

She was thinking of Frasier and a confrontation. What if he shows up?

~ * ~

Lord Murray Frasier Marquis of Bellmund paced the room he rented for the week. It was a small but adequate room in the heart of Glasgow. His heart raced when he thought on what he almost did to his daughter. Christ, but he could have killed her. The poison had been meant for the Turk who deserved to die after what he did to Alison. She was no man's concubine. Bloody hell, she was his daughter, the child of a marquis.

That night on the road was the first time he'd seen her. She'd been attempting to leave the sultan. Even before he gave Zara the poison to kill Arie, he'd looked into the matter and how his daughter became Arie's favorite woman.

Alison's mother promised to keep her safe. When he left Glasgow so many years ago, he left believing her mother would protect his daughter.

He felt as if he'd been betrayed, yet he was also responsible. He should have taken Alison with him. She'd been so young at the time. He didn't feel it was best for him to take her away from her mother.

"So how the hell did she end up in a brothel only to be sold to a sultan from the Ottoman Empire?" he murmured, distraught with all that happened. Yet he understood the man who'd been living with Ali's mother was the perpetrator of the crime. The act was all monetary.

He couldn't blame it all on the mother, yet Robin did fail in her job. The money he sent should have been put to better use. There were enough funds to hire a tutor for Alison as well as presentable gowns, enough to feed both women. What did she do with the money?

"Don't be so hard on yourself," Angus Stewart said as he sipped the Guinness and poked around at the fish they ordered for dinner. "You couldn't have known what would happen to the wee thing. Now we need to go about setting this to rights. Any ideas as to how to make that happen?"

"Don't know how to get Alison away from that man who has so many resources," Murray mumbled, thinking he needed to ride to Bellmund and see what was left of it after his father died and his older brother ran it to the ground. At least that was what he heard, what had been written to him. Come home as soon as you can book passage. You're needed in Scotland.

"Probably the first thing you need to do is find a way to make amends with the sultan," Angus said. "Explain what happened over the years. You don't want to get any farther on his bad side. Heard tell he has a mean way of dealing with his enemies. I'd be willing to guess, you're more an enemy than a friend."

"Bloody hell, I'm her father, her protector." Murray's hand came down hard on the table as he rose to pace the room.

"Keep your temper in check, Murray. It won't do you any good to anger the man farther," Angus said, drumming his fingers on the armrest.

"First thing I need to do is find a way to wrench my daughter from his hold. She deserves better, deserves a lord who will treat her right, not a sultan who will turn her into his personal sex slave."

"If you go about this in the wrong way you could end up naked in the town square," Angus sat back, his drink resting on his belly a broad grin on his too ruggedly handsome face. "Heard rumors."

"I should set up a meeting in a very public place. You have any ideas? I've been gone too many years. Glasgow has grown and changed.

Many of the old places I'm familiar with are no longer there."

"Heard Lucky Black's tavern is still in business. I'll have the men informed so it's not just the two of us," Angus said. "Can't take any chances with the sultan. Heard he's bent on revenge since Alison nearly died. Would have except for one of his slaves who knew what poison you used as well as the antidote."

He grimaced, running those words through his head. He was all too aware of the fact he almost killed his flesh and blood. "Tomorrow morning I'll send a message to the man. He's at the ship with her as we speak." Murray's fists clenched as he pounded the wall hard, knowing his daughter's virtue was in question.

"You can't take back all the years you missed. Hindsight is often overrated. You made your choices with what little information you received from this end. Robin never wrote that she was in trouble or that she might need you."

He understood his plans had gone awry. Years ago when he told his father he meant to wed Robin, a commoner, his father sent him to Virginia where they had land to farm. He effectively banished him from Scotland. Having fallen in love with the land across the ocean along with another woman. Mistakenly he thought Robin would be taken care of only to learn that after the first few years, his father did not give her the money he sent. His daughter was not educated. Instead, they were left to fend for themselves on their own.

Three years after he left, he learned he had a little girl by Robin. Her hair and eyes the same color as his. Thank his lucky stars the rest of her features were more like her mother's than his.

What to do now?

He, a marquis, a lord of the realm had a daughter who was owned by a sultan who would not give her up easily. She was the man's concubine. The gossip had been ripe this last week he'd been in Glasgow.

Rummaging through his things he found pen and paper then sitting down he penned a letter to Arie Demir.

When he finished, he read it to Angus.

"Arie," he began. "Don't want to start this message with words I don't mean. Just want this to be straight and to the point."

"You don't want to call the man, dear?" Angus laughed seeming to enjoy this part of his friend's predicament.

"Hardly," he cleared his throat to make the reading easier.

"We must meet and discuss your relationship with my daughter as well as my expectations for future behavior. Things cannot proceed in this way. I understand you've taken certain liberties with her, but now that I'm back in Scotland to protect her, these liberties must cease.

"I would like you to hand Alison over to me, her father. She is no longer a concern of yours and you will no longer see her."

He stopped to take a deep breath.

"You really think this man who is used to getting his way in every endeavor is just going to hand Alison over to you?" Angus asked, having grown more serious now. "He bought her and believes he owns her. You're going to have the devil of a time changing that fact. He could sail, take her from here. You would never see her again."

"Probably not."

Murray's sigh was huge. He didn't want to think of the meeting tomorrow if the man did agree to see him. "Alison is mine, my daughter. She doesn't deserve to be a concubine in this man's harem. I will return his money."

"He will tell you that you gave up all parental rights when you left and never returned. She is a woman grown now. What is she eighteen or nineteen? She can make decisions for herself. What if she would rather stay with this sultan than be returned to a man she doesn't know?"

"I will deal with that when she tells me so herself. She can't possibly intend to remain a sex slave to this man for the rest of her life."

Murray set the paper on the table, staring at it. He was assuming certain things that most likely were not true.

"You should prepare yourself for Alison's truth. She might despise you. I heard that her mother is on that ship headed to the Ottoman Empire to serve as someone's slave for her role in Alison's sale."

"I cannot help that. She was part of the plan to sell our daughter to a brothel. The punishment is just. I would not interfere."

"You dinna care if you loved her once?" Angus asked, one eyebrow rising in seeming speculation.

With a heavy sigh, Murray drank long and deep from his Guinness, pondering all that transpired in the short week after his return. “That was a long time ago. It was a past that never materialized into a future for either of us. What could have been didn’t happen.”

“Then so be it. We will see what transpires on the morrow.”

Chapter Six

Arie read the letter several times before finally setting it down on the table in disbelief. Alison would want to see what her supposed father wrote as well as the excuses. Indeed, she should know she had no options where her father was concerned even if she changed her mind about staying with him. Now that he'd had her beneath him, felt the raw delicious passion emanating from her, she was his for as long as time.

He would never allow her to leave.

Not in this lifetime.

Through the night she slept fitfully almost as if she knew something was wrong, something was threatening her existence. She should have an easy life from now on, but the sudden appearance of a birth father was making it difficult. He strode outside, inhaling the clear morning air. The sun was shining for the moment but dark clouds hovered lazily, promising rain later in the day.

A strange heaviness hung over him, a feeling that nothing would end well this day. His men would be there as he was sure the marquis would have men stationed around the tavern. The Scotsman could make things difficult if that was what he wished. Arie would expect nothing less. A man would not want his daughter in the possession of a sultan.

He wasn't sure what Ali would say or if she would change her mind about her father when he told her the man was a marquis, a lord of the realm. Perhaps the title would mean more to her than what he expected. Frasier was now the sole beneficiary of the Frasier wealth as well as the Bellmund estate. Alison could live a life of ease with her father if that was what she wished.

Victor approached slowly with an easy grin painting his face.

Leaning on the railing he stared out at the streets. "I believe for the first time in your young life, you might have met your match. You cannot send this man on his way with a bribe nor parade him naked through the town. At least not without repercussions you might not want to deal with."

"No, I cannot. It seems he has an abundance of wealth and power at his disposal. Still, it was not well done of him to leave his daughter in Glasgow while he spent the years in Virginia. She deserved better from him. Why did he return now?"

"Illegitimate daughter. That does not change the fact that Lord Frasier is here and intends to make amends," Victor said, reminding Arie of facts he didn't know what to do with. "If rumors are true, he only returned because his father passed away and his brother died a few years ago. He is the sole heir."

"I don't need reminding. A few nights ago, Alison made it abundantly clear she wants nothing to do with the man. She will have her wish whatever that might be. I've a second ship due into Glasgow in a day or two. We can always leave Scotland if she feels uncomfortable in any way. She didn't want anything to do with Murray Frasier before we discovered the truth about his heritage. Alison was so adamant I doubt if she would change her mind."

"I don't know her well," Victor said, his voice quiet yet reassuring. "However, I'm willing to guess that under the circumstances she wants less to do with him than she did before. Who would have use for a father who abandons his daughter?"

"I gather Tessa has been talking to you, relaying information Ali might not be willing to tell me. I'm glad to hear that Ali has someone to confide in. Have you asked Tessa to marry you yet?" Arie grinned enjoying the change of subject as well as the expression on his friend's face, taking his mind off the meeting this afternoon.

"I'm still weighing the benefits with the not so desirable effects of marriage," Victor said with a short laugh as he looked upward as if he would see her in a window. "Since Ali has come into our lives, Tessa is acting differently, more presumptive as if she expects certain things of me that she didn't use to envision. I'm sure Alison has put some new thoughts into her head."

"And," he paused thoughtfully, "is that a bad thing?" Arie asked his best friend. "The MacTavish girls as well as Ali have put strange notions into my head also. I just don't know what to do about my other wives when I ask her to become my wife. As you well know, I can't divorce or annul them. I don't want the children to lose their inheritance. I love them."

"There is little you can do. Shaming the other women would be a horrible punishment for women who have devoted themselves to you in many ways. As to your children, they would also suffer. It would not be seemly for you to do such a thing."

"Damned no matter what I do," Arie mumbled also casting his gaze upward. He longed for Ali to be in his arms. This meeting with Frasier had not been the way he wanted to spend a lazy warm afternoon.

His long drawn out sigh didn't go unnoticed by Victor. "Maybe that is why I haven't wed. Too many complications as well as all out problems come with that institution. As you well know a man doesn't have to marry in order to enjoy a woman in his bed or have children."

"Perhaps I've been a fool all these years. My father always impressed upon me the need to marry and have children. At the time I believed him. Three wives proved to be too many for me. Now, I'd be content with just one if she will have me."

"If she won't?" Victor queried, one eyebrow raised. "What will you do? Keep her anyway?"

"I find that I cannot see a future without Alison in it." The truth of those words hit Arie hard. For a moment he stopped breathing.

"But... I don't want to dwell on what might or might not happen," Victor said.

"Now, everything I ever assumed was true has twisted in the wind. I've no idea who I am or what I believe."

Frustration where Alison was concerned ate at his soul and gnawed away at his heart. In such a short time she'd become his world and after last night... what? After last night his universe changed even more dramatically. He didn't want to admit to any of it.

"Arie." Alison appeared unexpectedly on the porch, stepping up beside him. She was dressed in a lavender day gown, her eyes sparkling with unspoken pleasure. “I was looking for you. What are you doing outside?”

He wrapped an arm around her shoulders, pulling her into his body while enjoying the soft curves nestled close. His mind shot to the night before and the way she felt in his arms. She was warm and willing, compliant, filled with passion. Alison was his. He burned for her like no other.

His hunger for this woman nearly overwhelming him.

“What are you planning this afternoon?” he asked even though he had a pretty good idea.

Chelsea asked if she and her sisters could steal Alison away for the majority of the day. He agreed as long as Ali agreed. The opportunity to discuss the plan had not presented itself.

She smiled at him, looking into his eyes. Hers sparkled with what he could only describe as mischief, something new for her, something he might enjoy discovering more about as she began to feel more comfortable with him.

He tapped his finger to the tip of her nose. “I haven’t decided. Chelsea sent a note asking if she could visit with me. Said Cam would send a driver to pick me up but,” she turned her attention to Victor, “I only want to go if Tessa can come along with me. She said she needed your permission. I don’t understand why. I told her that she was not a slave to your whims. She informed me that was exactly what she was. Really, Victor, that’s just not right and you must comprehend that fact. This is Scotland. We are not slaves.”

Arie roared with laughter while Victor cleared his throat, looking to the streets. When he turned back, “Tessa may go with you and yes she does need my permission. I want to know where she is at all times so I can protect her. Is that so wrong?”

“Of course it’s not wrong to want to know where someone you love is, but you can’t dictate to her. She is a human being, an intelligent beautiful woman who has wants and needs of her own. She is quite capable of deciding where she wants to be at any given time of the day,” Ali said indignantly, her hands on her hips.

Arie laughed again, the humor of the situation so very evident to him. He was better equipped to deal with that than his friend. "You sound like Chelsea and you've barely seen or talked with the woman. I would swear the thoughts of the MacTavish women are wearing off on you."

"Well, she did show up yesterday at the ship when it was time to leave with a huge carriage. I didn't want to go with that man you assigned to drive me. I also wanted Tessa to ride with me, so we all went together. She talked my ear off on the way back home. I'm surprised your man didn't tell you about my change in plans as well as his dismissal. Don't they have to tell you everything?"

Arie was rocking on his heels now, his hands clasped tightly behind his back, displeased by Ali's revelation. "They do. It's wrong. This is the first time I'm hearing about your change in travel arrangements. I will speak to the man. I'm not sure I'll keep him on retainer. He better have a damn good reason."

"Don't flog him or send him naked through the town square. I really didn't give him much choice. Short of hauling me over his shoulder and tying me to the curricle, he would not have succeeded in driving me here." Ali finished with a long dramatic sigh ending with a flirtatious grin.

"If Tessa is to go with you, she has nothing appropriate to wear," Victor said as an afterthought. "Perhaps the two of you should reconsider. Tessa can have tea with you when you return."

Alison laughed. To Arie's knowledge that was a rare occurrence. "I'm lending her one of my gowns. We are very nearly the same size. It would be well done of you if you took her shopping. Ask Arie where he goes. Have several gowns made up for her so she does have an appropriate dress to wear when the unexpected occurs. She cannot stay confined to the house wearing her harem clothing. It is not good for her health. You do want her to be healthy when she has your child."

Arie watched Victor's face pale slightly. His woman was changing Victor in ways he never thought would happen. He laughed unable to stop himself. "You should do as the lady suggests."

"Or what?" Victor asked with a grudge.

"Or Tessa might not come to your bed," Arie said, studying Alison.

What would he do if Ali refused to lie with him? He didn't know.

Forcing her certainly wasn't a possibility, and Victor had had Tessa in his bed for years now. The options the men had seemed to be dwindling by the second.

Their world was changing and Arie was wondering that perhaps it was for the better.

"I would not allow that choice," Victor said with a following grunt. "If I want to sleep with the woman, I will."

"You would find a way to seduce her then because I know—"

"I would pick her up and carry her to my bed then she would oblige me in every way just as she has for the last few years. Tessa understands her place as Alison does not."

Arie watched as Tessa stepped onto the porch dressed in a dark blue confection that Arie bought for Alison. Then he turned his attention to Victor who looked as if Tessa just punched him in the gut. His mouth was open, seemingly astonished by the woman who walked toward him. Arie could easily imagine what Victor was thinking. Most of it was not good.

"I would not allow that," Tessa said with seeming conviction along with a twinkle of mischief in her eyes. "If you did that, I would not be willing. As soon as I could, I would leave your bed. Alison has told me that in Scotland women do have rights. We live in Scotland. Am I not right?"

"Scottish rights be damned. You are too weak and too small to win a skirmish with me," Victor said, his voice gruff with emotion, his eyes blazing.

"I'm stronger than you think," Tessa said as she followed Alison down the steps and to the waiting carriage her back stiff. "I might not win the first time, but I will persevere if you insist on this obtuse behavior."

"Obtuse behavior?"

Arie lifted his shoulders in a helpless shrug, hiding the grin that threatened. "That's what she said. What do you suppose she is thinking?" Arie asked, clearly amused by his friend's seeming discomfort. His life was turning upside down at such a fast pace, Arie didn't think Victor could keep up with the changes, "You might find yourself challenged tonight. Best you figure out how you mean to react when she tells you no."

"She will not. She is simply toying with my emotions." Victor seemed to be adamant on this issue. "Tessa is sweet and biddable. Besides, she likes sex with me as much as I do with her."

"So you say. You've watched the ladies and how they've influenced their men. They all have them wrapped up tight. As far as I can tell, Ali and Tessa are not going to be any different. The more they are around the MacTavish ladies the more difficult they will be to deal with. We will need to be creative in our endeavors to woo them and win their hearts."

"I've already won Tessa's heart. What about you?" Victor countered. "Do you have a plan?"

Arie grinned at his longtime friend then with another confidant shrug. "No, no plan as of yet except to give in to all her wishes as long as those demands don't put her in danger. I will happily do whatever she asks of me and my manly body. I am hers to play with." He knew that to be true. He felt a lot like Cam did when he was courting Chelsea. Cam would give in to any demands Chelsea made, even ones he severely disagreed with. Just as he gave into her whims the night she was kidnapped. Perhaps he should rethink his stance.

Women sometimes think with their heart not their minds.

"A man should decide the course of his woman's life." Victor seemed unbendable in his beliefs and how he would interact with Tessa, but Arie was sure he would change dramatically just as he had.

"Of course he should but the real fact is that here in Scotland that is not true so much. Now, your woman is being educated by the best and wildest, independent Scottish lasses I've known. Not that I actually know many. You must learn to bend with the times."

Arie wondered what tonight would be like. He was sure now after this brief conversation that Ali would even be more opinionated. He would have to tread carefully and consider every word he spoke to her.

"The MacTavish ladies rarely take their man's opinion as their own if they are already set on their course. I pray Tessa does not learn the lessons they are teaching," Victor mumbled seeming to get the gist of what Arie was trying to tell him.

"In any case we have a meeting to attend, one that should prove enlightening," Arie said striding toward the stables. "Can't say that I'm looking forward to discussing Alison with her father."

"Your men are positioned if this turns ugly. One cannot take chances," Victor said as he kept pace with Arie. "Has Cam been enlightened about the possibilities at his home? He should know about this in detail."

Arie found his heart pounding uncharacteristically as they rode to the tavern. Apprehension resided in the forefront of his mind. This was a different land than his. In this case he could not assume he had the upper hand. What Frasier would expect to claim, he had no idea. Eventually though it would come down to what Alison wanted. He would give her free rein once more in deciding her future. Just as he had that day a few weeks ago when she returned to him.

He was confidant she would stay with him. She did not want anything to do with a father who abandoned her.

Stepping inside the tavern, Arie stopped to allow his eyes to adjust to the muted light. Frasier stood, motioning him to sit. He, too, had men in the tavern and Arie assumed outside as well. Precautions on both sides were taken.

"Good day," Frasier said as he motioned for the barmaid. "A Guinness?"

Arie nodded, not feeling at all social, his gaze absorbing everything. This was the man who tried to poison him, a woman's method of murder. He was too used to making rules to fit his needs. This was not the case here. "No, from the start Alison has told me she doesn't want anything to do with you."

"Not even to speak with me?" Murray queried, leaning back, his hands resting on his hard belly. "I would think, well, not sure about any of this. Perhaps she is just shy. She must be a tiny bit curious."

"That's not what she told me. You abandoned her and her mother. She has no emotional ties to you, no reason to talk with you." Arie's voice was harsh and accusatory. "Her life was one of hardship. There were times she had nothing to eat, only ragged clothes to wear. Her mother would leave her alone for hours as she tried to fend for them. Where were you?"

A slow flush colored his face at Arie's words, clearly affected by what he learned. "If you don't mind, I'd like to hear the words from Alison. Don't know if I can trust you to relay her thoughts after all I've heard about you," Frasier said, now leaning forward, his arms on the table. Tension seemed to fill the air around him.

Arie grinned, slowly realizing he had more power here than he previously thought. Rumors seemed to help him in this case. "What would that be?"

Victor stood behind Arie, his arms crossed, feet apart and Arie welcomed his friend's presence.

"I've heard you bought my daughter. She was never for sale," Frasier grit out, his anger beginning to show. "This is Scotland, for god's sake, man, not some..."

"Best you don't finish those thoughts," Arie said, his voice smooth, seeming to apprehend where the man's thoughts were headed. "Women and children are sold in Scotland on a daily basis. I did buy your daughter but now she chooses to stay with me. We have come to an understanding."

"I want her to come home where she belongs. She's a Frasier and has all the privileges of such," Frasier said, his voice now taking on a menacing tone.

"She belongs with me," Arie gritted out before realizing those words were better off left unsaid.

Frasier was shaking his head, watching him over the top of his glass. "She should live with her father. If she eventually wants you to court her, I might allow something like that."

"You should have thought about that when you left Scotland over nineteen years ago without her or her mother. I will ask her again if she wishes to see you. If so, I will set up a time and a place. Keep in mind you abandoned her to the life she found herself in. Why didn't you care?"

"Don't know why I should trust you," Frasier said, ignoring the question.

"Because there is no alternative. Alison is at Lord MacEwen's townhouse as we speak. She is not held prisoner by anyone, especially not me." Arie recognized in some respects that was true. She could come and go as long as he approved, as long as she did return. He didn't intend to let her anywhere near her father unless he was present.

"Perhaps I should go by the home and see if the marquis will allow me to speak with Alison." Frasier stood, pushing back his chair. "I suppose this meeting is over."

Arie rose. Victor stepped around the table blocking Frasier's path from the tavern. "You will not intrude on Ali's visit. As I told you, I will speak to her and if she wishes to meet with you, I will send a message."

~ * ~

"So, tell me, how is life with Arie?"

Chelsea set a plate of ginger cookies on the table clearly appearing to pry into Ali's life. Stepping back, her smile broad, she seemed to wait for Alison to say something then, when she remained quiet, "Tea or brandy?"

Alison didn't know what to say. She knew if she were Cam, she would deny this woman nothing if she smiled that way at him. It wasn't as if Alison wanted to keep any secrets. It just she wasn't sure about confiding in another woman about what she and Arie did in private. "Have no idea what you are asking me. I suppose one could say it's normal." Yet nothing any longer seemed normal to her.

It appeared Tessa wasn't as shy about speaking her mind. "I'm sure Alison wants some privacy where her life with Arie is concerned. Wouldn't you? If you're asking about sex, I'm sure they've had it." Tessa smoothed her skirts, looking down for a moment then gracing Chelsea with a hesitant smile. "Isn't that what most men and women do when they are alone?"

Alison felt a rush of heat to her cheeks while moisture covered her forehead as she looked away unwilling to see any repercussions on Chelsea's face. Sweat dripped between her breasts. She wanted to hide somewhere, shrivel into nothing, vanish into the air.

"I wish Daryl would have made some of her famous cream puffs. I know Grams loves her ginger cookies, but I do prefer the puffs or éclairs that Daryl bakes over the ginger snaps." Lacie plopped down in an overstuffed chair, laughing and obviously in good humor. "If I were you, I wouldn't tell Chelsea anything about what you do behind closed doors. It's none of her business. I'm sure she just wants to lecture Arie if she thinks he's not proper. There is nothing proper about Arie Demir."

Ali smiled seeming to feel an immediate connection with the youngest MacTavish girl. She wasn't about to talk about something so intimate and private. "And why is that?" she reached for a cookie wondering about the cream puffs and éclairs. She didn't believe she'd ever had either. Chelsea handed her a cup of tea then poured a bit of whiskey in the cup.

Lacie gave a long drawn out sigh for drama's sake. "Chelsea will undoubtedly lecture Arie no matter what you say. My sister thinks he should be perfect. He can't be. He's only a man and because of that imperfection, perfection is impossible," Lacie responded, stuffing the cookie into her mouth as she reached for a second and a third.

"Only a man?" Ali felt a giggle threaten before she crammed it back into her throat. "If you are looking to lecture Arie, he has treated me right. I've no regrets about what has happened to me or between us. He has been patient and understanding, even gave me a choice as to whether or not I wanted to remain with him. I chose to stay."

"I hesitate to broach the way he obtained you and some of the things he believes, but I find I must. You do know he can't really own you. This is Scotland after all," Chelsea said. "You are not his slave."

Ali started to reply but was interrupted by Tessa, "Of course she is his slave. Arie owns her just as Victor owns me. It's a fact. What else is there to know?"

The disapproval on Chelsea's face was clearly seen in the sudden furrow lines in between her brows along with the thinning of her lips. "I will speak to him. This is just not well done of him. He has a valuable lesson to learn. I mean to be the woman to teach it to him."

Ali started to reach out to Chelsea but drew her hand back, "If you know Arie as well as you claim, you also know it will do no good to tell him what you think about his owning me. The lesson you seek to teach him will fall on deaf ears as well you ken. In truth you will be the one to learn."

Chelsea sat down in a huff obviously irritated by the turn of the conversation. It was evident to Alison Chelsea understood exactly what she was getting at. Slowly she sipped her tea, looking over the rim of her cup at Alison. "Well, that is just not what I'd like to hear and well you ken. However, my mind has not been changed."

"Don't fash yourself," Ali said her voice soft and filled with confidence. "I ken who Arie is and what he thinks. I'm fine with all of it. You need to let us settle our relationship in our own way. After all what happens is between the two of us. We don't need a very verbal third party. He has changed. I believe eventually he won't think of me as his possession, his slave. Not positive he considers me a slave, but Tessa insists based on her life and what she has experienced that I am."

"Enough of all this," Lacie waved a hand in the air, grinning playfully as if she knew the best course there was to change the subject. "I want to know about this supposed father who suddenly showed up to claim you," Lacie said. "Where did he come from and does he really have a title?"

"And after all these years," Chelsea pointed out setting the cup back on the platter. "What if he's a fraud and just doing this for some strange reason?"

"What does he have to gain by pretending?" Ali asked even though she'd thought about that very thing. "I've nothing to offer him; no wealth, or power. I'm a bastard if what he says is true. It would make no sense."

"Does he have proof? Has Arie asked him for verification of his supposed parenthood?" Lacie stood, walking around the room and peering out the window as if she expected to see either Arie or the hypothetical father marching to the front door.

"Not that I know of. Mother is no longer in Scotland to say yay or nay. Of course, she would have to recognize him first. I don't know if mother knew he was a lord. In any case she never said a word."

"Would he change so much in nineteen years. If he had an older brother, he would not have held a title?" Lacie asked grabbing another cookie. "Just curious, wouldn't want to fall in love with a man who grew a paunch. Is Daryl going to show up with something good to eat? I'm starving."

"You're always hungry and skinny as a rail," Chelsea said, looking her sister up then down, "Can't figure that out. Yes, Daryl was invited. Doesn't mean she will bring food although she always does."

"For starters I'm not pregnant. You cannot really compare us, now can you?" Lacie pointed out with a bit of a sigh. "Your belly is rounding nicely every day, although one can barely see it as of yet."

"And it's a good thing you are not considering how smitten you are with the duke. You cannot follow him around as if you're his puppy dog. You cannot give into his every whim or you will find yourself in my condition and unwed," Chelsea said indignantly, fighting to keep from further lecturing her younger sister who was apparently in grave need of lecturing.

Alison was heartily glad the object of the conversations was now directed between the two ladies. She was growing weary of defending herself and listening to Chelsea's complaints about the man she was slowly giving her heart to. The woman could say whatever she wanted about her husband, but she better leave Arie alone.

"Sorry, I'm late," Hope walked into the room, setting her bonnet on the stand as well as her shawl. "I wanted to meet you, Alison. You are quite fetching. I see why Arie is so taken by you. Don't let him walk over you. He will you know if you allow it. You must stand strong because he will cave. I guarantee it. After all, he is a man who when he is enamored of a woman, will give her everything she asks for, so choose wisely. Don't make more demands than he could possibly give you. Stick with what is most important."

"That's what Chelsea is telling me too. As you say Arie has not been anything but nice to me," Ali said, smiling and immediately liking this lady.

Ali's thoughts went back to the night before. She was falling in love with this man but knew she could never tell him her true feelings. She didn't dare.

"Well, he's had lots of practice where women are concerned. I can tell you there are other things needed between a man and a woman than sex. He's got to think of your needs before his. Will he do that?" Hope asked.

Ali couldn't help but lift her shoulders, slightly unsure of what Hope was speaking of. "I don't ken what needs I have that he should think about."

Hope sat down beside Alison taking her hands in her own. "I've known the man since we were children. Arie tends to be selfish. He's never been denied anything he wants. In his home," Hope paused. "In his land men simply take what they want. Arie wanted you so he took you. Now, this can no longer be about what Arie wants. You must figure out what you want."

"Why not?" Alison was truly confused now. She wanted to please him. Would do just about anything to bring that about. He pleased her in so many ways she couldn't count them all.

"What do you want, Alison?" Hope asked, "You should think about that. Before Arie bought you, did you have any dreams? What did you want when you were a little girl?"

Alison rolled her eyes, trying to remember her life that now seemed to be so far in the past it was murky tinged with fog growing ever denser. What had she wanted? "Truth be told, I don't remember having any dreams except perhaps to get married and have children. I wanted a man who loved me and children to love, little beings who loved me for me."

"Nothing else?" Chelsea asked, bringing out the wine now and pouring everyone a glass. "You must have wanted more. We all did." She looked at her sisters.

"There were times I just wanted to have food in the cupboard. With Arie I've never been hungry, never wanted for anything." She so recalled all the times she went to her bed with an empty stomach. "Sometimes I had nothing to wear that did not have holes. Arie bought me clothing and a horse."

"Really, there is more to life than possessions," Lacie said. "Don't you want to be happy and maybe do something with your life?"

"What would I do?" Alison had never been so confused. These ladies were asking her about things she'd never thought of before. "I've no talents."

"Except pleasing Arie," Tessa said then quickly covered her mouth as if sensing Alison's embarrassment.

Chelsea seemed to pay no attention to Tessa misspoken words. "My sister, Bliss, paints and she sells her paintings. She could, if she wanted to, live on her own. She doesn't need a man to buy gowns for her and feed her," Chelsea said, "Although I don't have any particular abilities. I think Cam understands I don't love him for his title and wealth. I adore him for who he is and how he treats me. I would give him anything he asked for."

She inhaled a very shaky breath, her heart pounding, "I'm sorry, but I've no talents. I can't even read or write."

Ali suddenly felt inadequate by these women's standards. Perhaps Arie needed someone more educated, a woman more like Chelsea. After all, when he purchased her, he knew nothing about her. In time he would soon grow tired of her.

"Then Arie needs to find you a tutor. That doesn't matter. Daryl bakes. I'm sure if she wanted, she could set up her own bakery and make her living," Chelsea pointed out. "Can you cook? You could always help out or perhaps you are an amazing seamstress."

"If she can keep track of what she's bought and sold. My sister is atrocious with numbers, so that's where I come into this scenario," Lacie grinned, obviously pleased with herself.

"I don't understand numbers either nor can I sew or cook," Alison said, her voice growing softer and more insecure with each beat of her heart.

She looked at Tessa as if the other woman would give her some reassurance.

Tessa was shaking her head as clearly distraught as Alison was. "I suppose I'm just as lacking in matronly skills. In the harem and under Victor's protection, I've no need of any of those skills. I know one thing and that is how to please a man in bed. Where I've lived there has been only that purpose in my life. Victor likes the things I do. He tells me how pleased he is with me every night."

"That will be so until he grows tired of you," Chelsea pointed out directing a finger at her. "You cannot let that happen if you love the man. I believe you do."

She did love him but she wasn't about to confess.

"Maybe not. Who do you think so little of, Arie or Ali? Men are not all fickle creatures. Just as a good Scotsman, if he really cares about a woman, he will not grow tired of her then send her somewhere else," Hope said smiling encouragingly.

"We can all band together to teach both of you whatever we can, whether or not it is baking or sewing." Chelsea said. "Or even painting. You might have an unforeseen talent."

"Tessa, perhaps you would like to learn how to read and write also. I'm assuming that you cannot write your name," Hope said, "but you also know other things such as..."

It seemed to Alison, Hope was waiting for someone to finish for her, but personally she had no idea where Hope was trying to lead them. Hope was actually looking to Tessa for the answers.

"I'm not sure what you mean," Tessa said seeming to hold her breath for the longest time.

"If you were to think, you might. I heard how you treated the poison given to Alison. If not for you and your knowledge along with your quick thinking, Alison would have perished. It seems you have extensive knowledge in poisons. I'm assuming herbs as well. That is a valuable asset in a world where men try to kill each other over the smallest of reasons. You can bargain with your man for more privileges if you still believe he owns you." Hope was smiling as she watched the play of emotions on Tessa's face.

"I just learned as I grew up," Tessa said. "In the harem where I lived this knowledge was imperative. No one took anything for granted. The man who owned my mother and me had many enemies. Sometimes the women grew jealous, wanted to get rid of a favorite woman."

"What other fields are you proficient at?" Hope asked, smiling. She paused for a few seconds. "You really don't know do you? It is a skill you take for granted because where you come from all women have that skill, but here in Scotland it is not so."

Tessa smoothed her skirts truly appearing nervous and

uncomfortable. "I've no idea what you're talking about. To me all this talk is a riddle I don't know how to solve."

"You're an accomplished midwife, at least I assume that for a fact. How is it I don't remember you from the harem when I was there? Ah, you said the man who owned you had many enemies. Arie's father did not so..." Hope thought, puzzled.

"I don't know you either. Victor... well he rescued me from the streets of Bagdad. There was a... I'm not sure what you would call it but a takeover by another sultan. He put some of the women out to fend for themselves. I owe everything, my life, to Victor and I would never be presumptive. As far as I'm concerned, he owns me, always will. While he doesn't treat me as a slave, that is what I am. I will never be anything else."

"I see," Hope was patting her hand. Her expression told Ali that Hope was in complete disagreement with Tessa. "I understand. However, you have important abilities, knowledge that is valuable here in Scotland. There is so much superstition based on unknown facts in this land. You could earn your way or at least contribute to a household if you ever wanted to leave Victor."

"I do not," Tessa said seeming to wave Hope and Chelsea's advice to the back of her mind. "I want to be exactly where I am."

"Do you want to learn how to read and write, either of you?" Chelsea asked, changing the subject away from Tessa.

Alison did nod in agreement. "I would like that. I'm sure Tessa would too if Victor will allow her to do so. In any case she won't unless he gives his permission."

"What is happening? I'm sorry I'm so late. Was waiting for the blueberry muffins to finish baking. Time just seemed to get away from me." Daryl strode into the parlor, the scent of her baking filling the air with good aromas.

Daryl uncovered the basket then passed it around the room.

"They don't really go with wine, but I'll make the sacrifice," Lacie said as she bit into the muffin, closing her eyes with the first taste. "Delicious. I think I've died and gone to heaven. You really do need to start your bakery. For this, I will definitely help you with the books."

"You say that every time I bring in food," Daryl said laughing at her little sister and her penchant for the dramatic when it came to food.

"Well, it's true every time. I did hope for crème puffs or éclairs though."

The knock came as a surprise to all of them, Arie strode into the parlor, a man they didn't know following. "My apologies ladies but Frasier wouldn't take no for an answer when it came to seeing his daughter. He wants to meet her despite the fact I told him Alison wanted nothing to do with him. So, might I introduce," Arie stepped aside, "Murray Frasier, the Marquis of Bellmund?"

Ali's breath caught in her throat, her mind reeling that Arie would allow this. Yet the man seemed determined and perhaps Arie was presented with no choice as he said. She understood how men could be. This presentation might be the lesser of two evils.

So, this was her father, the man who abandoned her before he even knew her. She should despise him. She recognized the man and wondered if he'd known who he'd been speaking with that day.

Cam appeared quickly, "Perhaps we should retire to the library and discuss this. The ladies were having an enjoyable time. This is not well done of the two of you to come here without an invitation."

Arie cleared his throat, seeming to look from Alison to Frasier, "I do believe the marquis wanted to meet Alison and see for himself she is well taken care of despite her unusual circumstances. Then he will leave."

"With my daughter." The resolve in his voice did not go unnoticed by Alison. "I'm not going anywhere without Alison."

Victor stepped in front of the man, facing him. Alison thought she'd never seen such a ferocious scowl on his face. She understood now why Arie kept him as a personal bodyguard.

"I've no reason to leave with a man I don't know, a man who claims to be my father. How do I know any of what you say is true?" Ali said, her voice weak, yet she knew there was an underlying determination.

"I won't have my daughter abused by this man, this sultan," Frasier said, gesturing to Arie, his hands shaking. "Or bedded without benefit of marriage. She will not sire a bastard."

"As you did," Arie pointed out.

"He doesn't abuse me. I don't want to have this conversation with you. As far as I'm concerned, I don't have a father, never have. In any case I don't want you in my life. None of this is your business."

Hope was suddenly beside her, "Come, we should let the men discuss this issue among themselves. I'm sure it will all come to a satisfactory conclusion," Taking Ali's arm she walked with her up the stairs to find a guest room.

Inside the room, the girls suddenly surrounded her. Everyone seemed to be talking at once. "What do you suppose they are discussing?" Ali asked as she watched Chelsea move around the bedroom. She was pouring wine for everyone.

"The men will make sure Frasier does not come after you," Chelsea said. "At least not tonight. I don't think we've seen the last of that man."

"After all these years I don't understand why he suddenly cares. Why would he decide to come into my life now?" Alison stood by the door wishing there was some way to get out of the house and away from her supposed father.

"With men sometimes it's an ego thing," Hope said with a gentle smile then with a slight lift to her shoulders, "With Frasier, who knows? Maybe he feels guilty for abandoning you before you were born. Perhaps he regrets leaving your mother to fend for herself. Too bad he didn't stick around or make sure you were taken care of. In my mind he has no claim to you."

"In his mind he does."

"Wants to make up for it now," Lacie finished for Hope and Chelsea. "Men they are truly strange creatures needing to have power over everyone."

"Is there another way out? Down a servant's staircase?" Alison asked looking at the bedroom door with longing. She felt closed in, needed an escape from all of this. Overwhelmingly, she wanted to run and hide.

"How would Arie and Victor protect you if you were to leave on your own?" Tessa asked then pointing out, "You need to stay here where it's safe. Remember the last time you left?"

Ali recalled all too well what happened and how she got lost. Victor rescued her but only because Arie made sure his men kept track of her. She remembered too that she saw her father that day and the way he acted. Did he know then she was his daughter?

"I do understand how lost I was that day. I was traveling in circles. In this instance I do think I know the way home and could get there on my own. It's not like there aren't any landmarks," Alison said still looking toward the door.

"You would have to walk there," Tessa reminded her. "It's not that far but you are not used to walking. You would have more blisters than one could count. Arie would be very unhappy."

"The two of you arrived in a carriage. I'm sure your driver is waiting to take the two of you home. You could go down the back steps and..." Chelsea said then seemed to pause to think.

Tessa cleared her throat, saying, "Arie will have men guarding every door. We would not get two feet from the house if we were to attempt something so ridiculous. I for one have no intention of walking home, so that would leave you by yourself. Nor do I wish to anger Victor by leaving without him even if it was in the very same carriage that brought us here."

"Tessa is right. I do recall the days in the harem and how well secured the women were. Arie grew up in that environment. Now he has a woman he considers precious to keep track of. I do know the man well. However, I could read his feelings by the expression on his face when he looked at Alison," Hope said calmly. "Even if he hasn't told you, he cares deeply for you. He won't let you go. Ever."

"Let's drink our wine and continue the conversation from before the men showed up and spoiled everything for us. They can be such downers," Daryl said grinning as she sipped what was left in her glass. "I barely got in on any of the conversation. Do you want me to go down the stairs and bring up the muffins and more wine?"

"I'd rather have some of those nice pastries and cheese cook makes. It's almost dinner. Perhaps she has a tray of them ready," Chelsea said with a tiny all-knowing smirk. "And while you are downstairs you can see what the men are doing or deciding or whatever manly things they do while they make sure they have their way in everything."

The huge crash coming from below stopped all conversation. Ali's heart seemed to be caught in her throat as she felt the blood drain from her face. She was horribly afraid for Arie then herself. After a long pause she rushed to the door, ready to careen unthinkingly down the steps and find out what was going on as well as if Arie was hurt.

"No." The urgency in Tessa's voice stopped her half way to the door.

A cold sweat broke out on her body. "I have to see. Can't stay here and wonder."

"You have to wait in this room right where you are, right where Arie expects you to be," Hope said her voice calm and restrained. "It would not do to rush into trouble. I'm sure Arie and Victor..." she stopped for breath.

"And Cam," Chelsea said.

"Have everything under control. They are merely ushering Lord Frasier from the premises, and he is resisting as would be expected," Hope said.

"Or my father has over powered Arie and Victor and Cam and he will drag me out of here," Ali said, her voice weak. "To God knows where. I won't stay with him."

"The marquis needs to worry about ending up in the town square without a stitch of clothing on," Tessa giggled. "I would love to see that."

Alison closed her eyes imagining just such a thing. A brief smile formed then, "We cannot be sure."

"We wait until one of the men comes to tell us it's all clear," Hope said. "That's the trouble with being a woman. We always have to wait."

"Well, I for one don't like to sit around waiting. As everyone kens, I've absolutely no patience." Chelsea stood up, Daryl following her as both headed for the door their skirts swinging.

"That would not be wise," Victor stood in front of the now open door. "Arie is taking care of matters. Alison, you have nothing to be afraid of tonight. Arie will explain everything when you have the privacy of your home or perhaps during the ride there, but I've a feeling he has something else on his mind for the carriage ride."

Victor was inside the room. The ensuing silence sent shivers down Ali's spine. This was not what she expected from this day.

~ * ~

It was only minutes later when Arie stepped into the room a smile on his face. Standing in front of Alison, he held out his hand, "Ali, you must come with me. Tessa will travel with Victor. It seems he has something important to ask her and would like some privacy. I told him to wait for a better opportunity, but he decided it must be done sooner than later."

Arie held out an arm for Alison. "Alright then," she said hesitantly while she looked from Victor to Tessa.

Victor watched as the pair left the room. Then, taking Tessa's hand in his, he helped her to stand. "Come along."

He wanted to laugh when Chelsea frowned at him but wisely chose to curtail his emotions. Looking at the worried expression on Tessa's face he understood her discomfort, doubting she had any idea why he wanted the privacy. In their world it was highly unusual for a man to ask a slave for her hand in marriage. She would be expecting a dismissal.

"You don't have to go with him," Lacie said unexpectedly. "You can stay right here. We won't let him hurt you or make you do something against your will."

"How nice of you but I cannot and even if I didn't want to go with Victor, I would," Tessa said, a tiny smile on her beautiful face. In a soft voice, "Victor would never willingly hurt me. He owns me, you know. Men don't hurt women they own."

Victor so wanted to reassure right now, but this was a private and special matter between the two of them. He'd waited his entire lifetime for this moment. He wasn't going to let anyone or anything spoil it. Tessa was right. He would never harm her in any way. He cherished Tessa.

Stiffly, Tessa walked beside Victor. When he wrapped his arm around her shoulder pulling her closer, he felt her trembling as well as the soft curve of her breast nestled softly against his chest. He bent close and whispering, said, "You have nothing to worry about, little pigeon, heart of my heart. You will like what I have to say. I promise you this."

He felt the gentle whooshing of air from her lungs almost as if she could feel relief from his words. He understood all too well what she might be thinking.

At the top of the steps he studied the entryway, looking for any sign Fraser might return. Everything was clear but he didn't trust the Scotsman. Fraser left just before he spoke to Arie and strode to the bedroom to retrieve Tessa. Cam gave him his carriage and driver for the occasion telling him to take as much time as necessary. So, with two bottles of champagne already in the vehicle he was ready, his nerves though beginning to fray around the edges.

He told himself she would not refuse his proposal, but he couldn't be positive. Tessa never complained, always understood her role, seemed to enjoy their relationship, which grew over time. What if she didn't want a change in status? Once more he asked himself what woman would rather be a slave than a wife?

They reached the carriage. He helped her inside. Climbing in beside her, "You've been very quiet tonight."

"I..." She turned to look at him, gently touching his face with her fingertips. "I'm just afraid."

"Of me?" he asked, not understanding her words. "I would never hurt you. You said as much a few minutes ago."

"Not intentionally but there are many ways a man can hurt a woman who is his slave." Moisture filled her eyes as she tried to wipe the tears away with the backs of her hands.

He didn't want her to cry. What she just told him was the crux of the matter. Tessa never thought past the master and the slave relationship. Truth of the matter was, it had been a very long time since he thought of Tessa as his slave. He felt so many things for her. Love? He wasn't sure but he cared deeply for her and knew he wanted her in his life.

Forever.

She pleased him in too many ways to count.

He pulled out one of the bottles of champagne and popped the cork. "Would you like some French champagne?" He poured two glasses. Her hand was shaking when she accepted the flute.

"What are you trying to tell me?" Her voice was whisper thin. "I wish you would just say the words so we can get this over with. Perhaps I would stop shaking if I knew what you were going to ask."

"So many things?" He grinned as the carriage began to roll, thinking perhaps she was right. They had been together for so long saying the words might be the easiest route. "This night is special to me. I hope to you too."

Tessa stared into her glass as bubbles floated to the top. Victor felt the moment slipping away. "When you finish the glass, I'll tell you why we are here together."

"I'm not sure my stomach will allow it. Can't you just get this over with? Please."

Just getting this moment over with was not in his plans, but her fear was real and changing the atmosphere he was trying to create. "Drink a sip first. It will relax you and then..." He drank half the glass then set his glass aside. "When you indulge, we can get onto more important matters."

"Are you taking me home? What are more important matters?" She parroted, trying valiantly to finish the drink. When she did swallow the last drop. He took her glass, setting it close to his.

"Feel better?"

"Tell me."

"We are not going home, at least not right away." Tenderly, he brushed her cheek with the back of his hand. "I don't know if I've ever told you just how beautiful you are, Tessa but I'm going to say it now. You are beyond a doubt the most beautiful woman I've ever known."

He wished he could see her eyes and the passion his words usually provoked in them. Gently he brushed hair from her face, smiling. Her skin was so soft. She smelled of roses.

"I don't recall." Her breath rushed in and out in short little pants.

He would have to say the words now. If he didn't, she might faint from lack of air. "Tessa." He held her hands in his. "You've always been my rock. Ever since I rescued you off the streets of Bagdad, I've needed you in so many ways. Always you've been there for me."

She started to reply, "You don't... I'll pack my things and leave."

Hush, he placed a fingertip on her lips. He was well and truly baffled. "Don't think you are listening to my words. I don't want you to leave me ever and I hope you feel the same about me."

"What are you saying?"

"I'm trying to tell you that I don't want you as my slave."

"Please... I'll do better. Tell me where I've gone wrong. I'll fix it."

He didn't prolong this farther, couldn't, "Little fool, I want you as my wife. You are my heart and my soul. There is no other woman I want in my bed or to walk beside me for the rest of our lives. I should have asked you a long time ago, but I was afraid you would turn me down. Still am."

"You are not afraid of anything," Tessa whispered softly.

Victor laughed then, feeling a small weight lift from his shoulders. "I am afraid of a tiny little slip of a woman telling me she doesn't want to become my wife. Say yes, Tessa. The sooner the better so I can breathe again."

"I don't understand. There is no reason for you to ask such a question. I would never leave you."

"You don't want to be my wife?" he asked, suddenly feeling sick to his stomach. Perhaps he misjudged her. Maybe she didn't love him.

Shaking she let out a long deep breath of air. "I do. I would rather be a wife than a slave, but..."

One dark eyebrow curved upward. "But?" He suddenly felt a tiny bit better.

"Why are you asking?"

"Haven't you been listening? I want you in my life, for the rest of my life. I don't want the risk of losing you. In my heart you are not a slave. Indeed, my heart is enslaved by yours."

"What are you talking about? You own me so you can't lose me," she spoke softly, her voice sweet and filled with emotions he didn't understand, couldn't fathom.

"I can lose the beautiful way you respond to my touch, to my kisses." With that said he lightly brushed his lips across hers, enjoying the slight gasp of air then the immediate response as he slowly deepened the kiss. "Is that a yes?" he asked as he put a tiny bit of distance between them.

"Yes," she breathed ever so softly, wrapping her hands around his neck and pulling him closer.

Chapter Seven

Arie stretched out on the lush pallet filled with pillows. Trays of food were located on nearby tables. In one hand he held a glass of champagne as he waited for Alison to join him. There was so much he needed to know. Wanted to know if she yearned in any way to see her father again.

He prayed she did not. The man represented a threat to their happiness. With words her father had the ability to persuade Alison to leave him. Arie didn't understand the emotion but he was strangely afraid.

This sudden appearance of a man from Alison's past unnerved him. Made him think of returning to his land with her so he could keep her to himself. He would make her his fourth wife. She would be his most treasured wife, first among the others. Yet he understood that running away would not solve the problem. There wasn't a doubt in his mind Frasier would follow. Once inside the harem, though, he would never get her back.

She wouldn't understand the status that title would give her nor would she understand the fact he would have to sleep with his other wives to keep a modicum of quiet and contentment within the harem. When ignored harem women could be brutal to one another. He didn't think she would like living among the other women in those circumstances.

At this point he wasn't sure of anything.

Alison walked into the room dressed in her harem pants and bolero jacket. He grinned, appreciating the site of her, of all of her. Nothing was left to the imagination. Sitting down beside him she accepted the glass he handed to her. "I see champagne. What is the occasion?"

"The celebration of several things," he told her, his voice gruff with emotion.

When he looked at her, with her beautiful woman's body revealed to him, his body grew hard with the incredible desire and passion she sparked in him so easily. He wanted her this instant but schooled himself to wait.

"Celebration? I suppose so. Hopefully my father understands that I never want to see him again. He has become a threat to everything I hold dear."

She shouldn't count on her father giving up so easily, but he wasn't going to tell her as much. Arie saw the glint in Frasier's eyes, knew the look well. They had not seen the last of that man.

"We can always hope," Arie murmured, wondering if tonight was the right time to ask Alison to marry him. He had a pretty good idea Victor had more courage than he did and was asking Tessa the very same thing. He drew in a long breath determined now to do the right thing for this woman who was slowly capturing his heart.

"Yes, we can hope." she leaned into him, stroking his chest, clearly wanting him, needing him as much as he did her. He trained her well, taught her so much.

He held her hand in his stopping her while he still had the ability. "You don't have to answer tonight if you don't want to but..."

She pushed away from him, clearly puzzled by his words as well as the sound of his voice, which was deep and gruff. For the first time since he could remember, he was unsure of himself.

"What is it?" Ali asked, watching him with her vivid green eyes sparkling with passion, her long red hair tumbling down her back in a tangled mass.

He cleared his throat, swallowing away his nerves best as possible. The pause before the question seemed to last too long. Finally, "Would you consider becoming my wife?" His smile was hesitant at best, his heart in his throat. Patiently, he waited for her answer.

"Your fourth wife..." She inhaled long and deep seeming to think during the process. "The fourth," she repeated.

"Yes, my fourth wife. I cannot divorce or annul the others. It would cast shame on them and my children."

The truth of his life was there for her to consider, yet he had no regrets. Would do the same if presented to him as when he was younger.

"Yet becoming your fourth wife places no shame on me?" she asked clearly puzzled. "I don't know how to deal with something such as that."

"Not in my country but in yours it might. I believe it might cause more shame to be on my head though. No one needs to know about my other wives except the two of us as well as my people. If we never return to my country, well then you will never have to deal with my other wives. As I told you before, they barely tolerate me."

"Save one," Alison reminded him with what appeared to be a hesitant smile. "I don't know what I want now except a wife is better than a slave. For now, here in Scotland, it would be just you and me."

"True," Arie laughed believing now Ali would talk herself into saying yes. "Just you and me together in this bed every night and during the day, well, you would never have to share me."

"Chelsea would stop lecturing you about the proper way to treat me." Alison went on to say with a tiny giggle. "She does ken you have other wives? Doesn't she?"

Arie pulled her close, as she set her head on his chest. He ran his fingers through her hair, undoing all the pins in the process, needing to show her just how much he wanted all of her. "This has nothing to do with the reason I asked you tonight. It's a secondary factor but if we were wed, your father would have no right to claim you in any way. I cannot bear the thought of losing you."

Once more she pushed away from him. "In my mind Frasier is not my father and has no rights where I'm concerned. If a marriage between us would stop him from tormenting us, then perhaps it is the right thing to do."

Relief sweeping through him, he let out a long breath of air. "That is not what Scottish law will say concerning your father. As your husband I have the right of decision. Yet I would pray you would wed me because you care for me."

Truly he yearned for her to love him. He supposed that emotion was too much to ask.

"You would take my decisions away from me?"

"Hush, never." He placed a finger on her lips following the action with a gentle kiss when he truly wanted more.

"Good then I will think on it. Perhaps in a week or two I will let you know my decision." She leaned back into him then rose above him, straddling him and smiling. "Make love to me and it will be easier to decide."

"So, my little harem girl, you want to seduce me to your ways. You full well understand that you would prefer to have me control your life than an absent father. I think you have learned too much from the MacTavish ladies."

She was fiddling with the ties on his shirt then pulling if from his waistband, running her hands along his chest. He would allow her these moments. They would be good for both of them as he felt the heat of her gentle seduction fill his body. Tempest, wind and fire swirled around the two of them. His blood raced through him in anticipation of her tender strokes.

Yes, he taught her well.

"I do," and she trailed kisses along his naked chest, licking and nipping as he had trained her. Caressing him everywhere.

"Those are the words I need to hear in front of a preacher," he growled as he felt the air rush from his lungs. In those few seconds she rid herself of the jacket and her breasts were naked to his touch. His hands were on her tiny waist, thumbs tracing gentle circles as he inched his way upward. "The sight of you steals my breath, entices my heart to thunder and roar. When I look at you, the sight makes me feel as if I've just seen the first flowers open in the spring after the snow from winter has melted."

"Perhaps you will. Maybe I would like to hear those words from your lips," she spoke as she leaned forward, the tight hard buds of her breasts, touching his lips, begging for him to take her into his mouth.

A few seconds later, they were both naked and then satisfied. He held himself above her, smiling at her and moving damp strands of her hair from her face. "Have you had enough time to decide?"

"I want you Arie so yes, I will marry you."

He felt a rush of relief at her words. This was necessary for her wellbeing. Even now time might be slipping away from them. "The sooner the better."

"I understand what you are trying to tell me. I never thought I would have a big elaborate wedding being poor and all, so I will be happy as long as you and Tessa are there," she spoke softly as she ran her fingers through her hair.

"That you will have and perhaps Chelsea, her husband and the MacTavish ladies as well?" he queried, hoping she would say yes to the added invitees because he already arranged with Chelsea to have the double wedding at the MacEwen townhouse tomorrow afternoon.

"I do like Lacie and Hope as well, but Chelsea intimidates me. I don't like the way she scowls at you when you say something outrageous or she disagrees with. She keeps expecting you be someone you are not and doesn't understand you."

"Sit up." He pulled her to a sitting position, laughing and thinking perhaps where he was concerned, she was a little tigress. "We can discuss this over more champagne then we can do other more fun things."

"I don't want to go to sleep tonight. In any case, I doubt if I could. I'm happy and excited. Truly, a few weeks ago I never thought this was possible, never thought I would meet anyone, especially a man, who could make me so happy." She did drink the bubbly liquid, grinning and leaning back on the propped-up pillows. "Where do you think Tessa and Victor are? It's strange that we haven't heard from either one since we returned. Don't you think?"

"Not tonight. I'm hoping they are having a private celebration of their own."

His thoughts went to his best friend and the words they said between them earlier about marriage. He hoped Victor's answer from Tessa was also a yes.

"What? Another celebration?"

She turned to him, her breasts swaying slightly with the sudden movement.

He reached out to cup one milk white globe in his hand, his mind working overtime. "Lie back," he told her, giving her a tiny push. "I've never done this before but I wonder what you taste like wearing champagne."

"Arie..."

Slowly he trickled fine droplets of the liquid on various erotic places, strategic places he knew would create havoc within her, heat her to a mercuric level, set a tempest of his making swirling inside her. He loved the passion and desire he could generate in her so easily. Then he set his glass on the table, sipping and licking the tiny droplets until she moaned with the pleasure of the sensations, tiny sounds coming from the back of her throat as her hips moved upward beckoning to him.

He wanted to prolong this, but it seemed she had ideas of her own taking over and touching him, exploring his manly parts until he could wait no longer. Her sheath was still small and so very tight, he nearly groaned when he entered her, drove inside until they were both wild with need. She gave him so much pleasure. All he wanted was to return the mercuric enchantment. Fascinated, intrigued, mesmerized, he didn't think he could ever get enough of her.

She was his through all time.

Perhaps she'd been his in another life. They were so drawn to each other it seemed unreal. The attraction was swift and potent.

When they were both sated once more, he looked down on her. Her eyes were closed. "Thought you said you wouldn't be able to sleep tonight," he whispered, touching her ear with his tongue and biting gently.

He could tell by her breathing she was only pretending. The small gasp when he touched her again gave him more reasons to smile.

"You know I'm not. What were you going to tell me about Tessa? It seems you wanted to change the conversation."

"And Victor? We both understand the man cannot be left out of the equation." He didn't think he'd ever been so happy or more pleased. He rolled over on his back, one hand behind his head.

"And Victor," she agreed with him, still touching him, running her finger up and down his arm as if she wanted him again. "I cannot get enough of you, yet I'm exhausted. You've worn me out."

"You need to stop or I won't be able to tell you about those two." Once again, they sat against the pillows, drinking more and eating a few of the fine delicacies set out by one of the servants.

She punched him in the chest and he respectfully grunted. “You’re the one who started it, last time pouring champagne on me, seducing me. Perhaps I could do the same to you. I want to lick champagne from every part of you.”

He groaned at the thought of her tiny pink tongue licking and sipping the champagne from his body. He stilled his thoughts, holding her hands in his. “Would you like to have a double wedding?”

She looked surprised then it seemed her eyes crossed. Tilting her head slightly, “Tessa and Victor? I can think of no others who might be getting married. Do you think she will say yes?”

“As you just said being a wife is better than a slave, although I know she was content in that role. She has always had a tender spot when it came to Victor. I believe she would give her life to save his if necessary.” He kissed her hands, the knuckles the palms then gently bit the tip of each finger. She was so small and fragile, yet strong in so many ways.

“I think Tessa would like that, but she never believed he would ask her. So, the two of you gave each other the courage to ask us to marry you. You big brute. The two of you needed courage for such a simple thing? What if one of you couldn’t bring himself to say the words? What would happen then? Would the other back out of the commitment?”

“If that happens, and I’ve no way of knowing yet, well then, we will not have a double wedding, but I will never back out from this commitment with you. I need you as my wife and the only way to keep your father out of yours is by our marriage.”

“Did you say we will wed tomorrow afternoon? Isn’t that a bit soon? I would like something nice to wear although,” she paused, “I know that’s impossible. I did say I don’t care about anything fancy.”

“Yes, I believe that was the plan. Chelsea has promised to have a minister at her home and Daryl has volunteered to bake us a cake, perhaps two if we’re lucky. Bliss says she will have a few flowers there.”

He watched her eyes as they sparkled with passion and something else he recognized all too well. She wanted his man’s body again and that was just fine with him.

“No one has ever treated me this well. I don’t know what to say.”

She kissed him on his chin then lower, lower still.

"Did you tell me yes?" he prompted, needing to hear the words more than once.

He discovered he always wanted her to say yes to him. Although the more time he spent with the MacTavish ladies, the more she would challenge him. Perhaps he would be willing to listen to a "no" once in a great while.

"Yes, Arie, I want to marry you tomorrow afternoon if that's what you believe to be the best course of action." Her expression turned inward.

"What is it?"

It seemed she returned to the subject of a gown. "Really, Arie, I don't know what to wear. Do I have something special enough for a wedding? I know I said I didn't care about all the elaborate planning and whatever else goes with the ceremony..."

"I so hoped you would tell me what I wanted to hear that I had a gown made for you. I believe it will suit you as well as the occasion."

"Thank you, thank you, I..." she paused then. "You were that confident?"

She punched him again. He caught her chin with his fingers and gently kissed her, ran his tongue along her lips hoping she would open for him.

She didn't disappoint.

Then his breath whispering so close to her, "Perhaps I was more hopeful than confident. The fourth wife fact I knew would bother you, but truly I've no plans to return home. There is simply nothing there for me."

For the first time since leaving Turkey, he realized this was his new home.

"Your children," she reminded him. "Do you want to be an absentee father like my own? Then show up one day in the distant future and because you're feeling guilty start dictating your children's lives, what they can and can't do, who they can see?"

"No, of course not but the fact is, I would rarely see them anyway. As I said my wives tolerated me for the gifts and trinkets I gave them. Children are all taken for granted by their fathers."

"There is no one there to give them gifts so if that's all they wanted from you, they must be angry or disappointed not receiving any now." She looked away from him then, "If we have children will you ignore them? I don't think I'd like that. Perhaps I have changed my mind."

He laughed then, "Why are you thinking of my wives when we have other more important topics to discuss? They are well treated and my father agreed to give them their rewards while I was gone. You see they are all most likely happy that I'm not calling them to my bed. Without me around they are left in peace. As for any children we might have, they will be raised by us. I've seen and like most of the European ways concerning families."

"I would not have been happy in that life. I would rather be in your bed than receive gifts from you. You are the only present I need or want."

He roared with laughter. "All you want is my body, little harem girl. I do believe I like that trait very much." He kissed her soundly and they made love again. This time he let her sleep while he watched over her.

He loved her. This marriage was right. The two of them would do well together. They would marry tomorrow. Her father would not interfere in their lives again. With a quick kiss on the cheek to his soon to be wife, he dressed and strode to the parlor where Victor and Cam waited for him.

Both Cam and Victor rose acknowledging his presence. "Never thought I'd be planning a wedding with you," Cam laughed, his eyes twinkling with mirth.

The two men looked relaxed as they spoke about the weddings to be this afternoon since it was well past midnight. Marriage, he'd been married three times before but this one truly meant more to him than anything else in his life. When Victor purchased her for him, he made the best decision of his life

Victor handed him a drink. They all sat again. "Here's to tomorrow and our ladies who have," he paused, when Arie nodded, "agreed to marry us despite all our bad tendencies and wicked ways."

"What can you tell me about Frasier? Do you think he gave in grudgingly to the fact his daughter doesn't want him in her life and will leave us all alone for the rest of his stay here?" Arie asked, hoping Cam answer would be yes.

"He went straight to his townhouse. So far by all reports he has not left Scotland or traveled to his country home. Men have been coming and going all evening. I'm sure he's planning something," Cam said his brows narrowing. "I don't trust the man, but I don't think his intent is to leave Scotland. He is the sole heir now and has responsibilities."

"I will have all my men stationed around my home." Arie began then thought better of the suggestion. "You should have your men there. I will make sure my men accompany the four of us to your home when we leave here."

"Chelsea has everything else planned. I think she has been waiting for this moment since we married. She knew all along that when you actually bought Alison after all her lectures, she was more than a purchase," Cam said, seeming to watch him for a reaction.

If he was truthful with himself, he wanted her from the first moment he saw her in the restaurant, sunlight dancing in her hair. Knew he would do anything necessary to have her and keep her. Now, all this infatuation developed into a wedding. He was pleased he found a way to purchase her. Pleased his home was preferable to a brothel even though he knew she would choose to stay with him.

"Chelsea has no problems with a double wedding?" Victor asked, seeming to understand Chelsea's feelings for his boss didn't carry over to him.

"Under the circumstances, no, she doesn't," Cam said laughing, "and neither do I. Indeed, I'm quite pleased Arie has found someone besides my wife to care for. When he is married, I will be the recipient of more of my wife's attention. By the way after the nuptials are said, would the two of you or even the four of you like to honeymoon at my beach house?"

"I believe that would be quite the thing. Thank you for asking," Arie said, remembering the place quite well.

"Then it is all settled and we should all try to get some sleep before one o'clock tomorrow afternoon," Victor said looking up the stairs to his bedroom appearing to think he'd like to get to bed and hold his soon to be wife in his arms. "Not really sure I'll be able to sleep with Tessa lying beside me and my knowing in a few hours she'll be my wife."

Ushered by two of Cam's men, tomorrow's minister walked through the door, a folder of papers in his hand. He cleared his throat as he looked between the three men. "This is just a formality that Cam thought of. I've known him since he was a wee lad. He's always been one to think of the worst-case scenarios, but he also never leaves openings for something to go wrong. This is just such a case. One cannot be too cautious."

Arie stepped forward relieving the man of his folder, looking from the minister to Cam "What is this?"

"The documents that need signing that say you are legally wed," he replied. "Cam thought the sooner the papers were signed the better, and he has direct knowledge that your ladies do not write."

"The women are asleep. I'm not sure I want to wake Tessa to put an X on a piece of paper."

"That's what Chelsea told me and that they both agreed to the marriage. No one will know the difference if the grooms mark the X for their prospective brides. Doubt if said brides will complain if their men do the signing. Are you willing to take part in a tiny bit of deception?"

Arie thought it a splendid idea. "I'm sure Alison will be thankful and Tessa as well. Where do we sign?"

The minister took a few moments to arrange all the papers while Arie produced pen and ink.

Arie read over the document before signing and nodding to Victor. "It appears to be in proper order."

"So, are we officially married?" Victor asked with a gruff laugh looking as a man well-pleased. "We do not have to dress up for tomorrow."

"It is official on paper but you must say your vows before God," the minister said with a smile. "You cannot think to get out of the ceremony by signing a few papers. It is not God's way."

Victor grinned with a masculine shrug and sigh to emphasize his feelings. "It was worth a try. I know Tessa will want to wear the new gown I purchased for her. I will also enjoy removing it later in the evening."

"My men will see you home." Cam walked him to the door.

"The duplicates will be put in the safe," Arie said not wanting to take any chances with the paperwork.

He headed to the safe and quickly put the papers inside relocking the steel box.

"The others will be filed away in the church archives for safe keeping. Let no man try to put asunder your vows. You are legally wed as of tomorrow at one o'clock."

After the minister left, "A drink to tomorrow and our new brides," Arie said refilling everyone's glass.

"To your brides," Cam said laughing.

Victor sat down letting his head settle on the back of his chair, his eyes closed. "I for one will be happy when this is said and done. I will feel so much better. I love her. This is what we both want but..."

"Tomorrow Alison will be my wife," Arie mused thoughtfully enjoying this moment of personal revelation. "I never thought to take another wife."

"Then why did you ask Chelsea so many times," Cam growled, downing his glass of brandy before refilling it.

"Because she knew the proposal was half in jest and I knew it would annoy you," Arie said looking up the steps and thinking it was about time he joined Ali.

Cam set his glass on the table. Arie was sure he was about to leave. "I will see you tomorrow at your wedding. I pray nothing goes awry but if it does, we will deal with it in a timely manner."

The crashing at the door stopped all conversation. Three English soldier entered through the now broken door with no explanation or apology.

Arie rose quickly and Victor stepped in front of him. "What do you want?"

"You'd better have good reason to barge in here. This is a private home," Cam stepped toward the English soldiers. "I'm Colin MacEwen Viscount of Rosehill. This is not well done of you. I will speak with your commanding officer and have your heads."

"We are here to arrest Arie Demir for the crimes he has

committed," the Lieutenant said, his voice calm.

"I've not committed any crimes," he said ignoring the fact he had kidnapped Fletcher and Leod Donovan before sending them on their way to become slaves. "Who says I have?"

"Murray Frasier, the Marquis of Bellmund. He accuses you of buying his daughter, kidnapping her and turning her into your slave."

"I am wed to the woman in question. I've the papers to prove it."

Yet he knew he'd find himself in the Glasgow jail before he could retrieve the documents. These men were intent on one thing, his arrest. Thank his lucky stars Cam was here and would be able to get him out. He would not fight this physically, a battle he could not win. He would have to wait. He hoped Cam could get them out before one o'clock tomorrow afternoon.

The soldiers grabbed Victor too. "You are both under arrest. We have orders to take the girl to her father. I assume she is under this roof."

Arie's heart froze in his chest. He couldn't breathe and he wasn't sure if it was caused by fear for Alison or anger at a man who he should have dealt with more severely the first time he saw him. He fought for calm rational though while his heart pounded erratically. This would not bode well for either of them.

Guns were pointed at Arie's and Victor's chest. Then Cam spoke up, "Go with the soldiers. I'll get reinforcements as well as the signed documents. You'll be free by morning. They have no legal recourse but to set the both of you free."

Helplessly, he watched as the men headed up the stairs to the master chamber. Heard the shriek as well as the cursing as one of the soldiers pulled Alison from the bed. "Lord, but he'd left her naked." His heart pounding, he strained against the men holding him but to no avail.

Before he could protest further, he was hauled from his home.

"Don't fight them," were Cam's last words.

~ * ~

Alison felt the covers ripped from her as she found herself unceremoniously hauled out of bed by strange men then suddenly let go.

The man's gaze raked over her body. "Get dressed. You're coming with us."

She scrambled for the covers, trying to cover her nakedness while she searched the room for something decent to clothe herself in. All she had in Arie's chamber were the harem pants and the skimpy jacket. For whatever purpose these men had in mind, she knew her harem pants and bolero jacket were not something she wanted men to see her wearing. Her hands clammy and shaking, she was desperate for these men to leave. Frightened for what they intended.

Where is Arie?

"I have to go to the dressing room," she told them as her body shook and her heart raced.

Perspiration beaded on her forehead and between her breasts, her hair in wild disarray around her shoulders. Where was Arie? What happened to him? If he was in control, he would never allow something like this. Her hand on her chest she struggled for breath.

"Why would I go anywhere with you?"

"We'll go with you to your room."

"No!"

She raced to her room. Holding a sheet around her she searched for a dress and proper undergarments. Then turned waiting for the men to leave her in privacy.

"Don't think we can do that, lass. We were told not to let you out of our sights, and we mean to follow the orders."

His sneer sent a shiver down her spine as he kept his gaze focused on her.

"You cannot possibly think to watch while I dress."

Her words echoed in short little pants around the walls of the room. She knew Arie would seek these men out and punish them. They had no right to be here or command her. Trying to hold the covers in front of her she attempted to put the clothing on.

One of the soldiers ripped the sheet from her. "Already saw you naked. Just get dressed. The marquis is waiting for you."

The marquis? Frasier?

In a matter of seconds, she was clothed. One of the soldiers wrapped his hand around her arm ushering her from the house and into a waiting carriage. When she walked through the house, silence was the only sound she heard. Arie was gone as was Victor.

Oh my God.

She knew her father was behind this. She also saw no sign of Arie or even Victor. Closing her eyes, she let the bumps of the carriage soothe her shattered nerves as it trundled through the city. She tried to keep her breathing calm and slow, tried to not think about the humiliation she just endured.

Blessed hell, what was happing now?

Alison didn't have to ask where they were taking her. She understood all too well that Arie and Victor misjudged the man, her supposed father. They were prepared for thugs not law enforcement. All too soon she would find herself standing in front of Murray Frasier. *To what end,* she wondered. She would not stay with the man who tried to claim her after all these years. If he expected that, he would have to lock her away.

This was not how she'd expected the rest of her evening to go.

A partial moon stood out in the cloudless sky. A few lights shone into the carriage as they passed along the street. An eerie silence seemed to reverberate around her. She had no idea the location of her father's townhouse. She would get lost if she managed to break free and try to return to her home. Moisture swelled in her eyes.

She would have to wait this out and let Arie find her... or Cam. He would discover what her father did with her, would come for her. Arie would never allow her father to take her away from him. Would Tessa know where she was? Where was Victor?

Her happiness seemed to have been short lived but now that she understood contentment and happiness, she would get it back. No one would stand in her way. She would fight this man, her father.

When the carriage finally drew to a stop, she thought about bolting from the door but she understood she'd be caught before she could run a few steps. She would have to be quicker in mind than foot. She was strong. Arie had made her strong. Her anger would be a weapon if she controlled it.

"Now you be careful with the marquis' daughter. He doesn't want her hurt."

Thank God for that. Well, that fact might give her a slight edge over these men and even her father. He didn't want her hurt, but he didn't care if strange men drug her naked from her bed and watched her dress. If he cared anything for her, it was not well done of him.

When they helped her from the carriage, her breath snagged in her throat for a few seconds. She coughed trying to breathe and think as well. This was not what she expected. She'd thought to stay in Glasgow. They were on the waterfront. A ship bobbed on the currents. He meant to take her away.

"No!" Panicked she did try to run, but she was hauled against a broad chest a huge arm wrapped around her. She struggled, lashing out with her arms and legs accomplishing nothing.

"Your father wants to see you lass, safe and protected. He just wants to keep you away from men like Arie Demir. You will stop fighting and come with me. This is all in your best interest. You'll see."

The vows would have been said in a few hours. In her mind he was. She lied, hoping to persuade. "Arie is my husband. You've no right to do this."

"Ah but the marquis believes he does have every right where you are concerned. Scottish law says so. In any case if Demir is your husband, you won't be seeing him again. He should have kept a closer eye on you." The man laughed, the sound harsh in the stillness of the night.

One soldier on either side of her ushered her up the gangplank to her father who was waiting, arms crossed in front of him, a harsh look on his face. He looked to the kidnappers. "Did you have any troubles?"

"None but the Viscount, Lord MacEwen, said they were wed. She just spoke the same words. If they are then you are kidnapping the lass and we are a part of it. Thought you knew what you were doing."

Frasier waved his hand in the air. "It's a lie. They've been at their home all day. No one resembling a minister arrived. I would have been informed in that case."

"When Arie finds you, he will make sure you never see your homeland again."

She was trying to project confidence, but she knew her words shook with the fear and loathing she felt. "He will find me wherever you plan on going. Arie won't stop looking for me."

"He can do little from prison. I'm hardly worried. If he does get out, we will be gone from here. If he tries to seek you out in the states, his efforts will be wasted. He will never discover your whereabouts." Murray smiled at her, his eyes narrowing. "Now, should we get you settled? The trip will take several months. I want to see you comfortable."

She closed her eyes, swaying on her feet. She would have crumpled to the ground but the man held her upright. "No, I don't want to go. I'm of age. I've a choice in this matter. Wherever you take me I'll turn right around and return here."

"Come, come, you will like Virginia. I will treat you much better than the sultan. The weather is nice most of the year. We do have snow occasionally in the winter, but the summers are refreshing."

"I will find a way to come back here. You cannot keep me a prisoner forever. There will be a time when you are not looking." She spoke slowly understanding everything she said would be true. "You are not my father and never have been."

He laughed again seeming to enjoy her discomfort. "This is all being done to free you from his power. He's cast a spell on you, made you his sex slave when you should have had a proper marriage to a Scotsman."

"What do you know of me? Nothing."

Her hands were fisted at her sides as she was forced the rest of the way onto the ship. Only seconds later the ship was readied for sailing.

She didn't know if Arie still had a ship moored here. His vessels came and went bringing goods from the Ottoman Empire. He'd told her once there was usually at least one in port. Now she prayed one was there and faster than her father's.

"We will have a lot of time to talk and to get know each other. I would like to learn everything about you."

His voice grated on her nerves.

"You can tell me all about your childhood later."

She turned from him, racing to the railing thinking to throw herself overboard. Swimming couldn't be too hard. The sound of his voice shattered her nerves even while she understood she needed to stay strong. Arie would come for her. She didn't have to tell this stranger anything.

Leaning on the rail of the ship she watched Glasgow disappear from sight. She'd never wanted to travel, never had the urge to see another land. Now it seemed she was being given no choice, forced to leave Scotland. She would have wed Arie. Now they were nothing to each other.

Murray stood beside her. She cringed, moving away. "I'm not a monster. Once you give me a chance, you will find me quite cordial. Most people like me. I suppose except for this Demir fellow I've no enemies."

I don't like you and you are my enemy.

"I've a room for you below deck. I've purchased some gowns for you. It seems the seamstress had your measurements on hand. So, the man who bought you decided to provide clothing for you. How interesting. I would have thought he meant to keep you in his bed all day and all night."

His voice was a throaty growl. She understood his anger toward Arie even though there was no reason for it. Perhaps Arie had been wrong to buy her, but this man was just as wrong to kidnap and take her against her will across the Atlantic to a land she'd never seen before.

"You don't want to talk? Ah, well I suppose it is just as well. You might not say the nicest things. In time you will thank me for what I've done and appreciate my actions. Your life will be much better."

"I won't be free."

"No, I suppose not. At least not in the near future, maybe in time."

She turned then, pushing him hard enough that he stumbled backward. "You believe that nonsense. I will never feel anything for you save loathing. You almost killed me, would have succeeded if it were not for Tessa. How dare you presume so much?" Her breath caught in the back of her throat as anger swept through her. "I will not be a willing hostage. I will never see things your way. If anyone should be in jail, it is you."

Anger threatening to erupt in more words of loathing, she strode across the deck to the other side of the ship, trying to keep her emotions inside. A few moments later he stood by her side again. His closeness sent shivers down her spine and goose bumps on her arms. A chill enveloped her. She didn't want to be anywhere near him.

It seemed to Alison he tried to ignore her words. Then pleasantly saying, "You also have a lady's maid. I do believe you will like her. Everything you could ever want will be yours."

Now he sounded smug. She wished she could throw him overboard, at the very least never look at him again. Her hands bit into the railing, physical pain easing some of the emotional heartache.

"She will not stay in that room. I don't want anything to do with you and what you buy for me, including a lady's maid. I 've never had one nor do I want one now. What would she do for me?"

She sounded petulant and indeed she was. She could hardly give back the clothing. Even now with the ship picking up speed, she was very nearly freezing to death.

"Very well, but I cannot toss her off the ship. I'm sure you will hurt her feelings if you act as rude to her as you are to me. In any case, she has an adjoining door so you can lock it if you like. Keep her out. If you won't talk to your maid, or me, you'll have a very lonely trip. Really, Alison, all I want is for you to be happy. Try to look at the brighter side. You will no longer have to grace that man's bed."

She wanted to be in that man's bed every day and night for the rest of her life. Her so-called father was too presumptive by far. "I can lock the door, both doors?"

She mused that over in her mind, thinking she'd like to lock her father out, but he'd already done all the damage he could possibly do. Until she set foot on land there was no way to escape this predicament except by death. Biding her time was by far the most practical avenue for her to take. She would wait for her chance.

"Of course, my dear, but I assume you will want to unlock it to receive your food," Fraser said, his grin more irritating now that he had control of her entire life.

Somehow it had not mattered to her when Arie controlled her life.

She loved Arie.

She nodded, understanding at least some her father's words were true. Until her situation changed, she should change her ways. "I'll try to be a bit less rude to my maid but where you are concerned, I've no intention of changing my attitude. Perhaps if you had taken time to listen to me and accept my feelings for Arie, I would feel better about you, perhaps be accepting. Now will you show me to my room? It's cold out here." For emphasis she rubbed her arms, trying to bring some warmth to her body.

The steps into the lower deck terrified her, her grip so tight on the railings she could barely move forward. When she reached the floor below, she inhaled a long deep breath in an attempt to steady herself.

"This way," Frasier moved in front of her. "In time, you will get used to the ladder."

"I won't be going up and down."

She turned looking upward. It was dark. She could barely see the opening. Her body shuddered, wishing she could stay above deck and knowing her words were false.

"You will want fresh air. You can always send someone to get me if you cannot find the courage to go it alone" Fraser smiled again seeming to understand he still held control. "I am here to do your bidding."

"Never," she mumbled, realizing he was right.

If the trip did take several months, she could not stay beneath the entire time. She needed the sunshine and light, to feel the wind on her face. She had to have fresh air to breathe. Staying strong for Arie was imperative.

He would come after her, yet she felt the tiniest bit of apprehension.

What if he didn't? What if he couldn't get out of jail?

When the door closed behind her, she sank down on the bed. She breathed in huge gulps of air as tears she managed to hold back began to fall nonstop. Letting herself wallow in her despair for a few minutes, more tears fell. Finally, she wiped her face with the backs of her hands, determined to weather this with all the courage she could find within herself.

The room was small but tidy. It had no windows. Suddenly, she felt the walls closing in on her. She closed her eyes, breathing deeply until she calmed. There was a trunk on one side of the room and a chair accompanied with a table. She supposed when she wasn't sleeping, she would be sitting or eating. Boredom crept into her soul with a raging purpose. What was she going to do with herself for months on end? Maybe she should reach out to the woman Fraser said was to be her maid. Her circumstances could be just as dire as hers. They might suit each other.

Curious, she opened the trunk. All different kinds of gowns and shoes lay inside. She didn't want to wear any of the things Fraser bought her even though it appeared he'd spent a great deal of coin on her behalf. Rummaging through she also found two nightdresses, stark white with buttons up the front along with high collars, prim and very proper.

She laughed softly. She'd grown used to sleeping naked, Arie holding her in his arms, her head nestled on his chest. Rubbing her arms, she stared at the cold bed. With a huge sigh, she turned in a full circle once more looking at everything that would be her new home.

No, her prison for the next few months.

Closing her eyes, she tried to recall everything she and Arie did since she first saw him, since he paid money for her. Since she found herself all alone in a room in the brothel waiting for her future, for a destiny she had no say over. For days she held herself back until loneliness and curiosity caused her to move ahead with her life. She found despite her efforts she could not stop the horrific trembling engulfing her.

An inhaled breath of air tore from her, sobs escaping. Here she was again, the same predicament, the same place. Would she have to change the course of her plans and move forward to make herself happy?

Yet this time she held the hope that Arie would come for her and she would be with him again. Once more he would hold her in his arms, whisper in her ear with seductive words as he came inside her. He would promise her happiness.

A voice from the other side of her door startled her. "Miss? I've got something for you to eat and drink. Captain thought you might be hungry as it's almost morning. He said you probably wouldn't be sleeping so I should bring the food now." It wasn't Frasier but an unknown man. Shivers ripped up her arms, her breath catching in the back of her throat while her heart pulsed frantically against her chest.

Terrified, Ali opened the door. The strong scent of coffee and bacon filled the tiny space. Despite the fact she wanted to refuse to eat, her stomach growled hungrily.

"Come in."

She stepped aside so the man could walk through the door. He was tall and dark haired with broad shoulders narrowing to slim hips. His eyes were dark blue, sparkling as if he was amused by something. His day-old stumble gave him a dashing look and his smile reassured her. He was a handsome man, his blue eyes twinkling with what appeared to be warmth and amusement.

"I'll set the tray on the table. When you're finished with it, just put the tray outside the door and someone will pick it up when they get the chance. If you need anything, leave me a message. There is pen and paper on the bedside table. During the voyage, I'm at your service."

A rush of shame swept through her. She looked down then decided she should only speak the truth. After she looked up, her voice was whisper thin, "That won't be possible. I cannot write."

For a moment the man appeared confused. "Then leave a blank piece of paper and I will know that you would like to speak with me. I'll come as soon as I receive your message. It will be our secret." He smiled at her then taking her hand in his, he placed a chaste kiss on the back before looking into her eyes again with sensual promise. "Your hair is very beautiful," he said, catching her by surprise.

The shame she felt earlier suddenly vanished, "Thank you. Fraser said I have a maid. Do you know where she is? I'd like to get to know her."

Talking to someone would be heaven. She'd only been on board the ship for a few hours. She missed Arie and Tessa, missed hearing a voice other than her own when she talked to herself. She did not wish to let this man into her life, did not want to forget Arie would come for her. He seemed so sweet and sincere. It might be hard to ignore his sensual smile, the way his eyes lit up when he looked at her. In her short life she'd known few men.

"Your maid is next door to you as I'm sure Murray, the captain, told you. See the adjoining door?" He pointed toward it. "The two of you can go in and out as you please."

"Do you think she'd mind too much if I went to see her?" she asked, "Do you know her name?"

"Names Tessa, I believe, and she's scared, undeniably more than you. Think she'd like someone to talk to."

"Tessa?" She sat up straighter, her spine stiffening. This was no coincidence. Her father kidnapped her too. How dare he?

"Yes, Captain said you knew her."

"I think I do." Her heart leapt as she moistened her lips, trying to think of things to say. She would be afraid yet resigned also.

"I'll go now. Remember, leave a piece of paper for me if you want to see me or even go on deck. I'll come as soon as my duties allow it." He began to back from the room.

She stood, watching the man leave her alone once more. When the door clicked shut, she raced to the adjoining door.

Knocking, "Tessa! Tessa, you there?" Eagerly, she turned the knob and slowly pushed open the door.

Unlike her room, Tessa's was dark, no candles burned to give it a tiny bit of cheer. She heard the soft sobs coming from the bed. Quickly, she returned to her room, picking up a candle.

"Tessa, it's me, Alison. Are you all right? No one hurt you, did they?" She set the candle on the table, watching her friend sit up and wipe tears from her eyes. "They will come for us, Arie and Victor. I promise you they will."

"No, they didn't hurt me. The man told me Victor was in jail. He would stay there and I would never see him again." She drew in a deep ragged breath, her hands shaking. "Am I a slave again?"

"Frasier is wrong. We will see Arie and Victor. No, you are not a slave, just a pawn in my father's schemes. They will come for us. Don't ever doubt it," she said once more trying to reassure herself. "Cam will make sure our men are released. He has a great deal of power and influence in Scotland. They will set sail as soon as they can. Arie always has at least one ship in port." She felt as if she was rambling, spouting words to make herself feel better.

"You don't know that," she said her voice weak. "You can't

possibly think the men will come after slaves. No matter how you think. After all we are only possessions."

"Even if that were true, men don't like to have possessions stolen right out from under their noses. Promise me you will not give up hope."

Alison knelt beside Tessa. With her hand under Tessa's chin she forced her to look at her. "Promise me."

Tessa nodded a moment later. "I promise." Her voice was weak, wavering as she spoke.

Alison believed her. "Victor asked you to marry him? You said yes. You are no longer a slave but a wife. Come, we need to get you dressed. It seems they were not as concerned about your well-being as they were mine. I'm sure Frasier never gave them an order to make sure no harm came to you or that you were properly clothed."

She nodded, still trying to stop the tears from falling. "That doesn't mean anything. I'm still his slave. He wanted children." With a feeble lift of her shoulders, "I was convenient. If he weds me, his offspring will be legitimate." She sniffed again, looking so forlorn. "I don't have any clothes, nothing to wear."

Ali tried not to laugh. "Did Victor tell you that? That you are still his slave? I'm sure he did not and speaking of clothing, I've more than enough for you too. We will share."

"No, but he didn't tell me I was no longer a slave or even that he wanted to marry me because he loved me."

"So, you wrote your own story. Not a good idea where men are concerned. Chelsea told me men don't like to admit to love so I wouldn't worry about Victor saying the words. He and Arie will come for us. I'm hoping it will be sooner rather than later. Come." This time she placed Tessa's hand in hers, tugging her gently to a standing position. "We must get you dressed."

"Do you really believe that? They will use their time to follow this ship?" she asked.

For the first time, Ali saw hope in her friend's eyes.

"I have to believe or I'll cease to breathe."

~ * ~

"Do you think Alison is adjusting to what I've done? It might be a hard road for her but I don't ken it. Why would she be so appreciative of a man who bought her?" Fraser asked his friend, Shea Devlin, the man who delivered the food to Ali's room. The man he hoped would capture his daughter's heart.

"She will come around. Her eyes were red from the tears she cried but they had stopped, unlike Tessa, her maid. Alison explored the cabin. The trunk of clothing you bought her was open. She has been through hard times in her life if what you've told me is true. This will be an adjustment, but she will adapt to her new circumstances. I'm sure of it."

"Good, you're right. My daughter is strong. I like that in a woman and where she is going she will need that trait. But I'm worried about the other woman."

Fraser paced his cabin, wondering and trying to do right by this mission and the course he set for his daughter. If he had any say in her life, she would not be the slave or even the wife of the sultan.

No, that would never happen. He wouldn't allow it. Yet he understood the power could well be taken from his hands. Murray knew he had to reach the states so he could disappear into the interior with the two women.

"You mean to take them to your plantation then. It is on the edge of the wilderness. The place might not be safe for women who are so out of their element. Alison has lived in the city her entire life."

"Yes, I understand it borders the wilderness, but I can't stay in Fredericksburg more than a week or two after we arrive. I can't risk Alison trying to find a ship back to Glasgow. Lord knows there are ones traveling to Scotland nearly every day. She has already threatened to do just that, leave for Scotland."

"She has no money to book passage," Shea reminded him. "There is no way she could achieve what she threatened."

Murray knew there were a myriad of ways for a woman to gain passage if she had no money. What terrified him the most was that she might try to sell herself. After all, Arie found and bought her while she was living in a brothel. Whoring wasn't new to his daughter. He had no idea what she would attempt.

"She might try to sell herself," Fraser muttered his fears beginning to pace again, feeling thoroughly frustrated.

He would have to remain attentive to her. He inhaled a long deep breath realizing just because she was on this ship, she was not safe from a man like Arie Demir.

"From what I've seen of your daughter, she is no whore. I truly believe the sultan is the only man who has bedded your daughter," Shea said as he looked out the window, his hands clasped behind his back.

"I hope so," Fraser spoke softly. "A father does not like to think of his daughter in that light."

"I could go on ahead and make sure everything is running smoothly. You did leave a good man in charge."

"I don't like this at all. She is going to try to run. We'll have to keep an eye on her all of the time. Don't know if that's possible."

Frasier did not want Alison running back to that man. The thought was untenable. He let out a long slow sigh, knowing that as long as they were at sea she was probably safe. As soon as they landed, he would have his work cut out. Until then he meant to get to know his daughter a little bit more thoroughly.

"You've got several months to convince her you do have her best interests at heart," Shea said, looking back to the stairs toward her room.

"You think you could come to care for her? Even wed her?"

"I don't know. She fancies herself in love with the sultan. It would be hard in a month or two to accomplish such a turnabout."

"She will not change her mind easily. Perhaps you can help, woo her gently. Alison would make a good wife for you. Do you find her attractive?"

Fraser had every intention of pursuing this match. If Alison was to fall in love again, she wouldn't run, and Arie Demir would no longer have a hold upon her.

Shea coughed, clearing his throat. It seemed to Frasier he didn't know what to say. "I..."

"Cat got your tongue," Fraser laughed at his friend's expression. "You need a wife. Yes, I understand the sultan used her but that is not her fault. Perhaps she can be swayed away from Arie. You are attractive and well spoken, extremely intelligent. You would make any woman a good catch. Do you have any other prospects?"

Fraser hoped this attempt at matchmaking would prove beneficial to his cause. He liked Shea. Would not mind having him for his son in law.

"So how much are you giving me permission to do? A kiss perhaps? Or would you skewer me through if I took her to my bed. I doubt if a woman who has been with a man such as the sultan and fancies herself in love would fall for another man who only kisses her."

"You might be right about that. However, I trust your judgment. If the only way to wrest her away from Arie Demir is by sex, you have my permission. Don't force her. She has to be willing, mind you."

"I will do my best." Shea laughed outright, his eyes sparkling.

"Don't hurt her."

Chapter Eight

"What took you so long?" Arie growled at Cam as he stepped into the dreary Glasgow day. The dark foreboding weather fit his mood and he was in a rush to see Fraser and demand his wife back. The situation as it stood was untenable. Yet Arie had a sick feeling in his gut. Knew this would not be easy. If he were Fraser he would not stay in Glasgow. He would hightail it out of here.

"If we didn't have the documents showing your legal marriage, you'd still be rotting in jail, which was my idea, need I remind you? A thank you would be nice," Cam said with a complimentary growl as he headed for the horses, putting on his riding gloves as he walked.

"Thank you, "Victor said, "and I speak for Arie as well. We are both very grateful for all your help and of course, you're right in everything you said. We would still be rotting in a cell if it were not for your timely arrival as well as the signed marriage contracts, which you thought of. The jail stunk. I for one am glad to be out of the hellhole. I'm looking forward to seeing how Tessa is doing. She must have been terrified when they came for her."

For a moment Arie felt contrite and almost decided to apologize, but he didn't want Cam to get the upper hand in their tenuous relationship. Despite their differences where Chelsea was concerned, Cam put out considerable effort to get them released this morning. Arie was sure the viscount spent the entire night working his connections in Glasgow.

Then, "Thank you. Now let's go see Fraser and find out what he's done with Alison. I'm sure it's not going to be as simple as finding her in his home. That would show little thought or creativity. Even Fraser is not that stupid."

"He might have her at the country estate. That's what I would do," Cam said thoughtfully. "Easier to keep her hidden. However," Cam paused, "there is an off chance he took her from Glasgow. Many of the lords have second homes, some at the ocean, some hunting lodges in the northern hills. He could even intend to return to Virginia."

"Some across the Atlantic," Arie agreed, wishing that wasn't one of the options.

"We should split up," Victor said seemingly eager to start. "I'll ride out to the country and stop by to see how Tessa is fairing. She must have heard something about what happened. I want to reassure her everything is fine. I'll be back soon. Her state is fragile as she still thinks of herself as my slave even though I told her otherwise too many times to count. If we have to leave the city, she is not going to be pleased. When and If we do, I'll take her with me."

"No need for that," Cam said as he mounted and started riding. Then looking over his shoulder at them, "The Fraser townhouse is on the way to yours. We can all stop there and perhaps garner some news."

Mounted and riding hard, time seemed to stand still for Arie. A frail sun peeked from the gray clouds for a moment before disappearing again. Heavy mist filled the air, subtly drenching them. He was terrified for Alison and for what Frasier might have done with her. She could be anywhere by now. Time passed, more seconds and minutes, still they failed to discover anything.

It had taken Cam all night and into the afternoon before he could free them and convince the authorities that the documents were legal along with the fact they were truly married. It would have helped if Alison could write her name. When he found his wife, that would be the first order of business, teaching her to write. He did smile then. She told him several times it was something she would like to learn.

Pulling up sharp at the townhouse, Arie was off his stallion leaving Cam to tie the horse to the hitching post. His heart racing double time, he two-stepped the stairs. His fist was raised to pound, but the door to Fraser's townhouse opened before he could knock.

"I was expecting you." The tall thin man stepped back, his hands clasped in front of him, holding what appeared to be a letter, "Lord Fraser left you a message. Can I assume you are Arie Demir?"

Arie nodded, his gaze focused on the parchment his heart pounding even while his stomach clenched painfully. "I am."

He handed the note over to him. "He wanted me to make sure you received it and read it thoroughly. I wasn't to give it to anyone else. Although he didn't expect you'd be here until tomorrow."

Looking at the other men along with a deep breath Arie slowly opened the letter. He cleared his throat before he began to read.

Mr. Demir,

God willing you will never see Alison again. I've taken her away, far away. If necessary, I will continue to move her in order to escape you. My daughter deserves better than the likes of a sultan who uses her for his purposes and with no regard for her tender feelings. I will make sure she finds a man who is dependable, will work hard, a man who will treat her with respect, not force her to his will, all things that are the antithesis of you.

Don't waste your time looking for her. You won't find her. I have invested considerable time and money to make sure she has effectively disappeared and will be out of your life forever. Move on with your life. Find another woman. The best thing you can do is forget about Alison. She is not for you.

Tell Victor Tessa is with Alison. I felt Alison would need a friend and a confidant during this crucial time of readjustment. Neither of you will see your women again.

Lord Murray Frasier the Marquis of Bellmund.

"Where did he go?" Arie turned to Victor whose hands were now fisted tightly then back to the servant. "My god man, if you know, you have to tell us."

"I'll kill him," Victor spoke slowly, his voice harsh. "If I ever find him, I'll kill him!"

Cam ran his hands through his hair until it was standing on end. Then to Arie, "My gut tells me he's taken the two women to Virginia. We need to go to the docks and find out when his ship left and if the women were passengers. Do you have a ship in port and can it be readied within the hour?"

"One came in two days ago. We're taking on cargo even as we speak. I'll get every available crew member on the task," Arie said, running, the words Cam spoke prevalent in his mind while trying to foresee any possible problems.

If he caught up with Fraser on the open ocean, Fraser would rue the day he stole Alison from him. He would blast his ship out of the water as soon as he saw Alison and Tessa to safety. Fraser was dealing with the wrong person now if he cared for his life. Before he left the Ottoman Empire to look for Hope, his crews were corsairs, feeding off slow moving merchant ships in the Mediterranean. He was sure Fraser's ship would be child's play for his men who were used to a good fight and seemed to miss the excitement. His body shook with thoughts of the impending battle, a battle he and Victor would win. There would be no contest.

"Have the cargo unloaded and stored somewhere close. I don't even care if we lose it. Give it to some deserving sea captain. We need to catch up to Fraser's ship. I don't want anything slowing us down. They've a twelve-hour head start on us," Cam told them walking swiftly to his horse. "Gather all your men. We'll meet at the wharf as soon as possible."

Now with a direction in hand, Arie and Victor moved with speed and purpose. The man, lord or no, didn't know what Turkish pirates did to men who captured their women. His fate wouldn't make a bit of difference even if he claimed he was Alison's father until he was blue in the face.

He kidnapped her. That was not well done of him. He would pay the price, perhaps the ultimate price. His life.

Cam placed his hand on his shoulder. "In this case you need to curb your instincts. You cannot kill these men or sell them as slaves. The repercussions for something like that would be far too serious. We will stop Fraser's ship and retrieve Alison and Tessa then make sure lord Fraser will not be welcome back in Glasgow for any reason. A threat you can probably not keep but it is worth the effort. Other than that, you cannot do what you are thinking."

"What am I thinking?" he asked, toying with Cam who couldn't possibly understand the black thoughts in his head. "You cannot conceivably guess my intent in this. You've no idea where my mind is going."

"Or mine," Victor spoke up. "Tessa must be terrified. I never wanted her to feel that terror again. When I found her..." Victor let his words trail off not seeming to want to talk further.

"At least they have each other," Arie murmured. "For that I'm thankful. Perhaps that is why Fraser took Tessa. He understood they would be a comfort to each other. It is something, I suppose."

"Conceivably, but more likely the deed was meant to anger me and try to teach some perverse lesson to both Arie as well as myself. Fraser is a pompous pig who thinks of no one except himself," Victor muttered, his voice vibrating with the anger emanating from him.

They reached the docks in record time then set about unloading the cargo that had just been placed on Arie's ship. Cam called in his men. Arie had his well-trained crew on board and waiting. With the wind on their, side they would make record time up the Firth of Clyde to the Atlantic.

Before they left, they made sure Frasier did indeed leave Glasgow with the two women, interviewing numerous dockworkers and sea captains. Many on the docks were willing to talk to the sultan, possibly remembering other times when Arie was displeased with a man. They didn't want to anger the sultan, Arie Demir.

On board, Arie stood stiffly at the bow, holding his breath at times while he watched the horizon for a sighting even though short of a miracle it would be some time before they could make up the distance, his mind running over all the things he misread concerning Alison's father. Taken off guard, he'd never expected a kidnapping. His nerves stretched to a breaking point, his heart pounding double time. He thought he might surely die if he didn't see sails soon.

He would not.

Victor stood beside him, his hands gripping the railing until his knuckles were white. "I want to hit that man and hit him again, keep hitting him until blood runs freely, until his eyes are so swollen, he cannot open them. After that I would like to throw him to the fish."

"After me," Arie gritted out, the wind whistling through the sheets.

The man cannot possibly believe he will get away with this travesty of justice. One by one the necessary sails were unfurled. His ship was fast and sleek, they would catch up soon, perhaps before the sun rose again.

"I want to hold Tessa in my arms and never let her go. I need to feel her warmth cuddled close to me."

Victor's eyes were closed. He was breathing deeply and Arie could only assume the myriad of thoughts rushing through his head.

"The two of you should get some sleep," Cam stood beside them, his back stiff. "I understand if this was Chelsea, well, then I'd be right beside you. Now I have to be the voice of reason. The two of you must remain calm, especially when we board Fraser's ship. Remember only necessary force should be used. It is my guess they will put up little to no resistance. Your almost wives will be in your arms sooner than you think. When that happens, we can sail home then get on with the rest of our lives."

"I cannot sleep until I have her back in my bed and by my side. Never realized how much I would miss her." Arie felt his gut tighten again.

"The same as I feel for Tessa. I am lost without her. She is my heart and soul," Victor said staring into the distance as he watched the land slide by them. "My best friend and confidant even though she never understood how much I rely on her."

The wind picked up as the ship moved through the water with more speed and purpose. Arie felt the cold. Found he was rejuvenated by the icy wind stinging his face and limbs. He was ready for a fight as were his men. They'd all been informed as to what was about to happen. If everything went as they hoped, tomorrow or at the latest the day after, they would see the ship on the horizon. Every member of his crew was alert. The men in the crow's nest would tell them as soon as a sail was spotted. At that point they would hoist the skull and crossbones.

The three men left the deck to settle into their rooms. Arie sat on his bed, staring out the window as the sun slowly began to set. It had taken longer than he wanted to get the ship readied, but now the lights of Glasgow had disappeared. There were only a few lights of the smaller communities as they sailed down the Firth of Clyde toward open water.

With a quick knock to let Arie know he was coming into the room, Victor entered with a tray of food and drink. "Best we eat and just as Cam suggested we should try to sleep. Mayhap a bit of wine will help dull the mind and allow a few minutes of slumber," Victor said.

Arie rose and joined Victor at the table. For minutes they ate in silence. Arie's thoughts continued to settle on Alison and what she must be feeling. He smiled remembering how she looked last night, sated from their love making, naked, her head resting on his chest. She would be in his arms soon, he decided. His lips set in a grim line he told himself; he'd never allow her to leave him again.

"After we retrieve our women, I want to send Frasier and his crew to Turkey. They would understand the power of crossing you." Victor rose, standing by the window staring at the ocean. "I understand we cannot do that. Cam would be held accountable as well. While neither of us care, Cam and Chelsea..." He shrugged his shoulders, his hands behind his straight back. "Fraser is a lord of the realm. We have to deal with him in a more refined manner."

"Even though Ali doesn't like her father, I couldn't do that to the man who sired her. I love her you know. Think I have from the first time I saw her if that was possible." He sighed deeply trying to come to terms with the newfound emotion. "Thank you for finding her for me and bringing her to me."

"You do not have to thank me," Victor said.

"In this case I want to," Arie said.

"As I also love Tessa, more than I can say. Still, I haven't told her. I've had such a devil of a time convincing her she is no longer a slave there has been no time to speak of love or more tender emotions. In any case she would most likely not believe me. She's a hard headed little thing."

"Do you think either of them love us?" Arie mused thoughtfully with a hesitant smile. "If they don't, the question is does it make a difference? In my mind it does not. I want her whether or not she loves me, and I do believe she enjoys my company."

Victor chuckled softly, seeming to think of Tessa. "Where our manly hearts are concerned our women have wound us up into tight hard knots. If they only understood how much control they have over us, we could be sorely misused."

"I believe I might enjoy being misused by Alison. The mere thought brings on all types of ideas," Arie smiled thoughtfully thinking of all the ways she could use or misuse him and how much he'd enjoy every moment.

"As would I. Do you suppose we can teach them how to do that?" Victor's chuckle lightened his heart for a moment. "Misuse and abuse us in very special ways?"

"I am sand in her hands. She can do with me whatever her heart desires, mold me and shape me anyway she likes. I would give her the sun and the stars, the entire universe," Arie said, his throat clogging with unshed tears. "All that my life needs now is to hold her in my arms once more."

Cam knocked and opened the door. It seemed he heard the comment, "Perhaps when we all return, I'll take you to the observatory and she can see the moon and stars in closer proximity. In a way you'll be giving them to her." He sat down pouring a drink and helping himself to some of the food on the tray. "Really, we all need to sleep."

"You don't feel the least bit of apprehension away from Chelsea at this delicate time?" Arie asked, understanding how much Cam was giving up. With the change of expression on his friend's face, he wondered if he'd said too much. When they were first courting, Cam had trouble when Chelsea confided in him.

"How did you know?" Cam asked, a bristle to his voice Arie hadn't heard in quite some time.

"I can tell, read the signs. There is much that goes on when a man grows up living in a harem." Arie laughed softly, knowing Cam would be upset with the knowledge and waiting until he voiced his feelings. "What is she, about three months along?"

"We think two and a half or three and yes, there is a lot of apprehension on my part after her earlier miscarriage. Hope assures me she is healthy. There is nothing for me to worry about. I'm also sure we will be back within the week so there is little to concern me over her health."

"With a pregnancy there is always something to worry and sweat over. Men are so helpless," Victor pointed out. "My first wife..." he suddenly stopped seeming to realize that telling Cam his wife died in the second month of her pregnancy from complications would not be well done of him. "It is nothing," he waved his hand in the air dismissing the conversation.

"Your first wife what?" Cam leaned forward. It seemed Cam wanted him to finish what he began.

"It's nothing really. We will be home soon. If there are any difficulties, Hope knows what to do in any case. There is also Chelsea's grandmother who is a good midwife. You would only be a burden if there was to be a complication," Victor said, uneasily running a finger around his collar.

"You're right. There is nothing to worry about where Chelsea is concerned, only that I could lose her." His voice turned husky with apprehension, his expression turning inward. "I don't believe I can live without the woman."

"We appreciate all you have done. You could have stayed in Glasgow," Arie said, thinking that would have been a great deal more prudent considering Chelsea's delicate condition. He also came along to make sure neither he nor Victor did something foolish.

"I couldn't leave the two of you to your own devices. I don't trust you to leave Fraser alone and let him go on his way once you board the ship and retrieve Alison and Tessa," Cam said staring hard at Arie then Victor. He stood then, "I'm going to my cabin to sleep. The two of you need to do the same. Morning will come soon. Hopefully, there will be good news on the horizon."

When the door closed behind Cam, Arie breathed a deep sigh of relief. He knew everything Cam said was true. If he wasn't here with them, and playing the voice of reason, who would know how he would seek vengeance.

Allah, it would be done.

"I'll leave now also. Don't know if I'll be able to sleep but I'll try. Tomorrow or the next day we should sight the ship. At least I pray that we do. If it goes longer than that, we will need more luck than anything else. If that happens, we might have to go all the way to Virginia to find them. That would not be good for Cam." He left then, and for a moment Victor turned to look at Arie, worry clearly etched on his face.

"I will see you in the morning," Arie said as he stood in an attempt to feel positive.

Looking away he, too, stared out the window. Rain could be clearly heard pattering on the deck and across the window.

The clouds and the rain would impair visibility.

It was not good, not good at all for them. They might sail right by the other ship without knowing.

Quickly he disrobed, leaving his close folded neatly and close in case the ship was sighted before morning. His breath caught at the thought. He must have dozed because when he opened his eyes again, muted sunlight slanted through the window. There was an insistent knocking on his door.

"Come in," he said as he pulled on his pants hoping the ship had been sighted.

It was the cook not Victor or Cam.

He sat down, slipping on a clean shirt then his shoes. "Any news?" he asked realizing it wouldn't be the cook at the door if there had been a sighting.

"Good morning, no, nothing has been seen as of yet. We are now heading out to the open ocean. We've unfurled two more sails. The ship is light and fast. It should catch up to them soon."

He set the food and tea on the table then at the door. "If we see anything, you'll be the first to know."

Disappointment washed through him as he sipped the hot tea and ate. He had so hoped he would wake and the sails would be in sight. Now he was afraid it might take longer and the ocean was huge. They could pass the ship without ever sighting them.

"No news," Cam walked in, Victor behind him. "Been on deck,

the clouds and rain make the visibility poor. We could pass them and not even know it. It might be prudent to take in a sail or two."

"Don't have to tell you what that means," Victor said. "We're charting a beeline course straight to Virginia. That's all we can do."

"I'd hoped," Arie said, searching Victor's expression and reading only fear and concern.

His brows were drawn tightly together. Tensions lines radiated around his eyes. He supposed he must look much the same.

"As we all did," Cam said "but we need to keep up our spirits. This should not take long."

"I'm going on deck. More eyes are always better." Arie put on his slicker and headed outside, the other two following him.

Days turned into weeks. Morale hit an all-time low.

Arie spent the days cursing and the nights trying to sleep.

~ * ~

Alison ran to the basin, losing the contents of her stomach for the third time this morning. The first week out she wasn't sick at all but Tessa was. Now it seemed her friend found her sea legs and was no longer tossing all her food into a basin. Ali hoped it was nothing more than seasickness and she would soon feel fine as well.

Bending over the basin she groaned, nausea swamping her. When the knock on the door reverberated through the room, it seemed her head pounded also. She moaned, wishing for death or at least for this insistent, horrible retching to end.

What more could go wrong? Kidnapped and at sea. Now this.

"Alison, can I come in?" Shea stood outside waiting for her to answer, the door still closed.

She couldn't speak, just moan.

"I'm coming in. You don't sound very well."

The door squeaked as he slowly opened it. She sat up, sipping water and wishing the awful taste away. "I'm sorry. Don't think I can go on deck with you right now. Can't keep anything down. I'll lose the water soon enough. This horrible sickness just keeps going on and on."

He laughed softly, "A walk in the fresh air will do you good and help with the seasickness. I promise. We won't do much, just look at the ocean." He looked worried and unsure of himself. "We can make sure there are strategically placed buckets on the deck." As it seemed he tried not to laugh while he also tried to make light of the situation.

"I don't know."

She watched the man who befriended her as she pushed hair from her face. He was her confidant now. She felt as if she could tell him anything. "Let me fix my hair. If you step outside for a few minutes, I'll put something else on, freshen up a bit. I feel as if I've worn this dress for days."

"Of course, but if you need any help with anything, give me a holler. I'll be right by the door."

His grin touched her heart. Shea Devlin was a very nice man and handsome as sin as her mother would have said. He was a man she might have been attracted to if she'd never met Arie.

Arie. Where was he? In her heart she knew he would come. In her mind she now had too many doubts to count.

"Just give me a minute or two. I'll be with you."

She lowered her lashes for a moment, unable to look at him knowing he could melt her heart if he tried. Guilt at the sensations raced through her as she drew in a long steadying breath of air. She was supposed to wed Arie. She should not be having these wayward thoughts.

With one last nod of reassurance and a devilishly handsome grin, he closed the door behind him. Quickly she rummaged through the trunk and found something suitable. Just in case she was getting sick, she pulled out a heavy shawl. She should have asked him what the weather was like, but she knew from previous excursions the deck would be cold and windy.

The sun must be shining or he wouldn't have made the trek down the steps to her room. He only came for her when it wasn't rainy and cold. At least she figured that was the case. He rarely asked her to walk unless the sun was out.

She poked her head into Tessa's room. "Shea came to see me. I'm going on deck with him for a few minutes. Do you want to come with us?" she asked hoping Tessa would agree and act as a buffer between them.

Tessa had been in the depths of despair since they left Glasgow. The sickness seemed to make it worse. Ali hoped perhaps she would agree to some sunshine. She needed to see her friend smile and laugh again.

"No, but you need to be careful of that man. He's not as nice as you seem to think. He has other reasons to take you on deck and walk with you. I've noticed the sparkle in his eyes when he looks at you, and I know exactly what it means. So do you." She paused with a heavy sigh. Then emphasizing her earlier statement. "You best be careful, guard your heart. You don't want to do something you will come to regret."

"What does it mean? He has other reasons." Ali let out a long slow breath of air as she watched her friend finally sit up.

"It means he wants you, wants your body to be more precise. Since you're no longer a virgin, he thinks he can take whatever he wants. Men are the same everywhere," Tessa said, lying back down and covering her eyes with her arm. "You've only known one man, but mark my words, Shea is just like every other man. He only has one thing on his mind. Sex."

"No, it isn't like that," Ali protested vehemently not yet willing to admit to the truth of Tessa's words. "He's been a gentleman. Hasn't tried to take any liberties. He just wants to be nice."

"I assure you, he will try. He's a man. You're a beautiful woman. If I didn't suspect your father's suggestion as part of what is goading this man, I wouldn't say anything. He needs to drive a wedge between you and Arie. What better way than with another man? If you were to fall for Shea's charms and wit, succumbing to him, Arie might not want you."

"I don't believe anything you're saying," Ali said but she did mull over in her mind Tessa's words. She'd never had one beau let alone two.

"Of course you don't. The only experience you have with a man is Arie. While I'm sure he wasn't a perfect gentleman he's all you ken." Tessa sat back up, warning her once again. "Be careful."

Ali waved a hand in the air, trying not to think about Tessa words. "Don't fash yourself. If he does have feelings for me, I don't return them. I only care for Arie." She smiled, realizing she did like the attention Shea lavished upon her. "Now I'm going to go soak up some sun and enjoy a little conversation with a nice man. Are you sure you don't want to come?"

"Only as a chaperone and from what you've said, if it's true, you don't need one," Tessa said, her words cutting into Ali with an icy disdain.

"See you in an hour or so."

Ali left Tessa at her door. She inhaled a long breath of air, tying to steady herself. She did miss Arie so much, wished he were here with her now. A walk was a diversion, nothing more. She told herself but didn't completely believe that to be the case.

"I'm ready," she spoke to Shea who was smiling and staring at her with shimmering lights in his eyes. In the sunshine, they seemed to shift and change color. At the moment they were a soft grey blue, amusement at something smoldering in their depths.

"You look beautiful today but then you always do." He offered his arm as they walked down the hallway. "If you get cold let me know. While the sun is shining the wind can still cause a chill. The day is perfect and hopefully you'll feel much better after the walk."

"I feel fine. I don't think I'm sick just seasick."

She tried to laugh but found the nausea was churning in her stomach again. They needed to get on top so she could breathe that fresh air Shea spoke of and feel the warmth of the sun on her face.

They walked to the bow of the ship, gazing out at the lazy ocean. Compared to the other days on board ship it was calm even though the crests of the waves danced with whitecaps, sunlight sparkling like jewels on the crests. Dolphins seemed to be following as well as several seagulls. She smiled as Shea stood close to her, his big body shielding some of the wind.

Tessa's words swept through her mind. Perhaps the man did stand too close for appropriateness considering she was almost a married woman.

Quickly she turned to look at him, his warm blue eyes glittering with the same passion filled emotions she'd seen in Arie's deep auburn eyes. Shaking her head thinking there was more truth to Tessa's words she moved away from him, suddenly terrified of herself and the sensations he set in motion with his heated gaze. Looking at him, she drew in a shaky breath.

"Something wrong?" he asked, his hand lightly resting on her shoulder, caressing, stroking gently, coaxing a response. "You suddenly looked terrified. I hope you're not afraid of me." His long slender fingers massaged her neck, easing the tension creating little shivers that whirled down her spine. "You need to relax. Everyone of your muscles is tight."

"Please don't," she whispered stepping farther away. "Please... I'm almost married, would have been and..." She moistened her trembling lips. "I don't think you should be touching me like that."

"I meant nothing by the massage. Just trying to make you feel better."

Then he bent close to her, his words whispering across her cheek, undoing all his massage had attempted to ease. She felt his breath, knew the minty sent. "Truly I don't believe he intended to marry you. I will honor your wishes for now but not forever. I want you, Alison. I'm not going to lie to you."

"All I want from you is to be my friend, nothing more. I need someone to talk to who isn't lecturing me." She felt her body shudder as his hand traveled slowly down her back, stopping at her waist before moving a tiny bit lower. She could barely speak. "You're not listening to me or you are not hearing me."

Moving away from her and resting an elbow on the railing he turned sideways. She knew he was gazing, staring at her mouth but at least he wasn't touching her anymore. She wanted to tell him his touch was repulsive, but in truth it was everything but. The betrayal stung her. Arie would never do something like this.

"I always listen to what a beautiful woman is telling me. I also hear every word even if I disagree." Slowly, he pushed a flyaway tendril of hair behind her ear. "Your hair is so soft, silken fire and every strand reflects the sunshine. All kinds of golds and reds shimmer in the light, intriguing and enticing my intentions."

"Now you're talking nonsense," she told him, even though Arie had said nearly the same words about her hair. "What would you think if I said the same about your hair?"

He shrugged his broad shoulders, still grinning, his handsome face bubbling with laughter. "Believe what you want? If you said anything the same about my hair, I would call you a beautiful little liar since it is far from red. The dark brown would never catch the sun." He turned back to stare at the water. "I do work for your father. He's a good man even though you don't agree with my assessment."

"I might have if my father wasn't so heavy handed with my life. He kidnapped me even though I made it well known to him I didn't want anything to do with him. Shea, I was happy. Did my father ever marry?" She wasn't sure why she suddenly wanted to know about her father but she was curious. She still resented him for not being there for her mother as well as herself. His disappearance caused a lifetime of hurt.

"Do you truly want to know?" he asked, his constant grin becoming infectious. "I'll tell you whatever I can."

"I do but I'm not sure why I want to torment myself. The fact is he left and didn't look back, proving to me he didn't care for me then, now making believe he has a hidden agenda or that he might indeed care in some strange way." It wouldn't do her any good to remind herself about her father's shortcomings.

"He did marry but his wife passed a little over a year ago," Shea told her, his words sounding sincere. "Your father loved her very much, but he never forgot about your mother."

"So that was when he decided to come back to Glasgow and search for my mother and his child. When it was expedient. How convenient for him. He could have searched years ago. Perhaps if he had..." She understood the bitterness in her voice could be easily heard, but she couldn't ignore her feelings. "This is not going well for me. Maybe we should talk about you instead."

He laughed and the laughter sounded good to her ears. She squinted at him, wishing he wasn't so handsome and debonair. It would be so much easier to ignore his potent charisma if he wasn't so charming. Tessa was right about one thing. She needed to take care of her heart and remember Arie. The sultan wasn't here. She didn't know if he was coming for her. Perhaps, maybe he didn't care as much as he told her. After all, weeks had passed since they left Glasgow.

"What do you want to know about me? I'll answer then I'll ask you a question," Shea said.

"You told me you worked for my father. What is it you do for him?" She smiled at him slanting her head to the side while she watched.

He lifted his shoulders slightly, his eyes twinkling as if he didn't expect her to believe him. "I'm a physician. Your father employs me to make sure the few slaves he owns stay healthy." It seemed he observed her intently and she didn't disappoint in her reaction.

"He owns slaves," her voice was tight, thinking of his response to her relationship with Arie... "That's not right."

Shea rubbed his neck, inhaling a long deep breath before he began, "Where to begin. As I said, your father is not a bad man but he does buy slaves. He needs people to work the land on his plantation. Everyone does."

"Then he should pay good people to do the work."

She turned away from Shea not wishing to hear anything more. Somehow all their conversations seemed to return to her father.

His hand on her shoulder, he turned her. "He does in a way. Pay them."

"In a way? What does that mean?" She asked, confused now that he was trying to tell her things she didn't understand or couldn't believe.

"He buys the men and women as well as their children when they have them. The slaves work off their debt then they are free to go or stay for real wages. That is their choice."

"Why does he buy them in the first place?"

Again, her mind went to Arie and the reasons he bought her. She didn't think they were anything the same. Still her father bought slaves. "My father is a hypocrite."

He shrugged his shoulders again, his gaze still focused on the ocean. "If he doesn't someone will. In that case they might not have the opportunity to work for their freedom. They might be mistreated as many of the slaves are. Isn't it my turn now to ask a question?"

Gently he brushed hair from her face. His fingers were callused. She wondered at that, not expecting someone like Shea, a doctor, to have work roughened hands.

She wondered how much more she needed to learn about the land where she was headed. "I don't understand anything you're telling me. I guess it's a good thing he lets the men and women work then live out their lives as free men." Holding her breath for a few seconds before she spoke again, "I thought Arie would have come for me."

"If you were really his wife, he would have never allowed us to take you. He would have raced hell bent to capture this ship. As did you, I thought he would be here by now. I don't believe he will come for you. You need to move on and forget the man. Perhaps you could move on with me."

"He isn't here." She reminded herself. Moisture started to fill her eyes. She didn't want to cry, but Shea's thoughts had also been hers. Too many nights she'd gone to bed crying for Arie and her lost life, her muffled sobs heard by Tessa.

"Do you love him so much you are willing to give up the rest of your life on the off chance he might appear on the horizon sometime? He won't. You do understand that. You were merely a possession. You can't be positive he would have gone through with the marriage." He moved closer to her, his hands around her waist. "We could find something together."

"No and yes, I suppose, I don't really know." We're not married. She didn't want to tell him that again or remind herself. "He isn't here. The ocean is big. What if he passed by us and didn't see your sails?" She could hope.

"Can you live your life on what ifs?"

"For a short time maybe. We've still a long way to go," she said her voice soft and he leaned forward as if trying to hear her words. "There is time."

"I've seen his ship. It's much faster than this one. Arie should have caught up with us right after we hit the ocean. It's been weeks now. You should forget about Arie Demir, forget everything about him and what you thought you had with him. I'm here now. You can lean on me, confide in me as well."

She turned into his arms as he wrapped them around her, holding her close, shielding her from the wind. Her sobs wracked through her body. She cried until she didn't think she could cry any longer. Her tears soaked through his shirt and still he soothed her, ran his hand up and down her back.

His heart beat steady and strong, his scent one of spice and liqueur, nothing like Arie. Nothing about Shea was like Arie. He didn't presume anything about her or that she would give herself to him. He told her truths as he knew them. Arie often ignored her questions, tempting her in other ways always coaxing her to his will.

When she pushed away slightly, he allowed the distance. Her eyes were watery and her smile unsure. She moistened her lips then caught the bottom one beneath her teeth as she could not keep her eyes from his mouth. He wanted to kiss her. Somehow, she knew that. Could tell by the way his eyes simmered when he stared at her.

"Arie's not coming for you. You need to get on with your life."

Slowly his lips brushed against hers. They were soft and the mustache against her skin felt different. He pulled away, smiling. "Are you warm enough?"

"Hot," she said waving her hand. "I'm not sure why. It was barely a kiss."

He roared with laughter. "If you like, I could make it more of a kiss. No, perhaps it's too soon. Murray didn't tell me much about you, only that you were his daughter. His father forced him to leave you and your mother behind many years before."

"If he truly cared about me, he would have found a way to stay."

Her words were bitter once more, and she felt guilty about the gentle kiss. She had to admit she allowed it. His words about Arie not coming for her, twisted angrily within her. She felt nauseas, wanting and needing yet somehow lacking.

"Murray never expected to inherit. He was the third son. When his father gave him the land in Virginia, it was his chance to be independent, to have and hold something of his own. He told me he tried to find your mother before he left. Said he wanted to take her with him."

"Not very hard," she murmured.

"I can't say, but the ship was leaving. His father made it clear to him, he had to be on it or lose everything. His father was a stern taskmaster. He held no room in his heart for failure. "

She was nestled now, close to him, his arm around her. She knew Tessa would lecture her if she found out. Tessa would tell her she was disloyal to Arie.

Arie wasn't coming for her.

Tessa never expected Victor to come for her. She was his slave. Now she didn't believe he ever intended to wed her. The depression sweeping through Tessa needed to be chased away. Alison was afraid for her. She decided right then she was going to face the real facts and try to find a new path for her life. If Shea Devlin was part of that path then so be it. She would allow fate to take over.

Arie no longer wanted her. He proved that by not chasing after for her. As her father told her, she was his convenient. Nothing more.

Perhaps a fine piece of muslin. Nothing more.

"Ach, lass, what are you thinking now? You look a million miles away and sad. I would change that if you would allow it."

With his thumb he brushed a tear from her cheek then shook her head while she tried to breathe. "I'm afraid you're right."

"Right about what?" he asked but she was sure he knew what she was thinking. He was probing, hoping to find out the depth of all her feelings.

"Never mind. Tell me more about yourself. Do you have siblings? Are they physicians too?" She needed to turn the conversation to something more pleasant.

His hand rested on her waist, his thumb drawing gentle circles there. When he looked at her, he seemed sincere in his concern for her. "I have a sister. She is married and has two children. Now I know you don't have siblings. Is there anyone besides Arie who cared about you?"

"No, just my mother and she stopped caring when Fletcher Donovan entered her life. She was more than willing to let him sell me to the bordello where Arie found me." She paused in thought, recalling those days, "And bought me. If he had not made me his slave, I would have become a whore. Father would have never rescued me then. That would have been impossible. Needless to say, he would not want to either."

"If my facts are straight, you were sold to a brothel and Arie bought you. You can see why your father took issue with the man. He wanted you for one thing and that was to grace his bed."

"My father buys slaves. I was never Arie's slave, if that is what you intend to imply. Can you say without a doubt father never took any of the slaves he bought to his bed?" She was quick to point out and her comment didn't go unnoticed.

After a bit of a grimace, "No. The rest is hardly comparable. Did Arie give you a chance to work the money off? No," he waved his hand in the air. "Forget I asked that. It's none of my business."

She waved her hand in the air willing to defend the man she loved with all her heart. "No, he let me leave with no payment. He gave me a horse and told me I was free to go."

"That was when you met your father for the first time."

"Yes, and got lost. After that I told Arie I wanted to stay with him."

All too well she remembered that night. It was etched vividly in her mind. She'd been confused and terrified. Of course, she told him she would stay.

"Except for the chance meeting of your father, Arie orchestrated the scenario. He wanted you to feel as if your only chance at a reasonable life was to stay with him. When he gave you that horse, he knew you would get lost, also knew under the circumstance that when you were found by one of his men, you would choose to stay with him."

"He would do that?" Yet she knew how ruthless the man was and how he did get everything he wanted. Unsurprisingly, he would orchestrate her life.

"Of course, he would. If he wanted you and knowing you these few weeks I understand exactly why. You are beautiful. Any man would want you in his life. He would be a fool if he didn't."

"You're talking in riddles. I don't understand."

She was shaking, a fine trembling taking over her body and she knew he felt the shuddering. Only a few minutes ago, Shea told her he wanted her. In his bed, she assumed. He said nothing about marriage. He wasn't any better than any other man she met recently.

"I want you, Alison. In every way Arie wanted you but unlike the sultan, I'm an honorable man and would never make love to you without your permission."

His voice was gruff with the same kind of passion she recognized in Arie. He wanted her in his bed. What about marriage, a life together.

"I'm a married woman."

Lord but Tessa warned her about something like this. She should have listened more closely.

"No, you're not but I'm going to give you a few more weeks to think about my feelings for you and yours for me." His hands were beneath her breasts. If he chose to do so, he could cup them in his hands. She might not say no. Her nipples hardened in anticipations as she silently cursed her unruly body.

She remembered Arie's hands. How they created so easily an intense enchantment within her, the magic unmistakable, the heat raging. She didn't know what to think now. If Shea was right, her life with Arie was over. Perhaps Shea could fill the gap he left.

"I don't feel anything for you."

She was quick to deny the rising passion as well as the inferno he so easily created, telling herself it was just because she understood that Arie didn't care for her. Yet she couldn't reconcile the fact he asked her to marry him.

Why would he do that if he could let her go so easily?

It was hurtful and mean. Not for a second did she believe that about Arie. He could have continued to take her to his bed, make sweet love to her without humiliating her by asking her for her hand and not meaning the words. By leaving her with a man he knew she detested. Perhaps he suspected maybe even wanted her to find someone else.

"Little liar, I could tell by your kiss you care for me. Your passion rises swift and hot. You cannot deny that but I will—" Abruptly his words were cut off.

"You keep your hands off her." Tessa was standing beside them, hands on hips, a ferocious glare on her face. "She belongs to Arie. If he finds out you've defiled his wife in any way, he will cut your balls off and send you to a man to use and abuse you."

"Is your friend always this fearless?" he asked, not stepping back or removing his hands. "I've no fear of the sultan. As you can see, he is not even here to claim this woman. Alison has done nothing wrong. Neither have I."

"No, I've never seen Tessa like this. It's growing dark. You should take me back to my room. Perhaps I'll see you tomorrow."

In truth she didn't want to leave Shea's company, but she had a lot to think about. He made her feel things for him she shouldn't. This man was creating a sweet gentle havoc in her body as well as her mind. Too much confusion muddled her thoughts.

"I would eat dinner with you. Perhaps enjoy a glass of wine." It seemed he didn't want to leave her either. She felt a twist of emotions she'd only felt with Arie. "You can come to my cabin."

"You flatter me but perhaps we need to call it a night. I will have dinner with Tessa and perhaps tomorrow night we can dine together. I would look forward to that."

It seemed to Ali she was just putting off the inevitable, but she wasn't ready to give up on Arie or give herself to Shea.

"If you are sick again, make sure you call me. Send Tessa if she will come to me given her feelings. Your sickness might not be caused by the swells of the ocean but something else," Shea said, concern in his voice.

"It is not. Don't you worry yourself about Ali's condition. You know nothing about women," Tessa lashed out with her words.

"What are you talking about?" Ali turned her attention to her friend. "What do you mean condition?"

"Exactly what I said and I'll explain when we have a wee bit of privacy and not one second before."

~ * ~

Shea sat in Murray's cabin drinking brandy, his long legs stretched out in front of him, his hand wrapped around the glass warming it. He wasn't sure where this was going with Alison, but she was easily manipulated. Bending her to his will, would be child's play.

The kiss was different though. The sensation reached to the tips of his toes and back up to center in his groin. While he wanted her in his bed, he had second thoughts and third ones as well about doing so. If Arie did show up, there would be hell to pay for both of them.

This was a young woman, desperate for attention, needing love and willing to give it in return. She was enchantingly beautiful as well. Just being around her for a few hours he wanted to see more of her. She didn't understand the fascinating hold she had over him and he could only assume most men. Without knowing her influence on him, Alison reached deep into his soul as well as his heart. He didn't want to hurt her yet knew that was a very real possibility if Arie did show up, if he took her to his bed.

"So, I saw the two of you on deck as well as the brief kiss. Are you making any progress seducing my daughter?" Fraser asked with a harsh laugh. "Never thought I'd want any daughter of mine seduced, but a marriage to you would suit her fine. It would please me as well."

"She carries Demir's child," Shea said, his voice soft as he stared out the window, wondering what that meant to him. If he carried through with this scheme of Frasier's, could he care for another man's child? Truly, he didn't know if that would be possible.

"Does she ken it?" Murray asked, tapping his fingers on the tabletop, his eyebrows squinting tightly together. "I don't like that fact. A child will bind her irrevocably to the sultan."

"No, not yet but I believe Tessa will tell her tonight. She implied as much, talking about her condition."

He should have probed more about her sickness, but he had other intentions this afternoon. Stealing a chaste kiss had been at the top of his list. Now that he succeeded, he wasn't sure how to proceed. What he did know was that he wanted more from her.

"Where you and a possible relationship with my daughter are concerned, how do you feel about that? It doesn't change my mind, but if Arie ever discovered the truth and she kept it from him, once again there could be hell to pay. He doesn't strike me as man too give up his child to another man."

"Most of the time she still insists she is wed to Arie, but I don't believe it. Occasionally she has let it slip that they were not wed. She has no ring and he hasn't come for her. If Alison was my wife..." he paused in thought, unsure of exactly what he wanted to say here. "If she was my wife, I'd move heaven and earth to get her back. Nothing would stop me."

"Ah, I see you appreciate her beauty, just like her mother. I could not resist that woman. Hence the child."

"She does draw me in ways I don't understand," Shea admitted, wondering if it was love he felt or pure lust. He brushed that thought aside, telling himself it was too early in their relationship to feel love. Yet his attraction to her ran deep and hot.

"Are you going to see her tomorrow?"

"I've plans to take her for another walk on deck and perhaps dine with her in my cabin. I'm hoping Tessa has not mentioned the fact her sickness might be caused by a child growing in her womb. The knowledge might change everything. I would personally like to ease her through the issue at hand."

"Perhaps you should go see her tonight. Do you think she would slam the door in your face if you suddenly appeared at her room?"

He spoke softly. "I certainly hope not." Maybe he should check in on her. It wasn't late and he did want to see her again, reinforce the burgeoning feelings she had for him. If the timing was conducive, he might steal another kiss, possibly one that was not so chaste this time.

The feelings he had for her. What exactly were they?

"I will see you later." He walked onto the deck, stopping at the stairway to the deck below for a moment then thought better of it. He laughed at himself and the sudden urge sweeping through him. She was beautiful but he wasn't about to give his heart away to any woman, especially not one who claimed she was wed to a sultan. That would surely be foolish.

At the bow, nearly where they stood earlier in the day, he watched the stars begin to shimmer. The air was crisp. The moon was very nearly full tonight. He somehow wished that Alison was standing by his side.

What to do?

His thoughts were in such a jumble. When he closed his eyes, all he could see was the passionate shimmer of her sparkling green eyes. When he kissed her, he'd thought he'd gone to heaven and it was just the soft brush of his lips against hers.

Never before had he felt such a jolt of pleasure at a chaste kiss.

What would happen if he deepened the kiss?

He turned then, meaning to go back to his cabin and drink himself to sleep. Regret it in the morning he would, but for the moment it was all he could do to keep the green-eyed vixen form his thoughts. He wondered if that was how her mother had affected Murray. Fraser did imply her mother was impossible to resist.

At least she was already pregnant. It had only been a few weeks. The sultan would want to know if this was his child. He would want confirmation. Thoughts of what that man might do if he believed it to be his gave him cause to shudder.

"Shea?" Her soft voice surprised him, her hand resting on his shoulder even more. "I couldn't sleep. Did you have the same problem?"

"You shouldn't be out here in the dark. It's not safe."

He didn't want to reprimand her as pleased as he was that she stood by his side. No, he yearned to pull her into his arms and hold her close, feel the soft curves of her body press against him. Yet what he said was true. She shouldn't be here. He might very well take everything she was willing to give, consequences be damned.

"Yes, you're right. I don't know why but I thought you might be out here. I wanted to see you, talk to you again."

Her quietly spoken words gave his heart a gentle boost of delight. "Well, you were right but you're shivering. Why didn't you wear a shawl?" He wrapped an arm around her pulling her close.

"I just." She looked down for a moment then met his gaze and with a swift deep breath and tiny lift of her shoulders. "I don't know why. I didn't think about it. I hoped you would be here."

"You were in such a hurry to see me you forgot?" He laughed at himself as well as his thoughts then pulled her closer for a quick hug. Releasing her, "Come, let's go to my cabin and talk. We can have a glass of wine or two. Even though it's beautiful out here, it's damn cold."

"Cam was going to take me and Arie to the observatory so we could look at the stars close up, the planets too." She leaned against him, staring into the clear night sky. "Chelsea says that Cam thinks about walking on the moon. Have you ever thought about anything like that?"

"Can't say that I have. Didn't think it was possible." He laughed again, enjoying the conversation as well as the way her body seemed to fit neatly against his.

He turned her then and led her to his cabin. Once inside, he wrapped a blanket around her to warm her, rubbing her arms. "You really had no business out in the cold and the dark. You're still shivering."

"I know. I just couldn't sleep. I kept thinking about you."

Inadvertently, his finger touched her lips. He hoped she was thinking about the kiss. He didn't think he'd ever been such a besotted fool in his entire life. She wove a silver ribbon of fascination around him, binding him tightly to her in such a short amount of time. What would a lifetime with her be like?

He was pouring brandy and hoping the truth would involve her thoughts about him, "Why?"

She held the glass in both hands, concentrating on the floor for the longest time before answering. "I was thinking about you," she whispered softly, "and the kiss."

"If you want another one, I'll be happy to oblige. We could test it you know, maybe a bit longer kiss."

He was thinking deeper and perhaps some tongue. He wanted to be inside her, taste her sweetness.

"First, I want to know if Arie is coming for me. I really can't decide how I feel and what I want from you until I know." She sipped and looked at him over the rim, the amber liquid swaying slightly with her trembling.

On another woman the look might have been flirtatious, but he was sure she didn't know anything about the art of flirting. "Only time will tell. Will you give up everything you might want in your life while you wait? How long will you watch the pleasures of the world go by until you come to terms with the fact you are not his wife. He doesn't care enough about you to come for you."

She stood then, placing her glass on the table and walked to him. "No, not everything. Not forever. I want you to kiss me again. You said if that's what I wanted you would do it. Well, I've decided."

She appeared so determined he wanted to laugh but knew that

would not be well done of him. “What kind of kiss do you want?”

“One that tastes sweet and makes my heart race. One that makes my body heat to an inferno. If you can’t do that then I know you aren’t the one for me and that I should wait for Arie.”

“Even if he’s not coming? How long will you put your life on hold?”

He wasn’t at all sure about this kiss and how much of himself he should give to her. If he succumbed to her obvious charms, he might well lose his heart in the process. Already he felt more for her than he should.

Her eyes were wide-open pools of trust and hopefulness. “If the kiss does what I asked, I think I’ll wait one more week. Then you can have me if you want.”

At her words, his heart jerked while his breath caught in his throat. When his breath finally returned to him, the brandy in his mouth spewed out. Quickly, he wiped the droplets from his shirt with a handkerchief.

“I’m not sure you understand what you just said.”

“Perhaps I don’t but before Arie made love to me, he spoke of having me. At the time I wasn’t completely sure of what he was talking about. Now, I understand that men want to have women before they actually make love to them. I don’t know why but I think it’s different. Arie waited a long time. I do believe in some ways he always made love to me even when he looked at me with his dark brown eyes simmering with desire and passion.”

Blindsided would be a proper word to use in this circumstance. “I’m humbled. Don’t know what to say.”

“If after the next kiss and we give Arie another week or so, that will be alright with me. You can have me. I won’t expect anything else in return.”

Shea was sure he just stepped into quicksand and was sinking rapidly. He cleared his throat, trying to speak then cleared it again. “All you said is true, but let’s take this one kiss at a time. Tonight is for just one more kiss and nothing more.”

He never expected his voice to shake with excitement while talking to a woman about kissing. Never actually talked to a woman about kissing before.

She stood in front of him, her eyes blazing into his, a piquant smile on her beautiful face. “Should we kiss now or later?”

Her bluntness shocked him to his toes. “I need another drink since most of the first one ended up on my shirt or the floor.”

He topped off her glass and poured himself more. He wasn’t sure how to go about this. It seemed she was seducing him.

“You don’t want to kiss me.”

Over and over he was shaking his head, trying to find the words this was so far from the truth he didn’t know what to say. He downed the glass in a gulp, grimacing a moment at the heat burning down his throat. “I...” he cleared his throat again. “I think you are a beautiful woman and yes I want you, want to have you beneath me, but I’m not going to act on that want.”

“You’re a man. You’ve needs and I want to—”

He waved his hand, stopping her. “You’re needs, a woman’s, are just as great as mine, a man’s.”

“Why do you say that?”

“Because I know. I’m a doctor. I know things like that.” He coughed at his lie. “Shall we stop talking and give that kiss a try?”

Several kisses and drinks later, Alison was asleep on his chair. The taste of her was so sweet and beautiful. He prayed Arie would not come for her, wanting her like no other woman he’d ever cared for before.

Carrying her down the steps to her room was not possible. He didn’t want anyone seeing him and her in this inebriated state and coming to untrue conclusion.

With a contented smile on his face he picked her up before setting her on his bed. She pulled the pillow close and let out a long sigh of contentment. He didn’t know how she would wake, most likely with a blinding headache and...”

He placed two basins close to her.

Chapter Nine

Arie paced the deck with Victor matching him step for step. They passed each other, grunted then looked to the crow's nest for some indication of a ship sighting. He was beside himself with worry and fatigue. This was supposed to have taken a day or two and now they were going on four weeks, a month. Over the past weeks he'd slept little, ate less.

Today the sun was shining, the air crisp with the breeze off the ocean. A few clouds dotted the sky but otherwise they should be able to see forever. If there was a ship on the skyline, the vessel would be seen.

Cam was beside himself with worry over his wife who was newly pregnant after a miscarriage. He spent most of this time on deck also pacing and searching the horizon for any sign of a ship. He committed to this trip. He would not turn around so he told Arie. Still there was guilt in his mind, fear for Chelsea as well.

The weather had stopped them, made everything take so much longer. Dreary cloudy days and rain falling nonstop had kept them sightless. They could have passed the American ship days ago without ever knowing. Arie gave the order to bring down a sail, hoping to slow their progress. The strategy was a guess, that was all. He tried to foresee everything. Fear for Alison grew daily.

"What has gone wrong?" Victor strode beside him, his anger apparent as he slammed his fist on the railing. "We should have had our women back days ago, no weeks ago. "I don't want to sail to America or travel overland to the man's plantation. I'm not cutout for the wilderness and battling Indians. Give me a ship to board and I'll gladly meet any man, steel on steel."

"Neither does anyone else," Arie muttered, frustration eating at his gut, "but unless we find them soon that's exactly what we are going to have to do, battle Indians and wild animals."

"Cam is beside himself worried about Chelsea and her pregnancy. Her miscarriage with her last pregnancy happened at about this time. He needs to be there for her while here he is, sailing the Atlantic with no end in sight."

"We are not turning around."

Arie's hands fisted at his side, understanding Cam's concerns but this was his life and his ship. When they finally caught up to the ladies, this vessel would return and Chelsea would be fine the baby would be fine, all would be fine. However, if they turned around now, he might never see Alison again, might lose her for all time. That wasn't going to happen. He would go all the way to Virginia if necessary, trek inland if there were no other choice.

"No, we are not," Victor agreed.

"Chelsea will be fine," Arie muttered.

"Unlike Tessa and Ali if we can't find them. They will be held against their will."

Arie started pacing again, thinking about Alison as well as the irony. Once he held Alison against her will. He wished they were wed, needed to know he could protect her as his wife. As it was despite the signed contracts, she was nothing more than his paramour and Fraser could use that against him. The documents were only legal once the ceremony was performed. It would be his word against Fraser's.

"Tessa will believe I don't care. I was having trouble convincing her how I truly feel about her. Now she will think she was indispensable, nothing more than a slave to me. They must believe we are not coming for them. Hence we don't care."

"Her life has been controlled by men. She is right to be insecure. You are the first man she could trust and look what has happened. At least Ali, although naïve, has more backbone. She has not been a slave her entire life so she has expectations and dreams while Tessa does not. Alison has always known freedom."

"Still, where men are concerned, she has little experience. That was why you so easily manipulated her to your way of thinking," Victor laughed for a moment seeming to forget the obvious distress he'd been feeling for weeks. "She was willing to do whatever you wanted and with only one kiss."

"It was a damn good kiss too." Then, "You're saying I took advantage of her?" Arie asked, knowing the truth of Victor's words. After all, Chelsea impressed that fact upon him the first time she discovered his actions.

"We both know you did but when all was said and done, she was willing, came to you with an open heart. You have nothing to look back on with any kind of regret, not that you would."

"I keep wondering what could possibly be happening to her. She's alone except for Tessa. What does her father have planned for her? Does he have a husband handpicked and waiting in the background? If so, would she allow liberties and accept that man if she believed I abandoned her? We have not wasted time here, but she will be wondering if I really do care."

"Sail ho," the call from the crow's nest put a smile on Arie's face.

It was what they had all been waiting for. To Arie the cry was music and the announcement gave his heart a leap. Shielding his eyes, he looked upward then focused his gaze on the horizon. When he finally saw the sail, it was behind them just as he had guessed.

"Your gut instinct was right," Victor said, his gaze riveted on the sails. "We passed them some time in the last few weeks."

"Keep the Turkish flag flying until I give the order. I want to make sure it's the American ship we've been seeking before we turn on them." Arie called out.

His order was echoed from one of the crew.

Closing the distance between the two ships seemed to take forever. Arie's heart raced when he saw the American flag, their own skull and cross bones rose on the mast calling out their purpose loud and clear. His men let out a roaring cheer as their target was well in their sights. It would not be spared. Alison and Tessa would be back where they belonged, Alison in his arms Tessa in Victor's.

He grinned anticipating the fight yet keeping Cam's words to heart. There would most likely be no fight. He suspected the merchant ship would surrender to them. Ah, it is what it is. His men would have loved to clash swords after all this time. He would have to take what he wanted then let the ship go on its way.

Cam stood beside him, his hands clasped behind his back, rocking on his heels. "You remember my words. We don't hurt anyone. Wouldn't want to start an international incident. Just our boarding his vessel with swords drawn could be considered outlandish and even an act of war not to speak of the skull and crossbones."

"I understand. I'm going above for a better look."

Arie made his way up the mast to the crow's nest. After taking the glass from the sailor, he peered at the ship. What he saw stopped his heart for a moment before ripping it apart.

Alison stood facing a man he didn't know. Her head rested against his forehead and she held clothing. The man kissed her on the forehead, caressing her cheek then ushered her downstairs.

His worst fears might indeed be coming to pass. She might have lost her heart to another man. Might have given herself to this American.

The first cannonball crossed the bow, spraying water in every direction. Shouts from the merchant ship echoed across the sea. Arie waited for the return fire. It didn't come. Instead the sails were unfurled as the ship slowly came to a halt in the water. There would be no fight. Bitterness assailed him.

The grappling hooks landed securely on Frasier's ship. Aire's crew scurried onto the other boat, swords drawn as not one American picked up arms.

Quickly, he made his way to the rigging. He'd done this many a time when the prize was not his wife. He and Victor moved upon the ropes with skill and speed and uncanny ease. In seconds he was on the deck. As his boots struck wood, he was making his way toward the staircase where he saw Ali disappear.

The man he'd seen her with stepped in front of him, sword in hand. "I must ask your intentions."

"I am retrieving my wife and Victor his wife. Once that is done, we will leave. Don't stand in my way." His voice was gruff and urgent.

Arie would welcome a fight.

"Alison is not your wife and you know it. She must agree to go with you."

"Or what? You will lie down your life for her." Arie's sneer did not go unnoticed by the man.

His sword wavered until the blade dangled uselessly by his side. "No, I would not because I understand she will go with you if given the choice." He stepped aside, watching as Arie moved down the ladder, jumping the last rungs in his haste to find Alison.

"Is Tessa down there also?" Victor asked, pushing past the man in any case not seeming to need to wait for an answer.

Arie strode through the corridor, pushing open doors and calling her name, Victor doing much the same. When Tessa heard her name, she barreled from the door, jumping into Victor's arms.

"You came?"

"Never doubt it my little houri," he whispered close to her ear.

It was a greeting Arie would like to receive also but for some reason he didn't think that would happen. When he pushed open Ali's door, she was standing in the far corner of the room, her green eyes wide with what he could only describe as terror.

He slipped his sword in its sheathe and stepped toward her. "Alison? You have no need for fear."

"I didn't think you were coming."

Her words were whisper thin. He would give anything to undo the last few weeks. She was quaking, her hands clasped in front of her.

"I was always coming. Did you doubt it?" He moved closer. He saw the fine trembling of her shoulders along with soft sheen of moisture on her forehead. He held out his hands, "You've no reason to be frightened of me."

"There are things I need to tell you. Things you won't like." Her words were softly spoken. "I didn't think you were coming. It's been almost a month."

He inhaled a rapid breath, trying to calm his emotions. He would have liked to think she would wait longer than a month for him. "You shall have all evening to talk but now we are leaving. Are you going with me or do you plan to stay?" He held his breath, waiting for an answer, knowing he had to ask.

Hesitantly she stepped forward. The step was tiny. He wasn't at all sure she was willing to leave with him. He watched her swallow then look to him; her hands clasped so tight the knuckles were turning white. "Yes."

He held out his hand, hoping she would accept the offer. His muscles tensed. When her fingers wound through his he said a silent prayer, his relief palpable.

When they reached the deck, Tessa and Victor were on board his ship. It seemed Victor sent men to fetch the trunk of clothing Frasier bought for Alison. The American ship was allowed safe passage. Arie watched the look on Fraser's face as they left. He hoped and prayed this would be the last he saw of her father.

Once in his cabin, "I have to leave for a few minutes. Relax. I'll be back as soon as possible. You can tell me everything that comes to your mind."

He hoped his worst fears had not materialized, wished Ali's greeting had been as enthusiastic as Tessa's for Victor.

She was nodding her head but still it didn't seem she wanted to speak. The smile that played against her face was hesitant. He would have asked Tessa to keep her company, but he didn't think Victor would give her up just yet.

With a last look at her, he left the room striding onto the deck, feeling rage and pain at Murray Fraser as well as the man who threatened his life to protect Ali. They could not go on this way. He stopped at the bow of the deck and was quickly joined by Cam.

"How is she doing?" Cam asked.

"She wasn't hurt in any way. The proper question is how am I doing. She's terrified of me. I don't think getting answers is going to be easy." He paused, massaging his neck. "When all I want to do is make love to her she is terrified. What did her father tell her to cause that fear?"

"Perhaps nothing. You should see the look on your face. If I didn't know you so well, I'd also be terrified. You've been through a lot. This waiting and you are anything but a patient man."

"That bad?" he questioned trying to hide his emotions with a quirk of his lips.

"More than that. You should pretend you are wooing her again. Bring her wine and soft pillows. Make her feel special and don't push her for answers. She will tell you everything you want to know eventually, in her own time," It seemed to Arie Cam was very nearly laughing at him.

"She was with a man. I saw them from the crow's nest." The silence between the two men seemed to linger. "He kissed her. I can't help but wonder what else went on between them."

"The jealousy is raging. So be it. I remember feeling that way and the jealousy was directed at you. Suppose what goes around comes around. Give her a chance to explain," Cam did laugh then as Arie scowled at him.

"I did kiss Chelsea didn't I? If you must know it was with the direct purpose to make you jealous so you would stop being such an ass. It worked too. This is different. This kiss, his kiss just to her forehead was tender and spoke of gentler things, more intimacies than I would like to believe she could have shared with another man. Just recalling the scene in my mind makes my gut tighten with pain."

"Talk to her. She will tell you the truth. From what I've seen of Alison, she is guileless. For me, I'm just eager to see my home and my wife. I'm proud of you for taking your women without incident. I know, given the circumstances that wasn't easy."

"That was not difficult. Fraser wisely retreated to his cabin. I would have been hard pressed not to challenge the man if he'd shown himself."

"If I were you, I would waste no more time on silly pleasantries with me. You need to go to Alison, let her explain what transpired over the weeks she was held captive. Listen well, my friend. Try to understand her position. It took us a devilishly long time to find them. Whatever happened on board the American ship could have been worse."

"She certainly didn't appear to be a captive when I saw her through the glass," Arie muttered, suddenly feeling a wee bit sorry for himself.

While he'd been worried about her, she'd been enjoying another man's companionship. While he wrestled with sleep every night, she might well have been lying in bed with another man.

"Go, I'll round up some food for the two of you and a couple of bottles of wine although I suspect you have something stronger in your cabin. It will take me a few minutes. If she decides to start throwing things at you, I will not find myself in the way of any missiles."

"Thank you," Arie said, "I see you've already turned the ship around and we're heading back to Scotland. Guess you've taken over my duties."

"Wasn't going to waste any more time than necessary. Was pretty sure you would be ensconced in the cabin with your lady. Didn't really expect to see you up here so soon."

"Had to step away and think. Didn't know how to confront her or how to change the terror in her eyes. Figured a few minutes away might help, but it could do the opposite."

"Wouldn't want to react, pull her into your arms and erase all her fears, would you? Kiss her. Show her how much you missed her. She will fall into your arms now just as she did before. Remember, you gave her the choice of staying with this other man or not." Cam laughed as if he was thinking of doing just that the moment he walked into his home.

Cam's words rang true. He had nothing to fear. Turning, Arie strode to his cabin, shaking his head and thinking Cam's words were exactly what he should have done. It's what he wanted to do right now.

When he opened the door, Ali was curled up on the window seat, staring at the ocean. Slowly she turned her head, a half-smile gracing her pale features.

"Food is coming if you're hungry."

He sat down behind his desk, the table a protective barrier between them even while he yearned to pull her into his arms to show her how much he missed her, longed for her arms around him, her body pressed close against his. His confusion seemed to carry over to Ali. Her fingers were wound tightly into the fabric of her gown and crease lines marred her beautiful forehead.

"Are you hungry?"

Tiny little shakes of her head had him wondering then, "I'm too nervous to be hungry, but I should be. I haven't had anything at all to eat since last night and..." She stopped as if the rest of the sentence was a secret that shouldn't be divulged.

"And?"

"Nothing," she murmured, shaking her head again. Her lashes were lowered, soft dark arcs fanning across her cheeks as she looked at her clasped hands.

"Thought you wanted to talk. We could start with last night. What happened then that has you tongue-tied?"

She looked away for the longest time. He wondered if this conversation was going to be one sided. At least now she stared at something other than her hands.

"A glass of wine would be nice." She cleared her throat then, looking back to the ocean beyond as if she wanted to see the American ship.

"As soon as it comes." He almost laughed at the disappointment he saw on her face. "You were hoping I would leave again? To fetch the wine?"

"That might be nice," she said softly seemingly unwilling still to look at him.

"I'll start with me. Would you like to know what happened that night you were kidnapped?" He hoped she would listen and learn how hard he tried to stop her father.

"When Fraser's men ripped me from my bed, if you recall, I was stark naked." Her voice was soft, once more filled with the humiliation she must have felt. He ripped away my cover then hauled me from the bed."

Anger surged through him at her words, his fists tightening. He reminded himself there was nothing to do about it now. He needed to comfort her. "I'm sorry for that. I would have killed those men, but Cam would not let me hurt anyone on Fraser's ship. Said there might well be an international incident if I did."

"I wanted that at the time. Those weren't the men who actually kidnapped me. I doubt if Murray would have condoned the brutality." She moistened her lips, staring now at his. "I wanted you to kill my father or send him off to some punishment he would abhor for the rest of his life. I hardly saw him the entire trip."

He almost laughed realizing without even knowing it she was coming around. "Victor and I were hauled off to jail for your kidnapping. We might still be there if it wasn't for Cam's quick thinking."

She still watched him. He expected her to ask about this but she didn't. He strode to a safe and unlocked it. "Documents," he told her and set them on her lap waiting for her to look at them before recalling she couldn't read.

She stared at them for the longest time while he rocked on his heels in front of her. "You know I can't read." She handed the forms back to him.

Then he pointed to the X, "That's your signature on our marriage document. Says we are legally wed. I'm going to teach you to write your name first thing when we return to Glasgow. I want to see your name on our marriage certificate."

"Are we married? I told Shea I was married to you, but I thought it was a lie. I don't think I was convincing." She lowered her dark lashes. "He called me a liar. Didn't believe me."

"It was a lie. We need to say our vows in front of a minister when we return to Glasgow. The papers served their purpose. We were released albeit twelve hours after your departure. We should have caught up to you just after we sailed out of the Firth of Clyde, but we must have passed you in the dark and dreary days.

"Truly, I didn't think you were coming, not after three weeks then four weeks passed. I lost all hope as did Tessa." She wiped the moisture from her eyes.

"So, Shea is the man's name. The man I saw kiss you before we boarded the ship."

He saw her quickly drawn breath of air, saw the color wash from her face.

She looked up, her eyes wide pools of despair, "You saw that?"

"I did and I'm not too patient when it come to my soon to be wife kissing another man." Despite his efforts his voice was harsh and he watched her flinch and once again look away. She pulled her bottom lip beneath her teeth.

She was his, had been for some time now. Why didn't she stay loyal to him? What did the man, Shea, offer her to make her want to kiss him? Did he just claim the prize? He reminded himself he only saw the man kiss Ali, not the other way around. His hands fisted tightly while he tried to even out his breathing. Terrifying her would not help him learn what prompted her actions.

"It was just a kiss on the forehead."

It seemed she tried to defend herself, but her words did nothing to soothe his anger and frustration, irritation that had been eating at him for the weeks he'd been chasing after her.

"No man should be kissing you except me, your forehead or otherwise."

She turned then to stare out the window and ignore him. Her back was stiff. Despite her usual compliance she wasn't going to do that now.

"We aren't married," she whispered softly. "The kiss was just to my forehead. You have no other hold on me. You don't own me."

He did own her. She would best learn that fact. Wed or not he owned her. "Engaged."

He needed to know why she sounded so defensive. It was true he should not be jealous of that kiss but it was the way he held her face with both hands.

He watched as she breathed in and out, the breaths swift and tight, "You're right of course. I had no business kissing Shea. I kened it. I didn't kiss him. He did the kissing if that is any consolation."

"Did you respond to him? Did your body heat with passion and your heart race as it does when I kiss you?" he asked even though he both did and did not want to hear the answer.

~ * ~

"I would like to... Arie please, I didn't want to do this. It was so hard. I thought of you every moment, but he was gentle and sweet. I was lonely and afraid. His kindness was my undoing. He didn't push me to do anything. He was willing to wait to make sure you weren't coming for me."

Tears were beginning to threaten. She wanted to push them back. Instead, they continued to fall. She'd been so wrong to let Shea kiss her. She understood that now.

The knock on the door gave her the reprieve she needed to clear her head while figuring out what she should say next. "Your dinner and enough wine to make it through the night." Cam entered the room, looking from one to the other. "I hope I didn't interrupt anything." Cam grinned seeming to know the answer without either of them replying.

"No, it's fine. I would like some wine. I probably should eat something. Thank you." She spoke before Arie could growl at Cam for the intrusion.

She understood some of the animosity between them but most certainly not all. Eating was important. She would probably loose most of what she ate tonight in the morning and how would she explain that to Arie? She didn't know why she was so sick each day.

Cam set the tray on the table a grin on his face. "Anything else I can get you? Tessa and Victor wouldn't even answer the door. I had to set the tray on the floor." He started to back from the room. "Have a nice evening."

For a moment Alison was puzzled by his words then she understood and knew he was goading Arie. "Perhaps... never mind. Arie and I still have things to talk over." Actually, she had too many things to clarify.

"We do." Arie said pointedly. "Ali was just about to explain why she let another man kiss her."

"I need a glass of wine and food. Truly, I'm hungry. Can't this wait?" Suddenly her stomach did rumble. It had been so long since she felt hungry or was able to keep anything down for more than a few minutes. The food looked amazingly good, the wine even better.

He sat back, his hands resting on his abdomen. She suddenly wished this was behind them, needing him to hold her and reassure her that everything would be fine. More than anything she wanted her life to be normal again. She heard the door close behind Cam, knew soon she would have no excuses now, no respite from his questions.

"Until you eat." He poured the wine for both of them, his body obviously tense then sat down.

"You have to eat too."

Her hand trembled when she held the glass of wine then her mind traveled back to the champagne and the way he tasted the droplets he placed strategically on her body before laving them with his tongue, caressing her with his teeth. She swallowed the wine quickly then poured herself more.

"I'm fine." He sipped his wine, studying her.

She felt the tremendous heat of his gaze. She swallowed the liquid and reached for something on the tray.

He didn't say anything for the longest time. "Try the berries. They are delicious, very sweet."

She did then paused, pursing her lips. She wanted him, needed his forgiveness not this cold unyielding. Finally, "Could you just forgive me my indiscretions and make love to me?"

"Indiscretions? Plural? So, there was more than one kiss." His voice tight with emotion he drank down the rest of his glass then poured another one.

"Please, I just want to get this over with then you can do whatever you will. I betrayed you. Yesterday he kissed me. It was nothing like your kisses. He brushed his lips across mine. His mustache tickled but I did like the way it felt and yes my heart did race a little." She inhaled then long and deep as if it was about to be her last breath of air.

"You kissed more than once. I'm reading it in your eyes. You've more to tell me."

He sat back then, seeming to school his features. She had no idea what to think. His arms were crossed over his chest, his ardent gaze fixed on her with disapproval. He wasn't going to touch her, not until she confessed to everything.

She looked down again then met his gaze, trying for courage she didn't possess. She didn't want to disappoint him, only yearned to please him. "Yes, there is more. After we kissed. He sent me downstairs to my room. Later that evening I wanted or hoped to see him again. So, I looked for him on the deck."

"He was there, staring out at the ocean. Such a coincidence," Arie said, his voice void of emotions. She heard the anger, the recrimination in his voice.

"How did you know?" She drew her brows together, her heart racing.

"A lucky guess, I suppose. It's what I would have done. Gone outside and hoped you would come find me. Smart man. What happened after that?"

"It was too cold to stay outside," she murmured. "I forgot my shawl you see, so we walked back to his room."

"Not surprising either."

"You seem too calm. You don't care?" she asked astonished by his reactions even though she'd prayed for just this thing.

"I'm not calm at all," he told her. "In fact, I'd like to go up top and turn around the ship. If I knew what you're telling me now when I met this Shea on board the American ship, I would have killed him. Cam would have a lot of explaining to the Scottish or the American government as to why." His voice was gritty and harsh. His eyes sparked with anger, the auburn turning nearly black. "For diplomatic reasons we would have been sent back to our homeland."

Ali understood he meant every word. "What more do you want me to say," she brushed flyaway hair from her face. "When we were inside, he wrapped a blanket around me. I told him I did want him to kiss me again but nothing else."

"So, he did kiss you last night."

"More than once. But nothing else. I drank too much wine so he must have put me on his bed because that's where I woke up in the morning."

"He slept with you." Arie stood so fast he knocked the chair he'd been sitting on to the floor behind him.

"No, he slept on a chair."

"That's all."

She nodded, smushing her lips together, staring at him, waiting. She'd never seen him like this, never seen how quickly anger could rise within him. "Nothing happened except a few kisses. You've slept with other women," she tossed back at him then covered her mouth thinking she should not have done such a thing.

"You're right, of course, but a man doesn't like to share."

"Women don't either," she told him once again wishing she would just leave well enough alone. Keeping her mouth shut would be much more prudent. It was not something she should have said to him. "I would be jealous," she spoke softly watching the smile spread across his handsome face, his eyes now alight with passion not anger.

"You've done nothing that needs forgiveness. Do you know how hard you are to resist? I give Shea some kudos for his restraint. If it were me and you, alone, I would have taken you to my bed. I would have made love to you, threat of a husband or not."

"You didn't though if you recall. You were patient and gave me time to adjust to my situation. I know now you wanted me the first second you had me in your possession."

"You paint the wrong picture of me. My patience was simply due to the fact I didn't wish to force you. Needed for you to come to me willingly, bathed and perfumed just for me."

"There is something else and you will know in the morning if you allow me to stay the night with you." She was plucking at her skirts, not understanding why she should tell him, but Tessa insisted.

He sat forward then, his forearms resting on his thighs. His grin huge, "What is that? More?"

"Well, it seems in the morning I can't, well, I lose everything I've eaten. Tessa said you would want to know, but I certainly don't understand why I need to tell you. It's quite obvious."

For a moment Arie's smile faded. He was scratching his head then a slight smirk formed on his face. "Thank you for telling me."

"Thank you? Is that it? Then why would Tessa be so adamant I should say something? Neither of you are making any sense."

She wanted to understand what no one was telling her. The secrets were about her so why wasn't she allowed to learn what they were.

He strode to her and picking her up in his arms he twirled around in a tight circle before settling her on the bed. He returned with two glasses of wine and sat down beside her, wrapping an arm around her.

"You've made me very happy, my little harem girl."

As his grin widened, he brushed flyaway pieces of hair from her face. He placed a gentle kiss on her lips, his hand resting possessively on her belly. He moved away from her, puzzling her even more.

She wondered at the expression on his face. Now his eyes were closed and his head was against the backboard.

"Why?" she asked. "Why would you be happy that I'm seasick? That's all it is, you know."

"If you are seasick why is the sickness only apparent in the morning?"

He turned toward her, tracing the line of her eyebrows. She shivered in response as she wanted more. Her hands rose to stroke his face.

"I don't know. Don't know anything about the ocean and sailing," she said indignantly, dropping her hand from him.

"Tessa implied you would be able to keep it from happening. Instead you just grin and chuckle." She gave her back to him. "I think..." She started to rise.

Quickly he stopped her.

"Come back here." He kissed her softly then a swift brush of his lips across hers, his hands on either side of her face.

Then whispering close to her, "Thank you for telling me everything. I knew you would as well as sharing about your sickness. You will be over it in a few months. Eventually you will not be able to see your feet or put on your shoes. You might waddle when you walk, but I'll still adore you."

"A few months." Swiftly she drew away from him, confused. "How long is it going to take to get back to Scotland? We've only been out four weeks." Then she mulled over the other things he told her.

"Less than the time it took to get here. My ship is faster than Fraser's," he said but his fingers were working the fastenings of her dress.

His lips were everywhere, stroking touching her in the most intimate fashion.

She shivered with passion and the heat of the inferno he created so quickly. It rose hot and swift, enticing, fascinating. The groan emanating from him, thrilled her, telling her he still wanted her.

His desire was potent and strong. She remembered vividly his body and how it felt above her, the weight and the passion the strength and the vibrancy. Her fingers found their way beneath his shirt. His flesh was smooth, hot, just as she remembered.

He stopped abruptly. Her eyes crossed as she squeaked. "You don't want me?"

"More than anything." His hand rested on her belly while his gaze burned through her.

"What aren't you telling me?"

An urgent need scorched her, a yearning to understand Arie's thoughts created something within she couldn't define. Now while she was happy and he seemed to forgive her, she wanted to ken what was in his mind.

It appeared he was not going to allow distance between them. Suddenly her gown was on the floor. The few underthings she wore joined the gown. She was not self-conscious but she wanted him to undress also. Yet he held her hands as his lips traveled the length of her. A tiny moan of desire rippled from her lungs as he bent his will to her.

"Arie, please let me touch you..."

Her voice seemed to disappear into a thin wail as he sucked a nipple into his mouth, nipped and laved the tip while she moved beneath him. His hands roamed, explored, leaving nothing of her untouched.

"Not now, not yet. Not until I satisfy you and show you how much I care."

His lips whispered across the tip of her breasts and downward. He kissed her belly before gazing at her again. What she saw was love in his eyes. She wondered at the emotion she never thought to see.

She decided it was her imagination. What she saw was just passion, yet his lips, teeth and tongue continued their foray across her until she cried out his name, her hips reaching for him yet he continued to deny her. Hot rapture tore through her. She yearned to give it back to him but still he held her hands away from him.

Moonlight slanted across his face. She saw the tension radiating from the creases around his eyes, his dark brown eyes. He was above her now, his weight only partially pushing down upon her. She needed him in ways she didn't understand. Another man would never do. It was Arie she yearned for.

He was inside her now, penetrating deep and hot, deeper still. He was moving, moving some more but too slowly, she needed so much more from him. Yet it seemed he continued the sweet torment, bringing her to a point of no return then backing off. She wanted to pound on his chest, to kiss him everywhere just as he did her.

He still wore most of his clothes, her hands were still held tightly by his. He had never created a hunger inside her so great. She'd never coveted anything so desperately. This was Arie. He'd brought her to the utmost pleasure, but this was a rapture she could never define.

Her body shifted and writhed to the dance he set, the patterns he expertly created in her body. His skill was perfection yet he did not let her down, did not give her relief. It seemed he wanted these moments to last forever. Perhaps he needed to impress upon her the fact that no other man could give her this savage desperate tempest of desire.

He still did not release her hands from his captivity, still did not allow her to stroke him and give him the pleasure she so wanted to deliver. Yet he drove inside her with a force and fury he'd never before shown her. She swirled with it, soared and she reached toward the stars and the heavens seeking and seeking some more.

Then the heat captured her. A raging furnace of longing and enchantment exploded inside her as shock waves swept through her, left her shuddering beneath him. Before she'd thought their lovemaking rapturous. This went beyond that. It was perhaps because they had both been afraid they'd lost each other. For a few seconds her breath left her then she discovered her hands were free. Now he was above her and straddling her. His grin was wide. She knew he was not done, that they would make love again tonight and perhaps more.

They were both drenched and slick with a fine sheen of moisture while it seemed he was about to begin anew. Instead, he pulled her close and held her in his arms. "There will be more tonight if that is what you'd like. I don't want to tire you, but by God, I've never felt anything so pure and selfless."

He smoothed the tangle of hair from her face, his expression filled with tender concern as well as a raw untamed desire.

"What I'd like is for you to explain to me what I don't know."

She touched his face with a fingertip. He didn't allow the touch to linger but claimed her finger with his mouth, sucking it between his lips and biting gently.

Slowly the inferno began again but he stopped abruptly, taking her hand and placing it on her belly as his had been only a little bit before. "This is what I've not told you. What Tessa did not say to you."

The warmth from his hand filled her and she smiled at him, wanting to laugh at his comment, which told her nothing at all. "Don't you think that is a bit vague?"

"You really don't have any idea?" he asked in seeming disbelief, shaking his head as his humor grew.

It seemed to Ali he questioned everything about her. She wasn't sure what to say to him now. Letting her fingers rest on his hard abdomen so close to his erection, she searched for time.

"I thought I was seasick. If not that, I've no idea. Why don't you end this torment and tell me what you think or perhaps know? Did I get some horrible disease and now I'll be sick even longer?"

"No disease."

Once again, he smiled, but this time it seemed to be tender concern that prompted the showing of his even white teeth.

"Then..." She punched him and he obligingly grunted. "I'm truly tired of playing games with you and everyone else. Tessa mentioned my condition to Shea. It seemed he knew what I did not."

His scowl returned, "Tessa and I both believe you carry my child. You have morning sickness that has nothing to do with the sea waves."

It seemed he waited for a response as she mulled over in her mind what he just said. She inhaled deep breaths, having never considered anything like this. "I'm pregnant?" she finally asked.

"I believe so. Yes, I'm sure you are."

"Is that why you're smirking? Does that mean you're pleased with this?" She didn't know how she felt having never thought of the possibilities of motherhood.

"Are you pleased?" he asked. "As pleased as I am?"

She tried to push away but he drew her closer. Closing her eyes, she tried to understand what awaited her. Then hesitantly, "I'm terrified."

Her words seemed to surprise him. "There is nothing to be afraid of."

"That is easy for you to say. You're a man. You will gloat and hover but you do not grow until your belly is huge and you can barely toddle from one place to the other. You do not have to birth the child, enduring the pain."

"I cannot see you toddling. I will never gloat but will appreciate your body as the baby grows inside you."

"I need more wine." She sat up despite the fact she was sure he wanted to make love to her again. "And food. If I'm destined to spend months losing everything I eat, then best I put food in my stomach when it will stay put."

"The sickness could be over sooner." He pulled her back, his hand cupping her breast. "Every woman is different."

"Or it could last even longer than a few months. I don't suppose anyone knows exactly how long the sickness will last."

"No, no one knows anything like that." He leaned back watching her, his hands behind his head. "You please me very much, Alison Demir. That is your name now. I will never let you go."

She nodded, liking the sound of her name linked with his. "Alison Demir," she murmured. In the past she never truly cared for her last name, did not like it linked to Fletcher Donovan.

"As soon as we reach Glasgow, we will find that minister Chelsea arranged to have come to her home. We will wed. There will be no one to take you away from me again."

Alison was surprised at the vehemence in his voice, pleased too. "I do want to be your wife," she said so softly he had to lean closer to hear.

"You will please me greatly when you are," he murmured.

"As it will please me," she told him. "Pleasing Arie, hmm... I doubt if your Chelsea will like that notion but I don't care."

"Neither do I but I mean to please Ali," he murmured before he kissed her again, setting all the fires within her blazing once more. "In that we will be equals."

Epilogue

They were wed three weeks later in a small church with Tessa and Victor as witnesses before his friend and concubine said their vows. Chelsea and Cam were also present to observe the wedding along with the entire MacTavish clan and their spouses. It seemed both Chelsea and Cam were very pleased. So far Chelsea had no problems whit her pregnancy. Arie always assumed Cam was more than grateful to see him wed and no longer a part of their lives except as a good friend. The only punishment Zara received for her part in the poisoning was isolation for two weeks along with a diet of food and water.

When the child was born, Arie was thrilled to have a girl child, her hair and eyes reminding him of his mother and the fact he would have to protect her, watch over her diligently as he well understood the ways of man and how easy it was for an unprotected female to fall into the hands of evil men.

Arie continued to watch over his friends, always eager to threaten retribution for wrongs committed against them. For the most part he and Alison kept to themselves. He was even able to reconcile his anger and accept Murray Fraser into their lives. Alison's father was present at the birth of his second child, his son. Arie even went as far as to promise the father he would when the boy was of age and if the boy wished to, allow him to visit Virginia and the plantation. Since the boy was the only living relative, he would become the next Marquis of Belmond.

Alison did please Arie for many more years. They remained in Scotland, Arie making only one visit to his home in the Ottoman Empire. He brought gifts to his wives and his children, setting them free if they chose to pursue other lives. None of his three wives chose to stay with him, keeping the title of wife. They all yearned for their freedom, which he willingly gave, with no repercussions to the women.

She was pleased then to be his only wife, pleased, too, that the women had all chosen other husbands and were not shamed.

With their two children playing around them, Arie took Alison in his arms. “Would you like to work on a third child? These two are no longer babes. I want to see your belly swell, watch you as you grow.”

“I suppose you just want to keep up with Chelsea and Cam since they have three now.”

Arie grinned lazily. “It never occurred to me.”

She punched him on the shoulder. “Of course it did. You are always competitive when it comes to Cam. Sometime you will admit to the fact.”

“Perhaps I am. I do enjoy making love to you. It pains me when I have to take precautions.” He tugged her closer, his hands finding intimate spots beneath her skirt.

“The children.”

“Ah, you must not have noticed that the nanny took them away a few minutes ago.”

Alison tried to sit in an attempt to locate them. She groaned when he rolled on top of her, his hands expertly relieving her of her underclothing.

He picked her up, carrying her in his arms to the rug next to the fireplace. Setting her down gently he proceeded to make short work of her clothing. In a matter of seconds, she was naked, firelight glistening off her skin.

“We will begin work this instant.”

“Never thought this was work for you?” she laughed, accepting his kiss, meeting him with the passion she always did.

“I will always seek to please you Alison.”

“Pleasing Arie, it is what I’ve always sought. I love you Arie Demir.”

“As I love you.”

Coming Soon by the Author
at
Rogue Phoenix Press

Graham's Wicked Kiss

November 1826
North of Edinburgh

Graham Chamberlin pulled Draco to a halt just as the large drive to the Chamberlin estate began. He'd spent too many weeks in Edinburgh. With luck on his side, he made it to his ancestral estate, gifted to him by his grandmother, just before the first snows of winter would start. What he discovered in the city was that the life of leisure and balls he was invited to didn't suit. Neither did any of the debutants he met there.

Leaning on the saddle horn, he looked over his soon to be home, Granville Manner. Over the years there had been little change on the outside. Now, he wondered about the interior. His brother, Donal Chamberlin, had been sending coin to keep the home well appointed. Yet he'd also heard rumors the home had fallen into disrepair at the hands of the current manager.

His brother's holdings stretched to the states. He had little time for this home or the surrounding lands. When Graham volunteered to check out the manor as well as the grounds and perhaps live here, Donal agreed whole-heartedly. This suited Graham just fine.

As he studied the lane and the row of trees leading to the front steps, he noticed three different heads poking out from three trees along with spindly arms and legs waving at him. He laughed outright remembering days long past. Times when he and Donal played in the same trees, usually not in the dead of winter though.

After watching for a few minutes, he nudged Draco forward keeping his attention on the lads and wondering just how old the boys were as well as who they belonged to. Clearly, they appeared to be at home in his trees. He pulled up beneath the first trees.

"Come down, lads. All of you present yourselves. Front and center," he called out in his sternest voice, hoping they would obey but not having any illusions.

They seemed to take his order to heart, all three dropping to the ground in almost perfect unison. Urchins to be sure landed sure-footed on the grass beside the lane. They all needed to be scrubbed from head to toe, possibly twice but they would clean up well. He needed to laugh although didn't want the laughter to come at their expense. So, he held the laughter he felt behind his teeth.

The threesome lined up in front of him, straight faced and stiff as boards.

The tallest and he assumed the oldest of the trio spoke. "We were told to watch out for you and welcome you home. Heard you were coming just last month." He inhaled a deep breath obviously meaning to say more but was interrupted.

"No one told us we'd have to be here on the lane for two weeks. Did you know it's cold out here?"

"I was never informed I had a deadline." Graham's laughter was unchecked this time.

"Well someone should have done just that or you could have sent a message." The tallest said indignantly. "Not like it's summer, ya know."

He'd just been properly chastised by the boy and meant to proceed with further introductions lest they think it okay to reprimand an elder. "Do the lot of you have names? I'm Graham Stewart." He waited for acknowledgement and perhaps some information if they were agreeable.

"I'm Dodge," the tallest said as he cleared his throat. "Been called that for a long time now."

Graham reckoned he must be nearing nine or ten years. He directed his attention to the next in line.

"I'm Ollie." The lad nodded, his hair falling in front of his face before he looked up and pushed it away with his hands. It was hard to tell Ollie's age while he was pretty sure the boy was younger than dodge, perhaps eight or nine, he had no way of proving the fact.

"And you?" This lad was small and seemed to need at least three good meals in his belly. The others must have helped him into the tree because he wasn't tall enough to reach the lowest limbs.

"Midget," the lad grinned, "Please to meet you, sir. We're supposed to make sure you have everything you need and show you to the house."

"Who sent you?" From what Graham heard about the estate, he didn't think anyone here would care if he was greeted or not.

The boys looked at each other sharing glances several times before they seemed to come to a silent agreement.

"Ria sent us."

Graham found himself nodding his head and rolling all the names around in the cobwebs that made up his brains right now and could not come up with one person on his list of employees who was named Ria.

He dismounted, intending to walk with the boys to the stables and discover a little bit more about their truths and how much more they would be willing to tell him. "Who is Ria?"

As he walked past them, he wondered if they intended to stay on the lane. Looking over his shoulder, Ollie was drawing circles in the dirt with one foot and Dodge was tugging on Midget's hand.

Once again, seeming to reach some form of silent agreement all three started walking.

"Ria's no concern of yours," Dodge said, his voice gruff and taking on a prickly edge. "We protect her so you don't have to worry about her or go near her."

Protect her? Bloody hell who or why would she need protection from. For a moment he thought to ask them for more information. By the slant of their lips he didn't think any more material about this mysterious Ria would be forthcoming. Instead, he decided to let them lead the way to the stables and give them time to become accustomed to him. Clearly they had trust issues.

A few minutes later, Graham stopped in front of the stable doors. "Do you know how to take care of a horse? Draco needs a brushing down then food and water. Any of you want to do that?"

"Don't know nothing about horses," Dodge said, looking at him as he had mush for brains. "Don't know how to ride neither."

"I'm afraid of the huge beasts," Ollie said, once again his gaze directed to the ground below and what he was doing with his foot.

"I'm not afraid," Midget volunteered. "Don't think I'm big enough to brush him."

"Then perhaps at least one of you should learn. What do the three of you do around the house besides wallow in the dirt?" The words were uttered harsher than he'd intended. Nonetheless he meant what he said. Everyone would have to do something in his household if they expected to be fed and clothed.

Once again Dodge, the apparent spokesperson for the trio, said, "I'd like to learn how to take care of your horse. It's the only one in the stable now but don't have the time. The others are in the pasture. Have to protect Ria and right now she could be in trouble. We've been away too long watching for you." His words were said defensively and to make a point of telling him he was at fault if anything happened to the mystery lady.

The boys looked at each other for a few seconds. Once again it seemed the silent conversation between them was understood. They took off at a fast clip. Graham watched them speed around the back of the house where the servant's staircase would be found emptying into the scullery.

If there were no horses in the stable, would it figure there was no stable boy? Graham led his horse around the house, resigned to the care of Draco. Entering the outbuilding, he searched for anyone who could help him.

"What can I do?" A man strode from a room at the far end of the building.

"Draco needs to be brushed down then fed and given water. Is that your job?" Graham asked, handing the reins over to the man, impatient now to discover what was going on in the main house and establish himself as the owner. Apparently there were things that needed tending.

"I'll take care of anything, sir. Nice to have you back in residence, sir. You staying this time?" the man asked.

Graham stared hard, his eyes narrowing. “Shamus, is that you?” He held out his hand in greeting. As lads Shamus played with him as well as his brother.

“It is and you’re a sight for sore eyes. I tell you. It’s about time someone arrived here to right the wrongs going on in this place.”

Graham clapped his old friend on the back, thinking he might have to take a few minutes more to find out a few things. “Got some questions if you’re up to answering them.”

Shamus looked over his shoulder as he rid Draco of his saddle and blanket. He took a few seconds to start brushing the stallion. “What do you want to know?”

Graham positioned himself against the stall, crossing his arms in front of him. “Let’s start with the lads. Who are they and why are they here?”

Shamus grinned as he stroked the horse several times. “The lads, so you met them. Not surprised that Ria sent them to greet you. What did they tell you?”

“Not much, just that their job is to protect this woman, Ria.” He waited then, studying the man.

Shamus hauled out a bucket of water and once Draco had his fill gave him his food.

“Dodge do the talking?” Shamus laughed.

Graham nodded, his brows drawing together as he waited impatiently for Shamus to be a bit more forthcoming.

“He’s the oldest. If you were looking closely without assuming anything, Ollie is a little girl and Midget of course is the youngest. They came with Ria one day. They’ve stayed although Ria keeps herself scarce with good reason. Not really sure why they stayed but the house is shelter for them.”

“Where did they come from?”

“If Dodge can be trusted to speak the truth, the worst streets in Edinburgh. Had to do things, if you get my drift, just to eat. I’m surprised they let on that Ria is a woman.”

“I’m beginning to understand a few things. Why does Ria have reason to keep herself scarce?” He didn’t like the direction of his thoughts, although there were a myriad of reasons why the lady might not want to be found.

"Around these parts the main reason is well known. I'd be hopin' that your first order of business would be to get rid of Leod, your manager of the estate. Don't recall his last name, whether or not I was ever told I can't be remembering. Think the lady is hiding from something that happened to her in the city but that's just my gut telling me things. There's no evidence I could be right or wrong."

"And why would I want to get rid of this man?" He didn't like the fact the questioning and answers began with Ria and ended with Leod. Again, his mind travelled in a direction Graham didn't appreciate nor would he allow.

"He's turned Granville Manor into a whorehouse. Pretty simple. Don't think it's what you would want for your home. Now, is there anything else I can do for you?"

"Answer more questions when I have them."

"Whatever you like."

"Millie still here?" he asked as he pushed away from his position, meaning to see for himself at the main house.

"Only because she keeps praying either you or your brother will show up and set this mess to rights. Suppose her prayers have been answered."

"Suppose they have." Determined, Graham strode to the manor, walking up the broad front porch steps. When he stepped inside, a man stumbled drunkenly down the stairway from above. His pants were unfastened and his shirt hung loosely from his shoulders.

This must be the man Shamus was alluding to a few minutes before. He spread his legs his hand at his side. "Who are you?"

"Leod is the name. I took up residency here when it seemed no one was going to claim the land and the crumbling home. Didn't ken why it should go to waste. So many in these parts are homeless."

"Graham Chamberlin, owner of this crumbling home is now in residence."

"You own this?" He asked as he quickly tried to put his clothing to rights.

"I do and, well, you'll have to move out. You're no longer welcome here in any capacity."

“How do I know you’re tellin’ the truth and you are who you say you are?” He stumbled a bit then hanging on to the back of the chair the man glared at him, his eyes narrowing in seeming concentration.

“You don’t, except for my word as a Chamberlin.” Graham couldn’t imagine anyone living here unless they were desperate. Everything was in disrepair and needed hard work and groats to make it livable. “You haven’t seen fit to make improvements? Have you been taking the money that has been sent your way?”

The man shrugged, his body seeming to relax. “No funds. If you’d sent money, I would have done something.”

“My brother has been sending funds for the last five years. Most likely you drank the coin away or spent it on yourself,” Graham mumbled as he studied the shabby entryway to his home.

A woman ran down the steps naked but holding a dress in front of her. Graham watched her leave the home. His breath nearly stopped as did his heart as he processed the scene. “You use my home as a whorehouse. I heard that from someone.” Anger began to simmer inside as he perused the rapid flight as well as the woman’s backside.

“She wanted it. I was just obliging her wishes. She came to me beggin’ for me to take her.” The man grinned as he too watched the woman.

“That’s why she was naked and racing away. Because she was asking for it. Get out!” With a shaking hand, he pointed to the door. “Don’t ever want to see you again.”

“My things...” the man started up the steps.

“I’ll have whatever is in your room put on the front lawn. You can have them picked up when you please. Don’t ever want to see you again.” Arms crossed in front of him both impatient and angry, he waited for the man to leave. As far as he was concerned Leod’s departure couldn’t be soon enough. The puzzle that was Ria was still before him. He meant to get to the bottom of that riddle as soon as he possibly could.

When Leod finally exited the house, Graham let out a long sigh of relief rumbling from his lungs. Striding through his new home, he examined every part of it, every nook and cranny. He was just about finished on the third and last stage when he noticed a movement, a tiny shadow push back against the wall coupled with the softest whimper.

He reached the spot in two quick strides then hunkering down he peered behind a lose wallboard. What he saw surprised him. Two huge blue eyes peered at him from behind a set of knees drawn to her chest. Her blond hair was matted and tangled against her scalp, shortly cropped and greased with black boot grease.

"Who are you?" He hunkered down beside her, wishing he could draw her out from her hiding place. There wasn't one doubt in his mind she was ensconced in this tiny corner because of the man he just sent packing.

She pushed back farther, her breaths almost nil as she was attempting to hold it in. From beneath her ragged skirts two sets of dirty, bare toes caught his attention. She pushed her grimy and disheveled hair from her face, but the terror he saw in her eyes was very real. While he watched and studied her, the apprehension seemed to linger.

"Cat got your tongue? He almost laughed but held the chortle back not believing for a second she was seeing anything humorous in this situation. In truth neither did he.

She was shaking her head, clearly terrified of him. In all his life he couldn't recall any woman every being frightened let alone terrified when he was present. His thoughts travelled back to the man, Leod.

"Did Leod hurt you?" He would have the man tarred and feathered if he harmed this tiny delicate woman in any way.

She was shaking her head no. To his surprise and pleasure, she seemed to be relaxing. Her back was no longer pressed tightly against the wall, nor were eyes blazing with fear or anger. He wasn't sure.

"Good then. Come on out and tell me your name." He held out a hand to her in hopes she would accept his peace offering. Was not surprised when she declined the invitation.

She pushed back farther. Her hands remained tight around her legs, which were still pushed up against her chest.

"I promise I won't hurt you," he paused realizing he wasn't getting anywhere with her. "At least tell me your name."

Her lashes fluttered for a second then she focused on him, appearing to come to some conclusion. "Ria."

"That's a fine name, Ria. Now tell me why you are hiding here on the third floor?"

"Leod."

He expected to see tears but there were none, only determination in the set of her jaw. "Blessed hell," he muttered. One look at the man and he knew trouble surrounded him. "You told me he didn't hurt you."

"Aye, but he wanted to rape me. The lads were able to keep me safe and hidden these last weeks that we've been here."

"I understand." Yet he didn't. He figured getting to the bottom of this would be easier with the children in hand than with her. They were more likely to let something slip that would give him a better comprehension of her circumstances. "Are you going to stay there or come out?"

She looked at her feet then back to him seeming to consider, however a few seconds later it didn't appear she was willing to leave her hiding place any time soon. "Suppose Leod didn't like to exert himself to come to the third floor."

"He got winded and had to stop every so often to drag in air," she said, her voice to soft for him to hear clearly but he understood the gist of it.

"A bit overweight you're saying?" He laughed hoping to reassure her enough so she would leave the place.

She nodded, her fingers winding through the fabric of her gown, her eyes focused there. "Yes, he rarely searched for me here. The lads always found a way to make it harder for him to walk to the third floor."

"The lads are protecting you from Leod then? They understand what he intends?" His speculation was true but would she admit it? He was watching her closely and realized the dirt was an affect also. Where her gown slipped a little he saw clean white skin.

"They shouldn't but they do. We've dealt with this for a couple of years now. Not Leod but..." She lifted her shoulders slightly, looking resigned to the fact she was addressing but unwilling to put before him.

"You know," she picked up the fabric of her gown then let it fall softly around her, "that I'm a fake."

"A fake?" He queried. "What on earth can you mean by that."

"I'm not innocent or naïve as you probably believe I am," she told him, her voice soft as she spoke the words. He had to wonder what exactly was behind her admission now.

"As long as you don't lie to me, I don't care. I'll wager though that the lads bring you dirt so you can paint your face and hands with it. Quite a clever disguise if you ask me, but then you didn't. Does it discourage Leod from taking liberties you aren't willing to give?"

"I don't know. It was Dodge's idea. I refused at first but wondered about the possibilities to give into his wishes. Well, he told me the dirt on my face wouldn't hurt when they weren't there for me. I agreed."

"You mean they don't stay by your side night and day?" He wanted to laugh but wisely refrained after seeing the expression on her face.

She was shaking her head. Her eyes wide once more, "They do some work for Millie when she asks. You aren't going to put us out, are you?"

"I don't know. What kind of work can you do?" He smiled, watching her closely for a reaction to his question. Where her mind went would tell him a lot about this woman who intrigued him more than he thought she should.

She visibly bristled at his unspoken suggestion. "I won't be warming your bed if that's what you're getting at, Sir." Instead of pushing back and cowering she rose. Her hands were fisted at her sides, eyes blazing.

He was quite pleased with her reaction. He showed her with a half-smile. Standing beside her, he wanted to show her he would control the situation but also that despite what would happen to her now was up to him, he would help her. "Do relax, Miss Ria. I'm not going to make you pay for your residency here in my bed. I'm not Leod, nothing like him at all. I appreciate a willing woman as much as any man. However, since you are obviously unwilling, we won't pursue this."

The sigh of relief was visible as well as the tentative smile she graced him with. "I can work in the kitchen with Millie if she'll have me. If not that, I'm quite capable of cleaning. Everything here needs attention from the floors to the stairs to the walls. At the convent I did a lot of cleaning."

At the convent?

"It's true. I believe it would take a small army to put everything to right by the New Year. Even then it might not happen." He wanted her to be a part of this and he wondered what skills she had that might give her at least a bit of a recommendation for something more than cleaning.

"Then I'd be happy to help." She turned to him then, smoothing the folds of her gown. "I don't have a place to sleep."

He waved his hand a bit, wishing to pursue the other line of his questioning a little more thoroughly. "Miss Ria..." he paused hoping she would provide a last name.

"Ashton."

"Miss Ashton, can you read and write? Calculate numbers?"

She nodded her head, seeming to wait for him to disclose the reason for his questions. "Yes. In two other languages. I've had schooling."

"At the convent."

"Yes."

Miss Ashton was inadvertently adding to the puzzle surrounding her. She was well spoken, could read and write as well as calculate numbers yet here she was under the protection of three little urchins. He needed to get to the bottom of this if for no other reason save he was curious.

"Then I'd like to put you in charge of the staff. I will give you permission to go into the village with me tomorrow. You may help me decide who we need to hire. Also," he held up his hand when it appeared she might protest, "you will be my second in command here. It will be up to you to make sure everyone is doing their job properly."

"What about the lads?" she asked, once again finding the folds in her gown with her fingers.

"You are aware that one of the lads is a lassie." He was tired of secrecy and would accept nothing but the truth from Miss Ashton.

Her face paled and for a second she looked away from him. He thought she might lie.

"Ah, I see that you are aware. Is Ollie in need of protection also?" he asked. "Does she have the same needs as you?"

He watched the line of her neck as she swallowed then looked at her bare toes. "If you don't mind my feet are cold. I'd like to know where we will be sleeping. If it's not too much trouble the children, well the... I'd like them close by."

Accepting the diversion for the moment, "Do the children have other clothing to wear besides the ones they managed to soil today?"

"No, I wash them out every night and hang them up to dry."

"They sleep with nothing on? That must be embarrassing for the lass."

He didn't wait for an answer but poked his head around the corner to motion for the children to show themselves. "I've an idea if all of you will follow me. We'll see to some used clothing for the children then I'll show you where you all can sleep."

"Thank you," she moistened her lips. "The children do need something else to wear."

"And you shouldn't have to wash their clothing every night. In any case that will be up to the new scullery maid we'll hire tomorrow. Follow me."

~ * ~

Ria wasn't at all sure following this man was prudent or safe, but she really had no other options. He told her he wasn't like Leod. Of course, she understood all too well that only the passage of time would tell her the truth of the matter. The larger question was if he was like the other men who had been in her life.

"It seems I've remembered that my mother used to fold up our outgrown clothing before putting them in storage up here in the attic." He pushed open a door at the end of the hallway.

She and the children stood at the opening all unwilling to enter into the darkness. He marched to the window at the far end, drawing up the window and opening the shutters. Light slanted across the floor as well as the myriad of trunks sitting in the room while collecting dust. Still in the doorway, she watched as he sifted through various trunks opening lids then closing them until he discovered the ones he wanted.

Finally, she stepped forward, standing beside him and peering into the trunk. "Just what are you doing?"

He held up several items, britches and shirts both small and large. "These should fit Dodge and these Midget. Don't have any dresses for Olivia though."

"Ollie," she persisted.

One perfectly arched brow rose a fraction as he studied for a moment. "I will purchase a few garments in town for her tomorrow."

"She would prefer to wear boys clothing," Ria said through gritted teeth, wishing she didn't need to accept charity even if it was for Ollie's sake and not hers. Otherwise, she would refuse it. "We do not need or want, nor will we accept your offer until I've the funds to pay for her clothing myself. Until then, maybe we could find some boys clothing that would fit her."

A tentative smile formed across his lips before he pressed them tightly together. "These clothes are used. They were my brothers and mine. There is no charity involved. They will earn these through the work they will start doing. As for Olivia..."

"What about the dress for Ollie? I don't have money. Besides she is safer for the time being if people think of her as a boy."

"Olivia need not hide behind britches any longer."

"Ollie."

Graham let out a long slow breath of air, his features rigid with what she assumed was anger. "In any case, she needs to be a girl now. I will make sure she is treated as she should be. You no longer have to worry about her or yourself. Other than perhaps what you would prefer to do during the day."

He strode to another trunk before pulling out a couple of dresses. "These were my mother's. Feel free to look through them. Pick out anything you'd like. There is something of everything a woman might want or need. Can't make any promises about the fit. I believe at least in height the two of you are of a similar size."

She was breathing hard. She knew despite his good intentions he couldn't promise anything of the sort. She put aside his offer of his mother's clothing intent on finishing the previous conversation first. "As long as he's alive, she'll be in danger as will I. You cannot think to gainsay me in this. As they think to protect me, I do my best to keep them safe as well."

Frozen and without a word in his defense, he watched her then went on as if nothing had been said to him to negate what he thought. Giving in to her wishes, he brought out a pair of britches and a shirt he thought might fit Ollie. He held them up, "Until I can purchase a few dresses for her."

He was of a mindset she couldn't fight so she chose to say nothing. Over his shoulder, she peered into the trunk, seeing a few pieces that might fit her. The door had not been locked. She decided she would make a trip up here some time when he wasn't home. In the second trunk she picked out a gown and a few other things for herself.

"Very well." With a submissiveness she didn't feel, she clasped her hands in front of her. "We will proceed as you dictate."

He laughed, his gaze focused on her as he crossed his arms. "Why do I get the feeling you don't mean to comply to any of my wishes?"

She lowered her lashes before looking at him, "As long as she has a choice, I won't gainsay you. If there comes a time when I feel Ollie is in danger, we'll leave."

"You're free to leave here anytime you like." His voice was calm but she heard the underlying irritation.

"Good, then we understand each other." She collected the clothing, handing the items to the children as they left.

"We don't, Ria. That's the problem here, but you'll discover the truth soon enough. Now, I'll show you to your rooms. I'm putting the lot of you in the south wing. My residence is in the north. You will have free access to anything you need."

Without another word he stepped in front of them, striding down the steps to the second floor and turning when he reached the landing. She still wasn't at all sure about his intentions, unwilling to test his words. There was no reason she could see that he should put them in some of the best rooms in the manor unless it was for his own purposes.

He stopped then, opening a door for her. "This will be yours, Ria. There is a sitting room as well as the usual bathing and sleeping rooms. I'll send enough hot water for all of you to bathe sufficiently."

"Thank you," she said but by the look in his eyes, he noticed her reservations to his good deeds.

"I suggest you let me bathe the boys. You can take care of Olivia... She will have a room for herself"

"Ollie," she said, understanding he was growing impatient with her insistence. "Even with a room all to herself, we'll probably find her curled up with the boys in the morning. In my recollection, she has never willingly left their sides.

He cleared his throat several times before continuing his speech. "I don't trust the boys to get themselves clean without aide. Since Dodge is far too old for you to be in the bathing room with him, I'll attend to the lads."

"I've a feeling you've jumped over some details. Are you going to force them into the tub when they bathe?" she nodded toward the room he'd pointed out was for the baths. "You will find them quite unwilling participants."

"If I recall as a lad, I wasn't willing either. Seemed I liked the dirt better than soap and water. Also didn't see what was wrong with a few well-earned smudges."

"Would you like us to take a bath there?" She pointed to the room in her suite. "Us? By that you mean Ollie and me. You and the boys will go somewhere else." Again, she was left in the dark as to what he was saying as well as his intentions.

"Yes, after my journey I'm also in need of a soak in nice hot water."

"You will not get a nice hot soak if the boys are involved in any of this. If you wish for peace and calm, your bath should be taken in your sleeping quarters, not here."

With what looked like disappointment, changing to a strange smile, "I suppose you are right but only after I see to Dodge and Midget."

Millie appeared suddenly as if she'd been summoned. Ria was sure she had been in some way. She was grinning at the lord and waiting expectantly for the orders that were sure to come.

"We need hot water, lots of it. The first water should come here for Olivia and Miss Ashton."

This time she refrained from correcting him, nearly biting her tongue to do so. He slanted her an amused grin before continuing his orders to Millie who curtsied and left. She understood he'd won this round. He would continue to address Ollie with her female name for as long as he chose.

He made himself comfortable in a wing chair in the sitting room. She wanted to know what he was thinking as well as expecting from them.

The control was absolute. She cringed at the thought. A few weeks ago she'd been under the power of another man. She'd vowed when she escaped that servitude it would never happen again. If the children were not involved, she would leave as soon as he retired for the night. With the children came intense responsibility she could never flee.

She chose to stand. In any case, sitting was an impossible task for her. Even when she was hiding, she kept herself off the floor. He motioned to the wing chair facing toward his.

"She can't sit," Dodge spoke out. "Don't expect her to do so."

"Or?" he queried with proper politeness that left Ria cringing.

"Or she'll leave tonight. I know it. She won't take us with her this time seein' we've got a respectable home to live in until we mess it up. She'll sneak out when no one is the wiser."

"You're not going..." Both Ria and Graham spoke at the same time. Ria, however was directing her command to the children, specifically Dodge who was the leader of the little troupe. She understood all too clearly if she left, he would try to find a way to follow.

"Just like Graham can't hold you here, you can't keep us from going with you. We're family. I'm not going to let you be out there, alone," Dodge's voice rose with surprising fury.

"Enough," Graham slashed his hand in the air, obviously frustrated with all of them. "Bath's first then we'll talk about dinner, Perhaps after that someone will explain to me why Ria cannot sit."

Dodge let out a soft whistle. He fastened his gaze on the window and something outside while Olivia shifted from one foot to the other her view of them doing the same shifting while Midget stood his ground his lip tucked beneath his teeth as if that was keeping him from spilling the information.

Millie led the way with the hot water. Two men followed her with buckets, left then returned to finish filling the tub. Ria nodded at Graham, telling him without so many words that it was time for him to leave with the boys.

"I will see you at seven when dinner is served." He led the two boys from the room, a hand on each of their backs.

"Do we have to take a bath?" Dodge asked as the door closed behind them. "Not really feelin' the need."

Ria couldn't understand Graham's response though she could guess at what he would say. In any case she would see Ollie to the dinner table, however she didn't plan on joining them and undergoing another bout of humiliating questions. Why she couldn't sit was none of his blessed business, and she was pretty sure the boys would stay quiet. When the question was posed, she shot Dodge the most stern expression she could summon.

"Come, Ollie, let's get you cleaned up."

"I would like that. Why don't the boys want to take a bath?" she asked as she stripped the filthy clothes from her body. "I hate being dirty."

Ria tested the water with her hand. "It's not too hot. You can get in." Then, "Don't know why. Boys are just like that."

Ollie lowered herself in the tub, playing with the soap and the sponge. Between her hands she squirted the bar into the air and giggled. "Watch." She repeated the process and they both laughed.

"Do you want some help?" Ria handed her the sponge.

"You can do my hair. It's so filthy and tangled I don't think it will ever be clean again."

"We'll get it clean. I promise you." Ria smiled at the little girl who'd become so precious to her. The thought of Ollie's life in Edinburgh brought tears to her eyes. She hoped this manor with Graham at its helm would be somewhere they could stay. Ria understood she would not have been unable to maintain the little girl's disguise much longer. When the men understood what she could do for them, she would have been pimped out. Ollie was beautiful so she wouldn't have been left on the streets or placed in a bordello. No, she would have gone to one of the expensive bordellos where only finest politicians and lords convened. Not that a situation like that was tenable.

"Are you going to get clean water?"

"This will do." Ria grimaced at the water that was growing a darker brown with every washing. "There now, let's rinse your hair and get you dried off. Then it will be my turn."

Ollie was sitting on the hearth dressed now in her clean britches and shirt while Ria was humming and finger combing her hair in an attempt to rid the little girl of all the snarls.

"Knock, knock, everybody decent in there?" Millie didn't wait for an answer but pushed the door open for a peek. "Good, here's some more hot water for you. Under the circumstances, thought you'd appreciate clean water for yourself."

The tub was emptied and filled again, just waiting for Ria and the hot soak Graham had spoken of earlier, but this one was for her. "Oh my, thank you. I thought I'd be using Ollie's water."

"You think I'd let you do that? Never. Now, I'll bring a comb up as well as few other things I can find. Besides the boys' mother, you're the first woman to live here. Most of my life, it's been a house of males. They could have put a sign on the doorstep, no women allowed"

Ria waited until Millie appeared and disappeared again before disrobing and stepping into the hot water. She sucked in a swift breath of air as the water hit her back. Millie brought her valise with her second dress in it a few minutes later and set it near the tub. Ollie combed her hair, tugging at the tangles until Ria saw tears in her eyes.

"You going to wash your hair?" Ollie stood over her. "You should you know. This black grease is ugly."

"I'd like to but I don't want to be recognized. You know that." She ran the cloth over her body. The soap smelled of lavender. She closed her eyes for a moment, wishing she dared wash the filthy stuff away.

"Who would recognize you? There is no one here except Sir Graham."

Ollie was right. If she didn't wash her hair, it would not surprise her if Graham didn't insist she do so in some overbearing way of his. He wasn't like any other man she'd known, but she hadn't known many. Her life in the nunnery near Edinburgh certainly didn't prepare her for the life afterward.

Ria ducked under the water for a moment to get all of her short hair dripping wet. When she rose she soaped and rinsed. With Ollie's encouragement, she washed her hair three times before it was finally devoid of the black stuff she'd rubbed into it.

Feeling clean and better than she had in a very long time, she rose and wrapped the towel around her. Standing by the fire she combed her hair until all the tangles were gone.

"Now we are both ready for dinner." Ollie's stomach rumbled hungrily, the sound generating laughter between the both of them.

"I cannot go as well you ken. Sitting in the tub was all I can manage for one day. Do you think you remember where the dining room is?" Ria inhaled a deep breath. "Perhaps you can bring me a little something to eat after the meal is finished."

"I can but you really think he will let me without investigating for himself?" Ollie asked, her hands on her hips.

"You are much too wise for a ten year old. However, we will deal with the repercussions when they are here."

"I'm nearer to eleven."

"And nearer to the age where concealing you would be all that much harder. I'm glad we left when we did."

"You did it. No one knew you were a girl," Ollie pointed out, a slight smile on her tiny face.

"We left because we were found out. Blue discovered the truth one night when I was careless. Staying in the city was out of the question. I would have lost you and the boys." Ria was determined to never go back to that life. Thinking about it sent a shiver down her spine.

"Is that when he beat you?" Tears slid down her cheeks and Ria brushed them away.

"Yes, yes it was. He was very angry. While I made a mistake, he made one too. That's when I took advantage. He didn't think I would be able to move because of the pain. So, he left me untied, unguarded too."

"If he wanted to pimp you out, why did he beat you?"

"He knew I would heal. He wanted to make me hurt as well as understand that I couldn't deceive him and get away with it. I know he had big plans for me. If he ever finds us..." She couldn't bear to think about that scenario. Ria made herself believe the man would never discover their whereabouts.

"I ken it." Ollie wrapped her arms around her, hugging her tight. "He won't find out because of me. If he finds you, he'll find the rest of us and I think I like it here."

"Now, I want you to go on downstairs and eat with them. Don't let on how I'm feeling. If Graham asks just tell him I wasn't hungry."

"The boys are going to insist they see you. They always need to make sure you have not been hurt."

"You have a question or comment for everything. Of course, they will, but they can wait until after dinner. The important thing now is that no one tells him about my back." She slipped into the cotton shift she pulled out of the small valise she brought with them. One of Blue's ladies gave her two dresses she'd outgrown and could no longer wear otherwise she would have still been wearing pants and a shirt. She had one pair of pants along with one shirt with her. Blue lashed her while she was still wearing her male clothing emphasizing with each stroke that she was never to ape a man again. If she did, this would be her punishment until she understood the orders. By the time he finished her clothing was in shreds around her and useless.

"I'll go now," Ollie said, "as soon as you lie down. I'll cover you up so you'll be all warm and toasty."

"I'd like that. Thank you. Now enjoy your dinner. You can tell me all about it tomorrow or tonight if I'm still awake."

She turned then to walk to the bed. The gasp behind her startled her. "You're bleeding."

Ria pulled at the shift, as it stuck to her back. Unable to help herself, she groaned. "Help me. I need to get this off."

Ria knelt down and held up her arms. Slowly the shift fluttered over her head. Ollie let it drop to the floor, tears in her eyes.

"You're back is all red. It's not just the blood." Ollie's voice was shaking. "It's your skin too. I have to tell Sir Graham."

"No!" The last thing Ria wanted was for Graham to see her back. If he was told she didn't have any doubts that he would force her to show him her injuries.

"Then..."

"Go, I'll be just fine. You know I will." Ria slanted her a shaky smile. "I always land on my feet. I'll sleep on my stomach."

Slowly, Ollie backed out of the room. Ria tried to get comfortable, struggling with the pillow until she had it where she wanted it. She managed to bring the sheet to her waist. The tiny effort proved to taxing to continue. She closed her eyes trying not to relive the events of her life.

She'd suffered far worse than this lashing by the hands of another man after he took her from the nunnery. Going back to that was not tenable. If it happened, she would once again find a way to leave. That day was bleak. She recalled every moment. Mary Margret tried to save her, gave her money and the means to flee to London. The sister even booked passage on a ship for her.

Unfortunately, she never made it on board. The man who wanted her intercepted her and hauled her back to his home in the city. Ria groaned softly, her back aching now that she had no obligations to take her mind off the pain. The lashes had been burning for the last three hours. Now the pain was nearly unbearable.

Ria didn't know how long she'd been lying on the bed in the dark. A soft breeze from an open window attempted to cool her back but was fairly useless. She supposed the air rippling across her back was better than nothing. Her head pounded as she passed in and out of consciousness. The clock in the hallway chimed eight times. Truly she didn't know if Ollie would keep quiet about her condition. She hoped she would. She was proud of the little girl and her efforts. Now, it just remained for her to return to the room and go to sleep. The boys would show up. She'd have to make them vow their silence.

She groaned again and it seemed the sound came from outside herself. The heat she was feeling touched all of her from the inside out. Moving her arms and legs was impossible now. Her eyes were closed. She thought perhaps she heard voices but that would mean Ollie told. She was sure the little girl would do as asked.

"Bloody eyes."

No mistaking Graham's voice or his anger. Fighting from the fog swirling in her head, she tried to sit up then remembered she wore nothing.

"Don't move a muscle," he said as he kneeled beside the bed. The back of his hand touched her forehead then he swore again.

"Dodge, go get a bucket of water from Millie and bring her here. Tell her it's urgent."

"You don't need to be here," she whispered, her voice barely a croak.

"Water?" he asked pouring her a glass.

"If I'm going to drink that you'll have to leave the room." Her head was turned sideways. She saw the stern expression on his face and the crease line between his brows.

"Not a chance. If you can push up a little ways I'll get the rim to your lips and you can sip."

"I'm naked."

"True, do you want some water or not?" To her, his voice sounded patient yet despite the earlier sternness she heard a touch of amusement. "I'd tell you I won't look, but if I don't all the water will probably end up on you as well as the bed instead of where we want it to go."

She pushed up and sipped then a few seconds later they repeated the process.

"Thank you," she mouthed and fell back to the bed, closing her eyes, understanding he wasn't the first man to see her unclothed.

"Now that you've been refreshed, who did this to you?"

If she closed her eyes and pretended to sleep, maybe he would go away or at least forget the question she didn't want to answer.

"Ria." His voice was stern and held the insistence that he wasn't going to let this go without an answer.

"Blue did it to her," Dodge spoke up from behind, his voice taking on a tone Ria had never heard before from the young boy.

"Who is Blue?" Graham spoke the words slowly.

"The man who was going to pimp her out," Ollie said her tiny voice filled with anger. "He would have done the same to me, but Ria was disguising me as a boy."

Graham didn't respond to Ollie. Instead, he lightly touched the slash marks then pulled the cover all the way off almost as if he remembered that she couldn't sit. She gasped when she felt the air across her backside.

"Bloody hell," he said again but this time the whisper held a touch of venom in his anger.

All the way to the tips of her toes, she felt the emotion emanating from him but didn't understand what it was. She'd never felt as if any man in her life cared one way or the other for her. Fending for her survival one day at a time since she left the abbey had been her predominate goal.

"Should I send for the doctor?" Millie asked.

"No, I'm going to tend to her. What I need you to do is get my saddlebags for me. Bring them here. It's in my room on one of the wing chairs facing the fireplace."

"Do you think it's proper?" she asked.

"No, no," he said. "I'm sure there is nothing proper about any of this. Nor was there anything about Ria's beating."

Ria heard the sound of Millie's steps as she left the room. When she returned. "Here it is, sir."

He rumbled around in the packs, pulling out things before letting them drop to the floor. Then, "Go brew some tea with this. It's willow bark. It will help with the pain. Do it as quickly as you can."

"Pain?" she groaned softly and wondered if anyone heard her.

She felt his breath across her cheek. "I'm sorry but your back is infected. I'm going to have to cut you in places so the pus will drain."

"No, no there is no need for that." He wasn't a doctor. What did he know?

"There is. I'm sorry but if I don't take care of you now, there is a good chance you'll die. Drink this." He handed her the bottle of whiskey he retrieved. Once more he held the bottle to her lips until she downed a few tablespoons of the liquid. From the corner of her eye, she watched him pour the whiskey on his knife. Her gut clenched as her entire body tightened.

He was gone for a few seconds then, "Put this in your mouth. Clamp down hard."

"Sh-sh-shouldn't you wait for the tea?"

"The whiskey should be enough for now." He told her as he began to wipe her back with a cool cloth. "I'm going to pull the remaining vestiges of cloth from the lashes. That's what's infecting you. Have to get rid of them or none of this will do you any good."

Other Books by Christine Young

Available at Rogue Phoenix Press

My Sweet Broc

Bad Boys Book One

He's a bad bad boy...

Broc Wallace is a fun-loving rake who never thought any beautiful woman could melt his heart. He lives life in the present enjoying the camaraderie of his friends and the pleasures of his mistress. When Bliss races into his life, he is ill prepared to deal with her secrets or give up the tenor of his life. When the truth is revealed, he finds himself unable to forgive and forget the betrayal.

... but she's sweet for him

Bliss MacTavish knows she's playing with fire when she refuses to tell this bad boy her name. He tempts her with sweet whispers of seduction knowing her innocent nature will be unable to refuse all he yearns to give her. Deciding to follow her heart, she finds the repercussions more than she bargains for when she gives herself to this bad boy.

Crazy for Cam

Bad Boys Book Two

He's a bad bad boy...

Lord Cam MacEwen, Viscount of Rosehill, tries his best to be proper and court the lady of his dreams in the acceptable way. The feat proves impossible when the lady in question uses every means at her disposal to tempt him. He fights his jealousy for another man as well as the need to make her his own, finally giving in to her irresistible passion.

... but she's crazy for him.

Chelsea MacTavish wants the bad boy she fell in love with and kissed just before her eighteenth birthday. With feminine wiles and irresistible allure, the sensuous lady plans to best Cam at his game of hearts and make him forget his need to court her properly.

Falling for Flynt

Bad Boys Book Three

He's a bad, bad boy...

Fascinated by Hope's loss of memory yet haunted by her sultry beauty, Flynt is irresistibly drawn to the stoic miss—and into her troubles with the sultan who wants her for himself. When he discovers she is the sister of his best friend, his pride keeps him from pursuing her and making her his.

... but she's falling for him.

Raised in a harem but now penniless, alone and without her memory, Hope must discover a way to remember all that she has lost. She finds a way to continue with her life as a servant in Flynt's home. The first sight of Flynt steals Hope's breath as well as her heart. Can she overcome her fears and give herself to the man she fell in love with.

Dancing With Donal

Bad Boys Book Four

He's a bad bad boy...

Once a bad boy always a bad boy, Donal Chamberlin's carefree ways come crashing down around him when he meets the ravishingly beautiful Daryl MacTavish, the innocent little sister of one of his best friends. He is determined to win her heart as he sets his sights on marriage and an heir. His past gets in the way of his quest when a woman he once loved threatens Daryl's life.

... but she's dancing with him.

Daryl has seen the control her sister's husbands hold over them. She yearns for a life where she makes decisions for herself. No man will have power over her. But no man kisses her the way Donal does. No man can make her forget all her goals leaving her helpless to give up her dreams. Yet Donal is determined to dance through all the barriers she thrust in front of him, pursuing her until she says yes.

Loving Leslie

Bad Boys Book Five

He's a bad bad boy...

Leslie Stewart, Duke of Southcliff is stoic, set in his ways, a spy who is used to having his life well ordered. He expects life to continue on in this perfectly conventional fashion. He assumes his bad boy status while keeping mamas and debutantes at arm's length. An heir is needed but Leslie has every intention of finding a woman who doesn't covet his wealth and tittle. He is irresistibly drawn to the headstrong young lady who becomes more beautiful as she develops into a woman.

...but she is loving him.

When Leslie kisses Lacie MacTavish, she knows even at the tender age of fifteen this is the man of her dreams. Forced to wait until she comes of age, Lacie withdraws into herself. Now she is eighteen and Leslie has returned from a mission for the British Government ready to claim her as his bride. She refuses him and he must find a way to seduce her and in the process create a burning passion within her, which she cannot deny.

Foolish for Piper

The pickpocket...

Piper has spent her life surviving the streets of St. Giles Parish in London, a den of iniquity and crime. Masquerading as a boy she escapes the whorehouses the young girls are sent to as they come of age. The day she encounters Brett MacLachlan begins the same as every other one. When she picks his pocket, she has no idea her life is going to change irreversibly.

... and the mark

Handsome aristocrat Brett MacLachlan has come to London for his amusement only to find his world turned upside down by a thief and her dog. From the moment he spots her, Brett knows there is something intrinsically wrong. In his arms, Piper discovers passion and joy. Yet secrets of her past haunt her, and a scar will tell the true tale as well as her identity.

Taylor's Destiny

She traveled to another time and place to change destiny...

Enjoying a day of sailing, Taylor Maxwell never expected after a suffering a concussion she would wake up in another century. A resilient independent woman in the twenty-first century, the blond beauty is ill prepared for life in the 1800s. Her first sight of the naval captain who rescues her makes her heart stop, giving her hope for her future.

His life is transformed by a woman who appears from nowhere...

Born to a life of ease, Reid Stewart defies the dictates of those born to aristocracy and chooses a life of adventure in the navy and as a spy for the crown. When he discovers a nearly naked woman on the bow of small sailing ship, his heart warms. His love for Taylor and his need to protect her from a man who pursues her might cost him his life as well as hers.

Caitlin's Duke

She played a fiddle in an Irish pub...

Caitlin O'Shea Is the most beautiful woman Roc Leighton has ever seen. With her blue violet eyes and long black hair she captivates him. In turn he mesmerizes Caitlin. Caught in the power of his gaze as he watches her, she is wise enough to know he desires her but will never give his heart to her. Caitlin has vowed to never be any man's mistress.

And fell in love with an English Lord...

Roc knows the first time he watches her play the fiddle and dance around the pub, she will be his next mistress. Despite her protest, he will find a way to convince her that her place is with him. While Caitlin's determination to keep her vows, fate takes a cruel turn and she is forced to seek refuge with Roc.

Catching Meara

Book One in the McKenna Clan Series

Meara Thorton was a feisty, world-class computer hacker—cornered by the FBI and shockingly given the chance to be their newly acquired technical analyst. Brilliant and intuitive, yet aching with the loss of everyone she has cared about, her restless heart led her to discover a love she fought and a world she didn't know could possibly exist.

Sweet Sexy Sadie

Book Two in the McKenna Clan Series

From the first time Sadie's eyes met those of Brody McKenna in the hot Sierra Madre Mountains, theirs was a potent attraction—not gentle, slow, and easy, but hot, hard, and all-consuming. The daughter of a dysfunctional family, Sadie had dreams no man could wrench from her with hot sex and an all-consuming passion. She'd challenge this alpha male with all the strength she possessed. But her red hair, fiery temperament, and indomitable spirit obsessed Brody... and he knew he had to find a way to show her he was more than he appeared and convince her to make a life with him.

Sweet Misbehavin'

Book Three in the McKenna Clan Series

Cast adrift after fleeing the home of Jokul, the ice demon, Atantsi, a firestarter, grew to womanhood as she moved through time to keep the demon from finding her. Though stubborn and courageous, she was ill prepared to use powers she had not been taught. Her first sight of the intoxicating Carr McKenna left her breathless, and her second encounter gave her hope for a future she never thought she had.

A playboy, a second son and a shifter, a man who thought his life would be carefree, Carr McKenna was shocked to discover the woman he'd paid as an escort is a firestarter who is running for her life. He is the leader of all the McKennas around the world and that he has multiple powers. His passion for Margo and the need to defend her might cost him his life as well as hers.

Sweet Talkin' Sugar

Book Four in the McKenna Clan Series

Lyonesse McKenna, was dreaming or was she? From the instant Lyn saw Deacon McClain across a black jack table in a crowed Las Vegas casino the unmistakable attraction sent Lyn's senses flying into overdrive. Her family of shapeshifters believed in soul mates. She'd always been skeptical yet she couldn't help but question the way her heart sped when he looked at her.

When Deacon appeared in Las Vegas he knew his first job was to save Lyn from a Sea Demon, but the next order of business was to convince her he would someday mean more to her than she'd ever expected. But her stubborn nature and unbendable spirit consumed Deacon... and he had to chase away all the demons real and imagined in order to win her heart.

Sweet Surrender

Book Five in the McKenna Clan Series

Ripped from her family at the top of Infinity Cliff, Kimi McKenna finds herself thrust somewhere into the future. Dark elements threaten to destroy the earth unless Kimi can work together with the white witch to stop the destruction. Confused by her mate's role in the conspiracy, she refuses to acknowledge the connection. But amidst raging fire and attacks on the people she is coming to hold dear, she allows Maska O'keefe into her heart.

Maska O'keefe has loved the beautiful shapeshifter for years. Unable to save her life years ago, he vows to watch over her as he is given a second chance to convince her that even though he is a witch and not a shifter, they are indeed soul mates. Kimi's divided loyalties between her family and the cause she is now a part of will determine their relationship. Only the part she plays as the messiah can bring this to a conclusion in the final battle.

Dakota's Bride

The first book in the Lakota/Pinkerton Series

When Emma St. John received her brother's letter imploring her to escape her stepfather's vengeful scheme and to trust Dakota Barringer with her life, she was willing to chance it. But the handsome, brooding riverboat owner Emma found in Natchez a danger of another kind. For Emma soon found herself surrendering to an unrelenting desire.

Raised by the Sioux when his parents were killed, Dakota had been betrayed once before by a white woman. He wasn't about to trust another, especially one claiming that her stepfather, a powerful U.S. senator, had framed her as a murderess. But he couldn't let Emma's intoxicating effect on him. Now Dakota would risk his very life to protect the innocent beauty who had seduced him with her tender love.

My Angel

The second book in the Lakota/Pinkerton Series

A BEAUTY IN BUCKSKINS

When her father decided to send her to a finishing school back East, Angela Chamberlain refused to be confined to stuffy drawing rooms. Instead, the daring spitfire who could shoot like a man and ride like the wind longed for a life of adventure and romance—and she knew exactly who could give it to her. Devil Blackmoor was a hired gun with a dangerous reputation. But Angela was willing to go to the ends of the earth to capture the handsome devil's heart.

A DEVIL IN DISGUISE

He'd come to America looking for excitement, but Devil Blackmoor got more than he bargained for when he encountered a beautiful rebel who answered his kisses with a wild innocence that touched his very soul. Yet standing between them were more obstacles than either ever dreamed. For Devil had strapped on a gun for the wrong man. And that made Angela his enemy. Now he'll have to choose between his duty and the woman he loves more than life.

The Locket

The third book in the Lakota/Pinkerton Series

The year is 1894. Seeking revenge for crimes against his family, Misha Petrovich follows a path that leads straight to Ariel Cameron's boarding house in Mist Harbor, Oregon. A family heirloom in Ariel's possession leads Misha to believe she is guilty. The locket has been handed down to the oldest girl in the Petrovich family for generations. Ariel is innocent of wrong doing, but her father is not. Misha is torn by his feelings for Ariel and his need for restitution against her father. Knowing that the relationship between them is fragile, Misha does everything in his power to protect Ariel's father. His efforts are to no avail when her father is shot. Ariel comes to realize Misha's steadfast courage and determination to protect her and her father despite what has happened to his family. Ariel's love and devotion heals Misha's heart.

The Talisman

The fourth book in the Lakota/Pinkerton Series

Running from a marriage that lasted one night, Dr. Moriah McKeown discovers the land she has settled on is coveted by determined and lawless men. Yet the proud young woman who once vowed never to abandon her home has second thoughts when her adopted children are threatened. Her only recourse is to enlist the aid of a dark, dangerous gun for hire.

Haunted by the past and a betrayal he will never forgive, Ian Civanovich uses his fast gun and his reckless courage to forget the faithlessness of a woman in his past. He will trust no female—nor will he rest until the threat hovering over Moriah McKeown is put to rest.

Forever His

The fifth book in the Lakota/Pinkerton Series

Struggling to come to terms with the part she played in Jacob St. John's death, Etta Barringer resigns from Pinkerton Agency and seeks peace and solace in a Rocky Mountain Cabin.

Jacob has vowed to discover the reason Etta has betrayed him, sold him out to his enemy and left him for dead.

Isolated in their cabin, they discover their love for each other and learn to trust. But the trust is shattered when Jacob learns she is married to his sworn enemy; the man who left him in the desert to die.

Allura's Secret

Twelve Dancing Princesses Book One

Allura McClellan is horrified by her father's decision to take out an ad in the Times awarding her to the man strong enough and smart enough to win her hand and uncover her secrets. She's an intelligent young woman who takes great delight in the freedom allotted to her by her father. She's well aware that marriage would effectively curtail the adventures she's shared with her sisters and cousins.

Hunter Gray is nothing like the other men who've arrived to vie for Allura's hand in marriage and everything that goes along with it. However, he is the first to refuse to concede defeat and pursue her despite her attempts to disguise her true appearance. It's her temperament that is of more concern to him than her looks. Hunter has worked all his life with the hope of someday owning his own land. Now that it looks like there's a very real possibility that everything he's ever wanted is within reach nothing is going to deter him – including Miss Allura's disagreeable disposition.

Amorica's Wager

Twelve Dancing Princesses Book Two

Amorica Hepburn was sent to London to find a husband. Finding a man was the last item on her agenda. With her two cousins, Amorica wagers she can dissuade her suitor before the others. Despite her efforts she discovers a chemistry that cannot be denied. Suddenly she is the arrogant man's wife, pledged to a marriage neither desire. But swept off to his ancestral home above the Dover cliffs and into his strong embrace, Amorica is soon possessed by a raging passion for the husband she had vowed to despise…

Damian Andrews couldn't afford to trust the emerald-eyed spitfire who happened upon his secret. Amorica's hatred of all men of his kind only inflames the war that rages between them. Still, he can not control the intense desire his stubborn bride inspires, or make her surrender to his will until he has conquered the headstrong beauty on the battlefield of love…

Ravyn's Marriage of Inconvenience

Twelve Dancing Princesses Book Three

A REGAL BEAUTY

When the duchess decides to wed her to a wastrel and a fop, Ravyn Grahm takes matters into her own hands and declares her engagement to another man. Instead of fessing up and telling her great aunt what she has done, she goes through with the pretense. Ariec Lakeland is the bastard son of an earl and has a dangerous reputation. But Ravyn is willing to do most anything to keep the duchess from discovering the lie.

A DEVIL-MAY-CARE SMUGGLER

He'd bought land in America, looking to put down roots and end his life of adventure, but Ariec Lakeland got more than he bargained for when he encountered a beautiful heiress who made a promise she didn't want to keep. But the promise could not be undone and standing between them were more obstacles than either ever dreamed. Ariec had made plans to spend the rest of his life in America and that was at odds with Ravyn's plan of living in England and running her father's estate. Now, he'll have to choose between his dreams and the woman he loves more than life.

Christel's Sunrise

Twelve Dancing Princesses Book Four

He Made Her An Offer...

Life has thrown Christel McClellan some experiences that could have devastated a less determined woman. Beautiful, self-assured and fiercely independent, she is trying to forget the loss of her stillborn child. But is the child alive?

She Couldn't Deny...

Life is carefree for Ryder MacLaren who loves to see what is on the other side of the sunrise. Laird of Clan MacLaren, he is wealthy, handsome and happily unencumbered... until stunning Christel McClellan enters his life. When he hears her story, he believes the child she thought dead has been sold to a wealthy buyer.

Storm's Passion

Twelve Dancing Princesses Book Five

SHE MADE A PROPOSAL...

Life strikes Storm Graham a shattering blow when she learns her father has bartered her to a man she detests. Storm is beautiful, self–assured and fiercely independent, and refuses to be a pawn in her father's schemes, yet she can find no way out of this bargain made in hell. Going on the offensive she asks the wealthiest man on the eastern coast of England to marry her, never believing she might fall in love.

HE TRIED TO REFUSE...

For Hadden Johnston life has provided everything he ever wanted, including a sanctuary for homeless children. He is wealthy, handsome and happily unencumbered... until stunning Storm Graham marches into his life and proposes a marriage of convenience. Yet this type of marriage to a woman who inflames his senses is far from acceptable. If he's going to be tied down, he will move heaven and earth to have this woman warming his bed.

Gotta Have Fayth

Twelve Dancing Princesses Book Six

A regal beauty with raven hair and piercing blue eyes, Fayth Graham is unwilling to parade herself in front of the wealthy Lords of England during the season. Seeking a means to dissuade any man wishing to wed her, she seeks a way to ruin herself for marriage. When she unexpectedly meets a man with sparkling gray eyes and an infectious grin, she decides this is the man who will keep her from agreeing to obey.

He returned from six months at sea, looking for a few nights of pleasure with a willing lass, but Jarret Kinsley got more than he bargained for when he met a beautiful debutant who responded to his kisses with a wild innocence that touched his heart. Yet the obstacles looming between them might rip them apart. Both had vowed never to marry, so when consequences of their dalliances got in the way, Jarret would have to choose between the life he's always desired and the woman he loves more than life.

Ella's Pleasure

Twelve Dancing Princesses Book Seven

A WHISPER OF PLEASURE

Ella Hepburn was an auburn haired debutant from the harsh Scottish coastline—a wild innocent to be seduced and tamed. A spirited beauty, she captivated Drake Montgomerie's jaded heart—while succumbing to the smoldering desire she felt for her unyielding suitor.

A WHISPER OF DANGER

In Drake Montgomerie's glittering world of money and privilege, young Ella discovered passion and desire could overcome everything she'd been taught to resist—entangling Drake, the heir apparent, in a lethal coil of aristocratic family intrigue. But grave peril would only nurse the sparks of a love that knew no limits and a magnificent ecstasy that would not be denied.

Eveleen's Seduction

Twelve Dancing Princesses Book Eight

A WHISPER OF SEDUCTION

A brutal attack on Eveleen Hepburn's cherished island off the Scottish coastline leaves her shattered and bewildered. Learning a man she once trusted can kill as easily as he can breathe even though the deed saves her life, creates questions that need answers. An innocent beauty, she enchants Logan Maxwell's cynical heart—giving in to the raging passion she feels for her mysterious suitor.

A WHISPER OF INTRIGUE

In Logan's Maxwell's world of espionage and privilege, young Eveleen discovers truths about herself she never expected, and a need for passion and love can overcome all her fears if she learns to accept certain truths. She finds herself entangled in a lethal battle for land that was once owned by French nobility, taken from them during the revolution and sold to Maxwell. But grave peril would unleash the flames of love that simmers, creating a magical union that cannot be refuted.

Tavia's Deception

Twelve Dancing Princesses Book Nine

WHISPERS OF DECEPTION

When her father decides to send her to London for her season, Tavia Hepburn resolves to see the world instead. The raven haired beauty decides to disguise herself as a lad and find employment on a ship bound for Barcelona as a cabin boy. But she never bargains on finding passion and love to a red haired sea captain who rescues her from certain death.

WHISPERS OF MURDER

For James Macmurra, the world is black and white until he meets a young debutante, who turns his world upside down. He's unable to deny Tavia's intoxicating effect on him. In a match tense with obstacles, unwillingness to divulge secrets, and unforeseen peril, irresistible desire and passion grows into undeniable love. James would risk his life to shelter and protect the innocent debutante who seduces him with her sweet love.

Larena's Fascination

Twelve Dancing Princesses Book Ten

WHISPERS OF FASCINATION

Fiery, free spirited Larena Graham never wanted to marry a duke. She is thrilled to be in love with the fourth son of an aristocrat, Gavin Broon. But when it seems Gavin ignores her, she set her sights on politics and bettering human life. Unsuspecting intrigue and a plot against her, she continues her dangerous plans despite Gavin's wishes.

WHISPERS OF TRUST

Gavin has every intention of properly courting the beautiful Larena until he must leave the city in order to put his affairs in order. Returning to London, he finds the woman he means to make his own is embroiled in political protests that could lead to a prison ship. Larena must learn to trust the handsome Scotsman whose most pressing mission is to protect her and keep her from harm.

Tira's Education

Twelve Dancing Princesses Book Eleven

WHISPERS OF EDUCATION

Learning how to build ships is Tira Hepburn's only dream until she meets Jamie Lundin and her world is turned upside down. With her raven black hair and vivid green eyes, she tempts Jamie and pushes him to defy his vows. She never bargains on finding an irrevocable love and a passion to a man who cannot fulfill her dreams despite his burning desire for her.

WHISPERS OF A BARGAIN

Arrogant and self-assured Jamie is brought up short when Tira captures his heart. All his carefully made plans are put to the test when he decides to teach her the art of ship building if she will spend a week with him alone on his ship. He is unable to deny Tira's intoxicating effect on him. When Tira leaves him behind unwilling to live with him without the benefit of marriage, he races after her. Jamie will risk everything to shelter and protect the innocent debutante who seduces him with her sweet love.

Aidan's Love

Twelve Dancing Princesses Book Twelve

Whispers of Love

Aidan McLellan has loved since she first set eyes on him as a young girl. Spontaneous, wild and eager to grow up, Aidan haunts his waking thoughts day and night, insinuating herself into his life. With her fiery red hair and sparkling sapphire eyes, she seizes Blade's heart even while he tries to resist the innocent child until she becomes a woman.

Whispers of Courage

Blade has waited what seems a lifetime to claim the woman who captures his heart as a little girl. Claiming his inheritance before his younger brother takes what is rightfully his, Blade must convince Aidan of his sincerity after years of avoidance and wed her before his father dies so he can return home, securing his rightful place. Everything is put to the test when his life as well as Aidan's is threatened by the man who once called him brother.

Twelve Days to Love

When Archer Steele shows up at Calanthe Durand's failing plantation with an alligator over his shoulder, Cali thinks she's never seen a more handsome man. During the war she had to defend herself and her servants from both union and confederate soldiers. Independent and self-sufficient, she vows to never marry.

But Archer Steele has different ideas. The first time Archer sees Cali in town, he feels an instant attraction. He decides he will do everything and anything to convince the beautiful Miss Durand he is worthy of her love. During the weeks leading up to Christmas, he gives her twelve gifts in hopes she will fall in love with him. Yet they are faced with challenges they must overcome before Cali can commit to a marriage.

Door to Heaven

Jessica Lawrence is the stepdaughter of a woman born in the twentieth century transported back in time to the year 1868. An acclaimed suffragette, she raises Jessica to believe in the equality of women. Jess Law believes everything she was taught, and when the time is right she becomes a private investigator. Courageous and impetuous, Jess finds danger in her quest to save all women from white slavery. Her passionate mission results in a wedding to Roc Newman, a man she knows can steal her heart...

Roc can't trust the sapphire-eyed spitfire who invades his home in search of secret papers and knocks him flat with her karate moves. Jessica's refusal to obey his wishes serves to inflame the war between them. Still, he cannot control the intense desire his reluctant bride inspires, or make her surrender her independence, until he has conquered the headstrong beauty on the battlefield of love...

Rebel Heart

HER REBEL SPIRIT DEFIED HIS OUTSIDERS SOUL... She was velvet and silk, eyes the color of a summer storm and amber hair. Victoria DeMontville, because of a promise and a codicil to her father's will, was forced to marry one man to protect her from another. She hated Cameron Savage with a fierce passion. But to hold on to her genetic research and find a cure for the deadly Signe virus, she must pretend to love the enemy at her door, come with weapons of fire to melt her icy heart...

HIS OUTSIDERS TOUCH IGNITED RAGING PASSIONS... He wore a mask, disguised as the Phantom, a true legend come to life. Even as war and debate over new genetic research engulfed them all, he would find his greatest adversary in the beauty who'd branded him an outsider and barbarian, the woman he was born to possess, his soul mate.

Safari Moon

Solo St. John, a wildlife photographer, is preparing for a trip to Alaska. Suddenly, Solo finds women of all sorts invading his privacy, his home and his office, all cooing nonsense words and blatantly throwing themselves at him. Solo doesn't know why, and he has no idea how to rid himself of the persistent women. He finally decides to beg a favor of his best buddy Nyssa Harrington.

In love with Solo for the past ten years and knowing he doesn't return her feelings Nyssa doesn't want to talk to Solo. She knows if she accepts his phone call, she will not be able to resist the temptation to hope again.

Straight to Heaven

Running from demons, Alexandra McMurdie stumbles into Forbidden Ground where up is down and elements of nature are contested. Though a strong independent woman in the twenty-first century' she is unprepared for life in the 1800s. Her first site of the formidable James Lawrence makes her heart skip a beat, giving her cause to reconsider her desperate need to find a way home.

Born with a silver spoon, James' life was torn apart during the War Between the States. Moving west he vows to put the life he once knew in the past. When he discovers a half-frozen woman near Gold Hill, his heart begins to thaw. His love for Alexandra and his need to keep her from a man who has pursued her through time might cost him his life as well as hers.

A Valentine's Anthology

The Lending Library-a fantasy by Christie L. Kraemer

Faeries try to fit into the human world when the forest where they make their home is destroyed by a mysterious enemy.

Chasing Rainbows-a contemporary romance by Genene Valleau

An eccentric aunt, an inventive uncle, a mother who wears poodle skirts, and a brother who wears pearls provide a hilarious backdrop for the courtship of a young woman who yearns for a "normal" family.

The Gift-an historical romance by Christine Young

A man and a woman on opposite sides of the Civil War get a second chance at love after one final battle returns soldiers to their war-torn homes to rebuild their lives.

A St. Patrick's Day Tale

Christine Young, C. L. Kraemer, Genene Valleau

Tumble through time…

…to Ireland in 1817, when tensions are high between Protestants and Catholics and fae people guide the fate of villagers. A lovely Catholic lass stumbles upon the weakly ritual fisticuffing between Irish lads. She falls into the lap of a handsome young Protestant. Family ties, grudges, and two conniving faeries threaten their budding love. But the faeries outsmart themselves when they hijack a time machine that has mysteriously appeared in their forest and are whisked to…

…Eugene, Oregon in the 20th century, amid a property feud between the local faeries and night elves. The conniving faeries from Olde Ireland try to stir up more mischief. However, a warrior gnome convinces the magic folk to control their own destiny, and forces the intruding faeries to take refuge in the time machine again, spinning their way toward…

…A modern day castle in western Oregon. An eccentric inventor is determined to reclaim his wayward time machine and save his beloved wife from her latest misadventure. If only they can travel safely past the black hole…

a May Day Anthology

Christine Young, C. L. Kraemer, Rosemary Indra, Genene Valleau

Highland Miracle — Christine Young

HURTLED THROUGH TIME, Sean Michael Sterling, landed in the midst of a May Day celebration he didn't understand, assuming the role of Laird Sterling.

ILLIGITAMATE CHILD OF NOBILITY, Reagan Douglas searches for a way out of her half brother's house.

Defying the Odds — C.L. Kraemer

The night elves on the hill aren't happy without their magic. They concoct a plan to punish those who were involved in the act that rendered them almost human. Meanwhile, Uther, the rogue night elf, has returned to woo the Librarian to be his eternal mate.

Love in Bloom — Rosemary Indra

When childhood friends reunite it takes two fairies and a matchmaking daughter to help them admit their true love for each other.

No More Poodle Skirts — Genie Gabriel

After drifting for years in the innocent age of the 1950s, a woman struggles to join today's world by finding a career and a new love, with some help from her zany family.

Once Upon a Christmas Moon

Christine Young, C. L. Kraemer, Genene Valleau

TWELVE DAYS TO LOVE

When Archer Steele shows up at Calanthe Durand's failing plantation with an alligator over his shoulder, Cali thinks she's never seen a more handsome man. During the war she had to defend herself and her servants from both union and confederate soldiers. Independent and self-sufficient, she vows to never marry. But Archer Steele has different ideas. The first time Archer sees Cali in town, he feels an instant attraction. He decides he will do everything and anything to convince the beautiful Miss Durand he is worthy of her love. During the weeks leading up to Christmas, he gives her twelve gifts in hopes she will fall in love with him.

BOOTS AND BLADES

An ancient evil from the old country has arrived in the high desert of Oregon. Gnome children are vanishing then re-appearing, showing various stages of traumatization. Tiamoon, warrior gnome, will put her skills to use alongside Killian, a handsome warrior, also in need of a cause.

CHRISTMAS PAWSIBILITIES

With their world destroyed and their space ship malfunctioning, the dogizens of Planet Canid have little choice but to crash land on Earth. They face tortuous experiments at the hands of the Geeks in Green... or they can trust an eccentric inventor and his zany family to deliver the Canine Queen's puppies and help them celebrate new lives.

www.ingramcontent.com/pod-product-compliance
Lightning Source LLC
Chambersburg PA
CBHW071449170626
46811CB00007B/2524

* 9 7 8 1 6 2 4 2 0 5 9 9 6 *